SCIENCE FICTION FILMMAKING IN THE 1980S

ALSO BY THE AUTHORS

*The Dreamweavers: Interviews with
Fantasy Filmmakers of the 1980s*

SCIENCE FICTION FILMMAKING IN THE 1980S

INTERVIEWS WITH ACTORS, DIRECTORS, PRODUCERS AND WRITERS

LEE GOLDBERG, RANDY LOFFICIER,
JEAN-MARC LOFFICIER, WILLIAM RABKIN

CUTTING EDGE

ISBN-13: 978-1-954840-83-6

Published by
Cutting Edge Books
PO Box 8212
Calabasas, CA 91372
www.cuttingedgebooks.com

To Dave McDonnell,
without whom almost none of this would
have been possible

CONTENTS

ACKNOWLEDGMENTS

Abridged versions of the interviews featured in the present work originally appeared in the following magazines:

Aliens: Interview with James Cameron & Gale Ann Hurd: Lofficier, Randy & Jean-Marc, *L'Écran Fantastique* #73, October, 1986; Lofficier, Randy & Jean-Marc, *Bloody Best of Fangoria,* Volume 6, 1987.

Blade Runner: Interviews with Hampton Fancher, David Peoples, Ridley Scott and Syd Mead: Lofficier, Randy & Jean-Marc, *L'Écran Fantastique* #26, September 1982; Lofficier, Randy & Jean-Marc, *Starlog* #184, November 1992.

Blue Thunder: Interview with John Badham: Lofficier, Randy & Jean-Marc, *L'Écran Fantastique* #48, April, 1983; Lofficier, Randy & Jean-Marc, *Starlog* #70, May, 1983; Lofficier, Randy & Jean-Marc, *Best of Starlog* #7, 1986; Interview with Dan O'Bannon: Goldberg, Lee, *Starlog* #71, June, 1983.

Cocoon: Interview with Tom Benedek: Rabkin, William, *Starlog* #107, June, 1986.

Dune: Interview with David Lynch: Lofficier, Randy & Jean-Marc, *Twilight Zone Magazine,* Vol. 4, No. 5, December, 1984; Lofficier, Randy & Jean-Marc, *L'Écran Fantastique* #53, February, 1985; Lofficier, Randy & Jean-Marc, *Twilight Zone Magazine,* Vol. 4, No. 6, February, 1985.

Interview with Raffaella De Laurentiis: Lofficier, Randy & Jean-Marc, *Starlog* #88, November, 1984; Lofficier, Randy & Jean-Marc, *L'Écran Fantastique* #53, February 1985.

Interview with Kyle MacLachlan: Lofficier, Randy & Jean-Marc, *Starlog* #89, December, 1984; Lofficier, Randy & Jean-Marc, *L'Écran Fantastique* #53, February 1985.

***Enemy Mine*:** On the set of *Enemy Mine:* Rabkin, William, *Starlog* #102, January, 1986.

The Unseen *Enemy Mine:* Rabkin, William, *Starlog* #104, March, 1986.

Interview with Wolfgang Petersen: Rabkin, William, *Starlog* #103, February, 1986.

***Mad Max* Movies:** Interview with George Miller: Lofficier, Randy & Jean-Marc, *Starlog* #98, September, 1985; Lofficier, Randy & Jean-Marc, *L'Écran Fantastique* #60, September, 1985.

Interview with Terry Hayes: Lofficier, Randy & Jean-Marc, *L'Écran Fantastique* #60, September, 1985; Lofficier, Randy & Jean-Marc, *Starlog* #99, October, 1985.

Interview with George Ogilvie: Lofficier, Randy & Jean-Marc, *L'Écran Fantastique* #60, September, 1985; Lofficier, Randy & Jean-Marc, *Best of Starlog* Volume 7, 1986.

Interview with Mel Gibson: Lofficier, Randy & Jean-Marc, *L'Écran Fantastique* #60, September, 1985; Lofficier, Randy & Jean-Marc, *Starlog* #97, August, 1985.

Visit to the set of *Beyond Thunderdome*: Lofficier, Randy & Jean-Marc, *L'Écran Fantastique* #59, August, 1985; Lofficier, Randy & Jean-Marc, *Starlog* #95, June, 1985.

Return of the Jedi: Interview with Richard Marquand: Goldberg, Lee, *Starlog* #71, June, 1983.

The *Star Trek* Movies: *Star Trek II:* Interview with Jack Sowards: Goldberg, Lee, *UCLA Daily Bruin,* August 9, 1982; Goldberg, Lee, *Starlog* #67, February, 1983.

Star Trek II. Interview with Nicholas Meyer & Harve Bennett & Sallin: Lofficier, Randy & Jean-Marc, *L'Écran Fantastique* #27, October, 1982; Lofficier, Randy & Jean-Marc, *Enterprise Incidents Special Issue,* 1985.

Star Trek III: Interview with Harve Bennett: Lofficier, Randy & Jean-Marc, *L'Écran Fantastique* #53, February, 1985.

Star Trek IV: Interview with Leonard Nimoy: Lofficier, Randy & Jean-Marc, *L'Écran Fantastique* #77, February, 1986; Lofficier, Randy & Jean-Marc, *Starlog* #110, September, 1986; Lofficier, Randy & Jean-Marc, *Starlog* #114, January, 1987.

Star Trek V: Interview with William Shatner: Lofficier, Randy & Jean-Marc.

2010: On the set of *2010:* Goldberg, Lee, *Starlog* #87, October, 1984; Goldberg, Lee, *2010 Magazine,* 1984; Goldberg, Lee, *L'Écran Fantastique* #52, January, 1985.

Interview with Keir Dullea: Goldberg, Lee, *Starlog* #88, November, 1984; Goldberg, Lee, *Newsweek on Campus,* December, 1984; Goldberg, Lee, *2010 Magazine,* 1984.

War Games: Interview with John Badham: Lofficier, Randy & Jean-Marc, *L'Écran Fantastique* #40, December, 1983; Lofficier, Randy & Jean-Marc, *Starlog* #74, September, 1983.

PREFACE

We've written hundreds of articles about the entertainment industry. We've talked to big-name celebrities and no-name losers, high-powered producers and fast-talking wannabes, major directors and minor auteurs. But each of them had something to tell, shedding new light on perhaps the most over-reported, and least understood, industry on earth.

If that sounds like hyperbole to you, then we've captured the true flavor of the movie industry. Unlike genuine talent, there's no shortage of hyperbole in Hollywood. And yet, there's a lot you can learn about movies by reading these interviews. We'd like to believe it's because we wrung such wonderful, insightful quotes from everyone. But the truth is, the real knowledge comes from the 20/20 hindsight of the passage of time.

Most of the interviews in this book were conducted while the films were still being made, when enthusiasm and expectations (not to mention hyperbole) were running high. Many of the people we talked to were in transition—on the cusp of imminent fame, refining or reinventing their image, or facing an unexpected plunge into obscurity.

Now we know how their films—and their dreams—turned out. We know what effect their success or failure had on their careers and the industry. This knowledge gives us an interesting, and informative, new perspective on the remarks they made so many years ago. The chasm between hope and reality, between prediction and hindsight, is where the real lessons lie—and that is the reason for this book (and its companion volume to be published by McFarland, *Fantasy Filmmaking in the 1980s*).

Each chapter covers an individual movie, often from several perspectives, and is preceded by an introduction that puts the film and interview in historical context. It is our sincere hope that these articles will help create a better understanding of this turbulent and exciting decade in the history of science fiction filmmaking.

LEE GOLDBERG / RANDY & JEAN-MARC
LOFFICIER / WILLIAM RABKIN
Los Angeles, August 1994

FOREWORD: WELCOME TO TOMORROW

BY DAVID MCDONNELL

The measure of our lives is the movies. In the movies we meet our heroes, men and women to match ourselves to, people whose character we idolize and strive to emulate. From the movies we learn lessons in life: how to live (adventurously), how to love (passionately), and how to die (nobly).

These fictional stories preserved on celluloid chronicle our history. And sometimes it seems they do it better than reality. Certainly, it's intriguing to watch newsreels of unsmiling Calvin Coolidge, triumphant Douglas MacArthur, professorial Albert Einstein; but that real documentary footage has an almost surrealistic edge. Because we've been brought up on the movies, the heightened reality of screen entertainment feels that much more true, much more real.

For instance, examine the New York City of the fictional films that were shot (mostly) on location there: Gene Kelly and Frank Sinatra stepping out *On the Town*; Burt Lancaster and Tony Curtis experiencing the *Sweet Smell of Success* in the Times Square nighttime; *Midnight Cowboy* Jon Voight and pal Dustin Hoffman ambling through a city of squalor; or Nancy Allen pursued down into a Manhattan subway by someone *Dressed to Kill*. The New York that is the background to those films is the New York I favor over the cold, gray streets of Big Apple reality.

Each of those four films, shot in a different decade, illustrates a different New York. Indeed, the movies have always reflected their own time. Stories lensed against then-contemporary settings—be it *The Gay Divorcee, The Man in the Gray Flannel Suit, Move Over, Darling,* or *The Silence of the Lambs*—offer time-capsule peeks at what life was like then (or at least the view fabricated from location shooting, stock footage, studio sets, and cunning production design).

The past has always been present in movies as well; cleaned up and polished, the dirt and filth hosed off, and sentiment spray-painted on. Look at the movies' imaginings of *How the West Was Won,* the Civil War of *The Red Badge of Courage,* that mythically sanitary Camelot served by the *Knights of the Round Table,* the London of *Great Expectations,* and the Hollywood of *Singin' in the Rain.* These are movie pasts to yearn for because there's no doubt that they were better, kinder, gentler than the reality of their time.

Of all the destinations that motion pictures take us to, the most fascinating is the future. It's a place always just beyond our grasp, a tomorrow that is forever, even when the next day dawns. Tomorrow: the day we will never reach.

Science fiction enables us to imagine that day. For more than a century, science fiction—as "invented" by Jules Verne, polished by H. G. Wells, and perfected by those writers led by editors Hugo Gernsback and John W. Campbell—has provided the passport to tomorrow. In countless novels and short stories, grand masters like Ray Bradbury, Arthur C. Clarke, Philip K. Dick, Robert Heinlein, Isaac Asimov, and Frank Herbert have described far-off tomorrows (as well as imperfect presents and elegant pasts)—planets where robots rule and sandworms roam, where doorways into summer offer nostalgic escape, and where small-town pharmacies are stocked with the scent of sarsaparilla and a medicine for melancholy. In these books the readers are in a collaboration with the authors, imagining the wonderful and not so wonderful futures they describe.

However, it took the movies to show those futures to us. And thanks to film, for the last 80 years we've seen those tomorrows, the days we will never truly experience.

The history of movies, science fiction, or even just science fiction movies *isn't* the subject of the present work. Those topics could fill an entire library with volumes like this one—and have. No, this book and its companion volume, *Fantasy Filmmaking in the 1980s,* address only one decade, sampling 30 of the genre films released during that period.

There's no attempt at completeness here; that would require several thousand more pages devoted to such varying fantasy fare as *Spacehunter: Adventures in the Forbidden Zone, Altered States, Quest for Fire, Inner-space, The Creature Wasn't Nice, The Dark Crystal, Labyrinth, The Thing* (1982), *Superman II* and *III* (and *Supergirl*), *Clan of the Cave Bear, Tron, The Man Who Wasn't There, Escape from New York, The Running Man, Firestarter, The Ice Pirates, Predator, Harry and the Hendersons,* and *Metalstorm,* just to name a few that come to mind.

In addition, these two volumes are not a "best of" look at a decade of SF/fantasy. How else could one explain the absence of, for example, *Brazil, Who Framed Roger Rabbit?, Terminator, Time Bandits, The Right Stuff, The Fly* (1986), *Raiders of the Lost Ark, The Princess Bride,* and *E.T.?* Or the presence of *Howard the Duck?*

No, this look at filmed tomorrows past is one that simply evolved throughout the decade. Not every film was or could be covered. Some are too borderline genre to worry about. Some were dreadful and therefore easily ignored.

Not every filmmaker was or could be interviewed. Some, annoyed at past real or imagined slights, simply don't talk to the press in general or certain writers (or publications) in particular. Others, fixated on secrecy, rarely discuss their work, preferring it to speak for itself. And still others give terrible interviews. They may have much to say on celluloid, manipulating images, creating effects, or acting alien, but they simply aren't articulate about their work.

And, of course, not every interview opportunity was presented to this volume's writers. Thus, other "lucky" journalists examined the making of, say, *Masters of the Universe, Flash Gordon, Willow,* and *Lifeforce.* Somebody decides who does what, and for some years now, I've been one of the genre magazine gatekeepers, directing the exploration of tomorrow's movies.

In the early 1980s I landed a job on the editorial staff of *Mediascene Prevue,* the film/TV magazine published by comic book writer and artist Jim Steranko. In 1982 I departed to join, as managing editor, *Starlog,* a publication devoted to science fiction films, television, and literature (founded, pre-*Star Wars,* in 1976). And in 1985 I became *Starlog*'s editor.

From those positions I assigned articles, bought already finished interviews offered on speculation, and recruited new writers. Through editing *Starlog* and various other sister publications (as well as a stint on *Fangoria,* which explores horror in entertainment), I've shepherded into print some 3,000 articles— including almost all of the interviews in this book.

In fact, I commissioned more than 75 percent of the pieces herein, dealt with studio publicists and agents, set up the interviews, and hobnobbed with my fellow wizards: the writers involved. The remainder were done for other editors and publications. Still, I feel like the foster father of them all.

It may seem remarkable that the interviews collected here (and in the subsequent volume, *Fantasy Filmmaking in the 1980s*) are all the work of just four writers, but then Lee Goldberg, Randy and Jean-Marc Lofficier, and William Rabkin are four remarkable writers. Let me employ a few words to take their measure.

Lee Goldberg appeared in my life the very first day I began work at *Starlog.* He was already there, so to speak, represented in the form of a manuscript lying on my new, yet used, desk.

I sat down to read that piece and a pile of other manuscripts submitted on spec and willed to me by the previous managing editor. Which should we buy? Which would we return unsold with those sickeningly polite rejection letters that writers dread? Well, today's memory plays tricks on the events of yesterday, so I no longer recall details. But it was clear to then-editor Howard Zimmerman and me that Goldberg had talent. He also had a story with a provocative title, "The Man Who Killed Spock." Reading it sold me.

And it might sell you, too. It's still a terrific interview. Judge for yourself: Lee's talk with Jack Sowards, the *Star Trek II: The Wrath of Khan* writer who really did kill Spock (though not for long), is in this book.

Quickly, as these things go, we bought several of Lee's interviews. Before long, UCLA college journalist Lee Goldberg didn't have to generate story ideas; we were calling him up to interview the likes of Roy Scheider. Just one issue after I joined *Starlog*, he was already a regular contributor.

Jean-Marc Lofficier and wife Randy debuted just three issues later. As the American-based correspondents for the French film magazine *L'Écran Fantastique*, they were old hands at interviewing genre filmmakers. Originally, they contacted Bob Greenberger, editor of our sister magazine *Comics Scene*, regarding writing about comic book creators, and they sold him at least one story. Alas, *Comics Scene* was soon canceled (to be successfully revived several years later, with myself as editor). It was *Starlog* that needed new blood—good writers—and, impressed by their work, we assigned Randy and Jean-Marc to interview director John Badham from *Blue Thunder* (included herein). Before long, they were profiling all sorts of people in almost every issue, becoming two of *Starlog*'s most prolific contributors.

It took Bill Rabkin a little longer. A friend of Lee's from the *UCLA Bruin*, he had expressed an interest in writing for *Starlog*, pitching me several story ideas that we didn't need and one that we loved: a piece on the abortive attempt to make a new Dick Tracy film. How this article fit into a science fiction-fantasy magazine we never quite figured out, but we didn't have to justify its publication since, as of 1994, Bill still hasn't written the piece. (Actually, it was mutually deep-sixed due to the difficulties of getting quotes from those associated at various times with the project—Floyd Mutrux, John Landis, Clint Eastwood, and Dan Aykroyd. *Dick Tracy*, of course, was finally made in 1990 with Warren Beatty in the starring role.)

But the unseen Dick Tracy didn't matter, because we quickly gave Bill a topic that didn't involve jut-jawed, yellow-coated crimefighters (the special effects of *Starman*, published 15 issues after Lee's debut). Before long, Bill Rabkin, too, became a frequent *Starlog* contributor. I even sent him to Germany to cover the making of *Enemy Mine*, a film that inadvertently provided us the chance to recast that Dick Tracy article idea. When director Richard Loncraine was succeeded by Wolfgang Petersen on the project, Bill wrote a terrific piece, "The Unseen *Enemy Mine*" (included in this volume), exploring just what Loncraine's version might have been: an alternate vision of another filmed tomorrow.

There are many alternate versions hinted at in this book and in the second volume. *Dune* might have been filmed by Alejandro Jodorowsky or Ridley Scott, not David Lynch. As the screenwriters of *Robocop* and *Blue Thunder* can attest, changes in their work made for somewhat different movies. Ray Bradbury, adapting his own classic novel *Something Wicked This Way Comes,* ended a decades-long friendship with its director Jack Clayton over "creative differences." The resulting film is not exactly what anyone intended. And *Blade Runner* certainly evolved on its way to the screen from the original novel by Philip K. Dick.

Randy and Jean-Marc Lofficier have written numerous cartoon and comic book scripts (for series such as *Dr. Strange* and *Hellraiser*). Jean-Marc, an authority on the British SF television series "Doctor Who," has penned several "Who" reference works. And for some time the Lofficiers have been partnered with one of the few indisputable geniuses I know, the gentle French comics artist Jean Giraud (better known as "Moebius"). They help manage his affairs, sell his prints, translate his work, and arrange matters so he can do what he does best—dream of new tomorrows.

Lee Goldberg and Bill Rabkin, meanwhile, partnered as working screenwriters. They've seen their greatest success in television: contributing scripts to "Spenser: For Hire," "Beauty and the Beast," "Hunter," "Baywatch," and "Diagnosis Murder." As writer/producers, they've served on the underrated "Murphy's Law," the syndicated "She-Wolf of London" and "Cobra," and the celebrated "Likely Suspects."

Me? I still edit *Starlog*. And these four writers, despite their other activities, all continue to contribute on occasion to the magazine. As writers and friends, like the movies, I can barely remember when they haven't been part of my life.

And, like the movies, you can never be certain of just what effect you may (inadvertently) leave on someone else's life. Case in point: Lee Goldberg. A decade ago I instituted a policy of, whenever possible, introducing all of our regular freelance writers to each other. As strangers we met. We wined and dined together as friends. In 1984 I introduced Lee and Bill to Randy and Jean-Marc. There have been countless by-products of that friendship and two results of special note. One is the volume of interviews in your hands.

As to the other: without that introduction, there surely would be an alternate version of this story. It all but belongs on film as a romantic comedy, complete with clashing cultures and a classic "meet cute" first encounter. When Valerie Bisson, a friend of the Lofficiers from France, was visiting Los Angeles, Randy and Jean-Marc asked Bill to show her the sights. But Bill was busy, so Lee replaced him. And in 1990, with Jean-Marc and me as smiling spectators, Randy as triumphant matron of honor, Bill as angelic best man, Lee and Valerie were married.

That's a tomorrow I certainly never could have imagined all those yesterdays ago.

New York City
August 1994

ALIENS (1986)

Rarely do sequels measure up to the originals, and it is even rarer still when a sequel can succeed in creating its own unique style. *Aliens* did all of that and more.

The original *Alien* was, at its core, a 1950s-style B-movie about an extraterrestrial monster running amok in a spaceship, killing off the heroic astronauts one by one. But in the hands of director Ridley Scott and production designer H. R. Giger, it became a highly stylized and unique thriller that outclassed its comic book origins.

It would not have been hard to churn out a sequel that aped the same style as the original film. Instead, 20th Century-Fox went to writer-director James Cameron, hot from his hugely successful thriller *Terminator.* Cameron came from the Roger Corman school of guerrilla moviemaking, and he was obviously influenced by Corman's audience-pleasing, unabashedly commercial philosophy toward film.

Cameron reshaped the *Alien* story to reflect his own apparent fascination with high-tech hardware and weaponry, and he ditched Giger's surrealistic vision for the industrial look of Syd Mead.

While *Alien* was an intellectual, moody interpretation of a pulp story, *Aliens* was a visceral delight, a dry run for the exhilarating, roller-coaster moviemaking Cameron would perfect in the 1990s with *Terminator II.*

Interview with James Cameron and Gale Ann Hurd

QUESTION: Ridley Scott's *Alien* was an incredibly scary movie. *Aliens* on the other hand, isn't actually scary, but it grabs hold of you about 15 minutes in, and never lets go. It's more suspenseful, like a roller-coaster ride ....

JAMES CAMERON: You captured exactly the distinction between the two films that we set out to do. In other words, that was our intention going in, to do a film that was not as scary ... it's scary, but it's not as scary, but more intense, and I like to use the word exhilarating. Because I think you get exhilarated by the intensity of the kind of action that's in this film. At least, when it's presented in a good theater, with a good sound system and so on.

Producer Gale Ann Hurd and her then husband and collaborator, writer-director James Cameron.

Q: You knew you had Sigourney Weaver?

GALE ANN HURD: We knew that it would be about the character. At the time Sigourney Weaver was not signed.

Q: So, you would, conceivably, have put another actress in the part?

CAMERON: No. Never, never, never! I was asked to write a story based on Ripley. Later on it turned out that everybody but us thought that the film could be made without Sigourney Weaver, which completely blew my mind, and was absolutely out of the question for us. So, as far as we were concerned, we started with Ripley from the end of the last film, and it was her story. We, fortunately, were able to overcome these obstacles in the minds of the other people involved. We had to fight very hard for Sigourney to be in the picture, which to me was crazy ….

Sigourney Weaver as Ripley, a role she played in three *Alien* movies.

HURD: Then it's not a sequel, it's something else.

CAMERON: It's another movie, and why bother.

Q: Was calling it *Aliens* your idea?

HURD: Absolutely.

CAMERON: It's funny. It was very much like ... I don't know Dan O'Bannon, but I read an interview with him that said that he was typing away one night at four o'clock in the morning, and he was writing, "the alien did this, the alien did that," and he realized that the word "alien" stood out on the page. It was very much like that for me on this film. I was writing away and it was "aliens this and aliens that," and it was just right. It was succinct. It had all the power of the first title, and it also implied the plurality of the threat. It also implied, of course, that it's a sequel, without having to say "Alien II." ...

Q: Did you have the idea of the Queen from the beginning?

CAMERON: I thought it was very important to have something beyond that hadn't been seen before in the first film, even though we have a number of aliens throughout the main body of the film. They're mainly a reprise of Mr. Giger's design. I thought it was important to show some new form beyond that. And, I think there's a lot of revelation going on there, as to how their whole social organization works. I think of the Queen as a character, rather than as a thing or an animal ....

Q: Someone raised the point that having the concept of a queen alien was in contradiction to the reproductive cycle of the alien as it was implied in the first film.

HURD: Where did the eggs come from then?

Q: From the humans that had been infected by the alien.

CAMERON: But, you see, that was never seen at all. Yes, it's in contradiction to the reproductive cycle that was in the original script of the first film. But it's not in contradiction to what you saw in the film. What you saw in the film was a thousand eggs, one of them hatches, one of them goes through its life cycle, becomes an adult, and is killed. There is no connection between the adult and the future eggs. Now, in the scene that was apparently shot and cut, and which I never saw, in which Tom Skerritt and Harry Dean Stanton are turning into eggs, that closed the cycle. But, to me, that was completely irrelevant to what you actually saw in the film.

Unless you're an ardent fan of the film and studied what was taken out, which to me is irrelevant to the group experience of this movie, it's not a contradiction, it's merely an alternative explanation. And a more plausible one, really.

Q: Obviously, you've given this point a lot of thought. This change was not made lightly.

CAMERON: Yes, it was a conscious decision. Had the first film appeared in its complete form, then I would have had to take a different approach to the story. But I felt only a responsibility to what people saw within the first film, not the intentions of various people behind it.

HURD: Few people knew this anyway. Most of the people we spoke to assumed the alien was a shape changer.

CAMERON: No, I don't think that's quite true either. Some people might have been misled, but I don't think everybody was. I never thought it was a shape changer.

Q: Why was Giger not actively involved in this film?

CAMERON: Well, there are a number of reasons. One, he was doing *Poltergeist II,* and we didn't know exactly how long that commitment was, but we heard that he was busy. But honestly, I think that if we had really wanted to fight for him, we could have worked around it. However, we already had Syd Mead, and Ron Cobb, involved. Both of them are designers who were also working on other projects at the same time. And I didn't want to deal with yet another designer who was also working on another project.

Michael Biehn, seen here as Hicks in *Aliens*, has had roles in James Cameron's *Terminator* and *The Abyss*.

The other thing is that I wanted to personally take charge of that aspect of the design. I knew Syd was going to handle some of the fantastic high tech hardware of the future; Ron was going to deal with the colony. I just wanted an area for myself.

Q: So you designed the Queen?

CAMERON: I did, with Stan Winston. I did the artwork, and he did the physical sculptural work. We tried to be consistent with Giger's motifs, but not necessarily enslaved to it.

Q: You saw the Queen much more in this film than we did of the alien in the first film. I thought she looked very good.

CAMERON: I think we had the advantage of her not being exactly an anthropomorphic figure, so she obviously is not a person in a suit. Your willing suspension of disbelief is aided by the fact that it's clearly not a performer in a suit.

On one hand, you know that it's achieved by a sort of puppeting technique, but the fact that you also know that it's not just a person dressed up immediately helps you perceive it as a living creature.

Q: I thought you showed a great deal of cleverness in shooting the Queen, too. In terms of lights, cuts, etc. ... it was all kept to a minimum.

CAMERON: You have to be not too in love with the effects, if you see what I mean. I understand why some directors choose not to hide the special effects work. They try to make it so compelling that it looks real under normal everyday conditions. But I think it's one of those logic traps. You become so enamored of the illusion that the story is no longer what's important.

Q: For the first movie, they had to find a very tall actor to put inside the alien suit. Did you have to do the same thing here?

CAMERON: From looking at the first film, I realize that all the work that they did was not always necessary. I mean, they were charting new territory. They were creating a lot of stuff from scratch. So they had a number of disadvantages, whereas I got to compare their original intentions with what finally wound up in the film. And you can see that the alien almost never appears, and certainly never appears standing side by side with a normal-size person, except I think in one shot, very briefly, and even then, it was not a full-figure shot. It was from the waist up, and he could have easily been up on something.

So I realized that we didn't have to find ten seven-foot-tall people. All the aliens you saw in the film were six-foot-tall, regular-size people, but very thin. They were the thinnest people

7

that we could get that had the physical strength to do the movements. A lot of it was done hanging on wires, which required a fair amount of strength and agility. What we tried to go for was more speed, rapid action, and physical agility.

HURD: The suits were redesigned so that they would allow more movements. The first suit had a very limited scope of action.

CAMERON: We had access to the remains of the first suit. We were able to study it. When Stan Winston and I first sat down right at the beginning to go over these things, we talked about it. The two basic improvements were not as much sculptural as they were mechanic. We wanted the actors to be able to move with a much greater degree of flexibility. We wanted the suits to be lighter, and less restricting, especially the heads, with better vision.

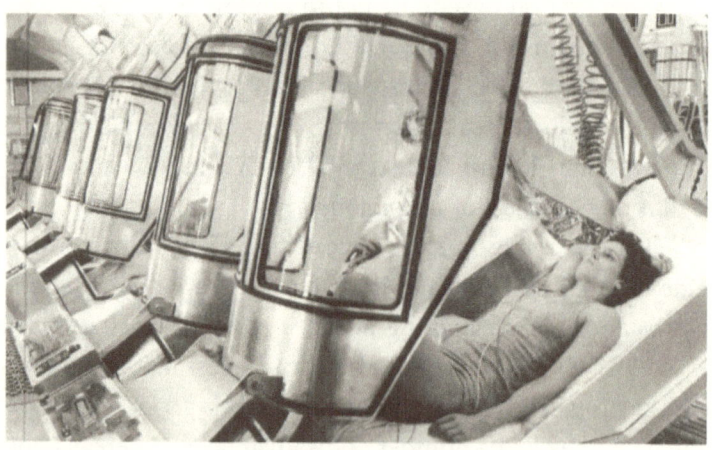

Ripley (Sigourney Weaver) awakens from suspended animation to do battle, once again, with the seemingly indestructible "Aliens."

I put the old suit on myself, so that I would understand from standing outside what it was like to be inside—you see what I mean? And I couldn't see anything. I knew that I would never get the kind of movements that I wanted from the actors with that suit. They had to run, crawl, leap from wall to wall, drop down, all sorts of things.

Q: Why does the dialogue of the film seem so much steeped in the 1940s, 1950s war movies style? Why not go the *Blade Runner* way and try to create a new futuristic lingo?

CAMERON: The sense of the dramatic relationships from these 1940s, 1950s war films, which sort of portrayed the common soldier, was more what I was looking for. The dialogue itself, the idiom, is pretty much Vietnam era. It's the most contemporary American combat "warspeak" that I had access to. I studied how soldiers talked in Vietnam, and I took certain specific bits of terminology, and a general sense of how they expressed themselves, and I used that for the dialogue, to try and make it seem like a realistic sort of military expedition, as opposed to a high-tech, futuristic one. I wanted to create more of a sense of realism rather than that of an interesting future.

Q: Like *Hellcats of the Pacific* in space!

CAMERON: Exactly! There is a conscious sense of reprising what would be clichés if it was an earthbound combat film. But because it's in an SF context, the clichéd aspects are taken away, because the imagery and the technology are new.

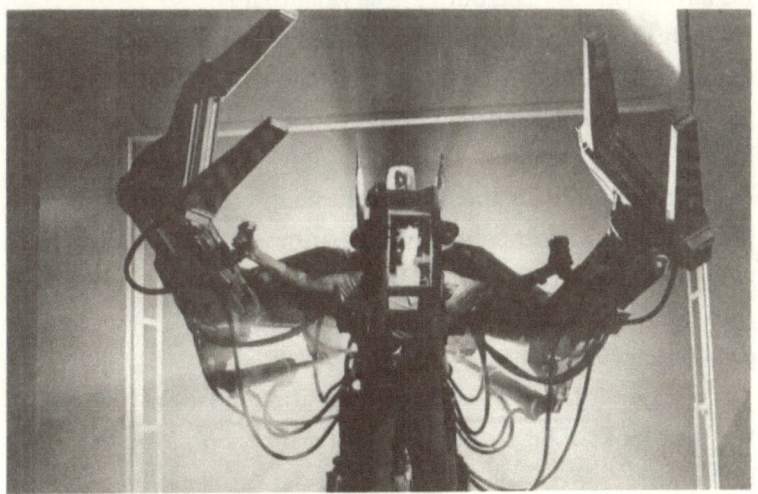

Ripley slips into a Power Loader to do battle with the Alien Queen.

There are two different arguments about the dialogue, really. It's 150 years from now. We may speak completely differently than we do now. But we don't know that. We don't know what it will really be like. But to someone living in that time, no matter what the language is, they will be at home in that language. So it's very important for us to be at home in the language that we hear in the movie. We're supposed to project ourselves into it.

It's like the idea that, perhaps, in 150 years from now, television sets may not even remotely resemble what we know as video today. Maybe they will be holograms, or maybe they will fill entire walls, or perhaps they will project directly into the brain, or whatever. We don't know what it will be, but it will be something different. And whatever it is, it will be familiar to those people, but if we were to walk into a room, we would very likely not recognize it for the equivalent of a television set.

If you're trying to create a textural reality within a film, you can't go to the extreme of suggesting what technology will be like. You have to keep it one step beyond what it currently is, but no more, so that you can look at it and say, "Right, that's a TV set! It's a futuristic TV set, but I know what that is."

HURD: Also with the electronic mass media today, there's less of a deviation in language now than there was a hundred years ago, from a hundred years before that. I think there's more homogeneity in the way we speak, and it's likely to continue.

CAMERON: That's the other argument. One could argue that the language has probably stabilized now, and will remain basically the same at least for another couple of hundred years. I don't think, for instance, that we speak vastly differently now than we did 40 years ago.

Q: The "lifter" exo-skeleton that Ripley uses at the end of the film looks a bit like a "Transformer" robot. Was there any influence?

CAMERON: I don't remember exactly the origin of the idea. It's based on a design that I created a few years ago for another story that never got made. That predated the Transformer robots, at least as a fad in this country. I think that the exo-skeleton concept has been used in a lot of literary SF.

In this particular film, the origin of it was that I wanted to have the final confrontation with the alien as a hand-to-hand fight. To be a very intense, personal thing, not done with guns, which are a remote way of killing. Also, guns carry a lot of other connotations as well. But to really go one on one with the creature was my goal. It made sense that Ripley could win if she could equalize the odds. So there had to be some way of amplifying her strength, in a way that was not a comic-bookish sort of concept, like taking a pill.

Q: Why reuse the ending of the first film, I mean, expelling the alien into space?

CAMERON: It seemed the only way to go. There was no other way that satisfied me. Crippling her to death would have been impossible. Remember, the acid blood … The image that I could not shake free was the idea of literally hanging, being suspended over an infinite abyss. It was not so much getting rid of the alien as the jeopardy that Ripley was in after the alien was already out. I wanted to have the image of standing along something, and the doors open, and there is nothing there but stars. Which I don't think had been done in a film. The closest thing was in *Alien*.

Q: Did you check if she really could have survived for such a long time, considering what she was experiencing, the decompression, the air rushing through, etc.?

CAMERON: It's artistic license really. I've studied enough physics in college that if I had sat down and worked it out, I probably could have computed the amount of volume of air that the room should have in relation to the size of the airlock. Or you could presuppose that all the air throughout the entire ship is being drawn out. Obviously, she was able to override the interior doors so that they would not automatically close when the outer doors opened, which is how a real airlock would have to work, safely. But one could assume that they had the capability of doing that so that they could load things in and out through that door, straight into the ship.

Ripley (Sigourney Weaver) protects Newt (Carrie Henn) from the mother of all aliens.

But I think it's very unlikely, not that she could breathe, because for the length of time that the air was going out she could breathe, but that she could hold on. The wind velocity would probably be somewhere around 300 to 350 miles per hour.

Q: There are several places in the film when, as a writer, you ask the audience to accept something that is not extremely logical, to suspend disbelief, to go along for the ride. Then, the director comes to the rescue and makes the scene so captivating, so enthralling that we don't ask ourselves any embarrassing questions—at least, until after we've left the theater. For instance, Ripley has just seen her friend be severely hurt by a splash of the aliens' acid blood. And when she goes back in to get Newt, she discards all her protective clothing and just goes in in a T-shirt. That does not make any sense. She should know better.

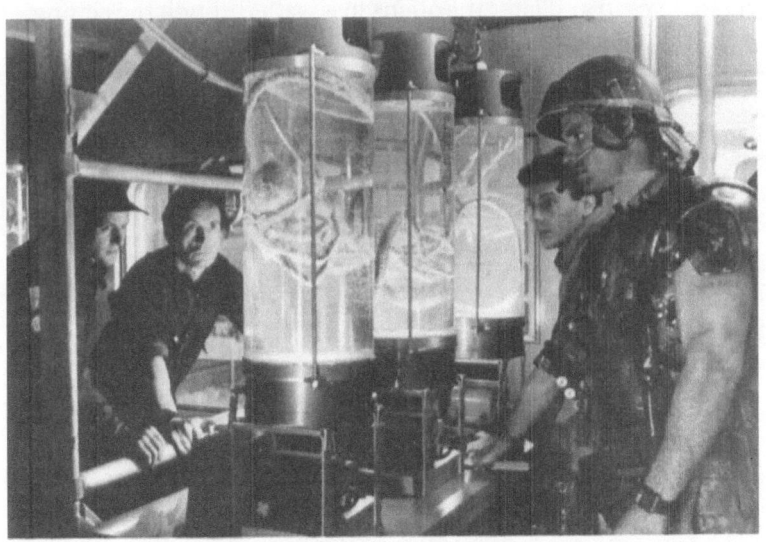

The crew examines the infamous alien "face huggers," which lay their eggs in human beings.

CAMERON: Actually, you can explain most of these things logically if you wish. In this case, it's the heat. She even takes off some of her clothes ....

Q: But she could die ....

13

CAMERON: Yes, but you can die from heat too! It was supposed to have been very hot, because the reactor is going to explode. I'm not sure that it was visually explicit that it was very, very hot, but it was supposed to be really red hot in there. Part of the problem is that a lot of the colors are cool, so that the inferno aspect of the scene does not come across as clearly as I would have liked.

Q: When you were writing the script, were you aware at any time that you were taking chances with the credibility of the story by coming up with something that's a little bit too hard to swallow, or did you just trust the director to pull the fat out of the fire? For example, there is the ending with the Queen coming out of the landing gear, or the scene when the crew barricade themselves in and later the aliens just walk through the ceiling— surely, they should have thought of that?

Ripley and Newt flee from a rampaging face hugger.

CAMERON: Being a visual person, I work backward from the imagery that I like. The logic of a scene, I believe, is secondary to the enjoyment of it. You have to assume that Ripley was dumb enough not to check the sub-ceiling, or you have to assume that she was so thorough that she thought she had accounted for everything, and there was something that she had missed or didn't know, or wasn't in the blueprint.

Yes, as a writer, you wrestle with all these things. It's not as much a question of whether it's illogical, it's a question of whether you need to put in so much expository material to explain the point. If you overexplain, you look like you're talking to the audience, which is not good. You're telegraphing. You no longer have the surprise.

For example, when the Queen holds on to the landing gear, and stows away inside the ship for the final sequence, do we show that? Do we show how she did it? No, because then you'd lose the surprise factor.

Q: Being both writer and director, it must make it easier to decide when to explain things or not?

CAMERON: The specific things we've been talking about were all pretty much decided at the writing stage. In this case, when you're writing, you're really predirecting the film, as opposed to a director who just arrives on the set. So you already understand the material when you come in as director. If I were writing for another director, I'd still try to second-guess the visual decisions.

Writer-director James Cameron at work on *Aliens*.

Q: How did you decide to have a little girl, Newt, being a substitute for Jonesey the cat in this film?

CAMERON: Yes, she's a surrogate cat, isn't she? It's hard to trace back some of those creative decisions. They just came up when I was thinking about the story.

HURD: I think it's important to have an emotional center to the film, hopefully to raise it above the mere level of action, science fiction, horror types of films that don't seem to convey that dramatics are as important as anything else.

Q: Did Weaver have any input in the role?

CAMERON: Absolutely. She had ideas about certain lines of dialogue, and certain things that she thought she could say. We went through the entire script with her, and did a sort of dialogue polish together. It was all those things combined: rehearsals, writing, etc.... The script didn't change very much, but it was fine tuned to her.

Q: Her relationship with Newt showed a great deal of her more human side.

CAMERON: Actually, those scenes didn't change at all. The scenes that she was most concerned with altering were the first three or four scenes when she gets back. And the scenes with Burke. She felt that my approach was too trusting toward Burke. That I had her put her trust in him too early. And I said that if you are completely mistrustful of this character, then our misdirection won't work. You will never go and there is no film. So at a certain point, you have to be convinced by him.

Q: Having her go back in order to get rid of her nightmares was an excellent idea, I thought.

CAMERON: I think some people missed the point. They think she goes because she'll get her job back, but that's not the case. There's no amount of money that could do it. One of my biggest problems writing the film was coming up with a reason why she goes back. It had to be psychological. One of the things that interested me is that there are a lot of soldiers from Vietnam, who have been in intense combat situations, who reenlisted to go back again. Because they had these psychological problems that they had to work out. It's like an inner demon to be exorcised. That was a good metaphor for her character. I did a bit of that in *Rambo* as well, but it didn't get used.

Q: How was the little girl who played Newt to work with?

CAMERON: She was very good. She memorized all of her scenes in advance. Basically, we were able to do complete takes of the entire scenes. She did most of her own "stunts," so to speak. Nothing dangerous, but a lot of exertion. Like in the scene where they are climbing on into the ship and it's lifting up out of the fire and explosions. That was really Sigourney and Carrie climbing up onto this ladder and being lifted up 30 feet in the air over the floor of the soundstage. Just because Carrie wouldn't let anybody else do it for her. She had to do it. We had stunt people right out of frame that were ready to grab her and that sort of thing. We rehearsed it pretty well too.

Q: How was working in England?

HURD: It's really a much different approach, even though we speak the same language. It's very different culturally. It's always difficult when you're taking on such a tough project to begin with, both in terms of what we wanted to accomplish and the fact that we didn't want to be a paler version of the original, the first film. Then, also, doing it in such a short period of time. So, to have to adjust, in addition, to different ways of working was difficult.

Q: Why go there in the first place?

HURD: There were two reasons ....

CAMERON: More production value ...

HURD: One was that the first film was shot there, and it turned out very well. There are really only three places in the world that you could have shot this film, England, Germany, and America. At the time, Fox did not have the stage space available, and we needed very large stages for a long period of time, and also stages adjacent, where we could do the effects. The company just did not have the spaces necessary.

CAMERON: Yeah, but I think you get more production value for your dollar in England....

Cameron with crew and actors in *Aliens.*

Q: The first movie was made almost exclusively with European technicians and artists. This time, you imported more American craftsmen?

CAMERON: Well, yes, Stan Winston was brought there because we knew Stan from *Terminator,* and we trusted him.

HURD: He used a very large British crew.

CAMERON: I'd say it was mostly a British crew. John Richardson, our special effects supervisor, who built the power loader suit and did all the practical special effects; Peter Lamont, our production designer, who worked on a number of Bond films; the cameraman, etc. With the exception of Stan Winston, and about three or four people in the miniature, visual effects department, we used mostly British people. Ron Cobb did most of his work in Los Angeles. He came over to England for a couple of weeks.

Q: Was there any incident during the shooting?

CAMERON: No, we had no accident, we had no stunts that were wrong, no stuntman was injured, no crew was injured and no sets were burned down or destroyed—other than, I think, that the Pinewood set laborers love to take the sets apart and burn them in that bonfire that they have behind the studio. So in case you need another shot, they have to build it all again [*Laughter*].

They will take the sets down and take them out and burn them so fast that you don't have time to say, "Wait!" I'm absolutely certain that it's a job security concept. If they burn the set, and you need another shot—and they know you always need another shot—so they will have to build it again. So it keeps them employed.

Q: What are your next projects?

HURD: I have one. We don't have one. Mine is not a genre film. It's a drama that deals with apartheid in South Africa. It's entitled *The Silent Man*. I'm waiting for the go-ahead.

CAMERON: I'm going to take some time off and do some writing. Perhaps I'll write maybe two or three scripts before we shoot another film together. Probably one or two of these scripts will be genre scripts, meaning in the fantasy or SF umbrella in the widest sense.

Q: Would you go back to being simply a writer, or will you direct all of your scripts from now on?

CAMERON: All my scripts will be for me to direct. Writing is difficult and takes a lot out of me emotionally. I can't write quickly enough for someone else. Also, if I write and I come across a really good idea, I know I'll put it in the script that I am writing, even if it's for someone else. I won't try to save it back for another script that I'd be doing. And I don't want to give away all my good ideas.

BLADE RUNNER (1982)

Rarely does a film overcome box-office disaster and critical drubbing to become widely regarded as a misunderstood classic. Director Ridley Scott's *Blade Runner* is one of those rarities: an ambitious, richly detailed, and stylized mix of science fiction and film noir that left theater audiences both awed by its imagery and confused by its muddled plotting. But an afterlife in art houses and on video (and in a restored, laser disk version) brought both new audiences and new appreciation to the film.

Blade Runner really started with a novel written by science fiction author Philip K. Dick, published in 1968 under the title *Do Androids Dream of Electric Sheep?* Although it is considered one of his lesser works, it was nonetheless dubbed "a marvelous and complex book, leaving all kinds of resonance in the mind" by Brian W. Aldiss, another famous science fiction writer.

Do Androids Dream is a fast-paced action novel which tells the story of Rick Deckard, a bounty hunter on an earth left devastated by World War Terminus. Deckard makes his living by hunting renegade androids and "retiring" them with his laser. His dream is to own a real, live animal—the ultimate status symbol in a world all but bereft of nonhuman life.

Interestingly, the term *Blade Runner* is not part of the Dick novel; it belongs to another science fiction writer, Alan Nourse, who published a novel by that name in 1974. Nourse's blade runners were doctors performing medicine in a futuristic world where only a few tax-paying citizens had a right to receive medical care. Doctors who were willing to treat ineligible persons in a sort of contraband traffic were dubbed "bladerunners."

There is an unfortunate truth in that when a book is translated to the screen, the finished product is seldom an exact representation of its antecedent. In many cases, this leaves the filmgoer, who was also the book lover, feeling frustrated and unsatisfied. This is particularly true in science fiction and fantasy, where in the books a great deal is left to the imagination.

When dealing with the transition of *Blade Runner* from print to film, it is, therefore, best to accept early on that certain themes and images, while totally valid and exciting in Dick's novel, were difficult if not impossible to realize in film. This is particularly true if the same sense of power is to be felt in both media.

Although the basic premises of *Do Androids Dream of Electric Sheep?* hold true in *Blade Runner,* the means of showing them are rather different.

For example, in *Blade Runner* the word "android" is never used. Ridley Scott thought that the word carried with it all sorts of preconceptions, and he threatened to break the head of anybody with a baseball bat who used it. The word used instead is "replicant," which was coined by cowriter David Peoples after a conversation with his daughter, a microbiology major at UCLA. The scientific origin of that word derives from the idea of replicating cells in laboratories. It adds a bit more of a futuristic feel to the film.

The ambiance of the story is also approached differently in film and book. In Dick's novel the earth is a barren, lonely place. Most people have parted for off-world colonies after the nuclear holocaust which contaminated most of the planet's surface. Everywhere are abandoned buildings and "kipple" (trash caused by disintegration and disuse), which rapidly encroaches on the inhabited areas. Buster Friendly, an omnipresent television and radio talk show host, constantly encourages people to leave earth before they become genetically damaged "specials," who will then be forced to remain.

Blade Runner presents a different picture of earth—specifically, a future Los Angeles plagued by severe overcrowding. The world's resources have been exhausted by greedy mankind, and the off-world colonies are places for further strip-mining and all-out profit wars between giant corporations. Strangely enough, this is very close to the visions of the world depicted in other books by Dick, such as *The Three Stigmata of Palmer Eldritch* or *Martian Time-Slip*. The buildings are retrofitted with high-tech trash to keep them in working order. Scott's future city, known among the film crew as Ridleyville, features crowded, booming streets, elegant executive offices, and gargantuan new architecture built atop the old buildings. The visual style of *Blade Runner*'s world is eclectic, full of familiar elements in bizarre contexts. In the words of Ridley Scott: "Like today, only more so!"

In the book there were ways for the characters to deal with the all-pervasive loneliness that Dick envisioned. A device called the Penfield Mood Organ allows persons to dial whatever feelings they desire at any given time. For those who cannot afford the Penfield, there is the religious experience of Mercerism. By grasping the handles of an Empathy Box, one is mentally linked with everybody else using the box at the same time. The users are transported to a surreal place where Mercer, another of Dick's typically flawed messiahs, constantly struggles upward from a pit of death and decay, while unseen hands stone him and eventually send him back to the pit, in a never-ending cycle. If any of the stones strike home, the box users are similarly injured—injuries which remain with them even after the empathy experience.

The Mercerism concept was discarded at the very onset by *Blade Runner* screenwriter Hampton Fancher, who did the initial drafts, because it did not lend itself to film and, from a practical standpoint, would have required lots of screentime to establish.

Empathy *is* the pervading theme of *Do Androids Dream of Electric Sheep?* and having it or lacking it is the only real differentiation between humans and androids. The idea is carried through in the film, but not to the same degree as the book. Empathy is symbolized in the book by the desire all the humans feel to own a real, live animal. Because the earth is such a dead place, animals have come to represent a life force and hope to everyone. The androids not only do not feel this need but they also do not have the feelings necessary to keep an animal alive and healthy. Rick Deckard is totally motivated in all his actions by his driving need to earn enough money for the purchase of an animal. He is unable to deal with the fakery of owning an anatomically perfect but "dead" electric replica.

This facet of Deckard's character, as well as the exploration of the true nature of empathy and, indeed, of humanity, provides the "meat" of *Do Androids Dream of Electric Sheep?* As Deckard examines his feelings, he discovers that there is little separation between human and android. After killing the renegade androids, he comes at last to the realization that everything, even an electric animal, has a life of its own to which it is entitled.

Blade Runner, although simplifying many of the themes due to the necessity of filmmaking, also explores the question of humanity. Even if the methods are different, the validity of its statement exists. What makes a human being "human," and can this quality be surpassed by an artificial construct?

However, to retain the same power as the book, *Blade Runner* had to lean heavily toward the visual aspects of the story and its thriller potential. Early on Dick was upset at what he perceived as a "destruction" of his novel. Fortunately, at a later stage a new draft screenplay (rewritten by David Peoples) was resubmitted by the studio to Dick, who gave it his imprimatur.

Ultimately, it is this very humanity that is the core of *Blade Runner;* it is the heart underneath Ridley Scott's visually overwhelming, high-tech future world; and it is what elevates the film from being remembered not as a stylistic extravagance but a truly great movie.

The Man Who Launched Blade Runner: *Hampton Fancher*

Cowriter Hampton Fancher is also credited as executive producer of *Blade Runner* because he is the man who, in 1975, conceived of the book as a film.

Fancher is an actor who has made about ten films and has been in a hundred or so television shows. *Blade Runner* was his first script. Although his attention was directed to Dick's novel as early as 1975, he had to wait until 1978 when the book (previously under another option) became available again. Fancher's treatment became controversial after one of its drafts was ferociously criticized by Dick.

From his house in Carmel, California, Fancher talks about writing *Blade Runner*:

Q: What first attracted you to *Do Androids Dream of Electric Sheep?*

HAMPTON FANCHER: I had been what you might call an underground filmmaker, and never got a chance to get anything that I'd written, and that I wanted to direct, off the ground. Over the years, I eventually learned that the way to do that was to do something that was commercially feasible. It was around 1975, and I decided to look for a property that had some kind of commercial feasibility. I'm not a science fiction fan, and I am ignorant of science fiction, but someone suggested that I read *Do Androids Dream of Electric Sheep?*. I saw in it a possibility. I didn't think of writing it or directing it, I just thought that, if I got something like that going as a producer, it would put me into more familiar ground with front office Hollywood. So I decided to option the book. Philip Dick turned out to be very elusive. His agent did not even know where he was. I ran into Ray Bradbury one day, after I'd given up trying to find Dick, and he gave me his phone number. So I called him. But he was very suspicious of Hollywood and of me. I met him, and we had three meetings over a period of a few weeks. Even though we made contact, he continued to be elusive, and though we liked each other, I felt that he thought I was a "Hollywood" producer. But I wasn't. I was just a filmmaker trying to do this because I felt it could be an interesting film. I didn't have an approach to it. I was naive enough to think that he might!

We didn't get anywhere, and finally I dropped it. Then a few years later, in 1978, a friend of mine, Brian Kelly, the movie's other executive producer, was looking for something to do, and I just mentioned the book to him, saying to do it if he could. He succeeded rapidly! I guess Dick needed the money.... There was nothing like what I went through. He just called the agent and within a day he owned the property, basically for very little money.

Brian was a fairly well-known actor, but had to drop out of acting after a motorcycle accident left him paralyzed on the right side. He wanted something to do, and films were his love. At that point in time, he had made two films with Michael Deeley, the producer, in Europe. So Brian took the property to Deeley, who read the book and said, "No way!"

Do Androids Dream was not the kind of thing that even someone who is professionally involved could easily picture as a film. Dick is very obscure and purposefully ambiguous in his writing; maybe it would take a filmmaker to understand how to deal with it. I didn't even see how to deal with all the components. I just saw one simple thing that you could hang a lot onto, and which I thought would be intriguing. That was the "bounty hunter chases androids" theme. There's a Kafkaesque atmosphere about the book that I enjoyed. But there was also a whiff of something else in the book that I thought could be turned into something that was close to my heart. I did not think that then, at least not consciously, but I must have subconsciously done so or else I wouldn't have pursued it so much.

But I didn't have anything to do with it at that point. Then Brian came back to me and explained that Deeley didn't like the book, and didn't understand how it could be done into a movie. "What can I tell him?" he asked. I told him to say this, and that .... So he asked me to write it down in an outline, which I did. It was basically a simplification of the novel in eight pages. He gave it to Deeley, who said no again. Brian came back to me distraught, and I felt guilty that I had tossed him into spending $2,000.

Then Brian entreated me into doing, if not a screenplay, but at least a treatment. I refused at first, but Barbara Hershey, the actress, who knew about all of this, told me it was a perfect way to achieve what I was trying to do. If I believed that this was what I wanted to do, and if I wanted to make it happen, then why didn't I write it? So I made a 50/50 deal with Brian, and I started to work on the first draft.

The first two drafts were very much in keeping with the themes from the book. A problem that you can run into in Hollywood is that, if it reads well, they don't know how to deal with it! But Deeley fell in love with it, and he made us feel that we had it made, and we felt that we had a producer with a lot of power, because he had just won an Academy Award, and a lot of people were romancing him.

Still, none of the studios would say yes. I realized later that we were going to make a movie that nobody understood. I guess there were four or five drafts. I lost my naïveté and got more experienced in what was needed, and adapted scenes that were already in the first drafts into better substance.

Q: Did you leave out the religion of Mercerism, for instance?

HF: I don't think Mercerism even got past the first draft. I was going to put it back in, but didn't because I finally didn't know what to do with it. The next thing that went—and that was terrible for me, for I still love these old drafts—was Buster Friendly, and what I had done with that.

Basically, at that point, the plot was that of a man trying to get enough money to buy himself a real goat. That was still in when Ridley came into it. Everybody liked it, but they were afraid of it. But I was dealing with people that didn't have the same commitment to mother earth. It was a bitter struggle and it took a year! In a sense, they won, but in another sense, the educational process for me in terms of writing was worth it. Eventually I came up with a much more important theme, which was even closer to my heart, the empathy theme, what is wrong with man.

Q: You mean that Deckard's character changed from someone looking to buy an animal, to someone who is now questioning his concepts of what is right and what is wrong?

HF: Right! I was always trying for that, but I finally got it more simplified and defined. It got so good by the last script I thought I was in good shape! But I don't think any of that exists in the movie now.

What got refined in the last three drafts was the theme of a man who was questioning his own conscience, or lack of one, and that the very thing the hero was trying to kill for being a machine was, in fact, less mechanical than he was! It was that discovery of his own soul, falling in love with the thing he had to kill. It was an agonizing process for that man, and a dramatic one too.

Q: How did Ridley Scott get involved?

HF: I guess there were four drafts written, and a very fine director came in for a while but had trouble with the studio we were dealing with at the time, which was Universal. That was Robert Mulligan, whom I respected a lot, a person who was very neat to work with. We did one draft together, and then we couldn't make sense financially with Universal. So Mulligan left, and then we left Universal. They weren't committed yet, and they wanted a happy ending. Mulligan and I wouldn't do it. Right around that time Ridley, who had been sent the script and liked it, but didn't want to do another science fiction picture, changed his mind and decided to do it. He, of course, was the reason it got made. We were in trouble because everyone said "you've got to have a director, because this is too weird of a film. You need a director to insure its value."

It was true in a sense, because two days after he got into town and talked to us, every studio in town called and said, "How much do you want, and when do you want to go?" So we made a deal with Filmways, and then they went "pffft!"

During that time, we all began to work: Michael Deeley, his assistant Kate, Ridley and his assistant Ivor Powell, and myself. Ridley is very imaginative and many-faceted, quirky and fun to work with, but difficult to tie down. I found myself getting excited about a lot of things, and disliking a lot of other things. We had a real basic disagreement on certain sentiments. It was an arduous process, as well as a fulfilling one, and certainly a very educational one.

Q: Was there no way to work out these problems?

HF: No way! I didn't think that, because he never made me think that. On a dialectical level, when it came to those areas that I disagreed on, and felt justified in disagreeing, I would usually win the argument and feel satisfied that my point had been proven. But two or three weeks later, we would have the same argument all over again! He was just steadfastly hooked into wanting things that I wouldn't do.

As preproduction began, and things really had to be nailed down, it got really hairy! I wasn't a hired writer, so it wasn't as if Ridley could say to me, "do this and that," and I'd do it. I was also a producer. Finally I said—because it was Ridley's film in the end—"If you're going to do that, you're going to have to get somebody else to do it, because I won't!"

I didn't think he'd do it, because the time was too short. We came up with what I thought, and what a lot of people think, was a very wonderful script. It has all those things that I wanted. But they did get somebody else, and it turned out to be David Peoples, just about two weeks before shooting started.

At the time, of course, I was very disturbed because I didn't know who David Peoples was. But I thought that they'd gotten a guy who was going to do anything Ridley wanted, and it was going to be too bad, because it was going to wreck the film.

Later, I found out that David Peoples did a really good job of translating Ridley's ideas into script. I was going to go into arbitration about it. I didn't know whether I wanted my name or his name off, but I was going to do something about it, until I got the script. Then I thought, "Hey, this guy is neat!" I really liked his work, and then the animosity, jealousy and all of that stuff disappeared. Now we've become friends!

What was disappointing was that I don't think even his stuff came across, because of how it was tampered with by people who weren't writers, but producers, secretaries, associate producers, directors. I think that there probably is a discombobulation, a lack of cohesion and coherency. Note that I say probably, because I don't know.

Q: What do you think of *Blade Runner* being promoted as a detective story of the future?

HF: That was Ridley's idea. That was the first idea that I gave in to. I hated it! What happened was that after literally three months of fighting, I gave in, and decided to fall in love with it instead, because it was, after all, a way to get everything through. It's a wonderful thing in a movie if you can, on a superficial level, get people to be hooked and then, just below that, have a message. I was against it at first because I thought it was a cliché and very unoriginal, but when I saw his graphic ideas about how to handle it, in a kind of Gothic or Kafkaesque manner, I started to think about it and I thought, "Wouldn't it be interesting, we could have a voice over narration, etc.... and all that kind of character." I originally had Deckard as a little bureaucrat, a guy who wasn't too sure of himself, but then I thought that it was better to have a guy who was extremely macho and then have him cut down so he doesn't know where he's coming from.

That's what I started doing by the sixth draft, and eventually I think I arrived at it in the last draft, number 10! But they didn't even go for that, and they left the underpart out. Ridley didn't want any vulnerability, but at the same time, he didn't make him macho.

The deepest thing I had was the love story. I don't think they ever saw it as a love story. For me, the most noble person in the film, the person with the most to lose and who was willing to lose it, was Rachael. I liked matching her against a macho jerk who was totally sexist-oriented in that stupid detective way. Then, through her, he becomes otherwise—but still loses her.

Q: Do you think that is why Dick is reported to have been displeased with your script? Because the woman was too strong?

HF: I don't know what Dick was displeased about, because I don't know what script he read, or even if he read a total script! I've seen at least three scripts that were extremely doctored, so I don't know what he got. But anything he got after script number four would bear no resemblance to his book at all.

Q: Why was the world changed from being empty to being overcrowded?

HF: I guess it was just looking at New York, Mexico City, etc.... and what's happening now. Which was a great idea!

A lot of Ridley's visual and atmospheric concepts are interesting. My atmosphere was much more naive. I didn't really create much of a world. You could have pretty much taken my first draft and put it on a stage. There wasn't a lot of exterior scenes, there wasn't a lot of hardware. It was basically a small drama that was going to be done for $9 million.

Q: Do you agree with Dick's rather bleak view of the future?

HF: Not necessarily. But the bleakness to me is watching a tourist suck an ice cream cone!

Any kind of art that moves or inspires you, and has something that's bleak about it, can be a strong inspiration and can make your life bigger. Definitely everything I did up to the last draft was a warning. I had to have something I was saying, or else I couldn't have written it!

I wasn't advocating bleakness, of course, I was warning about it, and empathy had a lot to do with it. But there was, always, even in the bleakest of my drafts, a lesson that engendered hope.

I wanted the last moment to be a thrill. I like proposing some hard questions that way.

Q: Are you nervous about the final version now?

HF: Yes, because although I think I have already accepted the outcome, the other day I saw the trailer and I was depressed for two days after that. I sort of pretend that I am not going to see the film, but of course I'll go.

David Peoples: Correcting the Aim

David Peoples cowrote and coedited an Academy Award-winning documentary feature, *The Day After Trinity,* which told the story of the making of the first atomic bomb. He also wrote the Oscar-nominated short *Arthur and Willy* and edited the Oscar-winning documentary feature *Who Are the DeBolts and Where Did They Get 19 Kids?*

A man of many talents, David Peoples's collaboration on *Blade Runner* started in 1980, at Ridley Scott's request, before the commencement of principal photography.

David Peoples lives and works in Berkeley, near San Francisco, where he explained his role in the writing of *Blade Runner.*

Q: How did you come to be involved in *Blade Runner*?

DAVID PEOPLES: During the period I was doing documentaries, I had written several original screenplays. I was actually working on rewriting one of these with Tony Scott, Ridley's brother, when Tony showed Ridley one of my screenplays and, I guess, spoke well of me. Ridley must have liked my work, because he called me, and that's how I ended up on *Blade Runner*.

Q: Did you know Hampton Fancher before *Blade Runner*, and did you actually work with him?

DP: No, I didn't meet Hampton until we had both finished working on the picture.

Q: Why did they bring you in?

DP: Hampton had reached a point, I think, where I don't believe he wanted to pursue it and make some of the changes that Ridley wanted. But he had written on it for a long time, and must have felt pretty tired of it. Also, there were some changes that I don't think he was very enthusiastic about. He just said that they should have somebody else make them, and Ridley thought I would be a good person to make them.

In many instances, I picked up right where he had left off, and did probably exactly what he would have done. There was a scene between Deckard and another character where I found that Hampton's dialogue, which he had written months before, and had not been picked up for one reason or another, was written exactly the way I would have written it!

Q: Had you read Dick's book prior to working on *Blade Runner*?

DP: No, and I did not refer to his book when I was writing. I referred only to Hampton's screenplay. From my point of view, Hampton's script was what I was working from. The script that Hampton had written before I got there was absolutely brilliant. It was just wonderful! When I saw it, I was terrified! I thought I was going to embarrass myself because it was just so good! The changes I made were really to make it more in line with Ridley's vision of that world.

It was definitely not the case of a bad screenplay being fixed up. Ridley has a very unique and brilliant vision of the world, and he wanted to fit more of that in there.

Q: Had Ridley much input into the script?

DP: Absolutely! Ridley *is* the author of the movie in every sense of the word. He is a complete author. It is his movie and he dominates every frame of it with his way of looking at things.

Q: How was it to work with him?

DP: He is very much a perfectionist, and you have to work very hard. But he couldn't be more charming, or a more pleasant person to work with. He surrounds himself with people who are pleasant people, and it's a wonderful atmosphere. He is also extraordinary in that he is open and receptive to ideas from everyone. He's always listening. He's polite enough to listen even when he knows he's going to do it differently!

Q: Did you find it difficult to write, considering the heavy emphasis on visuals?

DP: No. I didn't have that problem because Ridley was supervising at all times, and he understood the visual aspects perfectly. Sure, there were times when I didn't fully understand what I was doing, but Ridley always understood what he was doing and where he was going. I was doing what I was told to do, and it worked out fine.

Q: Don't you think that spectacular visual effects tend to take away from a story line or from the characters?

DP: Obviously, if they do, it screws up the movie. I would not say that it's truer of a special effects movie, although I have noticed it more in makeup than in the other kind of special effects.... I have noticed several pictures where the make-up seemed to be more important than the story or the characters. I don't think that's a good thing.

To a writer, of course, the story is always the important thing. But people go to the movies to see stories and spectacles, because you do have good stories on TV after all. So there has to be that balance where you're not only telling a good story, but you also have that sense of something special that makes it a movie and a theatrical experience rather than a television experience.

Q: Did you have any problems writing scenes around sets that had already been built?

DP: All along, there were things that were absolutely locked into the story, because people had been working on building this and that and so on. There were times when I would want to write something one way, and the set had already been built another way! At one point, I wrote out an ambulance, and someone told me that it had already been built! I don't remember if we wrote it back in, to tell you the truth! It wasn't a major problem, but it was a strange sensation to think that these things were happening even as you wrote the words down on the paper.

Q: Was there heavy pressure to get the script done on time?

DP: Yes, there was a lot of pressure because, as I just said, the sets were being built, the casting was under way, and the picture had to go on schedule because a certain amount of money was being spent every day, and you couldn't go into a holding pattern at that stage.

Q: From the time you started working on the script to the time the shooting started, how many months went by?

DP: Let me see… When I started writing the script it was November 1980. The picture was scheduled to start shooting in January 1981. However, the start date was postponed until March, so in fact, I was on it for about half of November and most of December. Then, I came back after Christmas, sometime in January, and worked all of February. I continued to work while the picture was being shot, until the writers' strike, when I left. After the film was shot, and the strike was over, I did some rewrites on some voice-overs which may, or may not, be used.

Q: How do you feel about the fact that Dick was pleased with the final version of the screenplay?

DP: I was happy that he was happy! I was embarrassed that he made it into a thing, as though I had saved something that wasn't in a good shape before I came in, because, in fact, it was a brilliant screenplay before I was involved with it.

I think it is a case where the force of Dick's ideas forced back the script toward some of the original concepts of his novel. It is often the case when you do a script based on a strong book to drift away from it, then come back to it. In fact, there were many drafts, and even the draft of mine that he read was changed.

Q: What do you think of his rather dark vision of the future?

DP: I think that when people do scientific stories, or future stories, what they're looking for is a way to talk about *now*. So I don't think we're talking about the future here. I think people are looking at *now* in an exaggerated way.

So when you talk about the future in *Blade Runner,* it's not a case of whether I agree with it or anything; it's a case of looking at the exaggeration of what is happening now. The cities in *Blade Runner* are bigger than the cities we have, but the cities we have are enormous! It's a way of seeing the present through different eyes. It's like an artist's rendering of something. If it strikes a chord in people and they say, "yes, that's what's happening," then the artist has really gotten to the people.

That's where *Blade Runner* is different from something that's a fantasy like *Star Wars,* where you're released from the present. I think *Blade Runner* is more vital in some ways, because it is not a fantasy.

Alternatively, if you showed a bright vision that rang true, then that too would be one you could agree with. There isn't one single way of painting the world. This is an extraordinary vision, and I think people will find that it strikes something in them.

Q: What would you say is the point of the film?

DP: The point that appealed to me was, when is a person no longer a person? Because he is not born from a womb?

Q: Wouldn't you say that part of Dick's point was about the nature of reality? Like this obsession with the electric sheep and so on?

DP: Ridley wanted to dwell on the animal theme, and I know Hampton's draft had a lot about it, but somehow we never found quite the proper way of making it an important part of the finished picture.

Q: Is *Blade Runner* SF, or a detective story that just happens to be in the future?

DP: I would say that it's a detective story all right, even more than it is SF. It's also a love story—all of that, but set in the future. I don't think it has ever been done before, at least in the movies. Unless you count *Alphaville,* and that is nothing like *Blade Runner.*

The Architects of Blade Runner: *Michael Deeley and Ridley Scott*

To producer Michael Deeley, Oscar-winning producer of Michael Cimino's *The Deer Hunter,* there are three types of movies: low budget exploitation flicks, medium range films that are better suited for television, and the "biggies," the handful of movies that are not just new releases but "events."

"I am in the event business," says Deeley. "I want to make films that no one has made before." What does a producer do to follow up a five Oscar event like *The Deer Hunter?* Deeley's answer is *Blade Runner.*

The production deal for *Blade Runner* was first made at a time following several mammoth flops, when most of Hollywood was understandably scared of big-budget pictures. Especially ones like *Blade Runner.*

"It was an unsympathetic financial atmosphere," says Deeley. "That's why I wanted to make the film, at the time, with very few large-scale productions to compete with."

Blade Runner's first backer, Filmways Pictures, the studio that produced Brian De Palma's *Dressed to Kill* and *Blow Out,* had been attracted by the presence of *Alien* director Ridley Scott. A budget was set up for the film: $15 million. Negotiations began with Douglas Trumbull's special effects company.

Unfortunately, Filmways fell prey to severe financial difficulties, and a new backer had to be found in a hurry. By chance, Alan Ladd, Jr., the top executive who at 20th Century-Fox had been responsible for the development of *Star Wars, Quintet,* and *Alien,* had just left Fox to start his own company, the Ladd Company. Though already engaged in the production of one science fiction picture, *Outland,* Ladd did not hesitate, and *Blade Runner* found a new home.

During the long, meticulous filming, Deeley remained virtually at camera side, always close to the creative eye of the cinematic storm. Deeley's first film, curiously, has become a cult classic in much of the Anglo-Saxon world. It is *The Case of the Mukkinese Battlehorn,* made at the age of 23 for $10,000 with two members of the cast of the famous BBC radio "Goon Show," Peter Sellers and Spike Milligan.

Ridley Scott's first film, *The Duellists,* on the other hand, was enough to establish his reputation immediately as one of the finest visual stylists in today's film world.

Scott was born in northern England in 1939. As a child, his interest in art compelled his parents to send him to study at the West Hartpool College of Art, and then at the prestigious Royal College of Art in London, where he excelled at painting and toyed with the idea of becoming a stage manager.

He joined a newly formed film school, and armed with a 16mm Bolex camera, he made his first picture, which starred his brother and father. The film attracted the attention of the British Film Institute, which gave him a grant to expand it.

After graduation Scott went to New York, where he worked in photography and observed documentary filmmakers at work. On return to London, he joined the BBC as a set designer.

After three years of working on such popular BBC series as "Z-Cars" and "The Informer," Scott left to direct commercials. He became so successful at this endeavor that he soon formed his own company with Ivor Powell (who, among other things, had assisted Stanley Kubrick as coordinator of special effects on *2001*).

Scott's company was responsible for over 3,000 commercials in ten years, many of them award-winning. Scott's first film, *The Duellists,* which starred Keith Carradine and Harvey Keitel, was originally a project for French television, but later evolved into a picture which won the Special Jury Prize at the 1977 Cannes Film Festival.

In his second film, *Alien,* Scott created a now classic blend of science fiction and horror, while making a highly successful thriller. *Alien* became an international smash hit, and one of the 50 top-grossing productions in film history.

Blade Runner was Scott's first Hollywood feature. According to all who worked on it, it was very much the director's own picture, reflecting his particular vision and concepts.

The following interview took place before the film's release.

RIDLEY SCOTT: It's a curious film. It runs on two levels. It's almost, in parts, philosophical. I hesitate to use the word with a commercial movie, but nevertheless, it is.

Q: How did you get involved with the project?

RS: Funnily enough, I'd been shown it a year and a half before, by Michael Deeley, who developed it. It was called *Do Androids Dream* then. I thought that the screenplay at that stage was very interesting. It was by Hampton Fancher. But the automatic reaction on my part, having read it, was to advise Mike that I thought it was a terrific screenplay, but that I didn't want to do it because it touched ground with what I had just done, which was *Alien.* So Mike automatically catalogued it as sci-fi.

I had let it go, but it stuck with me while I was working on something else [Dino De Laurentiis's production of *Dune*]. I kept picking it up and looking at it, and suddenly I decided that I knew a way of doing it which, oddly enough, would have nothing to do with what I'd just done! Because, in a funny kind of way, it's really like a contemporary movie, about relationships ....

Q: Were you familiar with Philip K. Dick's books before?

RS: I must admit that never in my life had I read a Philip K. Dick novel! I knew of him obviously. At one point, I tried one of his novels, and found it extremely complex ....

Hampton Fancher had actually done a very interesting précis of the book, so it made it much easier for me.

Q: Once you decided to get involved in *Blade Runner,* why did you pick Syd Mead for doing the designs—the spinner, the other vehicles and so on? ...

RS: I was a designer, and I still come very strongly from that direction with all the projects I do. It so happens that it helps tremendously with the kind of material and subjects that attract me.

I had been aware of Syd's work for two or three years. I had picked a book called *Sentinel* up about two years beforehand. I thought it was kind of very curious, a very brilliant sort of illustrations. You've got to look closely at the corners of those things as well, because there are some marvelous details in what's basically hardware. So when it came to this project, Syd just sprang to my mind as the one to do it.

He was an industrial designer, and I was certain that he would love to speculate on the way that industrial design could go, on a rather more practical level than on that sleek level. So I contacted Syd and he jumped all over it! He loved the idea.

We started with him designing the vehicles and then, eventually, he, in collaboration with the production designer, started to move onto all sorts of other things: the streets, the buildings, etc ....

Q: You must have collaborated together a great deal to define the "look" of the city?

RS: Yes. It's a kind of verbal sculpting process over a period of time. I usually collect a huge number of photographs and references, just in my day-to-day goings, as a part of my preparation of a movie. Immediately, when I start to think of a project, I start to get a sort of photographic room which becomes a pasteboard room filled with images of what could serve as references. Then, when the production designer comes in, I usually talk endlessly with him about the way I think it could go, and then they start to get sucked in, and then they start to contribute.

It's pretty well the same with everyone that I deal with in that area. I do have a lot to say about what I want it to look like, but at a certain point, I step back and, hopefully, I've chosen the right people and they then get on with it. They take it away from me and just keep making me presentations of various things, saying "what about this or that?" Then, we have other discussions, so the whole thing gradually builds up.

Q: In this instance, did you have any difficulties in getting the visualization of your ideas through?

RS: No, because one of the most valuable things I think I ever learned from my schooling is that I can draw very well. I was an art student for seven years so I should be able to!

So I can draw storyboards, sketches, etc.... The entire communications process is done not as a verbal communication, but rather as a pictorial communication!

Q: How much of the "spinner" concept was yours, for example?

RS: I originally thought the whole reason for me for doing this film, apart from thinking that the script was interesting, was that, again, in a funny kind of way like *Alien*, I could latch onto my own, personal views of how I wanted to do it, how I could shape the look of that movie in other words.

So that look I wanted entailed a lot of air traffic within the city. I had envisaged traffic jams in the air, which I never really got because it would have been too expensive. But originally, we had two really marvelous opening sequences where you witnessed the most immense traffic jam at highway level. Then, Deckard gets out of his car, because he's stuck, the police have called him to come in and he can't. He simply gets out of his car, and taps on a digital device inside the car—a kind of lock-in device—and the car moves off on its own. Then Deckard carefully nips his way through the traffic, which is still moving very slowly, like one mile an hour in a torrential rain, and he goes over the edge of the highway to what is in fact a huge, concrete mushroom. The mushroom reveals itself to be a landing platform, where he sits up there, having coffee out of a machine on the wall with other businessmen. They're all waiting to be picked up by air traffic from the lip of the platform. When his turn comes, the spinner arrives, and that was the introduction of that machine. That was also an expensive sequence.

Q: *Blade Runner* seems to have a lot of rain in it, why?

RS: For two reasons. The first was a practical reason, oddly enough! If you decide to do a movie the way we did it, where we selected the back lot of a studio to do the whole picture in, you've got to go to every [imaginable] length to disguise it. Because most back lots you see in films look pretty cruddy. They look like back lots really … I find that the use of rain on textures that we've created just kind of finely puts a layer on it, which pushes it over the edge into reality. It kind of glues it all together, if you like! So it helps, I think, in terms of the cost of the sets in a funny kind of way, because it helped make all of the street look more real.

The other side of things is that I thought of the idea of having a city with these monolithic buildings. … I guess you got the sense of scale in the city? … Now, you're looking at buildings which, on average, are the height of the Empire State Building or more … there are buildings which are twice that size … therefore, it has created its own weather storms at a high level. Because things are so huge, it creates its own weather program, with its own precipitations, within the city.

Q: I found a lot of the visual "look" of the film reminiscent of some of the strips done by Moebius for "Heavy Metal." Was that intentional?

RS: I get inspiration from Moebius all the time! I think Moebius is one of the great comic strip artists possibly ever! He's absolutely extraordinary. His drawing techniques, I think, are wonderful. His ideas, his observations and his humor—humor in every sense, whether it's in the architecture, the clothing, the insolence, etc.... it covers all grounds—are really brilliant. Yes, he's an influence all the time ....

Q: How long did you spend on the preproduction?

RS: Pretty short time, funnily enough, because we started with Filmways. Then, it became apparent that, financially, they were getting into difficulties. We were then in preproduction, and it started to alarm us. I had been working on the film for about four months, and to have the thing suddenly fall apart can be pretty frustrating. ... So we bailed out and we were taken over by the Ladd Company and Bud Yorkin and the people of Tandem. Naturally, that change of investors extended the production again, so I guess we were in preproduction for just over nine months.

Q: Did you storyboard the entire picture?

RS: Pretty well. We storyboarded the most important sequences. Then, we had to restoryboard certain sequences, because they proved to be too expensive in costing stage. So we had to rethink various things.

One of the big tricks was how I was going to introduce Deckard in the city. I wanted to do that in a spectacular way because I wanted to really demonstrate what the city was *then*, what our cities could grow to. One could have done the movie as a pure Moebius movie, where you're into pure fantasy. But it suddenly became apparent that there were too many elements in the screenplay which were comments, or statements, which referred most definitely to our reality. Therefore, I didn't want the future to get out of hand, so to speak, and get so far in advance that there was no point or connection with the present-day audience.

Q: Could you comment on when and why you called David Peoples to help you with Hampton Fancher's script?

RS: David came in finally when I think Hampton was onto another project, and I was still struggling with various aspects of the story, in terms of Deckard's detecting capabilities, some of the character references, the voice-over bits, and the vents during the detecting process.

I found that one of my problems with the screenplay earlier on was that the man did no detection! He seemed to be told everything, and I wanted to see some detection work. So Peoples came in and started to take over Hampton's place in terms of helping me with those roots, and also with voice-over narrations.

With a film like this, you can't just think up a scene and then hopefully do it in two weeks' time. That scene has got to be costed and prepared!

Q: In the screenplay, the world is portrayed as being overcrowded. In Dick's book, the feeling of alienation arose from the pervasive emptiness. Why this change?

RS: I hate the idea of cities being vastly empty! It's somehow a terrible downer—the idea of city wastelands! I don't mind the idea so much of a multinational, multipeopled textured city of the future. Somehow, it seems more optimistic! But looking at a terrible wasteland where people are hiding in pigeonholes, and where you see somebody only occasionally on the street or passing in a vehicle... now *that* sounds to me like a nightmare! So I don't think I'd have gone with that concept.

Q: How do you reconcile this overcrowding with Sebastian's large, empty building then?

RS: Well, the building was derelict, right? I believe his comment was something like "There's no housing shortage *around here.*" So, in other words, there *is* a housing shortage, but not in that building. Most of the floors were like the floors that Harrison

Ford crawls through, virtually uninhabitable. Sebastian's building is presumably in the "lower" part of the city.

Q: The importance of live animals to Deckard, and its world, was an important concept in Dick's book. It is mostly absent from the film. Why?

RS: That was a very tough concept to wrestle with…. We used to have that in the original screenplay, I mean have Deckard's desire to buy a real goat be his principal motivation. The idea that people will have animals on the roof of their apartment block as a kind of connection with the past—almost as a kind of therapeutic device because these things don't exist anymore—to me, that rang very dangerously close to being pretentious.

It works fine in book form, but when you present it on-screen, you've got to be very careful, because otherwise it looks like one is delivering a lecture, or a message, which I think is hokey, frankly.

I think it reads OK, but I don't think it *illustrates* OK, in the film sense, I mean. Funnily, enough, Moebius could probably illustrate it terrifically well… but I don't think it would work on film. You would have to spend the entire film explaining the presence of these animals, rather than something which is just part of the world that we happen to be showing.

Q: Did you feel that having just a few references would be sufficient to get the idea across?

RS: Yes, I think it was. At least, I hope it was! I would like to have done a little more, but I found that the obsession of the central character—the idea of getting a goat—just a little intellectual… and kind of cute, too!

Q: Isn't that kind of inconsistent with you showing pigeons in Sebastian's attic?

RS: That is a connection which was a little dodgy at the time [*laughter*]! I could argue that they were all artificial pigeons, but that would not make sense, would it? [*Laughter*] No, it would be kind of hokey. I think that in the world, there are certain types of animals, city animals, which are still in existence. In London, for instance, there are gigantic flocks of starlings which are destroying the buildings. So in a city like that, you may start to lose exotic creatures, but the animals that could survive, like rats and birds, would, even in the city environment. Then, you're looking at pigeons the same way as you would a rodent. In other words, like it's a pest.

Q: I found that the final scene, showing vast, unspoiled countryside, contrasted strongly with the premises of that bleak city.

RS: Sure it does... but there are huge, beautiful wastelands even today, in Alaska and Labrador, where only a brave soul or two exist. That does not mean to say that you or I are going to want to go up there and live there, or whether it's even practical to go and live up there!

So I guess these wastelands will always exist. Pushing city limits out to areas like that would probably be impossible.

There was a big argument about this. In a way, frankly, you are right. I would have liked to have stuck rigidly to the idea that the earth was then pretty well decimated and exhausted, and therefore, what you're looking at was a fairly bleak prospect, but these two characters were going to survive there anyway, somehow. Which is the romantic notion of the whole thing, because Deckard is essentially a survivor. But after the whole film, which I guess is fairly intense, to end up seeing them having escaped into an impossibly uncomfortable landscape would have been a real downer. I just didn't want to end on such a down note. So it seemed to make sense to end on the idea that there would be some unspoiled areas in the world still left.

Q: Why did you choose the title *Blade Runner*? It belonged to another book....

RS: I think I just liked it! *Do Androids Dream of Electric Sheep?* is good in literary form, but for a film, I would immediately be put onto an art circuit!

We contacted William Burroughs, and bought the title from him. He oddly enough had done a book in the 1950s called *Blade Runner: The Film.* And it was taken from that.

And just the terminology, as an occupation, sounded good. Not just because of the word blade, but the funny combination/energy of the word sounded just quite right. And, therefore, it just seemed to be a nice term to call the picture.

Q: Didn't you worry that Harrison Ford was too linked in the minds of the public to *Star Wars* and *Raiders of the Lost Ark*?

RS: Nobody had seen *Raiders* at that point. I caught Harrison way before *Raiders*. I wasn't concerned about anything, I thought he was dead right for the role.

Q: Batty is a far more compelling, charismatic character. Was that intentional?

RS: Well, I think that Deckard's character is very austere. Roy Batty, oddly enough, was the whole, not surprise, *turn of events* in the film. One thinks one is dealing with a kind of Frankenstein monster in character, but he really becomes more human than the average human as the film progresses, and therefore, in some respect, gains one's sympathy, possibly as much, or even *more* than the Deckard character!

Q: You tried specifically to achieve a film noir mood?

RS: Yes, I kind of saw Deckard as Humphrey Bogart. Well, the whole thing was influenced in one sense as a kind of comic strip anyway, originally. That was my "eureka" in reading the script, and feeling that I knew how to do it. That was one of the energies that got me moving into it. It was that we would most certainly do a sort of comic strip!

But in the process of it, the film became a lot more serious than I had imagined. So, when doing it, the seriousness of some of the aspects of the film emerged, and in some ways, that fought against it becoming a pure comic strip ....

Q: Why so little use of the Rachael character?

RS: She was there originally to present the predicament of the central character, who hunts replicants and then falls in love with one.

We had more scenes originally written, but never shot. Because the basic thrust of the movie just did not go that way. You've got to decide what your movie *is*. At that early stage, it was getting very drawn between a love story or an adventure. And even now, I find that aspects of certain portions of the love story elements are very good, but whichever way you look at it, it does slow down the film in those particular areas. I just don't think I could have done more. It would have gone against the thrust of the movie, it would have been making another kind of movie.

Q: Since this was your first Hollywood picture, would you care to comment on the differences between working here and in England?

RS: It is quite different, yes. Now, I'd like to live here [*laughter*]!

I think the process of filmmaking, in my experience so far, has given me more freedom than I was able to get in Hollywood. Therefore, I had to learn to construct a movie under some new rules. Basically, for instance, I am a camera operator, and I was not able to do that here, so I had to go through the process of getting visuals through camera operators, who were very good. That worked out fine, but it was all a learning process.

The hierarchies are different, but stronger. Finally, I gradually settled into that studio system, and I really enjoyed it. I liked the Burbank Studio a lot, I think it's a great studio. I just found that comparing it with some of our poor, old, beaten up English studios—there was no comparison, even though the capabilities are very much the same.

Otherwise, you get good'uns and you get bad'uns. You get good film units and you get bad film units, wherever you are. It's all according to the selecting process, and how good you are at hiring good people.

Q: Don't you think that in a case like *Blade Runner,* the elaborate special effects, the sets, etc., have a tendency to overshadow the picture?

RS: No. I think I kept it in place on this one. And, funnily enough, I think I kept it in place on *Alien,* too.

I think effects are there, especially if you're doing a film which involves a different time period. Then, obviously, if you *really* know what you're going to do, then you're going to be presenting your environment in a certain way, which has to look real, but has its place. Because if it upstages the actual contents of the movie, and the characters, then it becomes, usually, a lousy science fiction movie. The best science fiction movies in this area usually have a balance of things.

Q: Why was the anonymous city changed to L.A. in the final cut?

RS: I personally think that we just could have called it the city, but that was felt to be pretentious. I don't know why. There was a general overriding attitude that people seemed to like this thing that said "Los Angeles," probably because you could connect it to something.

Q: Any problems during the shooting? Did you manage to stay within the budget?

RS: Any filmmaking process, especially this one, which was a real difficult film to do, involves keeping everybody's energy up. We're looking here at almost 17 weeks of night shooting. To do that in 17 weeks is pretty goddamn quick!

As far as the release budget … I don't like discussing budgets. I don't think it's relevant to the movie anyway. But we stayed relatively close.

Q: Was Douglas Trumbull your first choice for the special effects?

RS: Oh yes, absolutely! Doug started it off, then he was involved in his own project (*Brainstorm*), so then I worked entirely with David Dryer and Doug Trumbull's team of guys at EEG (Trumbull's then FX company).

Dryer became essentially the special effects director, and did a brilliant, brilliant job.

Once I finished the shooting, I spent my time half editing, and half in L.A. at EEG. We had a fairly limited number of shots, but nevertheless, the shots were quite complex.

Q: Did you have the same hand in the score?

RS: The music is all by Vangelis. I would think that you could almost put the "street music" into being effects, but I was very happy with the track.

I chose Vangelis, but he's pretty much the kind of man you leave to it. We did a fair amount of work, changing various tracks around. But Vangelis very definitely works on his own.

Q: You have been described as a perfectionist by various people. Do you agree that you are, and do you feel that it is important?

RS: I think I am, and I think it's totally important. There are too many things that you lose hold of in the process of making a movie. A film can deteriorate fast because you've got so many people involved in it. It's a bit like running an army!

Q: Are you afraid of being typecast as a genre director?

RS: I think that was the instinct at first, but then, I'm beginning to wonder with everything else I've read, if frankly some of the best material isn't emerging from the SF field anyway.

I find that more and more, just reading the scripts I'm presented with .... I'm really looking at cannon fodder for cable TV most of the time. Some of the most original thinking and original ideas are in fact emerging from the SF genre.

So I've thought, why not? I'll just go into that particular area. I'm going to do a fairy story next, *Legend,* and that's pretty exotic, too. I don't think *Blade Runner* has really anything to do with *Alien.* In a funny kind of way, it's a contemporary film, really. So

I'm no longer concerned about that at all. Therefore, I embrace any ideas that come in from that direction.

Q: Do you personally like SF?

RS: No, not at all [*laughter*]! I don't read it. I just happen to have a view on how to do it. I'm now beginning to read SF, but I find a lot of it heavy going. Some of it has pretensions about idealistic futures and stuff like that, which is very dangerous.

Q: What were you trying to say in *Blade Runner*?

RS: With *Blade Runner,* I intended to entertain, but the film is also about the life of the living. If that message comes through, then terrific!

The Special Effects

The special visual effects on *Blade Runner* are by Douglas Trumbull. Since 1965 Trumbull has been instrumental in the creation and development of new technology in the field of motion picture special visual effects. His education and early experience in art, design, and illustration led him to work on such films as *2001, The Andromeda Strain, Close Encounters of the Third Kind,* and *Star Trek.*

As vice president of Future General Corporation, Trumbull was responsible for the development of new techniques, one of which is Show Scan, a high-speed cinematographic and projection system. Several years ago Trumbull founded EEG (Entertainment Effects Group) with Richard Yuricich, a professional cinematographer who has worked with Trumbull for several years and indeed shares the credits (with aide David Dryer) on *Blade Runner.*

Among the visual effects created by Trumbull and the EEG staff are an aerial view of the city for the flying spinner cars as they go by; hundreds of stories of futuristic architecture which were inlaid above the real street-level buildings; pictures projected on massive outdoor video screens and read-out screens in cars; cityscapes seen through windows, on the streets, and as a backdrop to the climactic final chase between Deckard and Batty; and—perhaps the most spectacular shot ever designed for a film—the aerial view of the hyperindustrialized suburbs of Los Angeles, year 2019, with the spinner's landing at the heliport, over 700 stories high, atop the gigantic pyramid of the Tyrell Corporation. The last panorama was rightly known among the staff as "Hades" landscape, or "Ridley's Inferno."

The bulk of those effects were accomplished through the use of enhanced mattes (mattes which combine paintings with rear-projected miniatures and special lightings), special motion control systems (used to animate the smaller flying saucers in *Close Encounters of the Third Kind*) and the sophisticated use of 70mm, a technique which is particular to Trumbull's studios (Dykstra's Apogee Studios, and Lucas's ILM use 35mm or 36mm Vistavision stock).

Trumbull described his collaboration with Ridley Scott on *Blade Runner:*

> We spent a lot of time with Ridley going over *Blade Runner,* and obviously everybody had their own mind's eye view of what a scene should look like. One of the most fortunate things for us on this picture was that Ridley is quite a good illustrator, and does many of his own draw-ings. He can draw for you right before your eyes what he wants to see, and from that, we can extrapolate what's special effects, what's foreground, what's background, and he can then guess at the length of the shot or the angle of a lens. From that, we make a plan of what the shot will consist of and hope it ultimately matches what Ridley asked us to do ....
>
> I think *Blade Runner* is representative of the coming of age of special effects. They are integrated into the film to support the basic premise. They are not meant to stand

self-consciously at the center of the stage. The effects are designed to support the story....

Blade Runner is really very accurate on a technological level. One of the things about this film is that it's absolutely filled with machines. It's just pervaded with high technology, and that's probably the way we're headed. *Blade Runner* has a very credible look in that respect.

Interview with Syd Mead

The major factor of the credibility of *Blade Runner* is the presence of Syd Mead, design concept consultant (he is credited in the film as the visual futurist) who created the many visual representations of the various machines and products of the future.

Mead, a famous industrial design consultant (his credits include Ford, Chrysler, Philips, and U.S. Steel), contributed to *Star Trek* and *Tron*. His book, *Sentinel,* presents a remarkable overview of this creative futurist's career. From his home in Hollywood, Mead told us about his lengthy involvement with *Blade Runner.*

Q: Working on *Blade Runner* must have been a new experience?

SYD MEAD: Yes, I'd never worked on a major production from zero to the finished print until this one. The little bit I did on *Star Trek*—designing the V'ger, its exterior, some concept sketches for the interior, etc., was at the tail end of the movie. But with *Blade Runner,* I was involved from blank paper all the way through the end, which was very exciting.

Q: What is your background?

SM: My background is primarily industrial design. I have been a consultant to Philips Electronics for 10 years, to late 1979. I've done consultant work design for Volvo, American Motors, Ford, and Chrysler. All of that because I did a whole series of large brochures, up to 95 pages, for U.S. Steel in the 1960s, and those went all over the world. Since then, I've been typecast as a vehicular, or a transport type of designer, but I've done product design and fantasy illustration. However, I had never worked on a major film before. When Ridley came to Los Angeles originally, with his group from England, Ivor Powell and Michael Deeley met them there, we had a first meeting and I was hired to do five vehicles. They had to be started on right away because they took the longest to make. That was the reason for hiring me, the vehicles.

My book *Sentinel* had just come out and Ridley had had his people in London accumulate all available publications from designers who slanted toward the technological fantasy field. That's how I was contacted.

Q: Did you have the desire to work in movies before?

SM: I had been contacted several times. The problem is that I have been a professional in my field for 20-plus years and I'm wired into a commercial pay level that movies don't usually match for production designers. So, I'd submit a quotation for working arrangements and I'd never get another call! They have a budget, naturally, and they'd start multiplying the number of days times what I charge per day, and they'd go over budget immediately—unless it's a large film ....

Star Trek was a very large picture, with a big budget, sort of in desperation, so they accepted my fee there. Then *Blade Runner* came along, also a large-budget film, and somebody made a decision to hire me at the rate I charged any corporation at the time.

Q: How did you grow to be more involved with the film?

SM: The first designs I submitted to Ridley and Larry Paull .... You see, I don't like to do sketches isolated on a white sheet. I like to bury the design into its setting so it looks like it's supposed to look when it's going to be in use. So I started putting in background indications, having read the script and heard discussions and started to get the visual feel that Ridley was after.

He liked some of the visualizations that he saw in the background behind those vehicle sketches, so he said to me: "Why don't you see what you can do with the street sets." And, at that time, they decided to use the Burbank studios to avoid the cost of flying actors, props, etc., around the country. So we redressed the New York set of the Burbank lot. I took photos of the street and just did a tempera sketch to show how I would dress those sets to match the look of the film. That progressed into interior sets, specifically Sebastian's laboratory, Deckard's apartment kitchen and bathroom. In each of those, there was a specific picture quality that Ridley determined and outlined.

Q: Have you read much science fiction?

SM: I love science fiction. My favorite author is Arthur C. Clarke. Isaac Asimov, too, because they both have a very solid believability. Both are people that write, but are also other things. They are familiar with chemistry and a broad-based scientific background. They don't propose things that are just for. the convenience of the story, which I dislike.

Q: How did you approach the design problems involved in *Blade Runner*?

SM: My background in industrial design helped in several instances. One, for example, was the entry system for Deckard's apartment building. We needed a dramatic device or sequence by which you had to get into this high-security building. The current state of the art is a magnetic card. That's not very dramatic or future-looking. So we refined it a bit. You push the card into a slot and the computer in the building identifies you and lets you enter that particular door, which means an enclosed controlled space. They can get a print-out which shows when you arrived, what rooms you went into, etc., but that was not dramatic enough for a movie. It does not look interesting enough, or does not impress you with the fact that this is a high security building. My knowledge of these kinds of technological accomplishments allowed me to fine-tune it further, with screens and voice identification, etc .... The device acquires an image which makes the audience (1) appreciate the technology, and (2) enhance the dramatic needs of that particular scene and piece of hardware.

Q: Why is the *Blade Runner* decor all old and dingy?

SM: We set up a sociological sort of theory of why the world would be that way in interpreting the original story, and then the script.

The theory was, that the heavy industry or high technology was concentrating so much on off-world accomplishments that it was taking all of the available capital, maybe as much as 70 percent of it, to accomplish what they were doing in space. As a result, the consumer base wasn't being serviced properly. You didn't have a new toaster, car, or shaver, a new device available for shelf sale every year like we do now. That then produced the recycling of old things, or redressing them to make them work better or longer, which meant that you had an aftermarket to supply bits and pieces of stuff, parts, technological add-on blocks, and you just put these on the car or refrigerator to make them work better because there is no new model available.

This approach gradually produced this accumulative sort of lumpy, knobby look, because everything was retrofitted with bits and pieces to make it work.

Q: Whose concept is this? Ridley's?

SM: Ridley would, in detail, describe what he was thinking about and what he wanted it to look like. He's very visual himself because he's an artist. He would draw sketches.

One striking example is the Voight-Kampf polygraph. He specifically said to me: "I want it to be very delicate, but look very menacing, sort of like a tarantula sitting on your desk." It had to be small enough to be a briefcase device. It had a thick cable underneath the desk going to a remote control box, but in essence, it was a very delicate device which sort of unfolded by itself. It had an optical thing that followed you and was centered on your face, because the idea was that it watched your iris

55

opening, because when you get very nervous, your iris contracts and it showed this on a small TV screen, and the person operating the device would watch the opening and closing of the iris, which is analyzed by a computer. Plus the fact that Ridley wanted it to look alive. So we had a bellows built into it. The idea there was that there is a science of smell. They suspect that there are molecules called pheromones that come off a person and your nose picks these up. So this machine would literally breathe with its bellows, very slightly, drawing in air samples and analyzing them along with the iris contractions. The end result was a briefcase-size device which looked very menacing and like it was alive. That was a specific crossover between Ridley's visual exact direction, and coming up with a workable prop.

Q: How did you interface with Lawrence Paull, the production designer?

SM: Larry's job was to have the things built. Everything, the vehicles, the sets, ... and have them built to something resembling a budget, and putting up with the changes in scenes! Some scenes were built or were in progress, then were written out of the picture!

I'll give you an example: I went to Europe and at the time I was designing a beautiful, Chinese tea machine for this restaurant where Deckard eats. When I came back with a sheaf of sketches, the scene had been written out totally! I think my designs ended up as a food cart on the street!

Larry's job was also to make the sets actually buildable. What I did was to supply some visualizations of the specific things that we needed to make the film look the way it does.

Q: Did you design things that could not be built?

SM: All the time! Larry did an amazing job because he had to have things constructed that were going to be very expensive. Of course, some things were just written out because of cost factors. There was a train scene, for example, that was in the original script. Deckard was on the train going toward the city that was at the time called San Angeles. That was written out because to rent an actual train, or to find an old one, and to redress it for a minute length of the scene was just not worth it!

Another example: originally, the ambiance of the film was going to be cold, but they found out what the cost was going to be to ship all the sets to Michigan or Wisconsin to get them to freeze and so, instead, it became misty, hot, with sweltering rains.

Q: Why do the streets look so crowded and poor?

SM: That look evolved progressively. One of the backgrounds of the vehicle sketches—I think it was the taxi—was reflecting the sociological theories we were discussing at the time. The city had grown to where buildings were 3,000 feet high. That was our theoretical figure. They're planning to build a 2,000 foot high building in Chicago right now, so that's not really too fantastic. I made a scale drawing showing the World Trade Center Towers—they're about 1,200 feet—then up to 2,000 feet, and then added another 1,000 feet because we're in the year 2020. When you start to get this scale, you realize that the street level would really serve as access to the building maintenance system. If you had to live next to the street, you'd see nothing outside your windows, except machinery and stuff. So I thought, "we'll have a rental service where you can rent a view!" Which means a box that you snap over your window, you have a flat-screen TV, which is technologically feasible right now, then you can have a nice jungle with birds flying or whatever you want!

Of course, when everyone has one of these, it produces a warehouselike look to old apartment buildings. It has a strange, noninhabited look. Yet if you had grown up with these, you'd know that these buildings have people in them!

Then you'd have big power conduits going up the outside of these old buildings. There'd be no use tearing down old buildings. You may take the whole inside out and remodel the entire interior.

Q: What do you think of creating a very elaborate set, instead of doing location work?

SM: Well, it depends on the reality you're trying to create. If you're trying to produce a reality that does not exist now, eventually everybody gets to know that brand new building in Dallas, or Berlin, or downtown L.A., or wherever, like they did in *Buck Rogers*, so you can't use that. You have to create a reality that doesn't exist, and that means either building it in miniature, or dressing a set.

Q: Aren't you afraid that the sets might become the stars of the picture?

SM: I don't think so. The cuts that I've seen emphasized the emotional reactions between Deckard and the other characters. Really, all that we did was construct an alternate reality as background. I think it really comes out that way, and I don't think the machinery competes with the ongoing story.

Q: What do you think of the world that you've created?

SM: Well, it's a possibility—if you're not too optimistic. Others have asked me this, and I have answered that this is only an illustration of a particular script. If another movie came along and the script was more optimistic, then I'd design a different future. You suit your designs to the story.

Q: Don't you think that going into so much research is too extravagant for a film?

SM: No, I think it's just professional. The amount of detail you can achieve depends on the money, of course. With enough time and money, you could duplicate the Taj Mahal.... In the old cathedrals, the back sides of the stone figures that you can't see were carved as well because whoever did them attached their own mentality to what they were creating. I think the density of detail is very important.

Q: Yes, but does it make any difference to the spectator?

SM: I think it does. The production people who were financing the movie saw the finished special effects composites that the

Trumbull group had put together, and they were so excited that they said "If you need more money to add more blinking lights down there on the matte shot, or another vehicle dubbed in flying along the street, go ahead and do it."

Because it becomes more believable, you see. If you look at a matte shot and you see traffic lights blinking, and you see a car fly by or a little rustle of paper down there, it might cost thousands of dollars for that one little movement, but it makes the entire thing more believable.

Incidental movement and details enhance the reality, which is what you're really trying to do.

Q: How much of your designs are based on valid scientific concepts?

SM: That depends. In doing Deckard's kitchen, we had to have things that looked like kitchen things. So if you have a flat surface, maybe that's a griddle. We had this fat sort of rolled-edge thing that was laying on it, and you don't know what that does—and I don't either [laughter]!

But it looks like something which belongs there. Like you buy readymade hamburgers, and they're stored in there, freeze-dried or something. All of these things are not scientific but produce a look and you can fine-tune that visual look anyway that you want.

Q: What about the spinners?

SM: Ah, the principle of that is scientific, it's the aerodyne which is an enclosed lift system. It's a valid principle, through which you just direct the exhaust downward and if you equal the weight of the vehicle, it lifts off the ground.

When Ridley and I had our first meeting, he said, "We have a flying car: that will be your biggest problem." It was because he didn't want rotating blades, or fold-out wings. He wanted a real car that would just lift off the ground and fly without changing shape. That way, it would always be more recognizable, and also it made more sense technologically to have something that could land and take off in its own space.

We borrowed the aerodyne principle and made it look like it could work in a car shape. It looks completely believable. I think it'd probably work in reality but would need some center of gravity adjustment for the exhaust.

Q: Is it easier to design sets for night shots?

SM: Probably, because you can get more mileage out of the existing fixtures, because you see less of them, and you can play with reflections, etc.... But you have to increase the color and make everything brighter to show up.

Q: Any designs that didn't work at all?

SM: Interestingly, yes. We had to design a special gun for Deckard. Ridley did not want lasers because that's been overdone. So we came up with a kind of projectile which maybe had its own propellant built into it. They went shopping around and found a kind of flare gun, big, heavy kind, and put some things on it to make it fancier. We tried various colored flashes out of the muzzle, blue, green, etc.... But my own original design for the gun was not used. In fact, it became a telephone because when the sketch was lying upside down, it looked like a futuristic handset telephone [*laughter*]!

Q: How was working with Ridley Scott?

SM: It was very nice. We got along well. Most of the concepts that I furnished were accepted on the first try, or certainly the second, except for the spinners, because it was such a central, focal point in the movie. That one did have to go around several times.

Q: Any ideas that had to be totally changed?

SM: Yes, Sebastian's truck. We had to come up with a truck that Sebastian, who was a tinkerer, might have built from things he found. The problem is what you'd find in a junkyard 40 years from now. I started off with a streamlined version of an old ambulance he might have bought, but it looked too much like a motor home! Then, we went into a completely new direction and assumed he might have gotten hold of an off-center cab chassis.

So we built a cabin on the back of it, and incorporated all sorts of technological scraps, and it grew just like it would have grown had he done it as we supposed.

Q: How was it to see your designs actually built?

SM: It was exhilarating! Most of the things I design are never built, because I work in a theoretical kind of area. But having something actually fabricated is fantastic because it does prove to me that my research, my ideas were correct.

The mean streets of Mead's and Scott's future are booming with life, full of texture and color. They include a total of 33 operational vehicles, all designed by Mead: seven coupes ("people cars"), seven sedans (including police cars and Deckard's personal car), four taxis (in the traditional, yellow-checkered American tradition), two vans (armadillo-like vehicles, including Sebastian's truck), and several old, retrofitted vehicles (such as a garbage truck, a gravel truck, and a disinfectant wagon, etc.).

Once the designs were completed, well-known California car customizer Gene Winfield was brought in to build the majority of them (Winfield's credits include work on *Star Trek*, "Man from U.N.C.L.E.," and "Get Smart").

Three spinners were built, a fully operational one for the street scenes, one "stand-in" and one for flying, plus a mock-up of the cockpit for interior shots of Deckard.

Mead explains:

> They painted the spinners different colors, although it's the same model. The idea in the film is that the spinner is a very particular kind of vehicle, to be used only by authorized personnel, or security forces etc.... The average citizen would not be allowed to have one.
>
> We built a five-foot-long spinner that was a complete duplicate of the big one that was used for the shots where you see it fly through the model sets. Then, there was a

smaller one, about two feet long, for the matte shots. These in addition to the three full-size ones, of course.

The entire look of the film was based on research and carefully thought out principles regarding the future of architecture, transportation, fashion, etc....

The architectural look of the city in which the story takes place, a city dubbed "Ridleyville" by the staff but later retitled "Los Angeles," was based on the principles of retrofitting etc., divided by Mead and Scott, and was actually built by Trumbull's EEG group.

The centerpiece of the film's bold design was the street complex known as the "New York Street" set of the Burbank Studios (also used recently in *Annie),* and redressed according to Mead's designs. The New York set was built in 1929 and provided the dark alleys and back streets that Humphrey Bogart and James Cagney stalked in so many Warner Bros. classics. They were a fitting location for a detective story of the future!

Interview with Lawrence Paull

For *Blade Runner,* production designer Lawrence Paull and art director David Snyder revamped the historic set into one of the largest sets built in Hollywood in recent years. It comprises elements of downtown Los Angeles's picturesque Little Tokyo, but also of New York, Hong Kong, Tokyo's Ginza, Milan, and London's Piccadilly Circus!

In *Blade Runner* the complex street set represents the Little Tokyo of downtown Los Angeles in the year 2019, with its nightclubs, sushi bars, etc. It also contains "Animoid Row," a street where replicant animals are sold, and the shopping arcade where Deckard shoots Zhora.

Following Mead's sketches, the production team built their arcades right out to the sidewalk and filled the streets with a variety of mechanical stuff: "trafficators," large video screens, bizarre parking meters, videophones and even "retrotrash"! Most of these gadgets were built out of surplus airplane parts, radar machinery, and missile parts salvaged from an air force base. The video-screen frames were made from bombers' radar-scope machinery, and the dome-lit parking meters were molded fiberglass, operated by key-cards.

At the other end of Ridleyville, atop a 700-story pyramid, is the office of Tyrell, where Deckard meets Rachael. Described by Paull as "establishment Gothic," it features 75 square feet of black marble floors, 20-foot columns, a black marble desk, and a huge picture window of the type described by Mead.

Deckard's apartment, by contrast, is done in Mayan cast-stone motif. The decor is high-tech mixed with antiques, with low ceilings and a beehive look. The exterior of Deckard's con-dominium complex is actually a house designed by American architect Frank Lloyd Wright in 1924.

The interior of Sebastian's apartment is eight intercon-nected and totally run-down rooms. It matches the location: the Bradbury Building, a famous Los Angeles building built in 1893 by architect George Wyman. Curiously, Wyman was inspired by a science fiction novel by Edward Bellamy, *Looking Backward,* set in the year 2000! The Bradbury was used for its outlandish Renaissance exterior, its geometric patterned stairways with wrought-iron railings, and its glass-block floor, glass-domed ceiling, and open-cage elevators.

Other exotic location work included a meat-storage room, doubling as a frost-covered scientific chamber where low temper-atures were necessary to make genetic parts, and where the film company bundled up for two days to work at seven below zero while the rest of Los Angeles was experiencing a 98° Fahrenheit heatwave!

Paull describes *Blade Runner* as one of the most draining and difficult projects he has ever worked on. For one three-week period, he never left the studios and had changes of clothes delivered to him! At the end of the shoot he had lost 15 pounds, and his long-term relationship with a lady friend had been completely destroyed, according to him. He adds that his was not an isolated case among the crew. In spite of this, he is pleased with the work he accomplished, and he relived with enthusiasm in his Hollywood Hills house his experience on *Blade Runner.*

Q: What is your background?

LAWRENCE PAULL: I've been functioning as a production designer primarily on feature films and TV films such as *How to Beat the High Cost of Living, In God We Trust, The Last American Hero,* and a lot of others. I just basically jumped around and freelanced.

Q: You haven't done any SF pictures before?

LP: No. One of the things I have to be rather clear on is that I don't consider *Blade Runner* to be a SF film. I have always considered it a period piece, it's just that the period we're doing is 40 years from now, instead of, say, 1940.

The only other thing close to SF that I've ever gotten involved with was a picture which unfortunately never got made. That was years ago at MGM, something called *Pyramid,* which Douglas Trumbull was going to direct. A good percentage of it got designed and we had storyboarded the entire picture, [but] the studio decided not to do it!

What I try to do for myself is not to get typecasted as doing SF films, or period pieces, or whatever. I try to do a mixture whenever possible, although I happen to *love* period pieces!

My background is architectural, as opposed to Syd Mead's which is industrial design, so we have a different attitude toward design. What I found interesting in *Blade Runner* is that it was set *only* 40 years in the future, so you're projecting forward as to what a city will look like, what the environment will be, the attitudes of the people, etc. ... So you build up a whole thesis really, before you sit down and start designing the show. It gives you a very concrete approach to the problem and the results can be good, or bad. If you take a look at the inner cities in New York or Hong Kong, conceivably, that's where the world is going.

Q: How did you get involved in *Blade Runner*?

LP: I was basically called in for an interview. I knew two people on the show already. I had previously been involved with Douglas Trumbull. That may have had some factor in it, since he wound up doing the special effects. Ridley and I were able to communicate and I gather he felt he would be able to work with me.

Q: Did you have any input in the background designs?

LP: Yes, absolutely. Syd was involved initially in automobile designs, and what I would call the design of the hardware. When I met Syd, when I first got involved in the show, he had already had preliminary discussions with Ridley for the look and the style of the vehicles. As time went on, the vehicles evolved. It didn't just happen by magic. What happened was that when Syd was doing some illustrations for some of the vehicles, he put in some of the city, pieces of buildings, etc.... Ridley and I liked what was happening so we took Syd out to where we were going to create the city. We sat down and did a lot of brainstorming.

Syd is an incredible illustrator, and he came back with a lot of interesting things that were drawn up. It was a combination of what I had said, Ridley's input, and his own.

Q: How did you achieve that retrofitted look?

LP: All of the hosing, turbine, and blocks of foam were added onto the buildings. The idea is that the mechanics of the buildings have deteriorated, and people go outside to buy additive types of mechanical devices to service them. Consequently, you get some of the style of the buildings where it just built up of layers.

We also tried to make the streets look very claustrophobic. We designed it in such a way that is in many areas similar to Milan, where the buildings actually come out right to the curb and they have these covered arcades with columns.

It was also the idea that it wasn't going to be all straight modern glass and steel buildings. Somewhere along the line, somebody had come and said "Let's get back to a more decorative type of architectural motif." Consequently, there were these massive columns holding up monolithic buildings in the city.

Then there were all of the interior spaces. Syd was also involved in these, designing the hardware. We collaborated on the decoration of Deckard's apartment. I had done rough designs which I gave him prints of. We also went through various types of research books.... We looked through electronic gadgets catalogues—a portable, battery operated vacuum cleaner was used as a hair-dryer, etc.... The purpose was to find things with a high-tech look and stick them here and there.

Then there is the rest of the movie. The responsibility for getting Syd's and Ridley's ideas done and designed right was mine. Besides the city, which was one set, there were 20 or 25 interior sets, which we sat down and designed basically from scratch. They were of the future somewhat, but not all. A lot of times we drew from the past, like making a composite.

Q: How did you get that dingy look?

LP: We didn't call it that, but all of the streets and the interiors of a lot of the buildings had a lot of trash. It wasn't just paper trash or garbage trash, it was all like high-tech trash. We used all sorts of airplane parts, engine parts, and just broke them all apart. We had barrels of them—55 gallons of high-tech trash! The point was that we had to have trash that looked like it was part of the buildings, of the cars, etc.... which deteriorated on the spot, and just lay there. It also gave us an added texture—it looks a lot different than if we just had taken paper and thrown it all around.

Q: Did you have any problems assembling any of Syd Mead's designs?

LP: The only thing pertaining to Syd that we had a difficult time with was the Voight-Kampf machine. We had a great deal of difficulty making the mechanics of it work in the size that we wanted to make it. We started over from scratch again a second time, and we finally got it to work.

We also had some difficulties with some of the vehicles because of the time factor involved. What we were asked to do was come up with five different types of vehicles in a five month span from design to finish. There were a total of 28 or so vehicles. When you think about that in terms of how long it takes General Motors to pull together a custom car—and we were talking about 28 of them in five different styles. They all had to run, they all had to be interesting, and they all had to be designed and drawn up from working drawings so that someone had something to go with on them .... Our biggest problem was time.

Blade Runner was so encompassing—what we were doing was really creating a total environment, from cars to what a city looked like, including parking meters, light standards, mail box chutes, whether you have newspapers or not, etc. ... In this instance, we took the premise that there would be no newspapers in 40 years. Everything is going to come over video machines. With the time limitations, such a total approach to design takes a lot out of you.

Q: Was starting with the New York Street set easier than setting up a new set from scratch?

LP: I don't think it was a matter of easier or not, it had to be done that way, period! A lot of the buildings on the set stayed as they were; the only thing we changed was that we would add the retrofitting, transformers, hosing, pipes, all these strange connectors, devices, etc ....

Had we started from scratch, we would have had to build the old buildings first, and then do the retrofitting on top of it. There are several factors to consider: time, the budget, but also: where do you build such a set? You have to find a very large soundstage that you can tie up for months, and that's *very* expensive!

Q: What came first, the street set or the vehicles?

LP: The vehicles. Then we got involved in some of the interior sets. I had put together an entire art department and we laid out a schedule of what our priorities were. I had three fellows working on executing drawings for just the street and another three doing just the sets.

Q: Was the fact that some designs were written out frustrating?

LP: It's somewhat frustrating, yes. But what's sad about it is you've wasted all of that money and that time.

I remember one specific, very large set that I designed—it was an interior set—and it got half built, then one day someone said we were going to put it out. Apparently, it was budgetary, and they were concerned about the flow of one scene through to the next. There was a lot of "shoe work" in this movie, people walking from one scene to another as opposed to just dramatically cutting. In this particular instance, even though I had already spent X amount of dollars, they felt that they just didn't want to spend the extra time—a few days—to shoot it.

With Ridley, there were always changes to be made. That's his modus operandi. Ridley likes to see things and then he'll start playing with them, and change them. So we had a lot more of that, instead of having something started and then totally yanked. We'd have something that was three-quarters or perhaps totally built, and then Ridley would change his mind. Sometimes, that would happen, but other times it would be fine.

Q: Did you enjoy the experience of speculating on the future?

LP: Oh yes, very much, because it was based on concepts in reality that we thought were valid, very valid. One of the things I like about the look of *Blade Runner* is that when people go to see the film, they'll be able to see the buildings that they still see today in downtown L.A., or Chicago, or whatever. So when they see the interiors, which are into 40 years from now, they'll be able to relate to them.

I found a lot of reality in the show, and it was a very stimulating experience.

Q: Did you have to design electric animals?

LP: We talked at one time about a white electric owl. We also made a bird, almost like a pterodactyl for an early, early script. We had a special effects team working on it. It had wings that were five feet long, made out of a tubular structure in aluminum, with a synthetic skin over it. It was almost like building a model airplane—and it had to work! We flew it by remote control. But all of a sudden, it was just another of those things that were eliminated from the script....

Q: Was there any problem in making things work, I mean, really work as they were supposed to?

LP: My only answer to that is—we are in the movie business, and by hook or by crook, one way or another, with the right people, I can always make it work!

The vehicles were especially difficult because we didn't have enough research and development time. Some of them leaked— we had rain throughout the whole film so water got inside! Some of the vehicles had exhaust leaks into the interiors. On most of the cars the window didn't work, because that's a whole big mechanical thing to arrange, and that takes time, so the windows were up, the exhaust and the rain leaked in—it was very uncomfortable inside! But nothing that we couldn't overcome.

Q: Did you work well with Scott and Mead?

LP: Oh, yes, I think so. There were tenuous times with Ridley because he's also a designer, but he's a very bright man and I've got nothing but respect for him. It was an interesting 14 months, I'll say that.

BLUE THUNDER (1983)

Beginning in the 1980s and climaxing in the 1990s, movies that relied on high-tech hardware became a genre unto themselves, a hybrid mix of cop stories and science fiction that began with *Blue Thunder* and continued on through the likes of *Robocop, Aliens,* and *Terminator II.*

It all began with a simple little thriller that played on the familiar themes of paranoia, police corruption, and lots of explosions—and added a unique twist.

Blue Thunder: a civil libertarian's flying nightmare. A helicopter capable of eavesdropping on conversations, peeking through walls, airborne reconnaissance and, of course, blowing up everything in its path with an incredible arsenal of high-tech weaponry. And although the film featured the likes of Roy Scheider, Malcolm McDowell, and Warren Oates (in his last role), there was no question who the *real* star was: the chopper. No one really cared about the story. They just wanted to see this ugly monster fly. And blow things up. Is it any wonder the series spawned not one but *two* television series ("Airwolf" and "Blue Thunder")?

But beyond inspiring imitations, it created a new hero, hardware: cold steel, iron, shiny chrome. He didn't demand top billing, a fancy dressing room, or catered lunches, but the studios were paying through the nose for him anyway because hardware always has the same costar: mayhem. As in explosions, and lots of them.

Truly the relationship of the 1980s was the marriage of technology and artillery, and if *Blue Thunder* is remembered for anything, it is for being the matchmaker.

Interview with Dan O'Bannon

If screenwriter Dan O'Bannon could get his hands on the *Blue Thunder* helicopter he created he would probably use its lethal artillery to level every movie studio in sunny Southern California.

And then he would hunt down *Blue Thunder* director John Badham and *Alien* writers Walter Hill and David Giler for a little extra target practice.

O'Bannon, to put it bluntly, is angry.

"It's a bad business, Hollywood, I'm just about fed-up," he says. "If I can't get something to direct soon I'm gonna get out of this business and be a novelist or something."

What O'Bannon wants is control, the power to make sure what he types is what gets on the screen. His scripts for *Alien* (with Ronald Shusett) and *Blue Thunder* (with Don Jakoby) were considerably rewritten—and not to his liking.

In addition, in the case of *Blue Thunder,* he was not exactly thrilled with the direction. "John Badham is lazy, a hack, and has very little film sense. He directs a $20 million movie like a TV episode," O'Bannon says. "He's a very mediocre director. When you actually see him on the set you realize how really lost he is."

O'Bannon says he was on hand during a day's filming when Roy Scheider, who plays the police pilot of a technologically and deadly new chopper developed by the federal government, forgot one of his lines.

"Badham said, 'It doesn't matter, it's only dialogue. Just say something and put the word shit in it,'" according to O'Bannon.

> Badham has the theory that the audience really doesn't understand dialogue. He's real dumb. After we slavishly and obediently made all the changes he asked for in the script, he quickly brought in Dean Reisner, who came in and moved around the commas.

7 1

But O'Bannon did expect his script would be rewritten. It is a basic part of moviemaking.

> Hollywood is just a machine, they have a process. There's this standing assumption among producers and studios that no script is any good. Every script that they buy or have written must be rewritten by several other authors before they'll film it.
>
> The trouble is most producers have no judgment and therefore if a given draft of a script is excellent and film-able they can't tell or won't make the mental effort to determine it. They'll automatically have it rewritten since most scripts in Hollywood are truly wretched. This process has a homogenizing effect and improves it. If the script is really, really good the process will lower the quality of it.

Guess what the process did to *Blue Thunder*.

> The political impact, and there was quite a bit, was toned down. In the original script, all the various outrages that were committed were done by the police, the LAPD. Before they would commit that to film those brave persons [Badham and Columbia Pictures] changed the police into heroes and made the outrages the fault of the federal government.

O'Bannon is obviously upset. "The idea of portraying the LAPD as blameless champions of individual liberty at odds with the federal government is strange."

They also had a different concept of what the ominous *Blue Thunder* should look like. "They envisioned it as a big, ponderous thing with crap hanging all over it while we saw it as a fast, black wasp—compact and deadly."

Blue Thunder was a child of O'Bannon's anger. He was living in Hollywood, back in 1979, and could not sleep at night because police choppers were constantly flying overhead and hitting his house with their searchlights.

"They were just driving me crazy. I was sitting around with Don in my place one night and one of them went over us. I just got very irked and said we should make a movie about that," he recalls. "Don agreed and got very excited. And that's how it began."

What can you say about police choppers if you decide to use the agile machine as a symbol for government intrusion in our private lives? You can say quite a bit.

> Helicopters, per se, I like. I don't particularly like them going back and forth and back and forth over the sky surveilling us and everything. The police have those things up there because they can prevent crime and they are very handy.
>
> The trouble is the police don't particularly care if they drive the rest of the population crazy or violate the rights of everyone else in order to catch a criminal. They don't care about preventing crime, they care about catching criminals. And toward that end, they will do anything to the rest of the citizenry. They don't care at all. That's what this picture was about.

The Blue Thunder is completely computerized, armor-plated, and armed with all manner of deadly weaponry. "There's nothing fanciful [about the chopper]. It just seems fanciful if you're not acquainted with it. There's nothing remarkable in that film, not when they have satellites that can photograph your belt buckle."

While there may not be anything fanciful about the chopper, some plot devices and a high-speed car chase at the film's end do tax a viewer's sensibilities.

Dozens of police cars are pursuing Candy Clark, Roy Scheider's girlfriend in the film, who leads them on a frantic chase through downtown Los Angeles. Badham eventually trimmed down the chase when Seattle preview audiences and others gave it the Bronx cheer.

> The idea of having a car chase has certain assets but what the hell makes his dumb girlfriend such a crack stunt driver? Badham saw the picture as a cartoon and what he was looking for in the end with Candy Clark running around like crazy was "Dukes of Hazzard."

John Badham, however, looks like an angel when compared to the portrait O'Bannon paints of *Alien* rewriters Walter Hill and David Giler.

> When they bought the script and took it away from me to make it themselves they tried to inflate it far beyond what it was.
>
> Hill and Giler did nine rewrites, each progressively worse. They said if you got a spaceship, it's gonna be the biggest spaceship in the universe. And then they changed that, they wanted a fleet of spaceships. I said "just one monster?" They said not one monster, we're gonna have 50 monsters and so on and so on. It finally reached a point that it was in such bad shape that it couldn't be filmed.
>
> Finally Giler was thrown off the picture because he wouldn't make the script changes demanded by Ridley Scott, who was hired at the last moment. He asked me to come in and try to pull it back into shape. I made some changes at that point and made it closer to the original.

What set *Alien* apart from other monster-in-space epics was the eerie and unnerving artistic work of H. R. Giger. It was

Giger's work which inspired O'Bannon, so it particularly angered the writer when the studio wanted someone else to design the creature and the sets.

> I fought for a year with Fox to hire Giger. I wrote the script so Giger could design those things. And when they picked up the script they said "naw, we don't want this guy. When has he ever designed a movie?" They wanted someone who was a good, solid movie pro.
>
> They hired Carlo Rambaldi to design the thing originally. He came up with something that looked like a half-molten marshmallow with a bunch of big, pretty blue eyes. For a year I kept thrusting Giger's work in front of them and they kept saying "This is some wingding who lives in Europe. What movies has he designed?" Only because Ridley was hired on was Giger hired. He took a liking to Giger's work. Without Giger, I don't think we would have had much of a movie.

Or as realistic a movie.

> Those sets on *Alien* looked so real. It wasn't as though they were trying to build something that would look good, but as though they were trying to build something that would survive beyond the pyramids and actually fly through space. It was extraordinary.

Also extraordinary, considering his success, is that O'Bannon does not particularly like writing. He finds writing far too solitary and feels there's a danger "you'll become neurotic and smoke too much." What he has been working toward is the director's seat and the "only avenue I could find toward that goal was to become a writer."

"It's very clear to me having worked on these two big pictures that the director's control over the script is absolutely immense," he adds.

Although he usually writes a script and then tries to sell it on spec, he developed a project with MGM entitled "The Sorcerer's Apprentice" that he wrote with the elusive director's chair in mind. Alas, it fell through.

> I still have high hopes for it. But, that's where I learned the pitfalls of writing on development, which means they hire you. You come in and they say here's X dollars, write a script. In this case, it was a deal for me to write it and direct it. By the time we finished it, MGM, the lion that roars, began to whimper and basically, for no real reason, they simply canceled the project.
>
> They may have indeed not have liked the script I wrote but their decision could not have been entirely uninfluenced by the fact that they were doing badly at the time.

Now "The Sorcerer's Apprentice" is sitting in an MGM vault where O'Bannon will need a powerful spell to get it back.

> That's why I became unhappy with development. It's tied up with MGM now and I have to extract it. I can't just cart it around town and say "Hey guys, ya wanna make this movie?" MGM owns it. Now we have to figure out a way to get them to let us make it elsewhere.

And he wants to. He genuinely likes the story and considers it one of his best works. "'Sorcerer's Apprentice' was something I wanted to do very much. It's lighthearted, it's fantasy. It's about a young man who wants to be a magician."

More than just any magician, the lad wants to be a great magician in the Houdini mold. When he is approached by a grand old magician from that very mold who asks him if he would like to learn magic, the boy quickly agrees. But the magic this old guy has in mind is not card tricks and disappearing rabbits. It is real magic.

Another project O'Bannon was grooming as a possible directorial debut was called "Bloody Noses," written by Bob Greenfield.

> It just didn't happen, I kept trying to promote it for me to direct and it just didn't happen. Then, all of a sudden, we got a glut of psycho ax-murder movies and as soon as that happened I said, no, it's too late now. ... It was a very extraordinary tale of a psychotic mass murderer but that can only play in absence of a bunch of other ones. But now we've got *Friday the 13th* "Part 300" and *I Eat Your Eyeball*. I'm disgusted by those movies now. Until those films have faded into the past and everybody has forgotten them I can't touch "Bloody Noses." I'm afraid it's a dead issue.

More lively are two adaptations of Philip K. Dick stories. His version of *We Can Remember It for You Wholesale* (later filmed as *Total Recall*) is being produced by Ronald Shusett for Dino De Laurentiis and "Second Variety" has been optioned by *Outland* designer Tom Naud for a film tentatively titled *Screamers*.

This year is also a year of big decisions for O'Bannon.

> I'm 36 years old, you know, starting to get kinda old, no longer a youth. Your body and mind are different. People are supposed to be middle-aged when they get to 50. Doesn't that mean middle of life? How long is life? If it's 70 years 36 years old is middle age. And my mind feels older than my body. Jack Sowards, the guy who wrote *Star Trek II*, a nice looking fella, kinda older looking, said in *Starlog* that he feels 19. Well, maybe he does but I feel about 70.

O'Bannon has always been into science fiction, and he proudly shows off his library in his Santa Monica home. "Look, here's *Snow Fury,* the first science fiction book I ever bought, I still have it, patched up by me. It's about snow that comes alive and eats people. Written in 1956. That makes me ten years old when I graduated from comic books to paperback texts. Not a well-known book, that one."

He is quick to point out he is no longer a science fiction buff.

> I was a science fiction nut and now I'm a science fiction filmmaker. I think there's a difference. It interferes with work to be both. It becomes very clubby and in-group oriented [your work]. Since I've become involved in making films I have to take a totally cold, jaundiced eye toward it. I think it's a real risk to just love the subject matter you're doing. I think it's dangerous.

The transition from buff to filmmaker was not easy.

> I went to four colleges, changed my major all the time, didn't know what I wanted to do. When I was 21 years old, I discovered I was on the verge of graduation from a Midwest college with a degree in psychology. And I thought, wait a minute, I don't want to be a psychologist. So, after a lot of soul searching, I could only think of one thing: I wanted to make movies.
>
> It was scary because I knew it was impossible but I knew it was the only thing I could stand doing for a living. I was sitting around a dorm room in 1968 and I had already exhausted the *Playboy* fold-outs so I was getting into the text, reading the *Playboy* adviser. Someone had written a letter asking where the best film schools were. I checked them out and applied.

He ended up at the University of Southern California and got his film education watching *Citizen Kane* and *Dr. Strangelove*.

> The actual production experience I got there was negligible. I got no encouragement from the faculty. The students there are all creeps, all extremely competitive loners. Nobody wanted to work with each other at all.
>
> There's a saying in Hollywood, I forget who said it. In Hollywood, it's not enough to succeed, your best friend must fail. That attitude begins at the USC Film School.

How did his parents feel about the career he eventually chose? After all, filmmaking is the least thing a lower middle-class, middle American couple would suggest to their only son.

> My father is not a man who speaks very much at all, a very inarticulate man, though he is a genius and a very funny guy. I've asked him about it and he just scratches his head. He goes to see them all [the films] faithfully and he collects the memorabilia so I'm quite sure he's proud and likes the films. But he doesn't know how to express it.
>
> My mother has always thought, from the time I was about eight, that I was a criminal. She always thought of science fiction not as an art form, literature, or as a substance. If sometimes I would take a science fiction book to school she would grab it from me and say "Don't take science fiction with you!" As if it was some kind of paste or putty.
>
> When I was about 20-21, she had me thrown in jail for smoking grass and tried to stop me from going to college. For the first two years I was out here while I was struggling, she kept trying to get me to be a civil engineer. She has only one real criterion for success: that's making money. So

when she saw *Alien* all over the country it was like puzzled dismay, she didn't know what to make of it.

O'Bannon pauses for a moment and then smiles. "It was a perversion to her that someone should make money off science fiction and movies. I think she sees me as the equivalent of a successful hitman."

There are some filmmakers who may end up seeing O'Bannon much the same way.

Interview with John Badham

The English-born son of actress Mary Hewitt, Badham moved to the United States at the age of five and settled in Birmingham, Alabama. He received an undergraduate degree in philosophy from Yale University, where he directed and performed in student stage productions. Badham's first jobs in the motion picture industry, however, were in the Universal Studios mailroom and as studio tour guide.

Badham spent the next three years in the casting department, then became assistant producer. In 1971 he started to direct for television. Among his works are "The Law," "Isn't It Shocking?," "Reflections of Murder" and six episodes of Rod Serling's "Night Gallery."

Badham made his feature film directorial debut with the critically acclaimed *The Bingo Long Travelling All-Stars and Motor Kings* (1976), a bright comedy (starring Richard Pryor, James Earl Jones, and Billy Dee Williams) about a black baseball player trying to start his own team. It was Badham's next film, *Saturday Night Fever* (1977), however, that helped launch not only his career as a big-time director, but also that of actor John Travolta.

Badham was also responsible for the film adaptations of two successful Broadway stage plays, *Dracula* (starring Frank

Langella and Sir Laurence Olivier), and *Whose Life Is It, Anyway?* (starring Richard Dreyfuss).

Q: How did you get involved in *Blue Thunder,* and when?

JOHN BADHAM: I got involved about two years ago, when the producer, Gordon Carroll, came to me with an idea from Dan O'Bannon and his partner Don Jakoby. The script was then developed and worked on for some months by myself, Scheider, and writer Dean Reisner, whom I had brought in. Reisner has worked on many Clint Eastwood pictures, such as *Dirty Harry,* over the years. He is a terrific professional that really solidified a terrific idea of O'Bannon and Jakoby, and made a good, focused screenplay.

Q: Did you do many changes from the original concept to what it is now?

JB: I think I did a lot of character revision and shuffling of characters about—this is Reisner and myself that I'm talking about—and focusing on the human beings. We had plenty of story and action there, but the human beings needed the most help. We worked on that quite a bit so that we didn't lose sight of the humanity of the situation. Sometimes, when you get all this great action going, you lose sight of humanity and you wonder why people don't care about the movie. Crashes, flying, and wonderful special effects don't mean a bloody thing if you don't care about the people. It's so easy to let that happen, and I get worried to death about it, because you see it so much.

Q: What was the hardest thing about making this film?

JB: The preparation, which went on for six or eight months. Planning to pilot the helicopters through the streets of downtown Los Angeles, 50 feet above street level, among the tall buildings—not down through a residential area but really in canyons—involved a tremendous amount of persuading, cajoling, planning, care, and so on, to avoid the incidents that happened with *Twilight Zone.* Not that we knew anything about it, because we were prepping a month before. But we were doing what was going to appear to be, and what was in fact, extremely dangerous aerial maneuvers.

We had to work on Sundays and things like that. You just can't go flying into these areas with motorists and pedestrians that aren't under your control. We would have to control whatever area we were in. Sometimes we would have to seal off twelve square blocks at a time, with police at every intersection, every alley way, and completely cordon it off so that nobody could go in.

We would do that for about three minutes at a time. Then we'd do what we were going to do. Fly in and maneuver all around and then release all of the traffic. Then, about 10 or 15 minutes later, we'd do it all again! It was very dangerous and very tricky work. But the care paid off, especially the day that one of the helicopters blew an engine 40 stories up and plummeted straight to the ground! The pilot was all right and had the tremendous skill to be able to put it down safely. But God knows what would have happened if there had been people under there.

Those helicopters, you can set them down when the engine isn't going, but it is like setting down a rock! The rotor is going, which is what gives you a little bit of a lift, so it is not completely a rock; however, you have no control at all. He dropped from 40 stories up, down to the ground in seconds. It was terrifying. I was right up there with it, in an adjacent helicopter.

Q: Was the helicopter totally destroyed?

JB: I'm sure that they could rebuild it. Put a new engine in it and fix up parts of it. It wasn't that bad. The pilot seemed to be okay. They get an immense amount of money for used helicopters! The parts are so valuable. For example, we bought some doors for a helicopter that we had to use on the stage. They cost $10,000! We also bought another wreck that was a totally crushed heap that had been lying in the woods. It cost $7,500 and looked to me like basic scrap.

Q: Are there special companies that specialize in helicopter stunts?

JB: Yes. There are trained pilots who are doing specialized stunt work and also very specialized aerial work. We employed what we thought was the best of these companies. In fact, that's a company that rents out helicopters for movie work and provides the pilots at the same time. We had one pilot with us the whole time we were preparing and the whole time we were shooting. He always knew all that was going on, and was involved in all of our planning.

He'd go with us when we went to look at locations to be aware of what was going on, and to see if he could get the helicopter in there and get it out. I know a lot about helicopter planning now, and can pick locations for helicopters, because I've listened to him and been so frustrated so many times. I'd find something absolutely perfect and he'd say, "No. We can't shoot here. And we can't shoot there because there are residential homes, or there are wires overhead, and there's this and there's that regulation and the FAA says this and that," etc.

Q: Now that the *Twilight Zone* accident has happened, would you feel more nervous about doing a helicopter movie?

JB: Yes, I would definitely feel more nervous about it. A few weeks ago, I shot a scene for *War Games*, where a helicopter is chasing two kids in an open field and keeps boxing them in, and finally corners them in one little area. We had stuntmen there and the same pilot that I had for *Blue Thunder*. Well, as careful as we had been on *Blue Thunder,* we were twice as careful on this one! Everybody was standing there chewing their fingernails the whole time, because God forbid anything should happen. We followed every regulation and precaution that we could.

Q: How do you feel about stunts, now that that whole tragedy has happened? Do you think that there are too many of them?

JB: No, I don't think so. I think you have to do them carefully. But you always had to do them carefully. You have to remember that you're not playing with tinkertoys, but you're dealing with life or death situations, and anything can happen. You tend to get lulled into a sense of false security because it's a movie set and it's make-believe. But, for years, almost any actor can tell you, that whenever they get involved with stunts, it's usually the simple stunts that get somebody hurt. The little silly falls where the actor says, "That's okay, I can do that myself." Then, the next thing you know, he comes up with a sprained wrist or a broken something else.

You always have to be careful with these things. A good stuntman is, in one sense, slightly crazy to be doing this; but in another sense, there is a tremendous amount of skill, care, and cold-blooded calculation in what he's doing. So it's not a wacko stunt. We have found that even the stuntman's union has gotten a lot of members in the last few years that are crazies, who are attracted to the publicity that they get, and who are not as trained and as careful as they should be. And then, there are these bozos who go out and do things for "That's Incredible," things that no rational stuntman would do. They're the same jerks who suddenly turn around and say that the stunt wasn't prepared properly, and try to sue the production company.

The way it properly works is for the stuntman to come in and talk with the director about what he [the director] wants to do. The stuntman will then say if he can do it, and what are the best ways, or that he can't do it and won't, but will offer an alternative instead. I've had that happpen with my pilot, Jim Gavin. That's a good way to handle it, so that when you decide on what you're going to do, the stuntman is setting it up in a manner that is totally acceptable to him.

You just have to allow the stuntman to set up a stunt in a way that is safe for him, and get it done so he's happy with it and not feeling rushed or pressured. A guy that won't put his heels down and say "Hey, guys, this is my life" is not a good stuntman. Part of a good stuntman's requirements is being stubborn and able to plant his heels down and say, "No! You want to fire me, go ahead, it's okay." I've wanted to fire Jim Gavin any number of times, I'd just get so angry, but something in the back of my head would say, "He's trying to tell you something and you have to listen to him."

Q: Did you have to change the script because of not being able to do a certain sunt?

JB: Only in minor ways. Sometimes I'll look at something which isn't as spectacular as I had hoped, or wasn't quite going to do. But I don't think I've ever had a real story failure because we couldn't make it do one way or another. You can usually make anything work. You may have to do it in three or four cuts, piece it together and not get that spectacular all-in-one shot that you want. But, curiously enough, when you get that spectacular all-in-one shot, by the time you get through editing the picture, you cut it up into banjo picks anyway. All the efforts you went to to get it that way were needless.

Q: Do you ever think that you could have done some of the things that you wanted by using miniatures, matting and special effects techniques, instead of live action?

JB: Well, I can tell you that the one section that was absolutely impossible for me to do completely live, involved F-16 fighter jets. F-16 fighter jets are not available unless the government approves your script. They control all F-16 jets. If you go to Israel, they'll let you use some, but somehow we thought that was a bit extreme since the jets had to be in the L.A. airspace!

So we were forced to look at all of those SFX techniques. We wound up using motion control techniques that have really been developed for *Star Wars* by ILM and by a much smaller but very good company called Dreamquest. It's a company of half a dozen guys that got going on their own and now subcontract from ILM, as well as doing their own things. They're very good, very inventive. We provided them with our storyboards and they built models of the F-16s, and we brought shoot plates of the L.A.

airspace. Then they matted them in using their techniques so the planes were flying through the space. The shots are very good—the wide shots. The close shots, where you really can see the ship up close, have given us a tremendous amount of trouble in making them as believable as the rest of the picture.

I think that, when you start dealing with an actual place in the daytime, you have real trouble with this kind of thing. If it was nighttime, you could get away with murder! You can't see matte lines, you can make everything blend a lot more easily. I used rear projection for most of the scenes where Scheider and Daniel Stern are in the helicopter. But we were doing it only at night....

For the daytime scenes, we mounted cameras on the helicopters, flew through the actual places, and shot their close-ups up in the sky. You can tell the difference, and it was worth the trouble. We did it at the very end of the picture, so that, God forbid something should happen and we had lost Scheider, we would have had a whole movie all put together. Which is something we all talked about at the time. In fact, I even went out, put the helicopter up on a stand, and shot some close-ups against blue sky so we had something. Then, once we had that, we went out and shot them in the real airspace.

Q: How did that work, and who flew the helicopter?

JB: You would shoot one close-up at a time. Those things are controllable from the left or the right side. Actually, it turned out that Scheider was flying the helicopter most of the time, because along the way Jim Gavin was teaching him how to fly. I have film that I shot myself—the camera was in my hands and I was shooting—of the first time that Roy took the stick. He did a lot better than me. I was learning how to fly too, but he was much better than me. He was even landing and taking off.

Malcolm McDowell was terrified of flying and used to get out and throw up after a flight, but he was professional enough to get back in. By the end of the film they had him flying the helicopter, even though he was scared to death. I had to go out and reshoot a few things, because there were some times when his eyes would get wide as saucers. He would come back and say, "I was just fine. I was terrified, but I held my composure all through the shot." But later, you'd look at the shot and his face would be all stern, except occasionally for these great big eyes. It was very, very, funny. His wife, Mary Steenburgen, said to us, "I don't know how you got him up there, I can't even get him in a 747!"

Q: Did you storyboard the film?

JB: I storyboarded all the flying sequences. Which means we storyboarded about half the movie. We were careful, especially with the action sequences because you can get lost without the storyboards, so that the crew doesn't know what you're trying to do. But storyboards tell them right away. You can also go and shoot way too much film. It's easy to get crazed and start shooting everything from every angle, much more than you need. At least the storyboard will give you the bare bones, and if you shoot a little bit more it will help keep you on track.

Also, for the Dreamquest sections with the F-16s, we had to be extremely precise. Their work was extremely costly, about $20,000 per shot. We contracted with them for around 27 shots, $540,000. I think the last shots were done in March, and we are still, on December 15, trying to get some of them exactly right, so that they'll fit into the film perfectly. I'd say most of them are just great, but there are three or four irritating little shots that still won't do.

They stick out like a sore thumb, no matter how much you try to make them blend in and work perfectly. This goes back to your question about miniatures. If one thing is ever so slightly off with those, the audience spots it in a second. I think we had talked ourselves into believing that they were as good as we could make them when we went to preview. We got the audience reaction cards back and they started talking about those phony planes, I got the fellows in the projection room and we looked at them closely. We saw that it was these three or four shots that sort of leap off the screen at you and don't cut with the others. It's daytime flying, blue-screen, where we had live actors in the frame shot against blue screen ....

Blue screen has always been a bear, and I just thank God that we didn't decide to do the flying close-ups at night that way, that instead we did them with rear projection. It's an antiquated, horrible old method that everybody tells you is awful and won't be any good. But I defy you to look at this picture and say that they look bad. The rear projection is just sensational. You'll be totally convinced that they're flying up at night in a helicopter.

John Alonzo, the cameraman, and I tested every process that we knew. That's how we came up with the rear projection. It had the flexibility and the instant accessibility that we needed. We could see our dailies the next day, not six months down the line, as I'm talking about with those three or four little shots, where I'm still trying to see a decent one. We could make our corrections and adjustments as we went along, Rear screen also has a wonderful flexibility of movement; we could move our camera all over the place. With the other methods, everything is locked down, nailed into the ground, nothing can move. However, since we could float the camera around, you always felt like it was in another helicopter, flying along with you in the skies at night. They're constantly shifting and juggling for position, which gives it a nice verisimilitude that you couldn't get with the other processes. That's part of the trouble with my F-16s. You cut from a real flying shot to one of those and it's really noticeable.

Q: There is also the problem that miniatures don't have any reflective light, and therefore the image is flat.

JB: Yeah, it just doesn't look right. We tried techniques to get around that, like having moving lights shining. With the rear screen, I made them bring in two machines. One projector for the rear screen, and one projector that took the same piece of film, or a copy of it, and would shine that right on the actors' faces. There was no screen, it was just shining on the bubble so there were these lights and things going over the bubble of the helicopter and their faces during the shot. So there's motion going on everywhere.

Q: Do you think you could make another film of this nature and lick the problems faster?

JB: I don't think you could lick them any faster. I kind of knew what was involved when I started, and I know better now what's involved, but I don't think I could do them any faster. I don't think there's anything that we could do differently. I think we did everything the best way possible. I did have people around me who had done lots of whatever we were doing, so it wasn't for lack of skill or knowledge that we had problems. It's just that we were really dealing in such a tricky area, where everything is all research and development. Every shot is R&D, and trying to get it right is horrendously difficult. This is very meticulous, especially if you're talking about special effects, stunts, and science fiction type of things that have to look real.

Our requirements as an audience, of what we will accept, is so much higher than before. Everybody's an expert. In the previews that we have, you'd think that all these guys had been to the UCLA film school, because some of their comments were so astute and they are so sophisticated about those films!

Q: Do you have a hand in the music as well?

JB: The composer and I worked together, He did the composition, but he very carefully spotted where it was going to go, what kind of music we thought was right. Usually, a good composer will be calling you up constantly while he's composing. Then you go over to his house, or wherever he's composing, and he has a video tape of the film set up right by the piano. He has you watch something and starts playing on the piano. Somehow you have to have enough musical knowledge or imagination to be able to translate what you're hearing on the piano to what is going to be a full orchestral thing. That can be really hard, even if you think you know music. Hearing a piano score drives me crazy. Sometimes it sounds flat and tinny on a little piano playing away.

Q: How do you feel about the film now that you've been away from it?

JB: It's a very exciting movie. It's great fun to watch. The last time I saw it with an audience it was terrific. It's a good audience picture.

COCOON (1985)

ocoon was the launching pad for two hot young starlets. One
of them, Steve Guttenberg, had been acting for several years
but was looking for the part that would break him out of the
"eager young guy hot to get laid" parts and move him into leading man status. The other, Tahnee Welch, was a true Hollywood
knockout, with a face and figure that eclipsed those of her sex-
goddess mother, Raquel.

So who emerged from *Cocoon* as the hot new stars in town?

Don Ameche, Wilford Brimley, and Jessica Tandy, not one
of whom was under sixty when the film was started, and all of
whom had their careers jump-started by the success of this sweet,
sentimental picture.

Ameche, a leading man of the 1930s and 1940s, best known
by this time for having played Alexander Graham Bell in a
biopic, had come out of semi-retirement for a supporting role in
the Eddie Murphy vehicle *Trading Places,* but he was hardly a
household name (except for aging wits who could not help wise-
cracking every time a phone rang that Ameche never should
have invented that infernal device). The role in *Cocoon* led to
an Academy Award, and the renewed career brought him starring roles over the next decade opposite Joe Mantegna in David
Mamet's *Things Change* and Tom Selleck in *Folks*.

Brimley, an old cowboy, had been discovered by director
Sidney Pollack for a small role in *The Electric Cowboy*. Although
the next few years brought him some meaty supporting roles,

after *Cocoon* Brimley became a genuine leading man, starring in the television series "Our House" and "The Boys of Twilight."

Jessica Tandy, who had been a star on stage for decades (she was Blanche DuBois in the original Broadway production of *A Streetcar Named Desire*), finally became a movie star, landing the lead role in *Driving Miss Daisy,* for which she received the best actress Oscar, and a starring part in the unlikely hit *Fried Green Tomatoes,* for which she was nominated as best supporting actress.

And, oh yes, there was one more star who emerged from *Cocoon.* Also an acting veteran of decades, this star used the film to cement his role as the hottest director of family oriented entertainment in Hollywood. Ron Howard, whom America had watched grow up from little Opie in "The Andy Griffith Show" into adult Richie Cunningham in "Happy Days," was coming from his second film and first big hit, *Splash,* when he undertook *Cocoon.* The film proved he was anything but a one-hit wonder—as *Parenthood, Willow,* and *Backdraft* would further demonstrate—and elevated him from the status of beloved boy-director to full-fledged filmmaker.

Tom Benedek

Two years ago, people called Tom Benedek when they could not unlock their doors, pay their rent, or get into their private parking space.

Now they call him when they can't figure out how to adapt the book they just bought into a script.

"I've been getting sent all the difficult adaptations," says the writer who turned an unpublished novel into the screenplay for *Cocoon.* "Since I did *Cocoon,* which was a difficult adaptation, it's been 'It's an impossible adaptation—send it to Benedek.'"

It is not a completely unpleasant experience for Benedek, who spent ten years trying to sell a feature script before landing the *Cocoon* assignment. Even the hardest adaptations have been more fun than his last pre-*Cocoon* job of managing an office building.

Benedek's newest assignment, however, may leave him looking back longingly at the office building. His job: to adapt Mark Helprin's mammoth 700-page epic fantasy *Winter's Tale* into a manageable script for producer Gene *(The Pope of Greenwich Village)* Kirkwood and director Martin Scorcese.

Winter's Tale is an epic love story that spans one hundred years in the history of New York and has at least a hundred characters. It's a huge, sprawling book by a writer who fills every line with intricate details. To reduce the novel's almost 700 pages down to a two-hour movie without losing its distinctive qualities is like trying to film the Bible—or *Dune*. It's a problem Benedek is well aware of.

> You *can't* put this book on the screen…. It's hard even to *imagine* the movie when you're reading the book. To film the book would give you a 20-hour movie with a $150 million budget. We really can't even let it be a three-hour movie, because those are so hard to get made.
>
> This is a particularly difficult adaptation because the beauty of the imagery is the key to the novel. The way things look is the most striking thing about the book. What's important is to stylistically retain the look of the book, to show all the visual elements.

But, Benedek says, in some ways the book's style makes the adaptation easier. "If you just tell the story, a lot of the book will fall away and seem unnecessary…. Without the visual imagery, a lot of the story simply wouldn't be that compelling."

The key to the adaptation, Benedek claims, is for the writer, producer, and director to understand the novel so well that they can make changes while remaining true to the book's spirit. "I think the trick is to respect what Mark Helprin felt when he was writing the book, and then take liberties with the book itself.... You have to develop a story from the book, and find what's the essence."

For Benedek, Scorcese, and Kirkwood finding the essence means following Peter Lake, the book's hero, throughout the entire film, instead of letting him disappear for 300 pages as he does in the novel. That means cutting down the other major characters, including the Penn family, who will play a more subordinate role.

One thing that won't change, Benedek predicts, is the role of New York City. New York itself is one of the most important characters in the book, and over the course of the novel it is ravaged by fire, surrounded by a mystical cloud wall, and crowned with a bridge of pure light. That will all stay. "We're playing up the city, the spiritual wrath of the city," he says. As difficult a job as this will be, at least Benedek has the comfort of knowing that the book's author supports his efforts.

> Mark Helprin realizes it's a difficult adaptation. He'd like to see his own vision on the screen, but he knows that's really impossible. There are some novelists who will only sell their books if they can maintain a certain degree of control: if they can choose the director or write the screenplay. And then there are some who just sell their books to a producer. That's what Helprin did. They asked him to write the screenplay, but he refused.

And even though it's a tough job adapting a popular novel to which thousands of readers will be bringing their own expectations—*Winter's Tale* was a bestseller in both hardcover and paperback—Benedek says it's not as hard as it could be. "*Winter's Tale* is a controversial book," Benedek says. "It's highly esteemed, but not all the reviews were good. It has its fans and its detractors. It's not imprinted in everybody's mind—it's not *Catcher in the Rye*."

As he gears up for *Winter's Tale*, Benedek is finishing up another adaptation of yet another fantasy novel.

> I'm doing an adaptation of *Sea Faeries*, from a book by L. Frank Baum, who wrote *The Wizard of Oz*, for Brian (*Splash*) Grazer. Ron Howard is involved, too. It's hard, too. It has people talking underwater. In fact, the whole movie takes place under water. It's sort of the *Winter's Tale* of summer movies. It's a very old book, written in 1908.

Whatever Benedek's current adaptations do for his career, they can't have the kind of impact *Cocoon* had.

> *Cocoon* was my first produced script, and it changed my life. I had been here in L.A. for ten years, working different jobs. I'd always had an agent, I studied directing at the AFI. I always had a script circulating. But when I was hired to write *Cocoon*, I was managing an office building. I always believed—or was deluding myself—that I was in the industry, but the phone wasn't ringing and I wasn't working. Then I was offered this thing to work on that already existed, that wasn't even my idea. Now I have this buzzing career.

Benedek's buzzing career now includes four screenplays he is currently working on and offers for more than he could finish in another ten years. But his affection for his first produced script, and the great fortune it is brought him do not blind him to its faults.

> The ending of *Cocoon* was *never* licked. The first hour always worked, we always knew what it was about. The

ending worked in the script, but the director never really committed to it. We worked on characters, resolved the characters, and had an emotional resolution, but then there was a second ending. I'm not the kind of writer who screams at every changed word, but I think they dogged the ending.

The second ending, of course, was the arrival of the flying saucer. It was almost universally criticized as redundant and familiar, even in the film's most positive reviews. Benedek says that scene was written to be not quite so familiar.

The shot everyone hated was the flying saucer coming down from eight other movies. The original part of the ending was that the saucer made weather changes, like an act of God. It didn't look like that. If the film had had a great second unit, if there had been brilliant, original special effects, the ending might have worked. It still wouldn't have been the most amazing ending ever—especially after E.T. and Close Encounters.

But no one ever came up with a better way to end the film. Robert Zemeckis, who was originally slated to direct, has said (Starlog) that he felt that the ending was never completely solved. Even Benedek still has questions.

Who knows, maybe it would have been almost better with no ending. But then the idea of transcendence would have been lost, and that's very important. Unless you had all the old people stay, and had this speech about Mother Earth, but that just would have been stupid.

Anyway, people didn't go to see Cocoon to see special effects. They went because they wanted the heart-warming story of the fountain of youth. It is Benedek's skill in creating likable, believable characters that made the film a hit. And Benedek is the first to admit that, if one ending had to be dogged, director Ron Howard made the right choice. "It's much better this way," Benedek says. "What was important was the emotional resolution, and that worked."

DUNE (1984)

One of the most eagerly awaited science fiction films of 1984 was undoubtedly *Dune,* produced by Dino and Raffaella De Laurentiis for Universal Pictures, and directed by David Lynch, the man responsible for *Eraserhead* and *The Elephant Man.*

Originally published in 1963 in *Astounding Magazine* (now called *Analog*) under the title "Dune World," *Dune* first appeared as a book in 1965. It quickly proved to be not only one of the most remarkable science fiction works ever written, but also an unprecedented best-seller. Today the *Dune* saga, along with Bradbury's *The Martian Chronicles,* Asimov's *Foundation* trilogy, and Clarke's *2001: A Space Odyssey,* is one of the few science fiction novels of fame which has spread beyond the genre and reached the general public.

Winner of the Hugo and Nebula awards, printed in millions of copies, and translated into more than a dozen languages, the saga of *Dune* has since been expanded into five sequels: *Dune Messiah* (1969), *Children of Dune* (1976), *God-Emperor of Dune* (1981) and *Heretics of Dune* (1984).

The year 1984 marked the twenty-first anniversary of *Dune's* first publication, and it was fitting that the anniversary would be celebrated by the release of a big-budget, feature film version. Yet the translation of *Dune* from the pulpish pages of *Astounding* to the Hollywood silver screens was anything but simple, and rivaled Herbert's fictional, labyrinthesque intrigues.

Naturally, *Dune's* colossal success quickly attracted Hollywood's attention. One of the first companies interested in

acquiring film rights to Herbert's novel was APJAC, a corporation formed by the late Arthur P. Jacobs, producer of the *Planet
of the Apes* pictures. According to an interview with Herbert,
published in the May 1975 issue of *Unknown Worlds of Science
Fiction*, APJAC planned to film *Dune* in an area northeast of
Ankara, Turkey, with Herbert himself as technical adviser. At
the time, only a treatment had been done, and no director or
scriptwriter seemed to have been chosen. For some reason, however, the project was abandoned, and *Dune* was left to wait for a
more determined producer.

Strangely enough, that person was not an American, but
a Frenchman, Michel Seydoux. To write and direct the film,
Seydoux called on Chilean-born writer and director Alejandro
Jodorowsky, whose previous credits included heavily mys-
tic-laden pictures such as *El Topo* and *The Holy Mountain*.
Jodorowsky's *Dune* was scheduled to begin filming in September
1975, but the incredible amount of work that the director put into
the preproduction held up the starting date almost two years.
Finally, the production cost, originally estimated at $6 million,
escalated to unforeseen heights. Unable to find new sources of
financing, Seydoux simply abandoned the project.

Jodorowsky was assisted during all phases of the film's
preproduction by the talented French comic-book artist and
illustrator Jean "Moebius" Giraud. Under Jodorowsky's careful
guidance, Moebius created over 1,000 pages of extremely elaborate storyboards and designs. "For me," said Jodorowsky in a
1976 interview with French magazine *Rock and Folk*, "Giraud is
a complete artist. He is not only a comic-book author, but he is
also a painter and a poet."

In addition to Moebius, the director also planned utilizing the talents of three other famous science fiction artists:
Christopher Foss, a Briton, celebrated for his ultra-realistic
depictions of spaceships and technological artifacts; Richard
Corben, an American, author of "Den" and other *Heavy Metal*

fare; and H.R. Giger, a Swiss, creator of 20th Century-Fox's *Alien*. Each artist was to create his own concept of one of the film's four planets. The golden, octagonal fortress-planet of the emperor was to be conceived by Foss. Caladan, the forest covered world of the Atreides, was to be designed by Giraud. The Harkonnen's leprous, corrupt stronghold of Gedi Prime was to be handled by Giger; and Corben was to bring to life the planet of the Bene Gesserit, with its weird, pyramidal edifices.

Music, too, was to be an integral part of Jodorowsky's vision of *Dune*. Different groups were also expected to contribute their own special styles to each of the planets. Pink Floyd had accepted the assignment of the Imperial Planet; a popular French band named Magma was to do the Harkonnen homeworld; and the British group Henry Cow was to bring life to the planet of the Bene Gesserit. Originally, the special effects were to have been handled by Douglas Trumbull. Later Jodorowsky, impressed by *Dark Star*, planned to entrust them to the care of Dan O'Bannon. O'Bannon went to France, where he met with Giger and Moebius, whom he later brought to work with him on *Alien*.

The filming of Jodorowsky's *Dune* was to take place in Tassili, in the Sahara Desert, with hundreds of actors and extras. Among the actors mentioned for the film were Jodorowsky's own son, Brontis, in the role of Paul Atreides. Salvador Dali had been mentioned for the role of the Padishah emperor (Moebius's original design for the character is a likeness of the famous Spanish artist) but, in a 1976 interview with French magazine *Cinema d'Aujourd'hui*, the director stated that he found Dali's political condonation of Franco's execution of several young Basque militants to be "so odious," that he preferred to tear up the contract.

The most interesting aspect of Jodorowsky's project was undoubtedly his personal interpretation of Herbert's novel. He told *Rock and Folk*

> I interpret and continue the book. I don't believe that one should take a novel and fail to put it at one's service. As the anarchists say, "Neither God, nor Master!" I take the torch and continue further on. If not, it's not really worth it.

Jodorowsky spent two years writing a scenario, which was then dialogued by French science fiction author Michel Demuth, Herbert's French translator.

In his screenplay Jodorowsky went beyond Herbert's book. At the end of his version, the death of Paul the prophet (in the Islamic sense of the term) "fertilized" Dune and turned it into a giant, collective intelligence, a living planet. This new Dune, in turn, gave birth to a living, intelligent galaxy, and onward, until the attainment of a communal, and completely spiritual, universe, one with man. Inherent in these concepts are alchemical themes dear to Jodorowsky. For the director Dune's spice is the science fiction equivalent of the "projection powder," or philosopher's stone, which has the power to transmute baser matter into purer elements. Alchemists have always held that that transmutation process is both physical and spiritual (at the level of the alchemist). Because of Paul's efforts, the planet Dune itself becomes a giant philosopher's stone, which enables the entire human race to realize its collective soul and become one with God.

The failure of the Seydoux-Jodorowsky project did not discourage other producers, and the film rights not only to *Dune* but the entire series were finally purchased by Dino de Laurentiis, producer of *King Kong* and *Conan*. Having discovered Herbert's novel on the advice of his daughter, Raffaella, De Laurentiis made her the producer of the film. He then asked Ridley Scott to direct. Scott, who had just completed *Alien,* worked on the film for many months, producing numerous storyboards and production designs. Unfortunately, after creative differences with

De Laurentiis, Scott abandoned *Dune* and went on to do another science fiction-inspired project, Philip K. Dick's *Blade Runner.*

Raffaella De Laurentiis then suggested the name of David Lynch, director of the underground classic *Eraserhead,* and of the widely acclaimed *The Elephant Man.* According to a 1983 interview in *Daily Variety,* De Laurentiis had liked *The Elephant Man,* but he was unfamiliar with *Eraserhead.* "Dino had never seen *Eraserhead,*" Lynch reported in the interview, "and if he had, he probably wouldn't have hired me. All his kids saw *Eraserhead* in his living room, and I think he just walked through and saw about 10 minutes of it at most."

In any event, Lynch was contacted and a contract was signed for him not only to direct but also to write the script. Not having read *Dune* before, Lynch set about "discovering" the book. In 18 months Lynch delivered a first draft screenplay. After more than half a dozen revisions De Laurentiis declared himself to be satisfied with the script.

For various practical reasons, Universal and De Laurentiis decided to shoot *Dune* at the Churubusco Studios in Mexico. The official budget of the film was set at $30 million, but some other sources have hinted since that the figure might actually be closer to $60 million.

Filming began on March 30, 1983. Frank Herbert was present, and it was he who gave the first clap of the clapboard. The shoot lasted for 23 weeks, finishing on September 20, but it was followed by an extensive period of postproduction, including the preparation of more special effects, of the music, and the mixing.

Since the beginning, *Dune* was surrounded by considerable secrecy, which only began to be lessened when Universal invited a large number of exhibitors and members of the press to inspect the sets built at Churubusco. Numerous confidential memos from David Lynch, dated June 1982, attest to the curiosity surrounding the film. This, according to one memo, "is like steam in a giant boiler. It is already building up considerable pressure. Any leaks concerning what we are doing on this project will decrease the curiosity factor and cause us to lose power. I beg you to keep this in mind." A second memo continues, "Remember ... they'll want to know right up until you tell them." And, in a third, "The walls have ears."

Lynch's script was relatively faithful to Herbert's novel. The original intrigue was made somewhat simplified, yet all of its substance was preserved. Few concessions to the general public were made. Indeed, a viewer not familiar with the novel might have had some difficulty in following the flow of Lynch's screenplay. At the beginning a Guild Navigator mentions the names of the planets Ix and Richesse (two planets which kept their technological civilizations after the Butlerian jihad), and that of Tleilax (the planet of the Face Dancers and the twisted Mentats). These planets were familiar to Herbert's readers but might have created a certain sense of confusion amongst the uninitiated.

Conversely, however, Lynch's script clarified the details of the plot against Duke Leo Atreides and his family. Jealous of the duke's popularity, the emperor was here, more clearly than in the novel, the instigator of the conspiracy, with Baron Harkonnen acting solely as his instrument. In fact, the character of the baron was much less dominant in Lynch's script than he was in Herbert's book. In any event, the plot remained the same: Exile from Caladan, arrival on Dune, the treason of Dr. Yueh, Harkonnen's victory, Paul's adolescence with the Fremen, and the final attack on Arrakeen. Certain scenes, most likely due to time consideration, were left out. Fans, for instance, might regret the absence of the famous banquet scene that takes place shortly after the Atreides' arrival on Dune, and during which Paul and his father lead a verbal duel with some of Arrakis's notables. Also missing in Lynch's screenplay was a character dear to the hearts of *Dune* fans: Count Hasimir Fenring, personal assassin of the emperor, and "kwi-zatz haderach" eunuch. Although it is true that Fenring is a minor character in the book, the final scene where the emperor demands that Fenring kill Paul, and where the count refuses after sensing the almost fraternal bond that unites him to the young hero, is one of the most memorable in the book. Finally, the Bene Gesserit's role was left relatively unmentioned in favor of that of the Navigator's Guild, which was portrayed in the film as the occult entity which manipulates the emperor.

Lynch's screenplay opened with the emperor expecting, and dreading, the visit of a Third Stage Guild Navigator. The description of the Guild Navigators, and how they functioned, was undoubtedly one of the most outstanding changes brought by Lynch. In his script Lynch divided the Guild into First, Second, Third, and Fourth Stage Navigators. At the beginning, hundreds of Second Stage Navigators descend from a Guild ship. They are humanoids with eyes that are entirely blue (an effect of the absorption of spice, which gives longevity and precognitive abilities, enabling them to guide ships into hyperspace), dressed in spacesuits containing an orange, spice-based gas, or "melange." They accompany a Third Stage Navigator to a secret meeting with the emperor. During this encounter, the deaths of the Atreides are sealed. The Third Stage Navigator is transported inside a huge, black metal tank which is more than 40 feet long. On the tank are various valves and regulating instruments. Chemicals drip and spill from underneath the box.

Guildsmen were not described in great detail in *Dune,* but one similar to Lynch's picture appeared in *Dune Messiah.* Obviously the product of mutations caused by a life in the spice-filled atmosphere, the Third Stage Navigator bears little resemblance to a human being. In the script he was described as "a cross between a pasty, pale human being and a fleshy grasshopper. The creature is over 20 feet long…. His head is enormous, almost four feet high and very fleshy, like a huge grasshopper head—the eyes are totally blue. His voice is a high, fleshy whispering, and an intricate, electrical apparatus in the front of the tank translates what he says into English and broadcasts it into the room." As to the Fourth Stage Navigators, which are even more monstrous, the film carefully hid their exact nature. In the script their presence is suspected when, conforming to the emperor's orders, the Atreides fleet leaves Caladan to go and take possession of Arrakis. One of the Guild's giant starships appears, and with its immense, articulated arms, it seizes the Atreides vessels one after the other and arranges them in its hold (which already contains thousands of other space vessels, en route to various other points in the universe). The size of the Guild's ship is such that it defies comprehension.

The scene then changes to the spaceship's 2,000-feet-high control room. There, swimming in a spice-filled atmosphere, 20 Third Stage Navigators and a hidden Fourth Stage Navigator hover around a six-dimensional, layered miniature replica of the entire Universe. The Navigators make odd noises, and electrical currents come from them, manipulating the miniature Universe. The miniature elongates, causing incredible, tonal vibrations. As the Navigators continue to make sounds, there is a sudden, huge roar and the Universe begins to curve into a "U" shape. The Navigators glow in a blue light. The ship's passengers also find themselves glowing with the blue light. Thus begins the voyage into hyperspace. Toward the end of the film, anticipating Paul's son's mutation in *God-Emperor of Dune,* the Fourth Stage Navigators are revealed in the script to be giant 500-feet-long, pale worms with humanoid faces.

Lynch's interpretation of Herbert's universe was certainly not as radical as Jodorowsky's; however, it was no less personal. For example, his description of Gedi Prime, the Harkonnen's planet, while undoubtedly impressive, could not help but bring to mind some of the sordidness present in both *Eraserhead* and *The Elephant Man:*

From High Above, looking down on a black steel shuttle landing field, in the middle of a vast sea of black oil. A small cable car zooms up toward us on an elevator of black steel. The car comes to a stop and is transferred to another cable and it begins rocketing horizontally across the black oil lake. In the distance can be seen a gigantic black city in the shape of a rectangular box over 100 stories high. Each level is lined with columns and passageways but no doors. Before the city there are rows of gigantic black steel towering figures atop massive furnaces. The figures serve as chimneys and black smoke billows out of their mouths.

In order to bring Lynch's vision to life, 75 sets had to be built on the eight soundstages of Churubusco Studios. The largest blue screen ever constructed (35 feet high by 108 feet long) was put onto one of the stages for front projection. Besides Gedi Prime and the interiors of the Guild spacecraft, other sets included the emperor's throne room and the Arrakeen palace.

A special color code was conceived both to avoid confusion and to better individualize each decor. For example, the throne room gave the appearance of having been constructed of gold and jade. It was decorated with superb mosaics mixing Roman, Aztec, Moorish, and Venetian styles. The decors of the planet Dune itself were done predominantly in black and sand. Dune's inhabitants, the nomadic Fremen, lived in immense, subterranean caverns that were carved from rock with the use of lasers. The idyllic ambiance of the Atreides' Caladan was created with splendid underwater forests and palaces with walls of beautifully polished wood. The baron's oily black world used Victorian architecture, created with forged metal.

The sets were conceived under the direct supervision of Lynch and the production designer, Tony Masters. Masters is known for his work on such films as *2001*, *Lawrence of Arabia*, and *The Deep*. Masters's sets were so remarkable that after *Dune* finished shooting, they were redressed and used in the making of *Conan the Destroyer* and *Red Sonja*.

Dune's exteriors were filmed in and around Mexico City; the parking lot of the Azteca Stadium served as a landing field; a 100 by 300 feet reservoir (to portray Fremen's secret water reserves) was built in a hangar in Iztapalapa; and a lava wall, 65 feet high, was erected at Las Aguilas Rojas. As for the numerous scenes representing the surface of Dune itself, these were shot in one week in the Salamayuca Desert, near Juárez. In order to make the desert as close as possible to the barren, lifeless Dune, it was completely cleared of all traces of plants and other organic matter before each take.

Filming *Dune* called for the services of 600 people, 105 of whom were imported from the United States. There were also 10,000 to 15,000 Mexican extras for some of the scenes. Among the more disagreeable consequences of shooting in Mexico were the conflicts with the Mexican administration. For example, special cameras for use in the filming of effects sequences were imported by Gregory Gorman and David Jacobson, and these were confiscated by Mexican officials. After intervention by the U.S. ambassador, the two technicians were able to leave the country with their equipment, but they had been unable to use the cameras on necessary scenes.

The impressive special effects required by Lynch's script were another problem. At one point, for example, the script calls for the landing on Dune of 3,415 Atreides vessels in rows of 50! John Dykstra (*Star Wars, Star Trek: The Motion Picture, Firefox*) was hired to create this and other effects. But after many months of work he resigned in June 1983. Dykstra cited the usual creative differences between himself and the producers as the cause for his departure. Van Der Veer Technical Effects was then asked to work on the film. Van Der Veer, along with Albert Whitlock (*The Birds, Ghost Story)*, created the many matte paintings needed in the film. Carlo Rambaldi *(King Kong, Close Encounters of the*

Third Kind, E.T.) created the giant worms of Dune and the Guild Navigators. Although the giant worms ("Shai Hulud") attained 400 feet in length, Rambaldi designed a reduced model of the creature, which was then built by technicians in Mexico. A 50-foot-long version, composed of foam rubber pieces, was assembled for the scene where Paul Atreides catches and rides the worm. This was later combined with mattes during post-production.

Also working on the technical aspects of the film were Kit West *(Raiders of the Lost Ark, Return of the Jedi),* who handled the mechanical effects, and Kiyoshi Yamazaki *(Conan, Beastmaster),* who supervised the combat sequences. To serve as director of photography, Lynch chose Freddie Francis, with whom he had already collaborated on *The Elephant Man.* Francis worked with many of the great British directors on other fantasy films, such as *Torture Garden, Dracula Has Risen from the Grave, Asylum, Tales from the Crypt, The Ghoul,* and *Legend of the Werewolf.*

In spite of all the effort and attention to detail which went into the production, the movie was a resounding box-office dud and critical bomb. Critics complained that while it was visually impressive, the film was dreary, confusing, and *long*—yet at 140 minutes the released cut was actually the *short* version, with over an hour of footage trimmed. A 190-minute version was eventually aired on television, though a disgruntled Lynch, who had nothing to do with the television reediting, opted for the pseudonym Alan Smithee.

Despite the resounding failure of the film, it has managed over the years to garner an ever growing number of devoted fans, and as time goes by, it is possible that Lynch's version of *Dune* will grow in respectability, and perhaps will join other science fiction films in the pantheon of cult classics.

In the end, audiences—even those who hated it—are more likely to vividly remember *Dune* than many of the more popular science fiction films of recent years. The reason for this is David Lynch's unique, stunning, and often disturbing vision.

Interview with David Lynch

If anyone deserves the title of cinematic genius, it is David Lynch. Ever since the first public showing of his black and white cult classic, *Eraserhead,* in 1976, Lynch has been a powerful visionary whose unique talent has stood alone in a world often dominated by clones. *Eraserhead* depicted the almost silent struggle of a lone figure in a decaying world peopled with mutants and monsters, and haunted by nightmarish visions. What made the film stand out was its sheer, totally encompassing sense of vision—truly a window into another world, another mind.

When looking at Lynch's work, one becomes immediately aware that a real artist is at work. In Lynch's hands film becomes less of a support to tell a mere story than an animated canvas of pictures, shapes, and sounds that the artist uses to plunge his audience into a total sensory experience. One might say that if Van Gogh could have become a filmmaker, his pictures, although greatly different from those of Lynch, would have proceeded from the same perspective.

The fact that with his subsequent films, The *Elephant Man* (1980) and *Dune* (1985), Lynch managed to retain and even reaffirm the originality of his vision is even more unique, especially within such a commercial medium as film. Although these two films were each made for someone else—Mel Brooks and Dino DeLaurentiis—and each could be said to be firmly rooted in someone else's vision—especially *Dune,* a book read and loved by millions—there is no doubt that the final results were David Lynch's films, and nothing but.

Q: First, let's talk about your early career. Why did you decide to make movies?

DAVID LYNCH: Well, I was in art school and every year they had an experimental sculpture and painting contest at the end of the year. The year before I had built this pinball thing where you dropped a ball bearing into a slot and it rolled down these ramps. The ball bearing activated these hair triggers. One of these hair triggers released a match down a strike pad and lit a firecracker, while other hair triggers were operating these little switches that opened this woman's mouth and lit a red light and made her scream and the firecracker goes off.

The next year I decided I wanted to make a film. I had always wanted to make films, but not regular films. I liked film but I really didn't know much about it at all. So I made this film that was one minute long, and was in a continuous loop. It went over a screen that I built. The screen took as long to make as the film. The film took quite a long time to make because it was animated and I had as many as 18 things moving in the frame at one time. The screen had three three-dimensional heads and arms, and the rest of it was flat. The film had six heads and arms, and three of them distorted over the three-dimensional ones, and the others were on the other. They grew in stomachs and their heads caught on fire and all these other different things started moving and then all of them got sick. Then it began again. A siren was the sound track.

I was real interested in animation and the idea of moving paintings. Every painting I did had an idea with it that wasn't able to be expressed, except I could say what it was, but it had a feeling, a mood, a smell, a sound, something more. It was just like one frame of a short, moving idea. But it wasn't like a film, it was a world that could have moved a little bit. So I got into film through that one-minute picture, because a millionaire named H. Barton Wasserman gave me the money to make one for his home. I bought a brand new camera, the camera was broken, I didn't know it, and I animated for two months and ended up with one blurred piece of film. He said, "Take the rest of the money and do whatever you want with it." So I made a four minute film called *The Alphabet*. With that film I won an independent film-maker's grant at the American Film Institute. I made that film, which was 34 minutes long and called *The Grandmother*. I got *The Grandmother* in 'sixty-eight, finished it in 'seventy, and on the strength of that I got accepted to the Center for Advanced Film Studies in Beverly Hills. I went there and made *Eraserhead*.

Q: There was a long period between *Eraserhead* and *Elephant Man*...

DL: Those were my shed-building years. I love building things, and I love going to Bob's. I had a paper route. I delivered the *Wall Street Journal* and I'd find things—wood—on my route on trash night. I was able to build several sheds, very good sheds. Some had electricity, plaster walls, skylights, and little windows and everything. There's nothing I like better than building and running wood through a saw.

Q: How did you first get involved with the *Dune* project?

DL: Dino called me and asked if I'd ever heard of *Dune*. I hadn't. He asked me if I wanted to read the book, I read it and I loved it, and that's how I became involved.

Q: When you read it, did you immediately have in mind how you would like to see it on screen?

DL: No. Always, when you read something, you picture something. But, a lot of the pictures that Frank painted...In some cases I didn't like them. It's not that I didn't like them, I chose some pictures over other pictures. Because I think almost every single thing in the script is based on something in the book. But Frank is very open to me picking and choosing, because I tried to be true to the book.

Q: The book was first printed in 1964. Did you find that in those 20 years the changes in society caused things in the book also to need changing?

DL: Maybe. I'm not like a political person either. I liked *Dune* because of textures, and I liked *Dune* because of different worlds, and because it dealt with an inner world as well as an outer world. I like things that go where you can't go. I liked all the different levels of the story. I liked the fact that it was more realistic than

Star Wars. I liked the basic story of it as well. It had a lot of things within the whole that were really exciting to me, in terms of what could be done with cinema and sound and all the rest.

Q: Several of the other people that have been interested in filming *Dune* over the years were interested both because it was political, and because it struck a specific chord in them, the mystic aspects for example. Did you share any of those philosophical feelings?

DL: The thing is, I know Jodorowsky is a mystic and all the rest, but a lot of times you can talk about something before, then when people see the movie they wonder what the hell you were talking about. It's not in the movie or it's so abstract, or whatever. I like to have people get something from something on their own. It doesn't really matter what I think. It matters what comes through on the film, and it's going to affect everyone in a different way. Some people, even though I'm not political, see every film that they ever see as a political statement, or everything is a mystical experience, because it's in those people. And that's the way I like it.

Q: Did you work with Frank Herbert when you were adapting the book?

DL: Not really. Frank read several of the drafts, and he's now seen a rough cut of the film. He would give suggestions or he'd answer tons of questions. He was very supportive all along, and excited about the whole project.

Q: Does he find that even though there may be specific instances in the film which are different than in the book, the ambiance has been maintained?

DL: Yes. He's real happy.

Q: How long did it take you to write the script?

DL: A year and a half. I'd have deadlines, then we'd have script conferences. Then I'd go back and have more deadlines and have script conferences. Then, during the script it wasn't just the script, it was starting to design the picture. The production designer came on, the costume designer came on, we started looking for locations and started casting. All this time I had to be writing too. It was plenty of stuff to do.

Q: The descriptions in the scripts are very elaborate. Were you always given as much latitude as you wanted to create the look you wanted for the film?

DL: Yeah, but it was real hard to get "a look" because there are four different worlds. In *Dune* there [are] a lot more worlds than that, but there are four that this story takes place on. And to get them so that they were different and real, and all the things that you saw within the worlds were logical to be in that world and fit and felt right, took a real long time. But it really evolved over a long time too. Tony Masters, who was the production designer, started working six months before we started shooting. We changed things three or four times before we locked into a thing. Then Bob Ringwood, who designed the costumes, had to design them within this world of the sets. Then the props and everything had to sort of obey these rules.

Once we got the world, and certain key things, everybody tuned in on that and it was set. Things would just come out and it was all right. It was a fantastic thing of discovering them.

The thing about *Dune* is that there are so many different things in it, that I don't know if one thing is going to stick out. It's like everything is different than our world. So, once you start getting into everything being different, everything is different. But, still, there was a long, long way to get it to where it is.

Q: Was it difficult to get the hang of, creating a world where everything is different?

DL: No, it was really fun. But even in a world where things are real, to me, you should concentrate on all these things anyway, because everything is important. So it's not that much more work, in a way. If you're real particular about every prop in a real film, it's the same thing. Except that you can usually find them. Or, if you build them, you don't have to design them so much and make them all new. It's harder, but I love ideas, and I love people who love ideas, and we had so many of them to run with things and let them grow and do their changes.

Q: Did you have a hand in all the design proceedings?

DL: Yes. A director has got to have a hand in everything. Anybody who doesn't, is crazy. But you are a filter, everything comes through you and is sort of shaped by you, but all these people have great ideas. It just has to go through the director and you have to be involved with everything. Otherwise it gets away from you.

Q: Do you have any design background of your own?

DL: I went to art school. I wanted to be a painter. So I have a lot of ideas. The visual side of the film is super important to me. I know that in film you need all the help you can get. Everybody on this picture helped make it what it is. It would never take these leaps if there weren't all these really great people involved.

Q: Were you trying to achieve any kind of personal style with the film?

DL: Well, it has to be sort of personal if it goes through you. But I don't have any kind of philosophy, except to be true to the material, even if it's an original idea. When you first get an idea, it has power. You have to remember that feeling and idea in its original state, and be true to that. If you read a book, and you're translating, you have to be true to the essence of the book. The book came from original ideas. Things can get watered down and carried away, then they lose their power.

So the material speaks to you, and every film is different and the style would change. In *Eraserhead* the world was so real to me I could sit in a room and I could picture the entire city it was in, which didn't exist outside the room, except in my mind. But it became real to all of us who worked on the film for so long.

In *The Elephant Man* it's a world that you can't go to any-more. It had to have a mood, it had to have feeling, it had to feel real. When you were on the set, even though there are a hundred technicians around, you have to concentrate and the mood has to be in all those things, the lighting and the feel. It gets that way, so you just have to make it believable and real.

Q: Is it different making the film in color, since you've mostly worked in black and white?

DL: Yeah, I don't like color. I wish there was ... I like it just fine, but black and white has more power.

Q: Did you ever toy with the idea of doing *Dune* in black and white?

DL: Yeah, but there are films that are color films, and this is a color film. The color does help separate the different worlds. The films I want to do next, the next two and if I do more *Dunes* they'll all be in color. But I want to do a black and white film again sometime.

Q: Was going to Mexico to shoot your decision, or was it a production decision?

DL: It was the only place to make the film. It was for pretty nearly every reason you can think of. When you realize all the things that the film needed, and you go around the world looking for different places, that's where we went. It's a perfect place to make the film for every reason.

We had 75 sets. We had eight giant soundstages that we filled twice. And the desert is right up the road.

Q: What about shooting in a country that has its own problems, both political and financial. Did that make it difficult?

DL: That makes it exciting! There's always something going wrong, there's always something happening, and always something to talk about. It's a fantastic world, real different. It's always good to see different things. And sometimes it wasn't easy to make the film there, but I think that everyone had a great experience in Mexico.

Q: How long was the actual shooting time?

DL: We shot principal photography for six months, and then postproduction ... we were down there shooting, every day, with four or five crews, for 10 months.

Q: When you first read the book and said you would do the film, did the scope of the film seem at all intimidating?

DL: Not really. I knew it was a big project, but every film is a problem to conquer, or to solve. And every film is just hell to get through, really. But there are so many things that I wanted to experience, that I was really just thinking about that. It seemed like a really important thing to get in and discover.

It's a very tricky picture to do. I think that everything that I've wanted to do, I've been able to do, and if I've failed at anything, it's not anybody else's fault. I was never forced into doing anything. Dino has a reputation for forcing people ... He's got strong ideas, but he's a really cool guy. He's not afraid to say he was wrong. He's not afraid to change something, and he won't ever force me to do anything, but he's still very strong about certain things.

Q: That brings up a question as to why you have been able to get along so well with Dino when many other people have not.

DL: I think my secret is that, let's say I write or shoot something that Dino doesn't like. Now you could either say, "Dino's stupid. He doesn't know what's good anyway, and I'm not going to listen to this," and you're going to have a real big problem and you're going to lose the battle. Or you can say, "Why doesn't Dino like this? Do I really like this and is it worth fighting for?" If it's worth fighting for and you can convince him, it stays. If it's not worth fighting for, if it's questionable and maybe he's right, it doesn't work or something. Or you can say, "There's a problem here." Now Dino might say, "You must do this or this," and you can say, "Wait a minute. Let me try to solve the problem." You go and put your thinking cap on, and you come up with the solution to a problem and maybe it's even better than the original thing.

That's what you try to shoot for. And that's the way I've done it every single time.

And a lot of times, there is a problem. Dino's got a sixth sense. He's like Mack Sennett sitting there. If it's boring he can't stand it. He doesn't always have the solution, but he always knows when there's a problem. And you've got to solve it. And if you don't solve it, he'll solve it. So you just have to think.

Q: This is the first time you've worked with major special effects. Was that interesting?

DL: It was a different experience, but in every shot of *Eraserhead* there was all sorts of rigging, even though it was on a small scale. On *Elephant Man* there were things that didn't seem like effects, but there were things that go on. You get used to things. There's just way, way more of it. Blue screen I've never done before, and I'd never done hanging miniatures. We had every kind of technique going. We didn't do red screen.

Q: Carlo Rombaldi was always involved with the giant worms, but John Dykstra left the project. Was there a time when you didn't have anybody set for the rest of the effects?

DL: No. John left and Van Der Veer's [company] came on. There was totally an international crew. We had blue screen guys from here and England, model makers from here, England, Italy, and Spain. Every department had people from all over the world. There was always somebody there. Everything was storyboarded, everything was broken down so people knew what they had to do.

What you really learn is, that whatever you can think of, you can do. There's a way to do it. It's just picking the way and hoping you have good people that can pull it off.

Q: This is your second film with Freddie Francis as your. You must have a very good relationship by now.

DL: Excellent.

Q: How did he help you with the look of *Dune?*

LEE GOLDBERG, RANDY LOFFICIER, JEAN-MARC LOFFICIER, WILLIAM RABKIN

DL: Well, Freddie's philosophy is that he tries to get inside the director's mind and find out what he's looking for, and he gives it to him. That's the way he helps you.

On *Dune* he used this thing called Light Flex. It's a thing that sits on the front of the lens and is like a filter, but it's not a filter. It's sort of like preflashing the film and gives a sort of unifying glue to everything. It's very subtle. It brings up shadows and you can see into shadows with it. And you can subtly add color with it to a scene. But, unlike a filter, it only affects the shadows and the highlights stay white. They don't turn color. It does a lot of different other things too. It makes the prints that are shot off the internegative better. It seems to go through second generation better. They don't build up so much contrast. You can use it subtly or not so subtly. Freddie likes it because it's just a subtle little difference to everything.

Q: For Paul you chose a basically unknown actor and there's been a lot of secrecy surrounding him. How did you find him, and why are you keeping him such a secret?

DL: The secret is not necessarily my idea. We found him, and we were very lucky to find him. For unknowns you always figure the guy must be handsome, but he probably can't act worth a nickel and you'll have to walk him through it. Kyle is a great actor. He's going to go places. He's got a real good quality on the screen, and he can act. He's got all the qualities that Paul had to have. If he'd been a famous actor, we would have picked him anyway. We're glad we found him, that's all.

Q: Wasn't he a big *Dune* fan?

DL: Yeah, he read the book when he was 16. It must be strange for Kyle. One person could play Paul, one person was going to be picked to play him. And for Kyle to be picked from a fairly obscure place on the planet, and having loved the book, it's like reaching into a barrel and picking out a winning number. He's from Seattle. But Frank Herbert is from Seattle, and I lived right down the road in Spokane. So it's kind of a Northwest movie.

Q: What about for the other actors? Did you have people in mind when you were writing the script?

DL: Not really, no. Casting is super important, like a script. I really love it. It's like maybe four or five people could play each role, but finding which four or five and finding the one that's going to do it is tricky, but it's fun. There wasn't anyone really in mind ahead of time.

Q: Why did you go for Sting, who's mostly known for being a singer?

DL: I had met Sting at Zoetrope, because he was down visiting Francis Ford Coppola. I was trying to get *Ronnie Rocket* going there. I met him and I knew he had been in *Quadrophenia* but that was all. I knew him as a singer. Then his name came up for Feyd, and I said no, because I was interested in somebody else. I said he was a rock star and all this, and he's just not right. Then I saw a reel of *Brimstone and Treacle* and I thought he was fantastic. That was it. But then we had to go see if he wanted to do it. I went to his house for dinner, we shot pool at his pool table, I told him about Gedi Prime, and he got excited about doing it.

Q: What kind of music sound are you going for with *Dune?*

DL: This is our idea. Old and new. *Dune* is old and *Dune* is new. So the music has to be the same way. We're talking about very modern, synthesized sound with a giant orchestra. To me it's got to be a giant, foreign, powerful sound that opens things up. It's a hard, hard, hard thing to have music that will work. The music is just starting. It's going to be like the look of the film; it's going to take time to evolve. Toto is right now working on the majority of the thing. They are all incredible musicians, and David Paitch's father, Marty Paitch, is orchestrating their stuff for a big orchestra. So far there's some really nifty things. They haven't cracked it a hundred percent.

Q: Do you ever have any fear about working on a film that people have been waiting for for 20 years?

DL: I live in total fear. But there's nothing I can do about it. I never like anything I do. It always falls short of what was basically a spark in the beginning. Nothing is ever right. That's just the way it is for me, and it's too bad, but there's nothing I can do. It's hell to have that. I guess one day, maybe a person could make a perfect film that would just work for you 100 percent.

Q: Is it different for you, working on a film that's not a personal film?

DL: Well, it is a personal film ... it is and it isn't. *Eraserhead* was a personal film. *Elephant Man* and *Dune* are more commercial pictures. Still, in *Elephant Man* I got into that world, and I worked with the material and I tried to get ideas and make it work. I try to do the same thing with *Dune*. But, everything is different. *Dune* has got to be the hardest film ... *Eraserhead* took five years, and every film is hard. But I think this has got to be absolutely the most work.

Q: Do you prefer working on something that started out as your own idea?

DL: Not a hundred percent. You see, your own ideas, you capture them, they're like fish. It's not your fish, you got it, you captured it. It's where you drop your hook and all this kind of stuff. You know which kind of fish you're going to get.

If I get my own ideas, a lot of times they're strange. If I get somebody else's ideas, and I add my things to it, I can kind of get the best of both worlds. I would have been stupid, in a way, not to have done *Elephant Man,* even though it wasn't my original idea. If I had kept doing films like *Eraserhead* I don't know what would have happened. I don't know if I would have been allowed to continue making pictures.

I want to do *Blue Velvet* and *Ronnie Rocket* and I wrote those myself, and I'm going to have a chance to do them. But I also want the chance to do other people's films. I want to do all different kinds of things.

Q: What about if *Dune* is the blockbuster that everybody has every reason to expect?

DL: Then, if *Dune* goes over, I'll do *Dune II* and *III* and they'll be done back to back. They'll be done, I don't know where in the world. Maybe back in Mexico, I don't know. Right now I'm writing the script for *Dune II,* which is totally *Dune Messiah,* with variations on the theme. *Dune III* is the one that's going to be trouble for me. I'm not wild about *Dune III,* and I want to read it again and see what kind of ideas I get, and get it so that I'm really dying to do it. *Dune II* is a very short book, and a lot of people didn't like it. But in there are some really nifty ideas. I'm real excited about that and I think it could make a really good film.

In *Dune II* it's 12 years later and a whole new set of problems. It's kind of a thing unto itself. The whole place where they live is different. It's the same location, but everything has changed. And it should have a different mood; it should be 12, very strange years later.

Interview with Raffaella De Laurentiis

Three weeks before the opening of *Conan the Destroyer,* Raffaella De Laurentiis took time out of her busy schedule to talk about her career, *Conan,* and most particularly, the long awaited film version of *Dune.* Rumors about the De Laurentiis family ran rampant throughout the film community, and the interviewer was unsure of what to expect in an encounter with Dino De Laurentiis's daughter. The surprise was a delightful one.

Ms. De Laurentiis is not only extremely attractive, with masses of blonde hair, but she is also charming and easily given to laughter. But it would not pay to take her lightly, for behind her warm brown eyes shines a light of intelligence and strong will.

Q: How did you become a producer?

RDL: I started working in movies when I was 14 or 15 years old. I was in art school. During the three-month school vacation in the summer, I'd usually take a month and a half vacation, and I'd be working in movies. I started doing props, wardrobe. I had studied architecture, set dressing, all that stuff at the academy in Rome.

When I was around 18, I worked with Visconti on my first serious job away from my father. It was a very enriching experience and it also paid better! I was assistant costume designer on *Ludwig*.

I think it was during that movie that I decided that I was never going to be a genius in the field I was working in. To do certain things, like directing, being a great costume designer, or being a great art director, you have to have a certain artistic mentality, which I found out was always against my practical side. I often made a decision because it was cheaper, more practical, more intelligent, faster, and never because it would have made it the greatest costume ever made. That's how I discovered that I would never be a great costume designer. That's when I slowly started moving into production, and I found it a lot more fulfilling.

I started as a production assistant, and slowly moved up. Then I went to Tahiti in 1977 and I handled all the construction for the film *Hurricane* and for the hotel that we had to build. That was the toughest production job I ever did because we had all these huge sets that had to be destroyed. Then, because we had been there and had equipment, and I had this damn hotel that by then was a real thing and you couldn't just walk away from it, I had to stay an extra year and a half in Tahiti. Because we had all that equipment there, we concocted a small little picture that we did very cheaply, and which was my first producing experience. We did that picture with 14 people and the natives. It was called *Beyond the Reef*.

Q: Were both of these movies for your father?

RDL: Yeah, *Hurricane* work was for Dino. See, Dino moved to the states in 1973 and I remained in Europe. I didn't go to Tahiti until 1977, so I worked on my own for four years.

Q: Was it psychologically difficult to go back working for your father?

RDL: No. When I went back I was ready to do so, because I had proved to myself that I could do it without him. So it would really have been dumb not to work with him. He's got so many projects going that he needs good people around him. As long as I preserve my freedom of doing only what I want to do, I'm perfectly content to work with him.

Q: Do you ever encounter any prejudice either because you're Dino's daughter or because you are a woman producer?

RDL: Not anymore. I think it was difficult at the beginning. More because I was Dino's daughter than because I was a woman. Because there is always this mentality saying, "Ah, here's this guy putting his daughter in this position." I think now, after all these years, people don't think about me as Dino's daughter anymore. I think I've got my own reputation now.

Q: How did you come to be involved with *Dune*?

RDL: It's a funny story and it goes back to Tahiti. When I left for what was supposed to be a weekend, [it] turned out to be two and a half years. I had just read *Dune*, and I loved it. I gave the book to Dino. The whole family, my brother, we all became *Dune* freaks.

Dino started to try and get the rights, which he did right before it was decided that I would stay in Tahiti. I left a note on his desk saying, while I was gone, even if it was for two years, don't forget that I want to make *Dune* and nobody else can make it while I [am] away! Then, many more years went by before we pulled it off, because we had problems with the script.

Q: You had Ridley Scott set as director for a while...

RDL: He worked on the script with a guy called Wurlitzer, but the script was not there yet; also Ridley wanted to do *Blade*

Runner. We said we didn't want to wait for two and a half years for him to do *Blade Runner* and then do this. So we parted company.

Q: How did you come to choose David Lynch as the director and the writer?

RDL: When I was finishing *Conan, Elephant Man* came out and we were still looking for somebody. All these big science fiction space movies were coming out. We felt that to make *Dune* after all these years, and to do it as a hardware picture would be a mistake. So we decided to go in a totally different direction: find a director that had proved he could cope with characters and feelings, and make you care for them. Everybody got tears in their eyes when they saw *Elephant Man.* So we figured he would be the right guy if we wanted to do the movie in that direction.

Q: Had you seen *Eraserhead?*

RDL: No, I saw it afterward. It's very unfair to judge *Eraserhead* if you know David as well as I know him. I was laughing from the minute the picture started to the minute the picture ended because, to me, it's filled with David's humor. Now, if I had seen *Eraserhead* without knowing David, I don't know if I would have laughed! I probably would have walked out. But because I know him so well, I found it humorous.

Q: You've obviously formed a good relationship with David. You're even planning to do future projects together …

RDL: Oh, we hate each other! *[Laughter]* David and I have spent three and a half years of our lives together. Nine o'clock in the morning to eleven o'clock at night, when we were shooting. We always say it's worse than a marriage. It has all the disadvantages of a marriage without having the advantages. We have about one serious fight every three months. That's about right. Maybe less, maybe one every four months!

Q: How do you feel about the film at the moment?

RDL: Right now, I feel devastated. I can't take it anymore, because it's the worst part of it. You get all the frustration, the aggravation of the 48 weeks that we shot. Every day costs hundreds of thousands of dollars, and you have that responsibility to bring that picture in. When that finishes, it's like giving birth. You say the worst is done, now it's in the can. On a regular picture, 20 weeks later, you've got a movie in the theater. Here you don't. Here you've got another year of aggravations, like: "Is that optical right? Is it wrong? Darker? Lighter?" You get to a point where you're so sick of even looking at it. So, right now, we're at the worst moment, because progress is so slow. We're all dying to see one more shot, one more this or that.

I suppose when it is all finished, it's going to be extremely rewarding. Because whatever happens at the box office, this is going to be a great picture. There is an effort there and it's on the screen.

Q: It's going to be hard to please all of the book's fans, worldwide...

RDL: We were very true to the core of the book. To the mood. It's been a battle from day one. Even if, many times, people told us, "Forget the book. It's a movie." You can forget the book to a certain extent, but you have to preserve the mood and feel.

I know that those millions of people that have read the book have probably visualized it in their head in such a way that nothing that is not their vision is going to please them. This is something that we knew we were going to face when we started. It's difficult, very difficult to try and do a movie out of this.

Q: It must have been very difficult to produce *Conan the Destroyer* at the same time that you were doing this...

RDL: It was a challenge that I had to take up, because people told me that it wasn't possible to do a picture like *Dune* and do another one simultaneously. But I couldn't stand the idea of anybody else doing *Conan*. I spent two and a half years of my life on the first one. I just couldn't stand the idea of somebody walking off and producing the sequel.

I called Dino up and said, "You're crazy if you're going to have anybody else produce this thing. I'm going to do it." He said,

LEE GOLDBERG, RANDY LOFFICIER, JEAN-MARC LOFFICIER, WILLIAM RABKIN

"How are you going to do it? You're doing *Dune?*" I said, "Don't worry. Just give me Arnold!"

So I did it down in Mexico, and I juggled things a little bit, but we pulled it off.

Q: Didn't you use the same *Dune* sets, redressed?

RDL: Not really. We used the same stage, and we did a lot of striking. We did do some extensive revamping. It's impossible to literally use the same sets. It would be like hurting myself twice. Then, we had a lot of locations on *Conan II* that we didn't have on *Dune.*

We did shoot together on one location, and it was very funny, because it was in the desert. It was a very beautiful location, and it also happened to be convenient. We were in this desert [in] the northern part of Mexico. On the dune on the right, we had Arnold on a horse, a barbarian with horns, and a skeleton of a mammoth, and on the dune on the left we had all the Fremen in still-suits walking up and down. It was a lot of fun. On the right I had these cavemen from the past, and on the left I had these cavemen from 10,000 years in the future.

For me, it was always difficult to keep a balance between the two directors. Especially because David is terribly jealous. So, if he asks a question, and I say, "One minute. I have to answer to Richard Fleischer," he goes pale. That was the trickiest thing. At the beginning I used to call Richard, David, and David, Richard. So that didn't work either!

Q: Why did you decide to film in Mexico in the first place? Was it an economic decision?

RDL: Partly. The reason why I really made that decision, is because it was the only place in the world where I could find eight stages that size that were empty. The government was ready to close those studios. So we got the eight stages which we needed. We used them all more than twice. And it had a desert, which took me a long time to find. It was an hour and a half away. Also, if you have extensive construction work, it's still worthwhile.

Because they're very good at working with wood and detail work. They do things that, if you tried to do them here, they would cost you dearly, because nobody knows how to do them anymore.

However, it was very difficult to shoot *Dune* in Mexico, because it's a difficult country to work in, and the technology is very backward. Their equipment goes back 45 years, so you have to bring everything in. It was not easy, but it was a nice challenge.

Q: Didn't you have some problems when some of the special effects people were bringing in equipment and it was confiscated?

RDL: We had something confiscated every day. That went on for two and a half years. They don't have a law for movies. In Tunisia, for instance, they passed this law that if you come in and make a movie, all the movie equipment can be brought in and customs approves what you bring in and what goes out. They don't have any laws like that in Mexico. The government says that they're going to help you, but then they don't. Also there is this bribery problem; they live by briberies. By confiscating stuff, they get bribed to get it out. It's a way of making a living.

Q: If you balance your savings in construction costs against having to import so much stuff, time wasted, etc., did it even out or did you still wind up saving money?

RDL: It depends on compared to what country.... Spain, for instance, is a great country to work in. Great technicians, great equipment, but it doesn't have any studios. If Spain had some, the picture would have been cheaper and faster to do there. Italy has great technicians and they have great studios, but they didn't have the studio space we needed and they certainly didn't have the desert. Otherwise, it probably would have been cheaper. The United States, definitely not. It would have been a lot more expensive here. England, we would have spent a lot of money in construction, so it probably would have been a little more expensive there, too.

Q: How many people did you have to take down there?

RDL: About 150 on *Dune* and about 55 on *Conan*.

Q: How did you keep them all happy for all that time?

RDL: That was the toughest part. Mexico City is the most unpleasant city in the world. It's overcrowded, it's overpolluted, it's over-high, you can't breathe, we all got sick. I had salmonella three times. We all had something going wrong with us most of the time.

Q: You had John Dykstra set up to do the effects at one point and that didn't work out. Why?

RDL: Because the way his operation works I had no control over the costs, and I can't work unless I know where I'm putting my money. He didn't want to work my way and I didn't want to work his way. It was better just to terminate it.

Q: Why did you finally settle on Van Der Veer?

RDL: Well, because I ended up doing my own shoot. At the beginning, I was scared. You must never be scared in life, because you end up making mistakes. I said to myself, "This is the biggest special effects movie ever made, and you can't do it yourself. You've got to get somebody in here that has done it a million times." I wanted to use ILM because I have a very good relationship with them and I like the people here. But they were very busy with *Jedi* and couldn't do it. So I ended up with John Dykstra because I felt I couldn't do it on my own. Then, when John left, I actually did end up doing it on my own after all. What these big companies do is they shoot your effects. They shoot your blue screen, your front projection, your back projection, your models, they build your miniatures, they shoot them, and then they composite them.

So I had to hire model makers, build my own models, hire my own camera crews, and shoot them. Van Der Veer would do the compositing. Instead of having one man, I ended up having 25 people, all of them heads of their specific departments. They all reported to me. Barry Nolan of Van Der Veer was always there saying, "It's very difficult for me to composite unless you change the background a little bit or make the foreground lighter." So he was always working with us, but they were only really doing the compositing. We did the whole thing ourselves. Which, if I had known better, is what I would have done to start with. It's just that I felt I didn't have the experience, and I wanted to rely on somebody who had done it before. But it turned out being not possible.

Q: Do you feel you know enough about special effects now to go on and do *Dune II?*

RDL: If *Dune II* goes, I'd do it the way I did this. Because, to be a good producer, you've got to have the thermometer of your picture. The only way of doing that is to know exactly where every penny is going and why. If you know that, then you know that maybe if you spend those $10 on this, you'll get an effect on the screen that is maybe worth $20. All you're there for is to put as much as you can on the screen. And you can't do that unless you're in full control of everything. I wasn't and I just saw this money disappearing and not knowing where. I couldn't cope with it.

Q: Did you do all your special effects shooting in Mexico?

RDL: Which was another thing that everybody told me I couldn't do. They said it was crazy to shoot special effects in Mexico. I said we'd been shooting there for nine months, I had trained personnel, everybody knew everybody. Why should I move back to somewhere else and start shooting again? We had our team, so it meant another four months of shooting in Mexico, which nobody was planning on.

I had to import all of the worms. We had first contemplated shooting the worms here, with John Dykstra. But when I called Carlo Rombaldi up and asked how he felt doing the worms in Mexico, he said, "My worms work. If they work here, they'll work in Mexico." He loaded them all in the truck and off we went to Mexico.

Q: There were never any problems because of the desert?

RDL: No, it worked out fine. It was tougher, because we had to do it in half the time that we should have had to do it. But

I'm happy with it. By doing things ourselves, we ended up giving more to the audience. We were ready to give up certain effects because they were too expensive. By doing them ourselves, we were able to reinstate them.

Interview with Kyle MacLachlan: Paul Atreides

Q: Could you give us some background on yourself?

KYLE MACLACHLAN: I'm 25 years old. I was born February 22, 1959—that makes me a Pisces. I went to school at the University of Washington, in their professional training program. I graduated in 1982 with a Bachelor of Fine Arts degree in theater. I went to Eisenhower Senior High School in Yakima, which is where I grew up and spent the first 18 years of my life.

I am the eldest of three boys. My middle brother's name is Craig and the youngest is Kent. Both are involved in the arts. Kent is a budding actor and he's doing his first summer stock work in Montana this year. Craig plays base guitar in a metal band down in Portland, Oregon. He's a headlining act down there.

My parents both live in Yakima, Washington. My father is a stockbroker, and my mother right now is on a leave of absence from her job as public relations director of the Yakima Public Schools. They are divorced and have both remarried, so I have twice as many birthday presents and twice as many gifts to give on Christmas. But it's wonderful, I have four parents now, which is great. And I've gotten a little stepsister in the bargain, through my father's marriage to his new wife. She's about 10 years old right now.

They're all very pleased, proud, and supportive. All the things that a great family should be, they are.

Q: When did you decide that you wanted to be an actor?

KM: It was actually a slow process. I had my first taste of being on stage in a theatrical situation when I was about 15 or

16. I was involved with a teenage theater group in my home town of Yakima. I did two productions with them, in various minor capacities. I was a chorus member in one, and a cast in another. I can't remember what it was. Then I went to high school and got myself a little more involved in the high school theater situation doing plays. I was still looking at theater in the sense of it being a real nice hobby to have, but concentrating my attention on two areas of study—architecture and archeology.

Then I got to college and began taking different classes. I found that I wasn't too keen on architecture and decided to take a drama class on a whim. That got me rolling again in the theater and led me to audition to the Professional Actors Training Program, also at the University of Washington, where I was accepted. All this time, I still hadn't really decided that theater was going to be for me, even after I got accepted into the training program and [had] gone there for a year. It wasn't until my second year in the three-year program that I really said, "Okay. I'm going to devote my life and soul to this now." That was about in 1981.

Q: What do you think it was that turned you around and finally made you decide that acting was going to be it?

KM: It was a combination of things. One was that I was happiest when I was doing theater, as far as I knew up to that point in my life. Everything that I had studied and thought about kind of led me toward theater. The catalyst must have been the role that I performed, which was Morgan Evans in *The Corn Was Green*; that I think was the final straw. Auditioning for that role and getting it, I suddenly said to myself, "I can't pretend anymore. This is going to become real life." I can even remember thinking to myself when I got the role, "Gosh. Now I have to be an actor!" All things had led up to that moment.

Q: How soon after that were you picked for *Dune*?

KM: I got the first call for the film just before New Year 1983. I had left school in March 1983 to go to the Oregon Shakespearean

Festival in Ashville, Oregon, for a season. So it was about nine months from the time that I left school to the time that I got cast in *Dune*, and about a year and nine months since I had made the decision to really devote my life—for now—to acting.

Q: Was *Dune* your first professional role?

KM: It was my first professional movie role, but I had been working constantly in the theater for about six years up to that point. Working in Seattle, working stock work and at a couple of regional theaters.

I had not yet made the move to New York City, but that was going to happen within a few weeks after I got my first call for *Dune*. That's how I was planning on going about it, and I was sidetracked down to Mexico City.

Q: I've read that you read *Dune* when you were very young, and that you've been a fan of the book for many years...

KM: Well, I read *Dune* when I was about 14 or 15, and really enjoyed it quite a bit. It was, and still is, one of my favorite books of that particular type. I was very familiar with it when they called me and said they were coming to Seattle and wanted me to audition for the role of Paul. So that was a great help in that.

Paul was someone who, when I was young, I had identified with very strongly. He was one of my book heroes of that period of time in my life.

Q: How did they come to find you?

KM: I was, in a sense, brought in. The production company had hired a casting group to go out and bring in people from outside of Los Angeles, and from within Los Angeles too. This particular woman, Elizabeth Lustig, was the woman who saw me. As a matter of fact, I was the only actor that she brought back from her particular tour, which included Washington, D.C., Seattle, and San Francisco. Meanwhile, her associate was in New York and in Chicago. They saw a whole bunch of people, then they came back to David and Raffaella and reported on who[m] they had seen, recommending that they see certain ones. Elizabeth mentioned my name, and David and Raffaella took a look at the photographs that she provided, and said they'd like to see me. That's how I made my first contact with David and Raffaella.

Q: It must have been kind of strange for you to get chosen for a part from a book that you had admired for many years.

KM: It was very unusual, I think. And the feeling that surrounded it was very unusual. It was very unusual to suddenly get a call for a role from a book that had meant very much to me when I was younger, and was still one of my favorite stories, and I was so familiar with it. First of all the knowledge that they were going to actually make it into a film was wonderful. And the fact that I had been called and was asked to audition for the role, that was something else that was kind of eerie, almost.

Q: How was acting with Sting in the movie?

KM: Oh, it was interesting. We didn't have a whole lot to do together; we just had one combat, fight type of scene at the end of the film. That went very well. He moves quite well, and he's had dance training, so he has good control of his body, and we were able to do a pretty good fight scene together. He was very considerate to me. In fact, he had brought with him into his dressing room a synthesizer, a rhythm percussion unit, and a guitar, and he said that anytime I wanted to I could go in and play, which I did. So that was very nice of him to offer that to me.

Q: What about working with not only Sting, but there were quite a number of very well-known actors in *Dune.* Were you starstruck at first?

KM: Not too bad. I was not much of a movie person before I was cast in *Dune,* so when they would mention these names, I wouldn't associate them necessarily with something I had seen when I was younger, and therefore I was not as susceptible to a starstruck type of response in meeting them. Which was fine. I admit I was taken [back] a bit when I met Max Von Sydow, simply because of his stature and his enormous power. The strength of him is quite overwhelming. Then I met a couple of actors whose work I had seen in films, particularly Jorgen Prochnow from Munich, Germany, who was in *Das Boot.* I met him and that was a wonderful experience, someone whose performance I had admired in the film, and here I was actually meeting him and we were going to do a couple of scenes together. Once you get over that, and you begin the actual work, there's no time for any starstruck anything to come in. You just knuckle down, get the script, and you begin to work on the scene. So it changes the tenor very quickly.

Q: It must have been fun to have such an international cast and crew to work with.

KM: It was, because they all brought in their own particular customs and ways of speaking and manners. For a young actor just out of Seattle, it was a real joy. Not only to meet these people, but to be able to work with them. There are some fine, fine actors that were involved in the film. Being the lead I had a great opportunity to work with them. Actually, that was one of the real great experiences about the film, meeting and being able to work with these people.

Q: What about some of the physical difficulties encountered in filming in Mexico?

KM: It was a difficult time, and a difficult place to shoot, because of the physical discomforts, and of course the emotional and mental ones that I was going through in the film. So I was taxed on about every level as a human being. I came through pretty well I guess. But Mexico City is not one of the more pleasant spots in the world to be.

Q: Raffaella told me about one day where *Conan* was filming on one side of a dune and *Dune* was on the other. Were you involved in that scene?

KM: Yes, I was. In fact, that was a return engagement for me. I was away in Europe and I had to be brought back because they needed some more scenes in the desert. At that time they were also shooting *Conan* in the desert at the same site. There was a lot of trouble with that, because lights were going to one set that should have gone to the other. And we couldn't shoot off some explosions sometimes and they had some explosions...It was one big mess. We got the shots, but I think it was a big headache.

Q: Was there any physical training that you had to go through for your role?

KM: I had a fight choreographer that I worked with prior to shooting the fight scenes. I was at a very good advantage, because of the training that I received at the University of Washington, which was far superior to anything I've come in contact with since then. So I was very well versed in weaponry. Besides that, I had studied martial arts for about five or six years when I was younger. So I had both backgrounds that were needed coming into this role. And the fight instructor took those skills and abilities and we directed them in one certain way, in the style that Paul uses in the film. I was able to do whatever he needed me to do, quite quickly. Also because of his expertise as a choreographer.

Q: Did they invent a different style of fighting to be more futuristic?

KM: Yes. There were a couple of different styles that were used during the filming. The one that took most of our time was developed from a samurai sword technique, kind of like the stuff you see in *Shogun*. And he got me going in some basic moves in sequence, like little miniature dances. There were 10 of those that he began training me in. Then we took the long sword and adapted it down to a dagger type of 27cm long, which is the weapon used in *Dune*.

Q: What happened when you first got to Mexico?

KM: Well, the first day I got to Mexico was the February 28. I was there about a month before we actually started our first day of shooting. There wasn't anyone there except for David and Raffaella.

I just spent those first 30 days walking the sets, getting myself used to my little neighborhood where I was staying, talking to

David about the script, going into all the different departments and seeing what was being done on *Dune*, sniffing around, investigating, costume fittings, some makeup and hair consultations, just a whole bunch of stuff getting myself prepared for our first days' shooting.

Q: Did you have any input into the character of Paul?

KM: A little bit. The script was in its sixth draft when I entered the picture. But as we would shoot, I would have some ideas, and would talk to David about changing some lines, adding some lines, deleting some lines, just shaping it as we went along, to clarify in my mind what David wanted and to put a little bit of my input into the character.

Q: Did you have any notions as to what you thought Paul was like? How did you feel when you read the script—did you feel that Paul lived up to your expectations?

KM: Yeah. The character certainly does. When I first read the script, I was a bit—not really disappointed, but I was wishing for more. But I soon realized that that was impossible because of the nature of the medium, and I realized that what David had created was really quite fantastic. Because, to take a book and make it into a script, as he did, and to make it as concise and include as many elements of *Dune* as he did, was pretty great. I was pretty naive as far as script reading for a film; I had never done it before. He did a real fine job putting it together.

I did think that the character of Paul was, for the most part, really together and well written, and [it] gave me plenty of stuff to work on. It's just that the more scenes there are in the film for Paul, the more variety of the character I can show. So I was disappointed that some of the scenes that I remembered had been taken out of the script since I first read it. It meant fewer opportunities to do what I wanted with Paul. What I was able to do was to take the script that David had there, minus the scenes that I really liked, and add to what was there.

Q: Were there things from the book that you particularly liked that didn't make it into the film and which you felt disappointed about?

KM: Before we started, I asked about all the things that I liked and that weren't in the script, and there were good reasons why they couldn't happen, which satisfied me for the most part.

For example, the whole thing about the hoods, having a complete still-suit and putting the hoods to reclaim the moisture lost through the head. The face masks on the stillsuits would have rendered the actors pretty well incapable of working. It would have been an interesting problem. I'm not saying that I'm totally glad that it turned out the way it did, but it would have been interesting. The fact that we didn't have capes on the costumes... that would have been a whole different thing to work with.

My general feeling about the Fremen was of a people that were real nomadic. They were a people that were able to move. Guerrilla warfare is essentially what Paul was trained in and trained them in. Guerrilla warfare means extremely rapid movement with a minimum of possessions. I had the feeling that the way it was designed it was kind of bulky. Plus, [there were] a couple of scenes that I thought would have been great to have in the film. But that's neither here nor there. It was impossible to put those in there, because they just didn't flow with the script. But those few things that I mentioned were some of the elements that I felt disappointed that they weren't able to include.

Q: What was different for you in working in a film as opposed to working on the stage?

KM: The major thing, of course, was the rehearsal element. In a stage play you have four weeks of rehearsal in front of a director, one person or a couple of people, then you go onstage and you have many, many people. Whereas on film, your rehearsal period is day to day. As you come in that day, the night before you've done a lot of intellectualizing about the script, and choosing some possibilities. Then you bring them in to the front of the camera, and you start to hone and refine in front of a camera, right there. Film seems to rely a lot more on spontaneity and the moment, unlike a stage play. So it's those two different approaches to the rehearsal. That was a major, major difference.

I don't mind so much performing in front of the camera as compared to performing in front of an audience. Performing in front of a camera is nice, because you don't have to think of the audience at all. You think about the camera, of course, but it's a different feeling, it's much more intimate. That, besides the fact that there's only 15 or 20 people on the film set in the real close vicinity, where the actors can relate to them. So it's much smaller than a stage play.

Q: What about the order in which you film scenes?

KM: They were real good to me, in the fact that they followed ... they didn't shoot it exactly chronological, but they shot it in three major sections. They stuck with one section, completed everything, then went on to the second segment, then went on to the third segment. As I broke it down in the script, there was the pretakeover by the Harkonnens, when Paul was young, just off Caladan and pretty naive; then there was the running into the desert until the taking of the water of life, the mystical change; then there was the mystical change on to the end of the film. And we shot within those three areas. That was extremely helpful to me. I thought a little bit about the chronological order; I had to think about what state my mind was in. But as you're going along, shooting the film, it seems just to happen. The director helps quite a bit too. Like I said, film is kind of a more moment-to-moment medium, so it's not quite as much of a problem as one would think.

Q: Did you find that the other actors, who had more film experience, were helpful to you, and were patient in trying to explain "the lay of the filmland?"

KM: There wasn't so much explaining that had to go on. I watched people work, but I didn't know how that would appear on film. I could watch the way Kenny McMillan shot a scene, I could watch his work from behind the camera, and then I would say, "that's interesting." But I didn't know how that translated to the screen, or whether or not I wanted to adapt or work in that direction, because I didn't know if that's the way I wanted Paul to appear on the screen. I didn't know how it would transfer. So I pretty well just did what I thought was right, and I trusted David more than anyone else, to tell me what he wanted.

As far as the other actors, probably the way they helped me the most was in working the scenes. The people I worked with are fantastic human beings and fantastic actors. So when you work with them in film, it's real small and intimate, which I really love, and just the fact that they were so good helped me. Whenever you work with a good actor, it's just such a joy.

Q: Were all of the actors around during shooting, or did people come and go, depending on the needs of the script?

KM: People came and went. They would stay for three, five, or one week, depending on what they needed to do. Francesca Annis was probably around the most. I was there the whole time, Francesca was there for a long period of time, Everett McGill was there for a pretty long period of time. It was kind of sad, Max Von Sydow was the first person who left. He finished first.

He's quite a man. He's very imposing physically, and he has an aura of power that radiates from him that's very strong. He made an impression upon me. He was one of the many that made an impression upon me.

Q: Who else can you think of that really made an impression on you?

KM: I have to preface this by saying that everyone I worked with in front of the camera, that I had direct contact with, influenced me in some way or another. And anybody who[m] I watched I was able to admire and enjoy. But as far as taking it one step further, outside the film into personal, I made some terrific friends. Everett McGill is a great friend, Patrick Stewart, we three hung around together a lot when we were all there together. Jurgen, who played my father, I count as a good friend. There are some real close friendships that were made. Maggie Anderson is a terrific lady who worked on the voice stuff with us. I have to say David Lynch too, because David and I are great friends outside the film.

Q: What was riding the sandworm like?

KM: It was shot in a whole bunch of different sections. One of them was on a rail track. They had built this very long, very high section, and they tracked the camera right along with me. That was the first section, with me chasing after the worm, then planting the hook. Then we went inside and shot on a blue screen.

Q: Did you have a lot of stunts that you had to do?

KM: There were a lot of fights that I did. There was one big stunt, a rock fall, that they brought a stunt guy in from England to do. Then there was a jump or two in one fight, where the guy had to land on a skateboard type of device, that I didn't do. But most of the actual fighting I did. I did as much as I could.

I had an iron fist control over the character, David and I both, and I just didn't want anybody else—[because] I was so conscious of everything, his speech, his movements—I didn't want the stunt guy to move differently than I thought Paul would move.

Q: Since you are so familiar with the book, you must have had definite ideas on Paul's character that helped you to bring him to life.

KM: Yeah, I guess so. I had definite ideas reading the book about what Paul was like, then I had some ideas about the script. Making Paul live and breathe for an audience became my concern. Before, when I read the book, I identified with Paul, but I kind of liked the whole story; I didn't really pick him out and examine him as closely as I had to when I did him on camera. And when I did pull him out and really put him under a microscope, I just really extracted from him what I thought I could convey in front of the camera, and went for that, with David's help.

Q: Did you get to meet Frank Herbert?

KM: Sure, I met Frank during the first couple of days, and then I was up in Port Townsend, where he lives, a few months ago doing a play. I saw him quite a bit. We palled around and had a good time together. I feel I can talk to Frank about a lot of stuff. He's a good guy.

Q: Did he seem pleased to see *Dune* finally make it to film?

KM: It's probably a real important moment in his life, to see something that he had imagined and dreamed up in his mind to suddenly catch fire like it did and become a film, after all the problems that it had incurred trying to become a film.

Q: Did you ever talk with him about your feelings on *Dune*?

KM: Not really. I was afraid that I'd probably get something wrong. I have some feelings about *Dune,* but I don't communicate too well verbally about things like that. I can't really pick it apart and say it's this, this, and this. It leaves me with a lot of different feelings and moods. When I try to put those into words, they always come out sounding wrong. I think I have a pretty good grasp of it anyway, and I don't need him to define for me what it is. I don't think Frank really likes doing that anyway. I wouldn't approach him and ask him what it's about. That's kind of an insult, like he didn't get his message across in the book. Since he's already told me what it's about by writing the book. And I wouldn't really talk so much about Paul; that was kind of David's and my world. I asked Frank a couple of questions about things that I wanted cleared up, about the direction that he saw it moving. Making a link between *Dune* and *Dune Messiah.* I asked him how he saw the bridges, preparing to move on to the second film, if indeed we do that.

Q: Can you think of a scene that was your favorite, and one that was the most difficult for you?

KM: One of my most favorite scenes is the painbox scene. One of the first big scenes that I shot with Siân Phillips. She's a terrific actress, and we did pretty good work in that I think.

One of the more difficult ones for me was a scene which was cut from the film. In the desert there was a fight scene with Jamis that has been taken from the film because of the flow. There was some stuff that I had a real difficult time with, and which I don't think I got, so I was kind of pleased to see it gone.

Q: Why do you think it was so difficult?

KM: I'm not sure. There was a tremendous amount of information that I had to assimilate as the character, and react to, and it was more than I could handle as an actor. It wasn't more than I could handle, but I think it was too much. I think David tried to condense an awful lot of information in a tiny period of time, and I wasn't able to make it work as a character. So I question if it really would have worked in the film. It wasn't a logical progression for me as Paul to go through. Because of that, I think, I balked at it. It was early enough in the filming that I didn't have enough confidence to say I didn't think it would work that way, and to stick up for the way I felt about the progression of the character. Something which I learned to do as I went along, got a little more confident and understood more about the filming process.

Q: Would you go on to further *Dune* films if they do them?

KM: They have me contracted to do a total of five *Dune* films, including the one I've just shot. In the books Paul is in the first three and not in the last two. So if they decided to make two and three, which I hope they do, then I will definitely make them.

Q: Where do you see yourself going with your career?

KM: I hope that my career will be … I like to think of it in terms of longevity … will be a long and very solid career. I would like to be involved with fine directors and fine actors, of course, as I move forward, and I want one that will encompass both stage and screen. There are a number of roles that I have still yet to do, and want to do very badly, onstage. I plan on doing those as well as, hopefully, involving myself in other films.

RL: What kind of roles interest you?

KM: For example, Richard in *Ah, Wilderness!*, a Eugene O'Neill play. I'd like to do Romeo again in *Romeo and Juliet*, and/or Mercutio. Those are just a couple that I would like to do. There are quite a few that I would like to still do while I'm looking young.

In film, I do like the films that tend toward the classic in style and in grandeur. And also in the adventure area, adventure with a twist. I think films like *The Three Musketeers* and *The Four Musketeers* would be fun to be involved with. Good adventure, and yet they are of a certain kind of period and hold a fascination for me. On the other hand, a film like *Road Warrior* which is also an adventure film, but hails from an entirely different period of time. Just about everything really interests me right now, because I've had contact with just one little piece, and there's so much more out there to explore.

ENEMY MINE (1985)

How could they have been so wrong?

Everybody at 20th Century-Fox was certain that *Enemy Mine* was going to be the smash hit of the year, the kind of science fiction spectacle that hurtles up the charts to the top of the all-time grosses list.

And they not only believed it, they were willing to act on that belief. The film was originally started under English director Richard Loncraine, but when his footage turned out to be unsatisfactory, the studio spent millions of dollars throwing out everything he had done and starting over with German director Wolfgang Petersen.

Yet when the film was finally released, it hardly caused a ripple. It was not even a notorious disaster like *Howard the Duck* or a high-profile flop like *2010*. It was simply ignored both by critics, who barely acknowledged its existence, and by audiences, who simply stayed out of the theaters. To this day, the only response the title brings from most people is "Enemy What?"

The film was so completely forgotten so quickly that it did not even seem to hurt the careers of those responsible for it. Both Dennis Quaid and Lou Gossett, Jr., continued their upward struggle toward stardom; director Wolfgang Petersen spent the next few years putting together financing for his thriller *Shattered* (a lower-budget bomb that might actually have hurt him more than this one, since thrillers were supposed to be his specialty).

But for the hundreds of people who worked on the film, *Enemy Mine* must remain a painful memory. To have been so certain that the film they were making would be not only a box-office smash but an artistic masterpiece as well, only to be ignored, is the cruelest blow of all.

On the Set of Enemy Mine

The deserted western town is covered in a deadening blanket of snow. On these streets where countless sheriffs named Hans and Fritz battled innumerable outlaws called Willi or Adolph, there is only stillness now. The town's silver mine crumbles quietly under the weight of Germany's winter. The world has lost interest in America's past, and the standing western sets at Munich's Bavaria Studios stand unused. Germany has discovered the future.

The future is Wolfgang Petersen's *Enemy Mine,* a $24 million science fiction epic that 20th Century-Fox hopes will be the big hit of the Christmas season. It is West Germany's first major science fiction film, and it has completely taken over the studio, filling nine of its 11 soundstages.

And so, on a soundstage near the rotting remains of the silver mine stands a new mining operation. No earthbound mine, this is the interior of an interstellar cruiser, a pirate mining company that travels not from town to town but planet to planet. It will be the site of the film's final shootout, not between sheriff and outlaw but between human and alien.

The transition from past to future has not been easy. The facilities necessary to make a modern science fiction film did not exist here before shooting began. The modern German cinema, most noted for small, personal films like Wim Wenders' *The American Friend* and Rainer Werner Fassbinder's *The Marriage of Maria Braun,* has had little need of stuntmen and special effects technicians. These people had to be brought in from England and the United States. A new soundstage had to be built just to house the enormous, elaborate sets a film of this kind demands.

The man responsible for bringing the German cinema into the future is Wolfgang Petersen, the internationally acclaimed director of Germany's previously two biggest films, *Das Boot* and *The Neverending Story*. Although both of those films posed tremendous logistical difficulties, they were trifles compared to the problems caused by *Enemy Mine*.

> To make a horrible, unearthlike ice storm on a stage with falling trees and meteorite showers and monsoon-like rain and fire on the water is very tough, very difficult. We have a lot of special effects teams working together here—English people, Americans, Germans. It's very difficult to get past that.
>
> There have been times a scene just didn't work out and we had to do it again and again. After 50 or 60 days of shooting, you are exhausted, the team is exhausted. It's a source of pressure on everybody, especially now because it's so cold outside.

The cold is an inescapable fact of life here. During the day, temperatures never rise above freezing. At night they plummet far below zero. The studio is covered under more than a foot of snow, which makes getting from stage to stage difficult and frequently dangerous.

No one feels the cold more bitterly than *Enemy Mine's* American star Dennis Quaid, who plays an intergalactic fighter pilot stranded on a dead planet with an enemy alien. The scene being shot on the newly constructed Wolfgang Petersen stage requires Quaid, standing on a cliff in a raging storm, to pour a bottle of fuel into a lake and set it on fire.

Director Wolfgang Petersen chats with the racing snail, one of the characters in *The Neverending Story.*

The rain starts and Quaid is quickly drenched. He struggles with the heavy fuel bottle, then, putting it down, whips out a flare gun and fires into the water. Nothing happens. Quaid throws his hands up in disgust and stalks off the set. It is never fun to walk the hundred yards from the stage to the star's trailer in the near zero temperatures of Munich's winter. Soaking wet, it is agony.

On the stage the crew scurries to fix the problem. A yellow metal platform rises from under the water so stagehands can check the gas lines. Yellow-jacketed production assistants sweep detritus away from the alien's lair. And the alien himself, dancer and mime Jack Luchino, who doubles for star Lou Gossett, Jr., squats, bored, under a styrofoam rock outcropping, trying to avoid the last residual drops of "rain."

Standing on the platform, director Wolfgang Petersen uses this time to discuss the shot with cinematographer Tony *(Brass Target)* Imi. Petersen is used to this kind of delay by now—after the nautical nightmares of *Das Boot* and the complications with creatures on *The Neverending Story,* creating an alien world is just part of the job. Petersen explains.

> You have to be really concentrated and know *exactly* what you have in mind from the very beginning. It's very difficult to make a big fire when you have tons of water coming down, but you have to be able to think past all that. You have to be able to keep in mind the dramatic story you're telling.

That task requires an enormous effort of concentration. Pieces of *Enemy Mine* are scattered all over the studio—you cannot walk three steps without coming across a section of planet or an artificially petrified tree gathering snow in its impromptu storage place. As soon as Petersen is done with the lake and cliff set, he will move to the mining ship on stage seven so that the 1,500 cubic meters of styrofoam used to create the volcanic cliff can be torn down to make room for another alien landscape. There is no opportunity for second chances.

Across the studio on stage seven, stunt coordinator Martin Grace tries to ready his British stunt crew for the climactic mining ship fight. Ideally, the fight choreography will be worked out by the time Petersen is ready to shoot it. Says Grace:

> We've brought most of our stuntmen in from England. We have some Germans, but they're very, very young and they're very, very raw. They can all roll around pretty well and you say, "Well, they're quite impressive," and then you take them out and try and throw a punch and they don't know what you're doing. These babyfaces can roll around on the floor, but they can't do stunts.
>
> I had a group of sixteen Germans who all said they worked on ten or fifteen films. They told me they had pictures of them hanging from helicopters. I said "You use a

harness?" "Oh, no, we don't need them," they said. I'm not silly. I rigged up a rope about twelve feet off the ground. Only two people out of twenty could climb up that rope. And they all had pictures. How they got the pictures I don't know, but one brochure had three people jumping out of the wreckage of a motorcar, and around the picture was a thick black line. They superimposed themselves.

Like the stuntmen, the effects technicians had to be imported. There simply was no German effects industry. Half of the film's effects are being done by Lucasfilm's Industrial Light and Magic facility, while the other half are being created by a British crew set up by Brian *(2001)* Johnson at the Bavaria Studios.

Although for their shots ILM will use, as usual, the newest technological advances, the British crew working at Bavaria are using the oldest of techniques: models on wires flown over cameras running at high speeds—in this case at 96 frames per second. High speed was one of the first special effects techniques ever developed and has been used in hundreds of films over the past 50 years. Although the technique has been slighted in recent years in favor of more high-tech methods, Petersen's crew feel it will work for *Enemy Mine*.

"We don't have motion control cameras. ILM has motion control," says Guy Hudson, special effects model supervisor. "When we first storyboarded, there was no need for motion control. On the space battles, they use ILM. Flying over the landscape is the most complicated shot we do."

The landscape is an enormous, volcanic plain erected on a wooden platform in Bavaria's stage six. At the moment crew members are laboring to remove one volcano from the range in order to put the camera in its place. Behind the landscape is a painting of an otherworldly skyline.

"We have to use a painted backdrop," Hudson says, "because the set is too big for a blue screen. It doesn't look like much on the set, but it works very well. We just fill up the stage with smoke and shoot."

On stage six the term "high speed" seems like a deliberately cruel joke. Most of what is being done here is waiting—waiting for the old smoke to clear out of the room so the crew can fill it with new smoke, waiting for the new smoke to settle the way they want it to. The smoke never settles the way it should. Eventually, the crew have to shoot anyway.

As the day goes on and the smoke from preceding shots grows thicker and thicker, the waiting becomes more and more unpleasant. The effects people have complained that they get frequent nosebleeds because they have to breathe the smoke day after day. Many of them wear surgical masks, which help keep the smoke out of their lungs but cannot do much about the stifling odor. There is no escape from the smell of the smoke; it gets into hair and clothes. The normal response would be to step outside for a breath of fresh air, but the bitter cold makes that alternative less agreeable than choking on the smoke.

Not all of the effects work is unpleasant, however. Even when it is being done on a million-dollar scale, high-speed model work is really just a matter of playing with toys. The model spaceships which dangle on wires from a pole that will fly them in a huge circle over the stage are a space-crazy kid's dream. Some of that atmosphere can be felt here on the set.

"Motion control isn't much fun at all," says an enthusiastic Moshe Asher, a special effects focus puller. "All you get to do is push a button. With high speed you get to fly little ships over the camera and play with them."

Asher and the effects crew demonstrate the joys of high speed. One crew member grips the end of the pole and pushes it across the room. The ship swings wildly around in a circle, just missing the top of the camera and the top of Asher's head.

"We risk the camera and the cameraman to do as much as we can in high speed. I'm not usually in much danger—I just turn on the camera and run away. But if the camera is hit, I'd be very sorry."

Back at the Wolfgang Petersen stage, the first unit is having much less fun. They've tried another take, and again the water has not caught fire. Quaid, furious and wet, has gone back to his trailer. Petersen, after conferring with Imi, decides to put an electric charger in the water to ignite the gas jets. This will mean a delay of at least an hour. With the rain turned off, an assistant fires a test shot into the lake. The water catches fire and burns brilliantly.

This is not the first time the production has had trouble with fire. A few weeks ago, the petrified forest set on stage 4-5 caught fire in the middle of a shot. In the scene Quaid and Gossett are running through a meteor shower. Meteors rain down on them. The meteors drop down on guide wires as the two stars run through the set avoiding the wires so it looks like they're just avoiding getting hurt. To make the chase more exciting, there is an explosive charge at the bottom of the wire. The charge made the shot a little too exciting.

"One of the meteorites hit the tree. The flames went up very high and started to burn the roof," Petersen relates calmly. "That was quite dangerous, but we got it under control."

The forest set was saved for the rest of its shots, but now it is being torn down to make room for another set. Burly workmen shovel the set's fake snow into wheelbarrows and take it outside, where they dump it in huge piles on the real snow.

The only time the real snow has been a help on the film was on this set. There was a scene in which Dennis Quaid had to come from out of the storm into the shelter, and he had to have snow in his hair. They tried the artificial snow, but it never looked right. Finally someone suggested that Quaid just go outside into the falling snow. He walked out for a moment, came back in with snow all over, and Petersen shot it.

While the first unit's electricians struggle to get the charger into the lake before the day ends, many of the rest of the crew have converged on the cantina, a small tent next to the Wolfgang Petersen stage that is the central distribution point for hot coffee, hot food, and, when spirits are high, hot gossip. The tent is "heated," which means there are a number of space heaters scattered around, but the cold seeps through the cracks between the floorboards and under the canvas flaps. Few people sit at the tables; most wander around flapping their arms to keep warm. The day is drawing to a close, and people are getting ready for Fasching, an annual German holiday which, if the stories circulating can be believed, is a cross between Halloween, a three-day drunk, and an orgy.

Finally, the charger is ready. A test with the rain has worked. The crew assembles. Quaid, in a dry uniform, climbs wearily up the ladder to his cliff. He looks at floor effects supervisor Karl Baumgartner and says cheerfully: "I'm going to burn your set down."

"Ruhe, bitte," Petersen calls. "Quiet. Start the rain."

The rain pours down. Quaid lifts the bottle and pours the bright red fuel into the lake. Out of the camera's view, two technicians pour another couple of gallons of the fuel. The water is stained red. Quaid lifts the gun and fires. Nothing.

"Motherfucker!" Quaid shouts. He throws down the bottle.

Petersen looks sympathetic. "I think you can take a break now, Dennis," he says.

As Quaid leaves, Petersen confers with his crew to try to figure out what went wrong. They have to get this shot on the next take. Says Petersen:

Sometimes it's hard to keep up your enthusiasm on a film like this. Sometimes you get a little tired. It's easier for me than for the crew, because as the director, I have the whole film in my head. I know exactly what I want to get, so one little success here and there and I know the film is like one of those puzzles that only comes together later.

> It's more difficult for the crew to keep their energy
> going. As the director, you have to give them energy, you
> have to give them enthusiasm. You have to show them that
> *you* don't give up. I try my best to do that.

As the yellow electrician's platform descends again beneath the water and the crew get ready for a final shot, Petersen waits patiently, attending to a dozen details and not betraying the slightest worry.

"In today's filmmaking," the director says, "if you want to have something really great and special and unusual on the screen, you have to go through all this. You have to take a little risk to get exciting shots."

Petersen surveys his huge crew. They wait patiently for his order to try the shot one last time.

"What we're doing today is only setting a little bit of the water on fire," he says with a small sigh. "Tomorrow, the whole lake will burn."

The Unseen Enemy Mine

In a strange, alien place, millions of miles away from earth, an American and an enemy alien have learned to be happy. By working together instead of trying to kill each other, they have turned a war zone on a hostile, volcanic planet into a virtual paradise.

In a strange, alien place, thousands of miles from Hollywood, 20th Century-Fox has learned to be happy. They, too, have turned what was once a war zone into a paradise.

This war zone, however, is a movie called *Enemy Mine,* a $24 million science fiction epic that is Fox's major Christmas release. As directed by Wolfgang (*The Neverending Story*) Petersen, the film looks to be one of the biggest hits of the year. *Everyone* at the Bavaria Studios in Munich, where Petersen has taken over nine of 11 stages, believes this is the best film they have ever worked on.

It was not always like this.

One year ago, *Enemy Mine* was one of Hollywood's most gossiped-about disasters. Behind schedule, over budget, with a feuding director and producer, and shooting in a country where filming is almost impossible, it was predicted that the film would never be finished, let alone released.

In a way, those predictions came true. The film Wolfgang Petersen is shooting now is *not* the same film that ran aground in Iceland. *This* film, everybody agrees, is a masterpiece. *This* film, everybody says, will be not only the hit of the Christmas season, but one of the all-time classics.

The other film, the film that started in Iceland, now sits in a vault at 20th Century-Fox. It will sit there, unseen, forever.

Enemy Mine got its start when producer Steven (*All of Me*) Friedman decided to do a science fiction project. He sent one of his two employees to a science fiction convention in Texas to find something. The employee came back with Barry Longyear's novella about an American star fighter and an enemy alien stranded together on a hostile planet. Something about the story appealed to Friedman enough to make him buy it. The next step was to find a writer. They chose Ed Khmara. Explains Khmara:

> When Steven Friedman was looking for a writer, I had *Ladyhawke*, another thing I'd done in the fantasy genre, in preproduction or whatever it was. Steve called me in and asked me to read the novella. I read it and he asked if I thought we could make a movie out of this. I, needing a job at the time, said yes.

Friedman took the novella, with Khmara attached as the writer, around as a pitch to the studios. There was no interest. The studios did not see the potential in the story Friedman knew was there. But Friedman did not give up.

"Finally, Steve hired me more or less on speculation from his own company to write the script," Khmara says.

Khmara set to work on bringing out the good in the story and eliminating the bad.

"The problem with making a movie from the book was that the book was not structured. There was no real ending," Khmara says. "I had to create a linear time structure for the story, because the book didn't have one."

One thing did not change in the adaptation. "The core of the story, which is the essential part of the relationship between the two characters, the alien Drac and the human, is quite a bit like in the book," Khmara says.

With the finished script, Friedman could now show others what he would seen all along—and that sold. Twentieth Century-Fox liked it enough to buy it. Then Friedman and Fox made what would turn out to be a disastrous mistake. They hired director Richard Loncraine.

"Richard Loncraine was a strange choice for a director," admits executive producer Stanley (*Outland*) O'Toole, who was brought aboard the project at the same time as Loncraine. "What can I add to that?" Loncraine *was* a strange choice to helm a $20 million science fiction epic. He had never directed anything of such epic proportions—his biggest films to date were Michael Palin's Victorian sex comedy *The Missionary* and the Stingstarring allegorical drama *Brimstone and Treacle,* which was a theatrical remake of a television play.

This was certainly no case of an ambitious director breaking into the big time with a low-budget smash; all of his films had received indifferent critical and commercial receptions in the United States.

But at first, Loncraine worked out brilliantly. He worked closely with Khmara on rewriting the script and, by everyone's estimation, made the script better. Admits O'Toole:

When I first saw that Loncraine wanted revisions, I thought "here's a young guy that wants to put his mark on a script." But when I read his revisions, I was floored. Richard brought out things in Ed I don't think Ed knew he had.

Khmara agrees. "Richard had wonderful ideas," Khmara says. "A lot of them improved the script and are still in the script." It was when the script was finished that the production started to turn into what O'Toole calls a "nightmare."

The majority of *Enemy Mine* takes place on a planet called Fyrine IV. Loncraine felt he had found the perfect location to shoot the Fyrine scenes on a small island off the coast of Iceland. O'Toole disagreed:

I never did want to go to Iceland. I wanted to go to Lanzarote in the Canary Islands. This made for a very agonizing decision on the part of the studio—whether to back the director or the producer. They decided we should go to Iceland.

Looking at the island of Haimey, it is not hard to see why Loncraine felt it could double for another planet. Says Khmara:

I hate to say this now, because in hindsight it sounds terrible, but at the time I was impressed with landscape. How unearthly it was. Here was a landscape we had never seen in movies before. Richard wanted a gray, barren, colorless appearance, and he got that in Iceland.

But to get that barren look would cost a fortune. Says O'Toole:

To go to Iceland is, to say the least, ridiculous. Iceland is a very expensive country. Running costs were so high. And it's not a filmmaking country as such, so therefore you have to bring everything in by ship: cameras, trucks, things you couldn't get anywhere else, even the catering. It wasn't worth it, and it never was.

Iceland is not only an expensive country, it is also not a great place to spend a spring. Says Hunt Downs, the film's director of publicity:

The living conditions were terrible. We were stuck on an island in the middle of nowhere. The weather was so bad they couldn't land a plane most of the time, so the only transportation to the mainland was a ferry that took four hours to get there and made everyone seasick.

Khmara agrees. "Conditions in general were harsh. The weather was terrible and the food was really bad. When you're cold and wet and miserable, the last thing you want is food that was left over from World War II."

The social life was not much better. Khmara explains:

We were in a little village on the island, and there just was not that much to do. To make matters worse, the locals resented the crew. It was the same old story—the crew was the object of attention. Because they were new, they were attractive to local ladies—and the local ladies *were* attractive. There was a single disco in the village where *everyone* went. There were fights in that disco on more than one occasion.

The disco was the only entertainment on the island. Aside from that, Khmara says, "we played a lot of Scrabble."

Most people who have worked on science fiction films have spent some time suffering in strange locales; after *Star Wars* was shot in Tunisia and *Indiana Jones* filmed in India, unpleasant living conditions have practically become part of the job description. There was one striking difference here, however. Says O'Toole:

> The time in Iceland was a lot of suffering for *nothing*. If you're going to make enormous visual gains, things nobody has ever done, especially in this kind of film, then of course you'd say let's go. But we were *never* going to do that.
>
> All that footage from this particular island where we shot the two protagonists meeting for some weeks looked like it was done in a coal mine in England. I could have gone out in the morning and shot it in Yorkshire. It would have been no problem; we would have gotten the same as we got.

Loncraine had achieved the gray, barren look he wanted. Unfortunately, he achieved it too well. Khmara says:

> The weather just turned *everything* gray. The weather in April was even less stable than in March, when we had last been there. In one day, you had fog, then the sun would come out, then it would snow, then the snow would turn to rain, then the fog would come in, then it would be sunny. It all happened so quickly, the director of photography, Ronnie Taylor, couldn't keep up with all the changes.

As the production went on, it slipped farther and farther behind schedule. The footage pleased O'Toole and the studio less and less. O'Toole and Loncraine began to argue. "It was all going wrong," O'Toole says. "I disliked intensely the way the film was going." Loncraine did not. "There is more than one way to skin a Drac," he says enigmatically, refusing to comment any further on his role in the production.

"Richard knew things were going badly," Khmara recalls. "Basically, he spent his time trying to catch up."

O'Toole did not like what was going on. He did not hesitate to let Loncraine know. And although the two tried not to air their differences in public, everybody knew of the conflict. The crew's spirit plummeted. Says Khmara:

> Morale was certainly not good. Everybody wanted to believe that all their hardships were worth it, so they believed in the film as much as they could. But a lot of the crew was not happy. The principals did a good job of keeping a stiff upper lip, but I don't think they were happy either.

Although Loncraine and O'Toole were hardly the best of friends at this time, they tried to work together to get the film back on track. But Loncraine refused to jeopardize the film he wanted to make. Says Khmara:

> Richard did everything he could to put it back together, *except* making certain compromises he felt would be detrimental to the movie. For instance, Stanley came to me and asked if I could make some changes in the script that would have cut out about two weeks of shooting in Iceland. I thought I could do it, but Richard wouldn't have anything to do with it.

Loncraine's unwillingness to tamper with his vision of the film might be seen as an admirable trait in an artist. Unfortunately, it was that vision of the film that O'Toole and the Fox executives disliked so much. O'Toole explains:

> The composition of the anamorphic frame was important here. It's important to consider how you fill the frame

when you're dealing with a normal widescreen 1.85 frame, but when you compose for 2.35 you've got a lot more to consider. You have that wonderful freedom to fill the frame beautifully or fill it horrifically or fill it however you wish, but whatever you do, fill it *interestingly*. Don't make it look like it's a background in Barnsley in Yorkshire where it's just black. That's exactly what we were getting.

Finally, O'Toole had had enough. He contacted Fox and told them to shut down the production. They did not. It *seemed* that the studio was going to stand by Richard Loncraine. What O'Toole did not know was that Fox had started shopping for another director. Recalls Wolfgang Petersen, the internationally respected German director of *Das Boot* and *The Never-ending Story:*

> I got a call in the middle of the night. It was my agent call-ing. He said he had just got a call from Iceland asking if I would like to take over a very big, very important film called *Enemy Mine*. I said no. At the time I was involved with the American version of *The Neverending Story,* and I'm not the type of director who takes the next plane and says "OK, next Monday I start."

That was not the answer Fox was looking for.

> A few hours after the first call, I got a call from Iceland, from Stephen Friedman. He called me and asked again if I would read the script; it's a great script and so on. I told him I could read the script, but I couldn't make it. Then I read the script. I loved it.

Enemy Mine dragged on for two more weeks in Iceland. The tension between O'Toole and Loncraine—who knew O'Toole wanted him fired—increased. And in Los Angeles stories of the film's woes were getting into the trades, along with extremely high estimates of how much the film was over budget. The production was in danger of becoming a *Heaven's Gate*-style embarrassment for Fox.

Then Stanley O'Toole got a phone call. "I got a call from some of the executives who had visited the set. They said, 'Shut down the production.' Since I had told them to do this two weeks earlier, I thought they were doing this very late."

Shutting down this kind of production is a dramatic move studios rarely take. After all, once a studio has dumped so much money into a film, they don't want to pull out without a chance of ever recouping any of it. And the first production of *Enemy Mine* did cost Fox a lot.

"We spent a few million dollars on the old production," O'Toole says. "I'm not allowed to say exactly how much. Although we didn't spend nearly as much as it was reported, it wasn't $50— it was a lot of money."

O'Toole went back to Los Angeles and met with the Fox executives. He wanted to know who the next director on the film would be. He was not worried that the film might not get made. "I never thought for one split second this film would die," O'Toole says. "More than any subject I've done in 25 years, I've always believed that this film was a winner if ever I'd read one." Forty-eight hours later, O'Toole was proven right. Fox was going to hire Petersen. O'Toole relates:

> Within 24 hours of finding out Fox was hiring Petersen, I flew to Munich and met with Joe Wizan, the then president of Fox, and Bob Cort, the executive in charge of the production, whose baby it was. We sat here and discussed it with Wolfgang, who was terribly honest, very firm, although he wanted the script so bad he could taste it. He said "I need time to prepare this; I want to do it right. I'll do it my way."

Usually, when a director is fired in the middle of a production, the new director is given a couple of weeks to familiarize himself with the script, then goes to work on the old sets. This is what happened when John Badham took over for Martin Brest on *War Games,* for example. This is exactly what O'Toole expected for *Enemy Mine.* "I thought it would be two, three, four weeks and let's make the most of it and get out of it whole, because, boy, were we in a hole." But Petersen wanted something else. Petersen wanted to start the whole film over. Petersen explains:

> If I was going to do this film, I had my conditions. I said the only chance is to start from scratch, with a totally new concept, with my people, in the Bavaria Studios. Push it back for about half a year, then start. That would be the reasonable situation to think about making *Enemy Mine.* I couldn't go on with the old concept and date of delivery.

So *Enemy Mine* went into preproduction for the second time. One of the first orders of business was scouting locations. Says O'Toole:

> Wolfgang said he wanted to go around the world and find where we could build this planet Fyrine and make it different from anything we'd ever seen on screen. I said fine. We had a guy out in South Africa doing this and somebody out there doing that. I said "Please, whatever you do, take a look at Lanzarote." He took a look at Lanzarote and there and then decided to go for it.

O'Toole was in heaven.

> Wolfgang Petersen has been the happiest surprise of my life. The more I got into a working relationship with Petersen, the more I learned, the more excited he got me.

I began to realize we were dealing with magic here. I got really trembly about it. This is the right way to make movies; I can't believe I'm here.

Khmara, too, was delighted when he started rewriting for Petersen. "Working with Wolfgang was very good work and a real creative experience that I'll cherish," he says. Petersen went out of his way to make writing as easy and productive as possible for Khmara.

If I wanted to create a sequence and Petersen liked it, we'd go to the production designer and he would make us some drawings or even some models so I could work from them. It's so much easier than just creating there's a that and a that and a that and being told by the studio they can't really film it. It's not very often a writer gets a chance to sit down with all those people and put all those elements together simultaneously and really see the thing evolve.

Petersen hired a completely new crew, headed by production designer Rolf *(The Neverending Story)* Zehetbauer and cinematographer Tony *(Night Crossing)* Imi. The only holdovers from the first film were in the cast.

I had the freedom to recast the film. But after seeing Dennis Quaid's and Lou Gossett's other films and meeting them personally, I said they're perfect for this. I recast all the other roles, with the exception of Brian James, who plays Stubbs. I took him along because I liked him.

Now that Petersen's film is cruising along just fine, O'Toole and Khmara have the perspective to reconsider Richard Loncraine. In retrospect, he looks better than he did in the grey weather of Iceland. Says O'Toole:

I think Richard didn't realize what an enormous undertaking this was as compared with most pictures. Had he realized that, he had the intelligence and the ability to deal with it. But I think it took him a little longer than it should have to realize it. Which surprised me, because he is that bright.

Ed Khmara agrees.

Richard's ambitions for the film were greater than what *anybody* would be capable of realizing. He had wonderful ideas.

I have very mixed feelings about Richard's leaving. [Khmara is delighted with Wolfgang Petersen's version of the film.] I felt great loyalty and friendship with Richard, but maybe that blinded me to his problems. Richard always believed he could get the film done his way if he was given the chance. At the time, my friendship inclined me to believe he could. Now I don't know.

Khmara also has mixed feelings about Loncraine's unwillingness to sacrifice his vision to save the production. "If the film had worked out the way Richard wanted to do it, this would certainly have been to his credit. As it is, who knows if he was right or just stubborn?"

Wolfgang Petersen Interview

It is not every night you get a frantic transatlantic offer from a total stranger begging you to take over a $20 million picture. Not even if your first feature won you an Academy Award nomination and your second was an international smash hit. When it happens, you listen.

Unless you are Wolfgang Petersen. When the internationally acclaimed director of *Das Boot* and *The Neverending Story* got an after-midnight call from his agent asking him to take over 20th Century-Fox's troubled science fiction epic, *Enemy Mine,* he hung up without a second thought.

It was the *second* call that piqued Petersen's curiosity. This call came from Iceland. It was from Stephen Friedman, *Enemy Mine*'s producer. He begged the director just to *read the script.* Intrigued, Petersen accepted but warned he was not going to take over the project. He had just finished *The Neverending Story* and he needed a rest. There was no way he was going to plunge into another huge production.

And then he read the script. Petersen recalls:

> The *dimension* of the script thrilled me. In a film of the science fiction/ action-adventure genre, there was a very personal, very emotional story taking place. What happens between this alien character and this human was so unusual, so moving, so touching in a way I'd never seen before in a science fiction movie.

Petersen was hooked. He insists:

> I never would have done just the next science fiction film. Never. I thought this was a chance to make something absolutely new: a science fiction film with great characters and a special meaning, a special depth, a science fiction film that tells something about relationships between people and not just a superficial story. Not just popcorn, but much more than that.

Petersen was still worn out from *The Neverending Story* but somehow, after reading *Enemy Mine,* it did not matter so much.

I think every filmmaker knows this feeling when you say "Now let's have a little rest and think about the future," and all of a sudden, Bang! There's a film and you can't say no because you love it and it's great. You do it. I don't regret that. I love it so much to work on *Enemy Mine* now.

But before Petersen would agree to take over the film, he had his conditions. Friedman had asked Petersen to come out to Iceland and pick up where newly fired director Richard Loncraine had left off. Petersen refused that flat out.

I'm not the type of director who takes the next plane and says "Okay, next Monday I start." I can't do that. I said the only chance is to start from scratch, a totally new concept with my people in the Bavaria Studios, push it back for about half a year, then start. That would be a reasonable situation to think about making *Enemy Mine*. I wouldn't go on with their original concept and date of delivery.

Much to his surprise, Petersen found himself in preproduction on *Enemy Mine* with writer Ed (*Ladyhawke*) Khmara and his favorite production designer Rolf Zehetbauer, who worked with Petersen on *Das Boot* and *The Neverending Story*. And a few months later, Wolfgang Petersen was shooting his third epic in a row.

There are few directors who can make a big logistics picture and still focus on the intimate human drama. David Lean, who started out making chamber dramas and Noël Coward comedies, is the master; David Lynch, who also started out with small, personal films, failed dismally when he tried with *Dune*. C. B. DeMille only would have known how many directors have let their stories get lost in the crush of extras, sets, and special effects. Petersen is one of the few who has successfully balanced the epic with the personal.

I had the same problems on *Das Boot* and *The Neverending Story*. I'm not really afraid about that because my main concern in these films is to concentrate on the characters. I don't mind going through all this special effects stuff, because it has to be, but my main concentration is always on the story. You must think ahead and know what you want to have and what you need to put it together later to have the story together and then it's fine.

Petersen credits this ability to his years of working as a director of almost 20 intimate TV movies.

I was so used to telling stories in almost 20 films, always dealing with people and characters and with a lot of concentration on actors. I think that was very important to me not to lose control over that area in these big films.

But even before he started in German television, Petersen was making movies. A fanatic devotee of American movies as a child, Petersen knew from an early age he wanted to spend his life as a filmmaker. He recalls:

From the time I was ten or eleven, I was thinking only about filmmaking. I made a lot of films at that time—8mm films: little cowboy films and ghost stories and so on. And then, of course, I was at the movie house at least twice a week.

After years of this informal training, Petersen took the plunge and enrolled in film school. It was not exactly what he expected. "When I started to work in the film school in Berlin, they were so surprised," Petersen says. "When I made my first small films there, they said 'What do you want to learn here? You know everything already.'"

With his film school education quickly ended, Petersen set out to look for work. Unfortunately, this was not an auspicious time for a German director who wanted to make American-style films. Says Petersen:

> This was in 1966-70, the very first years of the so-called New German Cinema. I was very much excited about what they did. But I was a little bit the outsider. They were doing—with great success, I think—what they called auteur cinema, making very personal stories. That wasn't really what I wanted to do or what I was able to do at that time—I'm not a writer really, and it was not my way of filmmaking. I was more a director, not so much a writer/director.

But if a revolution in feature filmmaking closed the theaters to Petersen, a similar revolution in television opened new doors to him. He explains:

> The seventies were a very exciting time for television in Germany. A lot of young directors of the time—Rainer Werner *(The Marriage of Maria Braun)* Fassbinder, Volker *(The Tin Drum)* Schlondorff, Wim *(Paris, Texas)* Wenders, and a lot of others—worked on TV before they made their first films.

German television allowed Petersen to make small, powerful films like "The Consequence," a drama about homosexuality, "Black and White Like Day and Night," about a chess player going crazy, and "For Your Love Only," a mystery thriller that featured one of Nastassia Kinski's earliest performances.

"I loved working in TV," Petersen recalls. "I always wanted a big audience for my films, and I got it there. I remember when I made the Kinski film, there was such excitement. *Everybody* was talking about it."

Petersen stayed with TV for years. Finally a feature project came along that promised the same mass audience Petersen's television movies would find. The feature was *Das Boot,* an agonizingly intense World War II drama set almost entirely in a submarine. Although the production required huge special effects and presented daunting logistical problems, Petersen found directing his first feature little different from his experience on television movies.

> The only difference was one of scale. My dream from the first moment on was to make movies. These first films for television were sort of training for me. The TV movies had smaller budgets and smaller scale, but it was no different for me at all. And if you see the five-hour television version of *Das Boot* (shown in America only on Los Angeles's prestigious cable Z channel), you don't see any real difference. They have the same style.

Soon after Petersen finished *Das Boot,* he was offered an even bigger project: a film based on the internationally best-selling fairy tale *The Never-ending Story.*

"I was looking for something light and warm and positive after three years' work on *Das Boot,*" Petersen says. "I was so happy when they gave me that novel. I really liked it. It was exactly the right stuff for me to do at the time." But the book presented major challenges—not only the usual logistical problem of making a big fantasy, but difficulties in adapting a much-loved but unwieldy novel. Petersen's decision was to film only the first half of the book.

> If I had done the whole book, I wouldn't have had a film because it's much too much. The big mistake on *Dune* was that they tried to do the whole thing in one film and it's so confusing it's no real story anymore. It's so complex that

> you don't understand what's going on. Exactly that would have been the mistake with *Neverending Story* because it's so much going on in that book. The book has a natural break in the middle. At that moment when Bastian flies into his own Fantasia, that is exactly the middle of the book. In the second part, we see and follow Bastian in his adventures in his creation of Fantasia. It was a very easy decision to make.

Creating a fantasy world full of bizarre creatures and awesome landscapes is a daunting enough challenge for any director. But in adapting *The Neverending Story,* Petersen faced a challenge most directors hate even more than they hate studio heads: working with children. The only three major human characters in the film are children. Petersen did not mind.

> It's no problem for me to be very patient with kids and to do it again and again with them. With little Barret Oliver, we had to do one scene 17 or 18 times. He was really not concentrating, he was playing around. So I played a little bit with him. We talked, then we looked at the tapes of what we'd done and discussed a little bit his mistakes, then we did it again. This sort of patience, being able to wait for the right moment, is very important when you work with kids. But you must really have a good relationship with kids to get that out.

Patience and understanding are just useful with children, Petersen stresses. They are the secret to his success as a director. He says:

> Filmmaking is really a lot of people. It means bringing together a lot of people and using their talents, bringing it all together and directing all that to the screen. I've found

out the best way is to motivate people and give them self-confidence so they feel you like them and their talent and their way of working. A dictator is not the best way.

Petersen has little patience with the Eric Von Stroheim/Otto Preminger image of the director as dictator.

The result is not good if you think all the time you're a genius and the others have no idea how to make the film at all. I can't see how that would work. You can see on the screen when the whole crew really had their hearts in the film, when they gave all their energy and their love to making that film. That's fifty percent of the quality of the whole film.

Even though America was the one Western country where the book *The Neverending Story* was not a hit, Petersen made the film very much with America in mind. Says Petersen:

The film was so expensive, we had to go to wide audiences like the English-speaking markets. So we shot it in English. We wanted to avoid dubbing the film into English because as you know that doesn't work. With a film like *The Neverending Story* you can't go with subtitles like an art film. We dubbed it for Germany, because in Germany dubbing's no problem—all foreign and American films are dubbed here, so people are used to it.

As it turned out, the film was a huge hit—everywhere *except* in America.

The film was a huge hit. It's still in its first run here—it's in its forty-first week in the same first-run movie house. It broke records in Germany and Spain, it's very successful in Australia. We're waiting to take it to Japan. And in Germany, it never ends.

But in America, it did end, and pretty quickly. Although the film grossed a respectable $20 million, it was far from a smash hit. Petersen speculates:

I think there are several reasons the film didn't do better in America. First of all, I think Warner Bros. did not do the best job with the film in the States. The opening date was a week before the Olympics, and the Olympics killed the whole movie business. All America was all of a sudden so excited about the Olympics. That was one of the mistakes.

But it may be also that the story has much more of a European temperament. In the summertime when the kids are used to seeing films like *Gremlins* and *Ghostbusters* and *Indiana Jones*—films with quite a lot of action and violence and fights and scary stuff, maybe *The Neverending Story* was a bit too sweet, too European for them. Also maybe it was a bit too sophisticated. A film about a boy reading a book—maybe it was not that perfect for the American temperament.

Even without a tremendous success in America, the film has done well enough that one immediately thinks about a sequel. The film was, after all, only half of the book. Petersen rules himself out of the sequel immediately.

I won't do the sequel, but the producer was thinking about it. I'm not sure they want to do it. *The Neverending Story* was very expensive for a German production—60 million DM—and the second part is much more difficult to visualize. There's no real world in the second half—it all takes

SCIENCE FICTION FILMMAKING IN THE 1980S

place in Bastian's Fantasia, with hundreds of creatures and everything. It would be very, very expensive to do that.

If the producers want to do a sequel, Petersen believes, they will have to hurry—

> The second half is still about Bastian and Atreyu, and that means Barret Oliver and Noah Hathaway. If you wait more than half a year or a year, they are not kids anymore. It is trouble if you have in the main roles kids who are no longer ten or eleven.

Although Petersen's attention is almost completely taken up with *Enemy Mine,* he still finds a little time to develop what he hopes will be his next project.

> My next film might be another film with Fox called *What Dreams May Come.* It's a life after death story. Right now I'm working on the script with Richard Matheson, on whose novel it's based. It's a love that doesn't stop in our life here—it goes over the border and takes place also in life after death. There is the chance that this could be the love story of all the love stories because it goes over the experience of our lifetime. Again a very difficult film to visualize, but Rolf Zehetbauer and I are both very excited about that. The plan is to shoot next spring, here at the Bavaria Studios.

Although *What Dreams May Come* sounds like a fantasy, Petersen insists it is not a genre piece. "It's not fantasy, it's not science fiction," Petersen insists. "It's a real story that deals with real people on earth here, but it deals with life after death. If you believe in life after death, it's not fantasy, it's not science fiction, it's real."

Although his big productions are full of logistical and organizational nightmares, Petersen has no desire to go back to the kind of films he made for television.

> I could see making maybe a film that's a little bit smaller—
> why not? But to go back to what I did earlier, no. Right
> now, I'm doing exactly what I wanted to do. Not to go on
> with even bigger, bigger, bigger films, but to make big,
> important films with budgets big enough that I can make
> all my dreams come true. That's a wonderful situation, and
> I appreciate it. I love it.

THE MAD MAX
MOVIES (1979-85)

With *Mad Max,* a 1979, low-budget, Australian-made picture, the name of George Miller burst upon the movie screens of the world, not with a whisper but with a bang.

Mad Max, which starred the now internationally acclaimed Mel Gibson, was a small, inexpensive film that in a somewhat rambling fashion, told the story of an Australian policeman's revenge against a gang of motorcycle thugs. The film was set in an indeterminate, lawless future, and it was made riveting by the amount of sheer energy packed within it.

If ever there was a film to substantiate the auteur theory, it was *Mad Max.* What raised the film miles above its humble origins and clichéd plot was the electrifying direction of George Miller. In *Mad Max* cars were not simply cars: they became personalized symbols of destruction. The bleak, deserted roads of Australia were turned into an arena worthy of medieval knights.

Mad Max, an Australian film about violence, vehicles, and vengeance, was a big moneymaker in every part of the world, with the exception of the United States and Canada. Poor distribution in those two markets kept it from grossing large sums at the box office, although the picture did well where it was shown.

Director and cowriter George Miller was pressured from all sides to do a sequel. However, the making of *Mad Max* had been a demoralizing experience for Miller, and he had no desire to go through it again. But he did.

Where *Mad Max* had originally evolved from Miller's desire to make an action-packed film dealing with Australia's car culture, *Road Warrior* (sometimes known as *Mad Max II)* was created as a deliberate attempt to mold the character of Max into a classical hero.

The 1981 sequel is, if anything, superior to its predecessor. It expands the mythical elements already present in the first film, raising them to the level of pure archetypes while focusing on a simpler, better structured plot.

With only two films to his credit, Miller had established himself as one of the best action directors in the world.

While touring the United States to promote the American release of *Mad Max II—The Road Warrior,* Miller was contacted by Steven Spielberg to direct one of the segments of a film, then under production, *The Twilight Zone.* The Australian agreed to his first studio assignment and chose "Nightmare at 5,000 Feet" for his segment.

When *Twilight Zone* was released, Miller's tale was generally accepted as the best in the picture. He was able to bring dynamism and excitement to the closed-in structure of a jet plane flying 5,000 feet above the ground.

After returning to Australia, where he made two critically acclaimed television series, Miller decided that the time was right for a third installment in the saga of his mythical hero, Max. In the 1985 *Mad Max III—Beyond Thunderdome* Miller's postapocalyptic world gained yet another layer. Although the film did not have the single-minded, tightly focused energy of its direct predecessor, except in the remarkable Thunderdome scene, it was much richer in its statements on life, history, society, heroism, and the nature of change.

The director does not discard the possibility of doing yet another *Mad Max* film under the wing of his Australian production company, Kennedy-Miller. This would make Miller possibly the only foreign director to build a successful Hollywood career while remaining true to his native roots.

A Few Days on the Set of Mad Max—Beyond Thunderdome

Dateline: Bartertown. Somewhere in the wastelands on the edge of hope. Time: the future. A bleak future where a nuclear war has forever changed our civilization. A future where one lone man becomes the agent of change. This is the world of Max, once known as the Road Warrior.

Cut back to reality. Bartertown sits in the center of the Homebush State Brickworks, the oldest brick factory in Sydney, Australia. Yet, sitting in the middle of this desolate quarry, surrounded by over 300 extras, all dressed in postapocalyptic clothes—not to mention the numerous goats, chickens, pigs, and camels wandering about—it is easy to project oneself into the future and imagine what life in Max's world might be like.

The first day on the Bartertown set is only slightly short of being as crazy as the future it portrays. The cast and crew of *Mad Max III—Beyond Thunderdome* has just returned from five harrowing weeks on location in Coober Pedy. Coober Pedy is a mining town located at the edge of the Great Stony Desert. According to the Australians, it is the opal capital of the world. Of it, Grant Page, stunt coordinator on the film, says, "It is one of the most notoriously desolate places on earth. Any desert that won't even support flies (Australian flies can lay claim to being the world's most pernicious, enduring, and aggressive) is pretty bad!"

Director George Miller, seen here directing his segment of _Twilight Zone—The Movie,_ was the guiding force behind all three of the _Mad Max_ movies.

The Coober Pedy location was used for most of the car stunts, which were carried out in broad daylight. Some days the temperature was measured at 146 degrees Fahrenheit. People lucky enough to stay in the shade of the tents still had to suffer a temperature of 117 degrees. "The first day we worked there," comments Page, "we had eighteen open vehicles, and the people wore black leather and vinyl uniforms, with most of their skin bare. The cars were out, working shot after shot, and so were the drivers! It inevitably puts a load that normally wouldn't exist. It's got an effect on your judgment. It's got an effect on the way you pad yourself. Normally, in a cool temperature, you pad yourself with wet suits and all sorts of things until you're so well protected that you won't get hurt. But out in 146 degrees, you can't do that because you'd last three minutes and you'd be dead. We had ten people collapse with exhaustion, and twelve cars collapsed too." After such an experience, the 90 degrees-plus heat in Bartertown seems almost like paradise to everyone!

Still, the first day back in the "civilization" of Bartertown starts slowly. The visiting reporter fortunately manages to enliven everyone's morning by taking an unrehearsed pratfall in a large and deep on-set mud pit. The sympathy of cast and crew is now acquired, but at what price!

Terry Hayes, coproducer and screenwriter, shares his excitement when telling the so far secret story of the film. *Mad Max III—Beyond Thunderdome* starts 15 years after *Mad Max II—The Road Warrior.* As Mel Gibson later comments,

> All the juice is now gone. What is left of society has reverted to an even more primitive level. Max himself is older, and more world-weary. He survived any way he could. He led basically a nomadic existence, coming across people and trading a few things ....

While traveling in the desert in his camel-drawn vehicle, Max is overtaken by a small methane-powered plane flown by the freewheeling bandit Jedediah and his son. Although the two characters bear no relation to each other, Jedediah is played by Bruce Spence, who was the much-loved gyro pilot in *The Road Warrior.* Jedediah succeeds in taking off with all of Max's worldly goods, leaving the hero to perish in the desert.

Max manages to survive until he comes to a sign that points toward "Hope," which in turn leads him to the city of Bartertown. Bartertown sits on top of "Underworld," a giant pig farm cum methane plant, which provides power to the city. According to production designer Graham "Grace" Walker, the central core of the plant is an old truck on rails, covered with a huge boiler and pipes going every which way.

Entrance to Bartertown is gained only by bartering rare goods against the town's supplies and services. Fortunately, Max, who has nothing but his skills, eventually succeeds in getting himself admitted. He is then hired as a mercenary by Bartertown's queen, Auntie Entity, played with gusto by rock star Tina Turner. Entity wants Max to kill her rival, a two-man team called Master Blaster (Master is a little person who sits on giant-sized Blaster's shoulders) who runs Underworld.

Max first agrees, but he finally refrains from killing Blaster after making a startling discovery. "He just cannot do something like that," comments Gibson. "It's something that would bother his conscience. It may be the only thing that singles him out from the rest of the scum."

Entity's chief henchman, Iron Bar Bassey, played by Australian rock star Angry Anderson of *Rose Tattoo,* has Max expelled into the desert, where he is found by the feral children of the Crack in the Earth, a deep crevice which contains a lush paradise at its bottom. (For the Crack, Grace Walker found a location in the Blue Mountains, 60 miles from Sydney.) Only a few skin houses and cave walls had to be built, as well as the rear of an old 747. To the children, Max is "Walker," a legendary figure that will lead them to salvation—in the guise of civilization.

In spite of Max's efforts, several of the children sneak away from the Crack to find Bartertown. In order to rescue them, Max must decide to leave his newly found haven ....

Mad Max III—Beyond Thunderdome sports a much more complicated storyline than the previous two movies. It takes Hayes over two hours to narrate it, or more accurately act it out. He succeeds admirably in conveying his sense of wonder and excitement, changing the level and pitch of his voice to suit the action. Although he prefers to let audiences judge the picture by themselves, Hayes even admits that there is a message in the film for any who care to find it—a rare admission in movieland, where few people these days seem to care about a story's moral content.

Whether or not *Beyond Thunderdome* has a message is not important to those on the set who scurry around, trying to set up a location that has not been used for five weeks. The town itself is an odd collection of adobelike, rounded huts and old, used metal bits that have been cannibalized from ancient machines. Parts of derelict automobiles are built into the sides of buildings. Everything looks so dirty and worn that it seems it has been there forever.

Grace Walker explains the evolution of Bartertown's shabby appearance. "In the beginning, George Miller sort of mentioned that it had a kind of African feel, and the design of the buildings came out that way. But then, it all changed and the crazy chimneys went up."

Because *Beyond Thunderdome* takes place 15 years after *The Road Warrior,* there was no desire or need to keep any similarities in design to the previous film. Walker explains:

> We didn't want to make anything similar. That's why our cars are the way they are. They've gone a bit further. Now, they're just engines with a skeleton frame. There are no auto bodies left, just bits of scrap. People live in them.

Building Bartertown was the responsibility of construction foreman Max Worrall, a tall, engaging man sporting a mohawk.

> The usual rule when you're building is that it should be plumb, square, and level, and you can't go wrong. Well, in Bartertown, nothing is plumb, square or level! On the other hand, that also means that you've got a little to play with. The finish is not so important, because the town is supposed to have a rough, medieval, postapocalyptic look—sort of like "The Flintstones!"

Although no one really lives in the strange buildings of Bartertown, Worrall made sure that people could walk on some of them. He explains:

The demands of the shot quite often mean that you have people where they shouldn't be. So you have to over-train for that. The town is made of light steel frames with chicken wire, covered with hessian, and then sprayed with concrete.

Spectators with good eyesight and quick reflexes will spot some injokes thrown to the fans and hidden among the various decorations of Bartertown. For instance, on a wall is a picture of a gremlin, and the feed and grain store has the words, "Proprietor: E. T. Spielberg" painted over its front entrance.

Dominating Bartertown, and located at its center, are two important structures. One is Auntie Entity's 50-feet-high penthouse, reachable only by a rickety, open-sided elevator. The other is what looks like a huge jungle gym. This is Thunderdome, the arena where all Bartertown disputes are settled in an exciting contest of strength, ability and pure determination. The battles there are always to the death. There is only one rule in Thunderdome, "Two men go in—only one comes out!"

It is in Thunderdome that Max battles Blaster. Hanging from the topmost metal bars on elastic ropes, the two men fight with such exotic items as a sledgehammer and a chainsaw!

Today, Thunderdome lies dead, waiting. The scene that is being filmed is one where Master Blaster demonstrates his power over Bartertown by causing the lights in town to flicker. The crew love it because it is being shot inside Bartertown's entrance tunnel which is also the only cool place on the set, as it is located inside a concrete and aluminum foil tunnel. In fact, everyone who does not have to be somewhere else crowds into the tunnel to watch the shooting.

The Collector (played by veteran actor Frank Thing), the impressively big man who guards the entrance to Bartertown, several guards, and Iron-bar Bassey are in the scene. Quiet is called for, but someone forgot to cue the chickens, which, tensing with anticipation, begin to cackle wildly. Throughout the shoot-ing animals will display that uncanny sense—making more noise as the humans get quiet.

For almost every scene the special effects team is called on to provide smoke and dust, making breathing in the cave difficult for everyone. On top of that, the ground is littered with sharp, pointy rocks. It can only be assumed that the extras really want to be in the film, since most of them walk barefoot, even between takes.

The mixture of these strangely garbed extras and casually garbed crew gives the place an aura of otherworldliness—a little like a particularly overworked immigration office of the future. Auntie Entity's punk-haired, leather-clad imperial guards lend a slight touch of menace to the whole scene—that is, until they start talking about the mundane realities of every-day life. Included in the guards is Max Worrall, whose impres-sive height caused Grace Walker to suggest him for a role in front of the camera as well—as long as he would agree to shave his head.

There are also women members of the imperial guards. One of them is Geeling, a beautiful, young, oriental actress who starred opposite David Bowie in his recent controversial video, "China Girl."

Max Worrall is not the only extra to have come to his part in a rather unusual way. Brian W. Ellison, for instance, started with the film as one of the nighttime security guards. Now he also plays the role of a knife twirling, snakeskin-dressed bodyguard to the Collector, the man who guards Bartertown's entrance. One night, as Ellison practiced a self-taught method of knife twirl-ing, which he calls BAOKOS (Brian's Art of Knives on a String), he was unknowingly watched by Frank Leonard of a company called Movie Stunts. Leonard told Ellison that his technique was good, but the young guard was still reticent about his skill and continued to practice in seclusion until stunt coordinator Grant

Page asked him if he would be interested in displaying his technique in the film.

"I was quite amazed," recalls Ellison. "But eventually, I went to see George Miller, who was impressed and said he'd like me to be in the movie. Then, I started to practice in earnest and tried to make my stunts as good as possible." Ellison warns audience members not to try doing what he does with apparent ease in the film: "It's pretty dangerous. I've got the scars on my hands to prove it!"

Ellison describes his part with gusto: "I attack Max with the knives, swishing them around, trying to cut him. He sees me coming, quickly draws a gun and shoots me. Then, of course, I'm subdued!" Although his character is not killed, Ellison says, "It makes me very aware of the fact that knives are no match for a shotgun!"

Being shot calls for Ellison's elaborate feather headdress to explode while it's still on his head. The first tests done with the explosives were tried on dummy heads and proved to be much stronger than expected. Finally, to Ellison's relief, a safe procedure was engineered.

While Ellison demonstrates his skills for this reporter, the second scene of the day, a direct follow-up to the previous scene, is being set up. Out of camera range sit the make-up people, the technicians, and several visitors. One of the extras wanders over and talks quietly with some of the crew. A double take later, it becomes apparent that the scruffy, long-haired, bare-chested stranger is none other than Max himself, Mel Gibson.

By five, the scene has not yet been shot. Cast and crew start to show signs of battle fatigue, with the exception of codirector George Miller, whose boundless energy makes him forget about time when he works. The scene is finally done, and a tea break is called. In the tea tent, when teased about almost spilling coffee on his leather pants, Gibson laughs good-naturedly and jokes that nothing can make them worse at this stage.

At 7:30 P.M. a third scene is set up, where some of Bartertown's "hopefuls" line up outside the cave entrance in order to gain admission to the city. Included in the group are the noisy chickens, which show no signs of exhaustion, two goats, and a large dog that has been conscripted to pull a cart.

The scene is rehearsed and rearranged several times, as are indeed most of the scenes in the film. Miller is open to suggestions from anyone who has a good idea, believing that filmmaking is a collaborative effort. This attitude carries over to the crew who display immense loyalty to the film and strive to do their best under difficult conditions. At least, most of them do, for at 9:15 (shooting is scheduled to go on for at least another half hour) several animal actors go on strike.

The dog, an Irish wolfhound, exhibits a perverse and so far hidden aspect of his personality, lying down every time Miller calls for "Action!" instead of pulling its cart as it is supposed to do. Not to be left behind, the goats plant their feet in the ground and refuse to be moved. Since there are 25 or more people who have to walk behind the obstinate animals, this quickly causes a massive traffic jam in the tunnel. Rather than fight the strike, Miller eventually decides to accept the goats' suggestion and calls it a day.

For the Australian film industry, a typical work week is six days, ten hours a day. So, although the next day is a Saturday, the Bartertown set is brimming with activity. Today is the day when Max's arrival in Bartertown is being shot. Although mostly undramatic to watch, the agenda for the day includes the scene where Max fires his gun at the knife-twirling Ellison. Great care is taken in setting up the shot. Shielding is being carefully placed, and all personnel have to stay in the safety zone.

All is finally made ready. Everyone is warned not to make any noise when the gun goes off. Gibson is prepared. He reaches into his costume—but finds no gun! One retake later, the scene (as well as the gun) goes off without a hitch.

Safety is a foremost concern on the set. While working with the cars in Coober Pedy, seven hours were spent in setting up one stunt. And because there was still doubt as to its safety, it was scrapped in the end; perhaps a great loss of time and money, but an admirable show of concern for safety over the exigencies of filmmaking. Page comments:

> We're at the end of the heavy stunts now. So far, there's been only one minor burn, and the man was back driving three days later. We've had a very, very good safety record on this film, same as on *Mad Max* where there wasn't one single injury.

On Monday everyone returns to Bartertown, feeling refreshed after a day of rest. This is Tina Turner's last day, and the production schedule calls for three important scenes to be shot. All deal with the eventual destruction of Bartertown.

The first one calls for 400 extras, a variety of animals, and multiple explosions. At 8:00 A.M. the extras wait outside the makeup tents. Some of them were found wandering around on Sydney's streets and are extremely proud of the fact that they do not need any makeup or costumes to look their parts!

At 9:00 A.M. the special effects crew start setting up their explosions on the hillside above Bartertown. Once everybody from cast and crew is present, a small demonstration of the explosive devices to be used is given. Three types of explosives will be employed: sound bombs, debris bombs, and fireballs. When the fireball blast goes off, it is much bigger than originally planned. Miller shows concern and eventually decides that its size will have to be cut down.

Because of the large amount of action scheduled to take place in the shot, as well as the danger, the setup is being very carefully prepared. The extras are rehearsed over and over. The animals are their usual uncooperative selves. The pigs, in particular, object to being kept in line by a dog; they eventually turn against it and chase it away—temporarily.

It actually takes seven and a half hours before everything is made ready. Several firetrucks are present should any of the fires get out of hand. The time is now 4:30 P.M. and there has been no break at all. The temperature is well over 90 degrees, and there is no shade. Everyone wants the shot to be over with, but no one forgets that it must be done right the first time, because there will be no chance for a retake. On top of that, there are still two more scenes to be done with Turner before the sun sets approximately three hours from now. The race is on.

Miller calls for action. Immediately, Bartertown takes on the appearance of a true postapocalyptic hell. With the explosions, the fires, the smoke, and the screams of animals and people, even the set observers begin to feel involved in the action.

"Cut!" is called. Miller immediately rushes to the side of an extra who has fallen and may have twisted an ankle. All the planning has paid off. There have been no real injuries, except for a stuntman whose bare toes were stepped on by a horse.

Excitement runs high on the set as everyone breaks for a much-delayed lunch. Miraculously, Turner's last two shots also wrap without glitches, making good use of the last of the sun's rays. As the singer-actress says her goodbyes to the cast and crew, everyone breaks into spontaneous applause.

Tuesday calls for the filming to be done on the quarry floor outside of Bartertown itself. It is so hot that crew members pour water over their heads in an unsuccessful attempt to keep cool. The rebellious Irish wolfhound is back, but after several hours of grueling heat, her owner finally takes her away. To make matters worse, there is a hot wind blowing dust in everyone's eyes....

All of the methane-powered cars have arrived from Coober Pedy by train. According to Page, many of them are on their last legs. "We got half of them to a degree where, if it weren't for continuity, we wouldn't be driving them at all," he explains.

Strangely enough, one of the vehicles is a leftover from *The Road Warrior*. Humungus's car has been carefully refurbished into a vehicle that now looks like a lobster pot.

Although the day's scenes are far less dangerous than the previous day's, the same attention to details and safety is given. Page watches carefully, although technically no stunts are being done. With an eye to the set, he sums up his feelings as to the differences between *Beyond Thunderdome* and the earlier Max films.

> Funnily enough, this one doesn't have as much car stuff as people would think. In fact, I think some of the traditional *Mad Max* fans might even wonder if this film belongs to the same series. It's broadened out a lot more, and there's more comedy.
>
> Being in the stunt game, one tends to be involved in a lot of very heavy movies. If you're involved permanently in death, destruction, and horror, it starts to get to you after a couple of films. It's really nice to do something with a bit of comedy in it. I must admit I've come out of the end of this, after many months, with a much lighter spirit than after *Mad Max* or *The Road Warrior*. I hope it will have the same effect on audiences.

Interview with George Miller

Q: How was making the first *Mad Max*?

GEORGE MILLER: To tell you the truth, it was a demoralizing experience. Two days after the shooting started, an automobile accident injured both the original lead actress and the stunt coordinator [Grant Page, who coordinated the stunts for all three films]. The accident completely shot my nerve. I felt that the film had failed creatively, and that it controlled me, instead of my having controlled it.

One of the things that bewildered me when I first started making films, other than the problems of realizing some kind of film, was the sort of will-o'-the-wisp nature of making a film. No matter how strongly you visualize something, there's always something else conspiring to get in the way of the shot that you wanted.

When I made *Mad Max I,* I was totally bewildered by this process. I had no control of what I wanted to happen and what was finally there on the screen. I thought at the time that it was only my problem. Therefore, I thought I wasn't suited to continue in film. And, of course, it's everybody's problem! No matter who the director is, the problems are the same every day on the set.

Q: What, in your opinion, made *Mad Max* into such a world-wide success?

GM: We realized that, inadvertently, we had fitted the film into a very classical, mythological hero genre. We were just retelling a basic story, only instead of there being a sword fight, we had a car chase! It seems that this has nothing to do with the individual. It's a collective thing. In fact, it's something that I never believed in until I saw it in operation in film.

Part of the usefulness of this mythological approach is ... its ability to take us down into a dark wasteland to confront the dark side of our soul and to, hopefully, be able to come out on the other side.

Q: What is it about the character of Max that is so special?

GM: Frankly, I don't know. That's a very hard question. I think, as a filmmaker and storyteller, that Max allows you—or the films allow you—to go almost anywhere. But they're not fantasy films as such. Everything, by and large, is based in reality. Except it's set in some future which allows you to play around with it quite a bit. It's much easier to get into those kind of stories, because you're not restricted by so much.

Q: *Mad Max II—The Road Warrior* contains a better visualization of the future world in which the characters exist.

GM: We started off with a basic story, even though in the film we were not really speculating about what the future would be like. If I had to do a documentary on what I thought the future would look like, I don't think that it would be the *Mad Max* films. But that look enabled us to have that sort of hyperbole, that stylized, simple story which had to be set in such a world.

Every element in *Mad Max II—The Road Warrior* was worked out from the present, and from the premise that, suddenly, there would be no energy, no electricity. So people would rush down to their supermarkets and take whatever was left in the refrigerators. They would find other people already there. There would be fights … We would have no gas for our vehicles. Very quickly, things would reach a Darwinian stage where people would have to survive as best as they could. Some would, undoubtedly, choose a brutal lifestyle, consuming whatever was left, since no more goods would be manufactured. There would be pockets of people who would maybe try to make a new beginning …

Q: Having children like the Feral Child for instance?

GM: Yes. People certainly would not be having many children at this stage, because a pregnant woman is less likely to survive. Even sex, in a tough world, is something that would be mostly recreational. Some people probably wouldn't even want it since they would be too worried about surviving on a day-to-day basis. There would, however, probably be some children that somehow would manage to survive. Children with a special something that keeps them going. These children would be brought up like wild animals, because no one would have the time, energy, or desire to care for them.

Q: What made you settle for the punk and leather look of the villains, Humungus in particular?

GM: We didn't start off by deciding to have a little bit of punk, and a little bit of S&M leather gear. It was more in the nature of seeing the character as if he, himself, had decided to become a warrior type. He would, therefore, need a bike for mobility, and also because it uses less fuel than a car. He would need to be pro-tected, so he would need some sort of weaponry. If he can get a gun, he can't find bullets, so he would fashion a kind of crossbow which he'd wear on his arm. That way, it's also easier to fire when he's riding a bike. He would need to look fearsome, because that way he wouldn't need to fight people. He would just scare them off. So he dresses up in the plumage to have a warrior look about him.

Q: What is your response to those who criticized the film for reasons of excessive violence?

GM: That's a very tough subject. I really think it's one of those things like love and death. It's such a comprehensive problem that you just can't deal with it by words or intellectual thoughts. If handled correctly, screen violence can be a way of dealing with aggression and other primitive emotions. It's one way of con-fronting those things which we normally would not confront in our day-to-day lives. At some stage in their lives, everyone must deal with the notion of death. If you like, the sooner it's done, the more mature you are. Some people never face it, and they have great problems...

I don't think that you'll find very many "ketchup" shots in *Mad Max II—The Road Warrior* or see anything in great detail. It's kept mostly out of frame and therefore becomes much more powerful. You get the ambiance of violence, the feeling that you're in a dark world, and it makes you want to sit on the edge of your seat a bit more.

Q: What are the differences in making films in the United States and in Australia?

GM: I was totally free on *Twilight Zone*. In many respects I was even freer than here. Because you could call on virtually anything. If you wanted a steadycam, we had Garrett Brown operating it [Garrett Brown is the man who invented the stea-dycam]. Though I could see that, if a film got into real difficulty, and you got into real political problems in the studio system, it could become a real nightmare. Then, most of your energy goes on anything but making the film.

Q : Don't you think that on *Twilight Zone,* part of that sense of freedom derived from the fact that Spielberg had a fair amount of control, since Warner Bros. really wanted him to make a film for them?

GM: Yeah. As I said, I don't think that that was necessarily typical, although it might have been. I really don't know. What it did do was surprise me with just how excellent filmmaking was in the States. I was very wary about working inside the studio. I thought all the technicians would be jaded. I thought they'd be people who just didn't care much about their work, and I found that it was quite the opposite. I found great enthusiasm and great expertise. But then, I find a good crew is a good crew anywhere, and a bad crew is a bad crew anywhere too.

Q: There seems to be an exodus of Australian directors. Once a director makes a film in Australia and that film does well, he goes over to work in the U.S. Yet you've come back. Why?

GM: Basically because in Australia you can be a little more experimental with the way you work. With a lot of my movies, I found I was learning more here than I did in the States. We'd done a television series called "The Dismissal," which was a highly collaborative workshop piece. What was interesting is that it was probably one of the most intense learning experiences that I had in filmmaking. I found that, if I could do something like that here, I could learn a lot faster. And if I sort of went in and worked on a studio picture ... Well, you know what I mean?

Q: George Ogilvie said that, when you met with him the first time, you were interested in finding out how to work with actors, how to get the best out of them, and that led into you having a very collaborative effort over the last couple of years ...

GM: Oh, very, very much. George has taught me an enormous amount. He's just a wonderful teacher. He's got that extraordinary thing of all great teachers. He's like a baby. He's open completely, so he's a great learner and a great teacher. You have to be both.

I think there's great mystery in most of filmmaking. The writing, the directing of actors ... I think acting is a great mystery, ultimately. By that, I mean it's finally, entirely intuitive. Not only intuitive because it's learned by doing a lot of preparation, but finally the performance is intuitive and open. It comes from somewhere else than the mind. I feel that I've learned much more about acting by working on this film than I ever would have before. I feel that, when I first started, I had not a clue about what an actor was. Now I think that I have some understanding.

Q: Mel Gibson said that you didn't think that you were a very good actor's director, but that you were wrong.

GM: Once I didn't feel comfortable with actors. Now I think I'd rather spend time with them than I would with anyone else—almost.

Q: How did it work, I mean, you and George Ogilvie directing together?

GM: Earlier on in the picture ... Now, we're doing more action scenes, so we've split up. But earlier on, until two thirds into the picture, we were on the set together most of the time. He would take one group of actors, and I would take another. When we fell behind a little bit, because I'm more experienced with this kind of picture, I'd take over camera a lot more.

But on the most important part of the film, the preparation was basically done by both of us, with George taking charge of the acting workshop for the children in the story—52 of them! He spent a long, long time with them, three or four months.

We worked with five directors on our television show, and it worked extremely well. One of them was George.

Q: Do you enjoy this collaborative process?

GM: Yeah, very much. It's one of the things I liked very much in *Twilight Zone*. If you really look at it, directors never really get the chance to work with other directors. They're the only ones who don't! Cinematographers work their way up with other cinematographers. But it's very rare when you see a director working with another director, or even observe another director.

Q: You seem very open to other people's input on the set. Have you always been that way?

GM: Yeah, because you can't do otherwise. You're all on the same train, on the same journey, so you'd be crazy to ignore any suggestions. Sometimes, you're desperate for them. When you have very good people working with you, it's a wonderful process, because so much good energy comes out.

Q: It seems to me that it is much more liberating to work with someone you know will listen to you.

GM: Definitely. I don't believe anybody can make a film and not be of a collaborative nature. A writer can write alone, without collaborating. But if anything is collaborative by nature, surely filmmaking is. It takes on its own life, like an organism.

What's interesting is that, the more you're collaborative with other people, the freer you are. Because of this, it's never been a problem to say, "No, that idea's no good." It's always accepted.

One thing I've noticed in the workshops we've done, and especially the acting workshop, is that I don't believe you can get a great performance unless it results from an ensemble. It is something that the group creates. Occasionally, you might have an individual performance that stands out. But I don't think you have a true piece of work until everybody's work is elevated by everybody else's.

Q: After *Mad Max II—The Road Warrior,* you told me you'd only do a *Mad Max III—Beyond Thunderdome* if you came up with a good story. But at the time you didn't really think you would. On the other hand, Terry Hayes has told me that he thinks Max has become a part of you, that you can't resist. What do you think?

GM: Yeah. It's sort of that way. I guess I'd have to give the same answer about a "Mad Max IV" now.

Q: But I imagine you wouldn't rule out the possibility that it could happen?

GM: No. But I'd still say, probably not.

Q: I know that you've read *The Hero with a Thousand Faces* by Joseph Campbell. *Mad Max II—The Road Warrior* was done to specifically fit into that mythology. But it seems that, in *Mad Max III—Beyond Thunderdome* Max has really become a messianic figure. The spiritual and metaphysical sides of this film seem much stronger. Are you trying to make even more of a point?

GM: No. That was the journey that was left for him. In the first story Max really descended into the darkness. I mean, he starts off relatively normal and gets real dark. Then, eventually, it gets really bleak. In the second story he kind of starts being very burned out and goes up a tiny little notch at the end of the movie. As Mel says, and I can quote him, "Max is a closet human being and there's a little creak of the closet door in *Mad Max II—The Road Warrior*." In *Mad Max III—Beyond Thunderdome* I think the door is opened pretty well. Max finally comes out of the closet as a human being.

Q: Is that why there is more humor in it?

GM: Oh yeah, definitely!

Q: Can't you have any humor if you're in the closet?

GM: No.... Partly, there's more humor because I think you have to be very confident as a filmmaker to have humor in your story. And the humor is in there because I'm getting better at making films. Also, the humor came very easily into the story. It's not something you can really force in.

Q: Have you toyed with the idea of killing Max off?

GM: We certainly did. We thought for a while that this might happen in this picture. But it just didn't play in the story somehow.... In fact, we went from one idea with him dying, to another with him disappearing and no one knew what had happened to him, and then to this ending we have. But he is a character that could die.

q: So you're not against killing off a character in a film?

GM: No, if it makes a good story.

q: We see Max as a hero because, in the end, he sacrifices himself. But he also goes into the functioning society of Bartertown and ends up destroying it. So couldn't you also call him the villain of the piece?

GM: Well, I don't think you should talk about heroes or villains. I mean, a hero is not necessarily the guy who rides around in a white suit. To me the hero is the agent of change, the agent of evolution. He is a man who shatters the world that he belongs to, and out of that shattering comes a new order. That happens to all things. They reach a functional ripeness. Often the people who are responsible for the building of something become tyrannical, or "hold-fast," as Campbell says.

Yesterday's heroes are all tyrants. They built something, then come to love it, come to own it too much. By desperately holding it, they become tyrannical, and then, it's time for someone to emerge to shatter that world again, so that there can be, yet again, something growing out of it.

If you look at the rhythm of the way elements are formed in the stars, the evolution of the stars, the evolution of organisms, the evolution of tribal groups, the evolution of society, the evolution of corporations, the evolution of just about anything, it's always the same rhythm.

So that's really what the hero, in the mythological sense of the word, is. Of course, to a lot of people, Max looks like a villain. But the so-called villain is really the tyrant who was yesterday's hero. The one who did build Bartertown and has come to love it so much that [the inhabitants] want to hold it forever. Whereas it was inevitable that it changes.

The world that the hero shatters is not a world that he shatters deliberately. He was part of that world. He shatters it because—surprisingly to himself—he has compassion. It's the compassion that shatters the world.

Q: Do you have an hypothesis about Max's future?

GM: Now? No.

Q: You don't think about what happens to him after he goes wandering in the desert?

GM: I just think he goes on to do other things.

Q: I noticed you used a video monitor while you were shooting. Dean said it was the first time you used one. Did it help?

GM: Oh yeah! I'm a very montage type of director. There's almost no static camera in this film. I'm particularly good from the point of view of cutting. What I find is—we don't have playback. If you have playback, you're very tempted to play it back and see what happened. So you get lazy. You must concentrate during the shot to make absolutely sure that you get everything as precisely as you can, to know whether or not it felt right. If you rely on the machine, you might get lazy in the observation.

But in terms of setting up the shot, it's much, much easier to look through the monitor and discuss it with the operator simultaneously [as] he's looking through the camera.

Q: I know you and Byron Kennedy were very close. Besides the obvious pain of losing a good friend, how has his death affected this film, and the company as a whole?

GM: Well, obviously, Byron was so extraordinary that it would affect us in all ways—in an extraordinary way. It all would have obviously gone in a different direction. Byron can't be replaced.

Q: Were you ever tempted to just stop?

GM: Yes. It was my first impulse actually, to say, "Well, that's it. I'm not interested anymore." But then, very quickly, it's one of the things I said no to.

I think, maybe, a few years ago, it would have been inevitable. But the thing is that almost the opposite happened. We went and started what was probably our most intense working period. We did twenty hours of very high quality television, and this film, all in eighteen months. So we've been really working very hard.

Q: Are you glad you've continued?

GM: Yes, very, very much. And I think that's part of it. Not to shrivel from life, but to attack it a little bit more, I think.

Q: In what direction would you like to see yourself and your company go?

GM: That's pretty open. Go with the flow. It's a little bit like the filmmaking is becoming now—much more organic. Go with the flow.

Q: Do you think it's important to have some kind of philosophy to hold on to when you're making a film?

GM: Yes, definitely. I think it's ultimately why you make a film. I think it's the impulse that sort of drives you. There are feelings and ideas and a kind of sense of the interconnectedness of all things that really make the filmmaking and the storytelling. I think that's what keeps you active in it.

I've come to realize that filmmakers and storytellers are very honorable [professions]. Not necessarily filmmaking, but storytelling, in whatever format, is a very worthy work.

Q: Do you feel proud of what you've been able to accomplish? It's kind of far away from being [an] M.D.?

GM: Well, there's two types of proud. One is the personal kind of creative satisfaction that you get very rarely. Then there's the proud of what people from the outside looking in must see. Which doesn't mean sort of that much, surprisingly. But there are moments of pride ... I think that the things that give me the most pride are the times which happen so rarely, when you have the sense of mastery over the work, when you suddenly begin to realize that something really did work very well. I'm not talking about the whole film, just little moments in the film.

Q: Do you have any regrets about *Mad Max III—Beyond Thunderdome* so far?

GM: Not a lot. I think you do on everything. I mean, silly things. One day, we were filming, and there was an absolutely stunning, really stunning sky that we wanted. And we didn't have our cameras with the right ingredients to get it. It would have been wonderful to have.

And then, there are other things … One day, there was that incredible dust storm. They hadn't seen anything like that in five years. We just happened to have our helicopter with a camera, and the aircraft which is in the story up at that moment, so they got it. But we didn't know they were getting the shot! They were going for something else entirely. I thought they had lost it, but there was a young camera assistant up there and, God bless him, he got it!

Q: What do you like best about filmmaking?

GM: I like the writing. I'm coming to really like the writing! I like the preparation and the editing. The shooting, I don't think I could describe as likable. It has its moments of joy. The problem with shooting is that it's such a continuous pressure of time.

Interview with Terry Hayes, Producer-Writer for Mad Max III

Even when he is being pulled in 50 different directions, with chaos reigning over the Bartertown set of *Mad Max III—Beyond Thunderdome,* Terry Hayes always appears to be smiling.

Tall, lean and blond, Hayes looks like the stereotypical Californian—or Australian. Actually, he was born in England but, along with his parents, emigrated to the land down under when he was a child. The operation was, as they say, a success, and Hayes now says "goo'day, mate!" with all the élan of a native.

The Australian film industry is, in many ways, more relaxed than its American counterpart. Nothing points this out more clearly than Hayes's own involvement in filmmaking. A onetime journalist, he met with director George Miller to discuss the novelization of *Mad Max I.* The two men hit it off, and Miller invited the writer to work with him on screenplays. The two have worked together ever since.

When one gets to listen to Hayes tell the story of *Mad Max III—Beyond Thunderdome,* it is easy to understand why Miller was so taken with him. Hayes is a born storyteller, whether on film, on paper, or in person. As he sat at a table at Bartertown's Hard Rock Cafe, he shared his excitement by acting the parts and miming the characters....

Q: How long have you been with Kennedy/Miller?

TERRY HAYES: From just before the first film was released. I did the novelization of *Mad Max I,* and that was how I met George. The publisher asked me if I wanted to write it. So I met George and we sort of liked each other. He seemed to like some things about the novelization, so he asked me if I wanted to write screenplays with him. I said, "Yeah, all right," and we started doing things together.

I was a radio producer at the time. I used to be a journalist. So I'd work from five o'clock in the morning until two o'clock in the afternoon at the radio station. Then from like three to about ten at night writing scripts with George. I don't think the scripts were that good, but we seemed to be learning a lot, so I gave up my other work eventually and just became a full-time script writer.

We did quite a number of things. There was one thing in particular which we wrote and are relatively happy with, but which we haven't made as a film yet. Then the next project was *Mad Max II—The Road Warrior.* There was a lot of work that went on before that, but that was the first produced film that I did with George.

Q: When you were working on *Mad Max II—The Road Warrior,* had you read *The Hero with a Thousand Faces* as well?

TH: Yes, but that predated *Mad Max II—The Road Warrior* by a long time. I think it's fair to say that I introduced George to all of that stuff. All that mythology is pretty interesting. It's basically just storytelling. So I thought, "If you're going to be a screenwriter, you better learn as much as you can about storytelling." All the myths are stories that have survived the longest. So it seemed to me to warrant at least some exploration.

Q: By *Mad Max II—The Road Warrior* had you formulated that there had been a nuclear war?

TH: Yeah, I think so. There's no mention of anything like that in *Mad Max I*. There was basically just that title that rolls up at the bottom: "A Few Years in the Future," or whatever it says. I don't think there was any thinking at that stage that there had been any sort of nuclear disaster. I think that George's theory was that it was a progression of the world of today into some form of anarchy.

But, interestingly enough, when we came to do *Mad Max II—The Road Warrior, Mad Max I* wasn't out of sympathy with there having been a nuclear disaster. Working backward, you could quite easily assume that there had been a limited exchange of nuclear weaponry in the northern hemisphere. What had happened in a place like Australia was that there had been a breakdown of social order. People started to grab everything and just became crazy, because of what they knew was coming. So we were fortunate in that regard. But number two was a much different film, much more into fantasy.

Q: I know that after *Mad Max II—The Road Warrior* there was a feeling that there would be no *Mad Max III—Beyond Thunderdome*. Obviously, at some point you felt that you had a story to tell. How did that come about?

TH: Well, there was never going to be a *Mad Max III—Beyond Thunderdome*, ever. Then George and I met again in Los Angeles. We'd both been traveling around different parts of the world, partly vacation and partly work. We were just having dinner, not talking about Mad Max at all, but when you've sort of worked on these films, they become part of you. It's hard to stop thinking about them. I think part of recreation between George and I is to sort of prattle on about Mad Max. It's like a member of the family that you talk about. And, in the middle of dinner, I said to George, "You know, if there was going to be a third film, Max ought to find a tribe of lost kids and take them to the city."

George said,

> Gee, that's an interesting idea! And then we could have this…. They could have got there by plane, so we could have this wrecked plane…and then, you know, we need somewhere where people are chasing them, so what about some sort of really bizarre frontier town.

It just started to arrive from there. By the end of dinner, it wasn't a story, but we thought we were on to something. I think that was when the decision was made that it could be a film.

Q: How long ago was that?

TH: That would be eighteen, twenty months ago, toward the middle of 1983.

Q: How long did it take you to finalize what it was that you wanted to do?

TH: Eighteen months [*laughter*]! It's been a long, old haul.

Q: I noticed that when George directs, each scene gets played through several ways before a final version is decided on. Do you work on the script that way too?

TH: Yeah. It's an organic thing. You know the conventional way of filmmaking. Someone sits down and writes it. Then it becomes a script. A director gets it and changes it and turns it into something that he feels happy with. Then the writer and the director have a terrible argument and swear that they'll never talk to each other again. The producer steps in and takes sides with somebody, and then quickly finds out that the director is a lunatic and wants to spend twice as much money as they can afford. Everyone ends up hating each other and it's a total adversary relationship!

Well, it's important to remember that the script is just a tool in the making of a film. It's somebody's best guess as to what will constitute a good film, what will be dramatic, what will work as scenes. Now, in the actual process of filmmaking, lots of things change, which will either enhance or detract from the film. So you turn up on the set every day and you find out that one of your major actors is not well that day, or is having difficulty with certain lines, or special effects can't get certain things going that you thought they would have going, so you adjust.

There's always that, which happens on every film. I think that's the great thing about the way we work. The film I eventually see is one in which I've been involved in the decisionmaking process all along. I know why things have been changed. I'm not in that unhappy position that a lot of writers find themselves in, whereby they write a script, they imagine what the film's going to look like, they go to see it, and it doesn't relate to what they wrote. Because they weren't there every day, seeing why decisions were being made. So, obviously, we change and adjust for all of those extraneous things that happen. Every film does that, but also I think we change it just for the way the story is going.

For example, in our script this guy Pig Killer was going to die during the chase. He was definitely going to die. It wasn't until we started to see the performance—he was so good—that we thought, "We can't kill him. The audience would never forgive us." Films are an organic thing. They grow and change and they take on a life of their own. You start out making a film thinking that you're in total control. Halfway through, you realize that all you're doing is you're on the back of this monster, and the only thing to do is to ride it, stay on board.

I think George would agree with me. The script is probably the most important element in filmmaking, but you've also got to be ready, prepared, and willing to listen to other people and to change and adjust. Not to lose the storyline or drama, or anything like that, but to improve it. People are always coming up with great ideas, better ideas of how to do things. So I think we've tried to stay very much away from this compartmentalized view of filmmaking, which is: "He's the director, he's the writer, he's the stunt coordinator," etc., and tried to make it more of a community effort. We listen to anybody who's got script ideas, because often they're very, very good.

Q: What about your two hats? Do you ever feel torn between being a producer and writer? You see something as a writer, but as a producer, you know it's going to cost a fortune?

TH: No, because whether or not you have the title of producer, it really doesn't matter. Any damn fool can write that Ben-Hur wins the chariot race. Always when you're writing you've got to give a mind to what is achievable. I think part of the discipline and part of the fun and part of any talent that you might have, is how to achieve things cleverly, without spending millions of dollars on special effects and all that if you don't need them.

That's one of the good things, probably one of the only good things about filmmaking in Australia. In Hollywood we have a system that's evolved over a long period of time, and people tend to work in various compartments. They see themselves having a certain function in the filmmaking process. They have to defend their area of expertise against all comers. So you instantly have adversary relationships. In Australia, because it's a very young and basically cottage industry, you tend to get experienced in a vast number of fields, because everybody pitches in and does all sorts of things. I don't really see myself as a writer, although that is a certain sort of way that I got into it, or a producer or anything. I don't think George sees himself as a director or a writer or a producer. We're filmmakers, and that means that you need a whole battery of talents or knowledge about things. Whether it's wrangling kids, picking up kids and carrying them, or talking in detail about scheduling, or trying to save money, or trying to work out.... Basically, there's one way you really save money on films, and that's cutting the script. It really comes from the script. And, I guess, I know where you can cut and when it really starts to hurt, where you might start to lose the patient because you're cutting so seriously. It's filmmaking, it's not writing or directing or anything like that.

Q: Do you think there's more freedom in Australia than in the hierarchized American system?

TH: There's pros and cons to everything. We have unions in Australia, too, that are difficult to deal with at times. The studio system, obviously, has great advantages. You get an enormous amount of support. I mean, I often said to George, the only difference between us and Warner Bros. is 4,000 people! There are great advantages in it, especially for some sort of films. There are just films that you couldn't make in Australia. Big, special effects pictures would be impossible to make here. There's just not the expertise in the country to do it.

George found this when he was doing *The Twilight Zone.* You get an enormous amount of support from that studio system. I'm not talking about psychological support, I mean support staff. Things are available. There's a great professionalism because it's an industry that evolved over many, many years and that has attracted the best in the world, there's no doubt of that.

The disadvantages are, I suppose, that you don't tend to have such a broad experience in filmmaking, and that you probably don't have as many people looking over your shoulder in Australia. That's a trade-off. But I'm not opposed to making things in the studio system. It's horses for courses. There are films that can only be made that way, and are very, very fine films. The world is probably better for having them made. And there are other films that can be made independently. It's assessing what your film is, and what will serve it best.

Q: You certainly have more opportunity to come in here than in the States?

TH: Sure, it's easier to meet people too. In a country of fourteen and a half million people, if you have a shared interest, sooner or later you meet. Whereas, of course, in America, it's different.

I suppose the thing that's the worst in the Hollywood studio system is the whole use of agents. I don't have an agent. George doesn't have an agent, or anything like that. Here, you can cut out a lot of that. It's more relaxed. You want to "take a meeting" with someone, you just call them up on the phone and say, "Hey, do you want to have dinner?" Or you see them around.

Q: I know you don't want to get into the horse race of discussing budget, but this is a pretty high budget picture for Australia, isn't it?

TH: Yeah, it would be considered that, for an Australian film. Everything's relative. You can see that by looking around. I suppose that the best thing is most of it is up on the screen. But as I've said before, there's no correlation between budget and quality. Never in the whole history of filmmaking has that been the case.

Q: With the kind of location work that you've had to do, has it been difficult to keep it within your budgetary limits?

TH: Yeah. It's always a battle. I mean, you're always out there on the edge. You're always working toward the very limit.

It's a certain thing about filmmaking. You'll see this in directors especially, it's pretty obsessive behavior. Wanting the best all the time. Always pushing. Not settling for eight cars instead of twenty. Traveling to far locations is expensive. Accommodation is expensive. But then, you can't do a desert chase in the middle of Sydney. So, you don't have much choice.

Q: How many people did you actually have up in Coober Pedy?

TH: One hundred thirty. Cast and crew, including stunties. Not many cast. Mostly stunt drivers.

Q: When you chose that location, had you realized how difficult it was going to be?

TH: Oh yeah. There was really no choice in the location. There's not many places, even in Australia, where you have desert, flat landscape without much desert scrub, a train line through it, which we could use. There are places which have train lines, but you can't use them. And no power lines or signs of habitation. So it really came down to being one place, and that was Coober Pedy.

There were other places, actually, but they had no towns around them at all. I mean, you would be camping out in the desert. That just seemed impossible. And Coober Pedy did have some hotels, because they have a lot of tourists through it. So it could support us.

Q: That was the most difficult part of the shoot, I imagine?

TH: Black Heath, up in the mountains, was pretty awful. It was so bitterly cold, and fifty-two children dressed in next to nothing that had to be kept warm. That was very, very tough. That was two weeks. It was the beginning of the shoot, you see, so everybody had a fair amount of energy. The thing with Coober Pedy was that it was a long way into the shoot and we were all worn out.

Q: It seems that the film can be taken on many levels. Either as a pure action/adventure piece, but also the messianic thing is much stronger. Was that a conscious decision?

TH: Yeah. When I first spoke to Mel, I said, "Look, don't take this the wrong way, but I'll tell you what the story is." He said, "What's that?" I said, "Listen, mate, it's Jesus in black leather." I don't know whether messianic is the right word. ... I mean, hero stories all have that messianic quality to them. The messianic quality to it was not the aim. It just so happens that messianic stories are hero stories, and this is a hero story, so obviously they have a common background and geneology. The really interesting thing is, that lurking within us all, there's a hero. I'm not talking about doing brave acts. There's plenty of courageous people. I'm talking about people who go on a real journey. Of course, with the character Max in this film, I don't think you can get much more of a journey from a guy that goes from being a mercenary—he's going to kill a man for material goods—to a man who's willing to lay down his life. Not for himself, but so that some children on board a plane can fulfill their great desire and go to freedom. It's a real journey. A real journey in change and growth for him as a man.

I think that's what the hero stories indicate to us. That we all have the potential to grow, to evolve into something else, to find the good in ourselves. I'm not sure it's whether or not you believe in religion, or God, or any of those things. I suppose, to a large extent, that's the currency of the story of, say, Jesus, who is an ordinary guy who's a carpenter, who maybe isn't the son of God, but lays down his life for something. Now that's a real journey for a character. An ordinary man who does something extraordinary. And, of course, that's the journey of Max. He's an ordinary man, wandering in the wasteland. He does something absolutely extraordinary.

I think the wonderful thing, and why I have an interest in telling those sort of stories, is that, within all of us, there's the potential to be extraordinary. We do have that potential to do it. And I think that [is] why the hero stories have such a currency and just survive on and on, and are told and retold in different guises. That's why audiences go along and listen or watch them, because it touches that note in them, of what you can be.

This story wouldn't be a hero story, if Max didn't start off as an ordinary man. It would just be a story of some extraordinary guy. That's the problem I have with, say, the Conan stories. You take one look at Schwarzenegger, and he looks anything but ordinary. So, from the first frame to the last, he's extraordinary. Those films obviously have an audience. All I'm saying is that that's not my interest to tell.

Q: Max's appearance, when he first arrives at Bartertown, with the long hair and robes, looks like what we imagine Jesus to have looked like. Although Max isn't pure...

TH: No, he's definitely not pure. But then, there's three moments when he shows that he's different from other men. And it's not overt. It's only under great conflict that he exhibits what he is as a man. I suppose that the function of all drama is to reveal people.

The first moment that he reveals what he is as a man is in *Thunderdome*. When it's such a clear-cut choice between worldly goods and something which he believes is immoral. And, boy, oh boy, in this world, there's not much which is immoral. But, he can't do it. And I think—I've often said this to Mel—I think he's really annoyed with himself, that there is still this glimmer of humanity within him, this glimmer of compassion. So that's the first compassionate act.

The second one, and I think he's really angry about it too, is when he sets off after the kids, out of the desert. For the third one, he's no longer angry. He lets go of all worldly things and just does something which is not for himself. And that's why I like the back part of the film. Even if he survives, he knows that he's lost. He knows that the best possible result is that he'll be left in the wasteland. It's very hard for Max's character, because he's really come to love those children. I think he really wants to go with them.

So it's a real journey for him, and it's a real journey for the audience. We go through this story totally from Max's point of view. Hopefully, we take the audience on that journey. The audience will judge it in the end.

Q: You leave it with some hope...

TH: Absolutely, yeah. I don't think George or I wanted to do something which would have an ending that would be so happy that it would be unbelievable. On the other hand, we didn't want it to be too bleak.

Q: At least you didn't kill him ...

TH: No, it was originally intended to. And, as I say, you get halfway through writing the story and you're not its master anymore, you're its servant. We just couldn't kill him. I honestly didn't know how to do it to get the story to work. So he survives.

Q: Do you think there will be a "Mad Max IV"?

TH: Everybody asks. If the story was good enough, yeah. If we could come up with a story that was worth it. You know, it's two years of your life to make a film. From the day you start to put words down to the day you see the answer print can take two years. Well, you know, I'm thirty-three now and two years is not something to be squandered lightly. When I was eighteen, I wouldn't have cared much but now ... *[Laughter]* So it would have to be a story really worth telling. If we could come up with it, sure. If we can't, well I'm not going to have any regrets. But we definitely wouldn't remake this film.

Q: When you look at the three films, each one stands out very much on its own. The only thing that holds them together is the character of Max. Do you think that Max in this film is the same Max as in film two, or are they just tales about the legendary figure of Mad Max?

TH: Yeah, they're chapters in a man's story. Except that there is one other core through it. In the first one it's the story of a man who's just an ordinary guy driven into the closet by what happens to him. In *Mad Max II—The Road Warrior* he spends the whole of the film as a closet human being, but toward the end he opens the door just a fraction and looks out at the world. *Mad Max III—Beyond Thunderdome* is really the story of a man deciding to walk out of the closet and go for something.

Now, it's a difficult film to do, because part of the baggage of the mythological hero is that he's enigmatic. So you're always walking a very fine line between that enigmatic quality and giving him really identifiable qualities. So it's been difficult. But there's been that progression. If there was ever going to be a chapter four, you would have to take into account what has occurred to him in this film. You couldn't all of a sudden revert back to having him as a closet human being, like in number two.

Pauline Kael said a very interesting thing in her review of *Mad Max II—The Road Warrior.* I got a sense when I read her review that she couldn't make up her mind about the film at all. She said that one of the things that worried her about the film was that it was joyless. Which is sort of a funny thing to say, because in one way it wasn't, but I know what she means. I think that what she was getting at was that there was no joy in Max as a character. I think that's right—not because I try to keep Pauline Kael happy—but there is a joy to him in this one. There is a vitality and stuff, and it's right in this film that he has that. I don't believe it would have been right for him to have had it in the last one. It wouldn't have sat right. He's changed a lot. But I can see the progression through.

If there was ever going to be a "Mad Max IV," he would have to have even more vitality than he's got in this one. You just have to take cognizance of what's happened here. He's found an affection about human beings again, and there's no doubt that he's proven himself to be clearly a compassionate man. You couldn't just ignore that.

Q: What about the kids that are left in Crack in the Earth; couldn't his compassion have drawn him back there?

TH: Well, I guess the kids that are left in Crack in the Earth are those of us, most of us in our life, who don't have the courage—it's what Carl Sagan calls the compulsion to ultimacy. The one thing that characterizes human beings, that compulsion to go on into the unknown. That's the same thing that took Columbus to wherever he thought he was going. It's the same thing that sent man into outer space. It characterizes us as a race, and it's wonderful that it does. But people have it in different measure, and I suppose the whole thing with Crack in the Earth—it would have been totally unbelievable if fifty-two of them had decided ... They all wanted to go to the city, and Savannah says this to them at one stage, "What we know now is, it's not going to be a free ride." They were all happy to go when they thought that you walked out and got on the back of a plane and somebody flew you there. When they realized that you had to walk out there, across the desert, and there was a good chance that you were going to die out there, well you know, you saw the level of their faith. It became not that important.

I come from a migrant family. Well, you know, Australia's been very, very good to us. But my parents had the courage to come here. Lots of people didn't. So I guess the reward is commensurate with the effort that's put into it. I suppose that's what happened to the people in Crack in the Earth. I imagine while the others are in the city, they're having a really lovely life. In Crack in the Earth they'll never know any different, and they won't grieve for what they don't know, and they'll just stay there. But Savannah and the rest of them are the ones that will build a future.

Q: Could you tell me about the way you see the allegory of Bartertown versus Crack in the Earth?

TH: When you do the story, you come up with lots of ideas and story points, and you can get lost in it all. You've got to keep stepping back and try to find that precision, find the focus of why you're doing certain sequences or scenes. What the total story is about. And, I suppose, our intuition had led us to so much of the story, that it wasn't till we looked at most of what we had, that we found a really precise focus.

That was the idea that Bartertown is really our world today. A world which is vital, lively, funny, grim in many ways, totally relying on commerce and trade and all those things. People trying to live their lives the best way they can. Very little concern for what might be termed "spiritual values" in Bartertown. Of course, it's a heightened version of that. I think what you look for in films is not a reflection of things, you look for the essence.

Films in many ways are closest akin to poetry, where you always try to get the maximum amount of meaning in the minimum number of words. Well, it's the same in film. You try to find the maximum amount of meaning in the minimum number of images. So, Bartertown is really our world today in a very heightened way, and also done in a really pop culture sort of fashion. Comic booky to a large extent, and fun, I hope.

Crack in the Earth is a place which would appear from the outside to be idyllic when we first get there, and it's sort of mystical in a way. I suppose that you would guess that it has a rich spiritual life and all those things. But its real undercurrent is superstition and fractured knowledge and ignorance. It looks wonderful, like *Swiss Family Robinson,* and all your dreams as a kid of growing up without adults and all of that. And it is spiritual, but it's also got all that superstition and ignorance.

What I think you realize is that no world can flourish like that. Crack in the Earth could never flourish, it's too fractured. It has no knowledge. It can't make the connections between things. Everything's got all mixed up. So, as wonderful as it might be, it's in its own way as barren as Bartertown.

There's a wonderful saying, and I don't know who said it— and it wasn't about this film, but it just fits so well—"One world already dead, another unable to be born." Well, the world that's already dead is Bartertown, and there's one that's unable to be born, which is Crack in the Earth. Well, the man that moves between those worlds, the catalyst for the whole of this story, is Max.

What he does of course, is he's exiled from this world of Bartertown to Crack in the Earth, and he takes what is good from Crack in the Earth, what is good and positive, that compulsion to alter, that innocence, whatever those spiritual things are as well, and combines that with the real world. I think that what you get a sense of at the end of the story is it's not the city being resurrected, it's not an old thing being patched together.

It's something new that's going to be born out of the ashes of the old. Because those kids have inherited whatever there is and are different to us. They're much different. They're better suited, probably, to the future than anybody in Bartertown.

So, that was where the focus came from, to decide to really sink Bartertown straight into what this world is today. So [there are] bars and pigs and technology of a sort, and industrial complexes and singles bars and girls on the make and guys fighting, and all of those things. And there's a real fractured knowledge in Crack in the Earth. So that was how we arrived at those things. Let's hope it works.

Q: What does *Mad Max* mean to you?

TH: I don't know, to be quite honest. It's a story. And when you tell stories, there's only one thing that matters—the audience. If you're a storyteller, then, unless you've got an audience, you're a race horse without a jockey, a car without a driver. It's a symbiotic relationship, storytellers and audiences. To me, *Mad Max* is a story, and what worth it has as a story won't be determined by me or any of these people here today. It will be determined by the audience. I'm not talking about box office, I'm talking about their attitudes and what they get from the film. It goes out there all alone as a film. You give it your best shot, but it's totally out of your control.

Q: Kind of like giving birth...

TH: Yeah, there's nothing you can do. All you can do is do the best you can and hope that it hits a note in that collective unconscious. That it's a story that people want to hear. And if it's not, then there's no way out. You're not much of a storyteller.

Interview with George Ogilvie, Codirector of Mad Max III

Q: I was going to ask you about your background?

GEORGE OGILVIE: Theater has been my life. I was an actor for 10 years before I began to direct. I never imagined for a moment

I would do anything but theater. I was perfectly happy. I never really wanted to do film, nor was I a film fan. Theater was my life. I knew theater and I've been doing drama most of my life.

Then, over the last 10 years, I began to do opera and ballet, because I trained at those and was really interested. I went to Paris where I spent a few years studying under Jacques Lecoq. All that seemed to combine with a tremendous interest I have in space and actors in movement. So I began to develop workshops with actors.

Finally, what really interested me more than anything else, and still does, is the preparation I like to go through in order to create and make a performance happen. That's really where my obsession lies.

In some degrees I love the film business because actors prepare in a different way than they do in the theater. I've been studying and trying to observe these ways, looking for something essential, something that would apply to any actor, any medium, anywhere, at any time. That's why I began to develop these workshop methods.

So I began these workshops and people became interested in it and it's through that I came to meet Terry Hayes and Byron Kennedy and George Miller. They were doing a series about political life in Australia, "The Dismissal," and they were interested in trying to get some more competent acting into their films. They were looking for a way of doing it that wasn't just ordinary, in the sense that a rehearsal is ordinary. I mean, you expect a gang just to rehearse the line, and then you expect them to do it.

They wanted something more. So we had lunch, and that's how it all began for me. I was fascinated with the idea of developing some workshops for a group of actors who were to play the parts of politicians. Then they insisted that I begin directing as well. I said, I didn't know the back end of a camera. I didn't know what they were talking about, but they insisted, and it was wonderful.

To have directed a part of "The Dismissal" was a very wonderful and important thing for me because it involved me, as you can imagine, much more so than if I had remained a fairly objective observer. Because I became one of the directors, it was much more.

Since then, for two and a half years, I have literally been working in film, apart from a short break to do *Death of a Salesman* on stage, and an opera. It's been fascinating.

Q: How did you know what to do as a director, the first time?

GO: Well, I didn't! But don't forget, I had four other directors to work with, who were all really experienced in film and television. So it was really the most wonderful kindergarten to be in. I suppose it was just a sort of give and take. We helped each other along the line. It was quite wonderful, and I had the opportunity of watching two episodes being directed before mine came up. So by the time my episode came up, I had a crew that knew me and that buoyed me up to such a degree that it was a wonderful time.

I think I also discovered that one of the reasons that I think I took to films was that I had been fascinated by the frame all my life. A theater frame, certainly, but a frame in space, and how you choreograph within that frame. This virtually applies in the same degree to film or television.

Q: What about the differences of framing for a theater audience, where the picture needs to be broader, larger, and for film, which is a more intimate medium?

GO: Let me put it this way, I've directed theater in every size of theaters. I've directed theater where the actors have had to project enormously because there were 2,000 people watching, and opera is a great example of this, where it's a huge feeling; but I've also directed plays with fifty people watching, and that's truly intimate.

Whereas, when it comes to film, however, there's another difference, and it's fascinating to find it. For me, that difference is that in theater the actor has to express what they feel. In cinema they have only to feel, and the camera picks it up.

Q: Did it take you some time getting used to looking at things through a monitor?

GO: You're right, it did! The only thing that breathes and lives in the film is what's in the frame. That's what you're working for, and there are some great lessons to learn. Ever since "The Dismissal," I've always worked with the same director of photography, Dean Semler, and I couldn't have a better teacher. He's taught me so much.

Q: How do you make actors feel? How do you make them act better?

GO: Things have changed over the years. About eight years ago I had my first experience with meditation and that turned me right around. Later, when I began rehearsing opera, I found a very particular way of centering. I think that the whole preparation for an actor lies in being, not just an attitude, but in being in a physical emptiness, so that the next moment fills you up. In other words, to create a space whereby you can be spontaneous.

I think that if an actor is filled with the role, with instructions, with details, then there's no room for him to be spontaneous. One of the people who put it very succinctly for me was Meryl Streep in an interview I heard. She was talking about *Sophie's Choice* and how she prepared, and she said that she went away and did her homework for months and months. She did a lot of homework and I expect every actor to do a lot of homework, a lot of thinking about the role, away from the set. But when they come on the set, they have to chuck it all away, throw it away, totally forget it.

In other words, they have to have enough courage to know that their homework is there without having to bring it up again on the set or in the theater. That way, you get the feeling of something not prepared, something being totally new all the time. That's the only way.

One of the ways I have found to help an actor become empty is meditation, which helps in allowing everything to go, to create that emptiness and then teach the courage to know that emptiness is a good thing.

Q: Do you find that actors need different forms of preparation for different media?

GO: The idea of emptiness does apply to everybody because of the very nature of the work of an actor. An actor has to have that kind of preparation so they can have tremendous freedom.

On the other hand, the homework is where they differ. Some actors like to do their homework so that every detail is in their head. It's done like a diary. Other actors can't do it that way. They're just feeling in a particular sort of way.

I think it's very important to know your actors long before you have to work with them. That's why I think it's impossible for an actor to arrive suddenly for a big role on that day, meet their director, and do it. That's rare, in fact. You might get a good performance, but you won't get the actor enveloped in the world in which they're supposed to be.

Any actor, if they're good and have good technique, can walk on a set and act. I've seen it many times. I think American television is filled with that sort of performance, very clever, very shallow, very sharp, very sudden, very quick; but I don't believe them. I believe the performance and I don't believe they're who they pretend to be, and I don't believe the world they're living in.

Unfortunately, television is getting to the stage now where they're manufacturing the play even to suit that sort of performance, so that everything becomes shallow and easy to come off.

Mind you, I don't blame the actor for this at all. I've seen several actors in soaps that I thought to myself, they've got talent but they're not allowed to show it, to use it. Everything is formulated for them.

Q: The films you did before *Mad Max III—Beyond Thunderdome* were all small films. How did you feel having to cope with a superproduction?

GO: It was just like doing an opera. I had a chorus of 90 with *Othello*. *Mad Max* had no problems for me in that way. I've done 300 extras before. Again, if you're used to working in a theater holding 2,000 spectators, you're used to size. So all that didn't worry me at all.

The things that did, or at least that were foreign to me, were the stunts and the special effects. Obviously, we have some on the stage as well, but nothing comparable to the size of what they have in films.

Nonetheless, I think that *Mad Max—Beyond Thunderdome* is actor-oriented, performance-oriented, and it was therefore very important for us to get a group of really good actors, and not only that, but also to feed them properly. By this, I mean to try and make sure that they felt that they were contributing, not only as actors, but to a role that was important to the whole film.

Q: How did you help the actors get into the postapocalyptic world of Max?

GO: We had workshops, particularly for the children, every weekend for weeks and weeks before we even began rehearsals. During these workshops, we tried to have the other actors along with the children, and talk and do games and all sorts of things, and find different attitudes.

What is this world? Where's the difference? What's interesting is by the time that we started to film with the children, they were already a group of children who understood not only what they were doing, but they understood each other. They weren't strangers to each other. It made the shooting much easier because you'd just have to signal and they would respond in a particular sort of way.

Q: Did you have trouble getting the children to think, to live the fact of this world?

GO: No. Children fantasize all the time. We found that many of the children we'd chosen were even ahead of us, and that their suggestions actually colored the world that we were trying to establish. It was much more the establishment actors who had problems than the children.

Even for an actor's imagination, to imagine this world was very difficult. I think it's because nobody wants to imagine it. They can only think of such a world with fear. Yet we had a group of characters who didn't fear because that world has been established for generations. So this fear is gone. We're postapocalyptic, not apocalyptic. We're going through it, we've gone through it, we're on the other side, so that we're already looking at an attitude that's well ahead. That had to be stated carefully.

Q: I can see conveying this to a core group of actors, but what about the 300 extras?

GO: It wasn't much of a problem inasmuch as we began with the Thunderdome scene, which is a big fight. Everyone knows what a fight's like and getting the traffic clear was one thing. I did a lot of talking. We left time for a lot of talking to try and show them and just let them know what we wanted. We treated them in that way like actors. They had a world that they had to be in, and they picked it up very quickly.

I had discovered before that, if you treat extras with that sort of respect, they'll give you a lot, because on [the] whole, most of them that's why they're here: to give…. They're not there for a boring night, just earning their whatever it is. They're there wanting to be part of something, and the more you give, the more you'll get back.

Q: How did you work with George Miller?

GO: In truth, I have no idea. We don't like to split up. I admire him and I know he admires me and my theater and what I do with the actors and all the rest of it, so we just supply each other with what we know.

I shot some scenes in the film where we split up occasionally, but we didn't like splitting up. Being together has been very valuable on the set in every way. George sees everything. He's obviously in charge of the set and everything that goes with it, and I work with the actors. But we're together, we talk about the scene.

I wouldn't be working for Kennedy-Miller if that feeling hadn't happened on the first day I met them. Something clicked because they were all seekers. If you're seeking, I think the most important thing in life is to remain pure in doing what you do. That's their feeling too. Then you just come together.

Q: Would you say you're an actor's director first?

GO: Yes, I can easily say that because my first application is always to the actor. Everything else later.

Q: What about the action part of the film. Have you learned from George on that?

GO: Oh, fantastically. It's been the most wonderful schooling you can imagine. I even shot one of the stunts, and I can't believe it, but it was really successful. It really worked, but I only applied the sort of rules that I'd been taught.

Q: What kind of rules?

GO: Well, clarity for one thing. It's got to be absolutely clear, absolutely simple, and the rhythm is more important than anything. What is the peculiar rhythm you have to film to. And all those things are helped technically, of course, with the set, the ambiance....

You could write down whole pages of rules and say stick to those and something might happen. I think also, the *Mad Max* films have their own particular flavors, and that flavor begins to seep in.

We started to use that word seepage in "The Dismissal" quite a lot, and I think that's got something to do with it. Don't just learn the rules and do it. You've got to be able to learn the rules, certainly, and then let a lot of other things seep in. It's a hard thing to do.

Q: What about the experiences that you actually had in Coober Pedy and on the Bartertown set?

GO: With "The Dismissal" and "Body Line," of course, a lot of it was indoors in what they called controlled location. When you come to a place like Coober Pedy, or here, nature controls it. It's hot or it's cold. It's too anything you can imagine!

My goodness, I never realized before that film crews in fact suffered so much. It's amazing and it becomes more and more important how everybody works together, as in a film crew ensemble. They must really enjoy working together because they have to suffer together so much.

To some degree, when you're doing a film like this, something like that physical suffering really works to your advantage, particularly if the film requires it when you're going through it. I realize that there's nothing like the real thing at times to suddenly give you the right feeling.

Our first day at Kurnell, in the sand dunes, we had all the machines and everything to create a sandstorm, but we didn't need it because there was already one—and it was such a bitter cold. The children were crying. It made you think. We had to protect the children. How can we get them to do what they should be doing at the same time.

Q: Do you feel the character of Max was changed and has a little different focus because of your being there?

GO: Not specifically. I always think of the first *Mad Max* as being a film of descent, of descent of a man. There's no ups and downs, it's just descending into a nihilistic state of bitterness.

Mad Max II—The Road Warrior is just an incident within that line of bitterness, but it also shows that just occasionally there was hope for the man. Just momentarily, in the film you knew that there was probably some hope.

Mad Max III—Beyond Thunderdome shows the hope. I think in that way there is definite development. Because I think the filmmakers themselves have developed to such a degree within their film, not just their idea of Max, but I think their idea of life, the philosophy of life they hold. They develop as men do. And because they're seekers, they're seeking some sort of development not only in themselves spiritually, but in the films they make.

Q: Do you think that there being some hope is important to the film?

GO: Oh, absolutely. I think it's absolutely essential because if you didn't, I think you'd be betraying the human race. I really believe that.

Q: Do you think that the *Mad Max* films have a special meaning to Australians?

GO: That's a really difficult question. I don't really know how to answer that except to say that because the film is made by Australians, in Australia, with Australians, and to a great degree within the film itself are people with Australian attitudes, it's bound to be for Australia in a very particular sort of way, even though it's made for the international market.

I think that the more universally one sees oneself as a human being, the more you're going to approach all sorts of things. The next movie I'm going to make is about the marriage of an Aboriginal man and a white woman in Sydney. It's probably the first one to be made here about that theme.

But you see, I don't see that as specifically what it's about, even though it is very much about their life and is written by an Aboriginal. We're going to make a film specifically about that, but because of our own feelings about racism and what it is to the world, we hope that the film itself will do much more than justify itself to the Australian condition, but will speak to any prejudicial condition the world over.

Q: How would you sum up your experience on *Mad Max III—Beyond Thunderdome?*

GO: All I can say is that it has taught me more, which is wonderful. Which means that I can remain a pupil, and there's much more to learn. Every day I seem to learn more, not only about shooting film but how to be with people during those times, and about the respect you acquire for everyone if you're really going to make something worthwhile.

Interview with Mel Gibson

It was refreshingly cool inside the tunnel passageway between the Bartertown set and the rest of the Homebush State Brickworks in Sydney where scenes of *Mad Max III—Beyond Thunderdome* were being shot. Because of the almost unbearable heat that reigned outside, everyone who did not have to be on the set was in the tunnel, unsuccessfully trying to get comfortable by lying down on the rocky floor or sitting on one of the various objects lying around.

Extras, looking like refugees from some war zone, wandered here and there. At one point, one particular scruffy fellow with very long, dirty, greying hair came in and sat down, wiping the sweat from his face. He was wearing only a pair of torn leather pants. Resting there, among the colorful crowd, there was nothing especially striking about him. Few fans indeed would have readily identified this bare-chested man as the star of *Mad Max III—Beyond Thunderdome*, Mel Gibson.

By watching him on the set, one quickly realizes that Gibson gives no impression of feeling self-important or being a star. He waited there for the shot to be set up, as uncomfortably as everyone else. He joked and talked with the crew, exchanging banter about the harshness of the previous five grueling shooting weeks in the Coober Pedy desert. In short, he behaved exactly as one of the guys.

When it was finally time to shoot his scene—Max's arrival in Bartertown—Gibson got up and walked to the set. It was fascinating to see him transform himself from an amiable set companion to the cold and deadly desert wanderer known as Max.

Gone were all the earlier good-naturedness and play, replaced only by steely self-control and a sense of menace. Never had the craft of the actor been so obvious.

Later, at a tea break, Gibson was once more chatting with the crew and various set observers. When teased about almost spilling coffee on his "lived-in" costume, the actor jokingly replied that nothing could possibly make the costume worse at that point!

This conversation, and the ensuing banter that followed, revealed an unsuspected side of Gibson. An almost paradoxical side. The actor is known not to like interviews, and indeed he made his dislike of journalists clear several times during the *Mad Max III—Beyond Thunderdome* shooting. Yet, when finally approached after several days of being together on the set, he graciously gave his consent without a moment's hesitation.

This contrast was highlighted by the actor's physical transformation. The first conversation took place during another 15-minute tea break. Gibson was dressed in full Max regalia: torn robes, long and dirty hair, weapons hanging from the belt, et cetera. Later, after he had finished shooting for the day, Gibson asked to be excused in order to refresh himself before carrying on with the interview. The man who returned was wearing no grey wig, no dirty clothes, and no weapons. Max was gone and had been replaced by a clean, almost shy Gibson, dressed in shirt and jeans.

Gibson shows a fierce concern for his personal privacy, mixed with the normal desire present in each actor to communicate with his public. Before and after the interview, while the tape recorder was off, Gibson chatted comfortably about Shakespeare, local politics, and the Los Angeles traffic. Yet, with the tape recorder running and himself being the focus, Gibson seemed to retreat behind an intangible barrier. This is Mel Gibson. A star who almost would not want to be one...

Q: What do you think [are] the changes in Max in this film, as compared to the way he was in the first two?

MEL GIBSON: Well, for a start, he's older and he's more world-weary. I think he's also a lot more open, open to change.

Q: Do you think he's a better human being?

MG: Yeah. Well, that's a process that happens during the film. It's his journey of character, if you like.

Q: What do you think of the concept that Max is a villain to the people of Bartertown?

MG: But that society, even though it works for these people, still takes a deviation right at the top.

Q: But they could still look at him as a villain…

MG: Sure, they should. He's a killer.…

Q: The success of the *Mad Max* films has contributed to helping Australian films get released elsewhere in the world. Do you think that these films have a particular meaning to Australians?

MG: No. I don't believe that, precisely because of their success. Other Australian films have been successful as well. It may have opened the awareness of the people to the Australian film industry, but that's about all. A film has to be good on its own merits.

People now are a little more likely to take Australian films seriously, not ignore them so much. But then, they've got to back it up with a good product, with a good film.

Q: How do you prepare for your role as Max?

MG: It's your basic sort of any kind of preparation. You read, you discuss, and you just draw on ideas in a pool. A lot of people just sit down and chat it over.

Sometimes it really doesn't come to a finished thought until just before you do it. Sometimes not even then. Sometimes it happens by mistake. But if you have the basics, or the foundations of this particular world that your character is in, when you set up how one in this environment would behave and react, well then, of course, you're halfway there.

Q: Have you hypothesized what happened between *Mad Max II—The Road Warrior* and *Mad Max III—Beyond Thunderdome*?

MG: Yeah, but not in great detail. Just the way the world finally ran out of juice. And Max went out and caught some camels and survived any way he could. Shot little animals. Came across people, and they traded a few things. There's not much civilization out there. It's just basically a nomadic existence.

Q: Do you think he's done things he's ashamed of, or doesn't he feel shame anymore?

MG: No. It's purely survival now. One thing about the character, even though he's a killer, he does have a code of ethics. But you see, that code of ethics allows him ... That code is one that—how will I put it?—is adjusted for that environment where killing can be justified.

Q: Angry Anderson said that he felt that Max and Iron Bar are really very close together morally, except that Max wouldn't do something like killing Blaster, while Iron Bar would ...

MG: No. Max would kill Blaster, except that something makes him stop. He himself doesn't even know what that is. He hates it in himself. It's his weakness, or he thinks it's his weakness. But, in fact, it's probably the only thing that singles him out from the rest of the scum.

Q: Do you think that Max thinks back to his own family when he sees the kids?

MG: Not necessarily. I think his family has become something that's from another era, another world, something that he now finds abhorrent. He just cannot do something like killing Blaster. It's something that would bother his conscience, okay; then he'd feel ashamed. Maybe not.

Q: After *Mad Max II—The Road Warrior,* were you concerned about being too stereotyped if you would do a *Mad Max III—Beyond Thunderdome?*

MG: No. I don't worry about it. I know it's four years apart. I always fill in the time with lots of other roles.

Q: Would you do a Mad Max film no matter what, or would there have to be a script that you liked?

MG: It would definitely have to be something that was going somewhere else. Like, for instance, *Mad Max II—The Road Warrior* was removed from the first one. It was better, it was neater, it was a different kind of story. And I think that *Mad Max III—Beyond Thunderdome* has evolved into something much bigger. It's a much broader tale and it's a lot deeper as well. So it's not like doing the same story again. In fact, it's a very different kind of film.

Q: Although Max is the obvious link to make the films into a series, they're all so different that he could almost be a different character, dealing with different societies.

MG: He is. What each of the films [is] trying to say, I think, is different. Yet I feel you could almost show them in one block and they'd still kind of work as one whole big story.

Q: When you choose films to do, do you have certain roles or types of films that you like better than others?

MG: Well, I have to like it better than a lot of other things in order to do it. I don't have a preconception of what I would or what I wouldn't like to be in. You could mention an idea to me, and I'll think it sounds absolutely shocking. But if I get it, read it, and ponder about it for a while, I might get very excited about it. Or it might work the other way around. I'll look at a script that doesn't really turn me on and it's the idea maybe that sorts of get me going. I don't know. It depends on when you read the thing.

Q: Are there certain genres that you haven't done that you'd like to try? You haven't done a comedy, for instance…

MG: This film is the closest thing to a comedy I've done [*laughter*]!

Q: Do you like it?

MG: What, this? [*More laughter*] Yeah, I like it! I really do think that this is a comedy.

Q: A lot of people are saying that. The other two films were pretty grim.

MG: Ah? I thought the second one was pretty funny myself. But not as funny as this one. The first one wasn't funny at all. It was almost a little relentless. But *Mad Max II—The Road Warrior* approached comic proportions. Just the way the whole thing was over the top and divorced from reality. You would sit there and laugh while people were having their fingers chopped off by Humungus. No, really! I think it was funny.

This one has got the same sorts of things in it, like bad taste jokes almost. I think it's much funnier.

Q: Would you like to do an all-out comedy?

MG: I don't know. I'd like to have a crack at something funny. I don't know if I could pull it off [*laughter*]. That's the hardest thing of all.

Q: Most of your films have an adventure aspect to them. Do you think that, if you did a comedy, you'd have trouble breaking through the public acceptance?

MG: No. I don't think so at all. All you've got to do is make them laugh. You have to have an angle. You have to come from no place, and I don't know how I could possibly do that. So it might be beyond me.

Q: Do you have any favorite book that you'd like to do if the opportunity came up?

MG: I've had a ponder at certain things. There are a few things I'd like to have a crack at, but I'm not sort of willing to jump into it just now. It's a big undertaking and I want to make really sure...

Q: Would you like to branch out and get involved in things other than acting, like directing?

MG: Yeah, but not directing. That takes a lot more organized mind than I have. And to do that, you'd have to learn. I think the key to directing is really learning how to edit. Provided that you have all those other things, you know, about motivation and camera technique. There's a lot involved and you've got to get that all together.

Q: I've noticed that you go over and look at the monitor, while they're setting up the shots. Does that help you pick the nitty-gritty details?

MG: Sure. I understand what it's all about. I've been doing it for a hell of a long time, so I use the camera. But it all helps. I mean, you learn every day. The minute you quit, it gets kind of boring.

Q: So what would you like to do—produce? Write?

MG: None of the above. Not even direct. Only if it happens. If you know what I mean. It's a good notion. But I don't know whether I'd be any damned good at it.

Q: You didn't know if you'd been any damned good at acting either, when you just started out…

MG: Of course not. But that just happened. I didn't push it. I'm not into planning anything.

Q: What do you think of your costume in *Mad Max III—Beyond Thunderdome*? You look a bit like Jesus….

MG: Yeah, I sort of noticed that myself. I didn't realize I was looking that way until I saw a couple of shots. It looks a bit like the 40 days in the desert…. It's not a bad thing. Max also looks a bit like a knight, sometimes later in the film, after his hair gets cut.

I like the look of it. It looks fantastic. I mean, Norma's done a fantastic job with the wardrobe. She always does. She didn't do all three Max films, but she did the last one.

These films have influenced so much music, the look and the style of music. They've influenced a lot of people.

Q: One of the things about *Mad Max III—Beyond Thunderdome* is that you can accept it just on the action aspect, or look into it more for what George and Terry are trying to say.

MG: I think what they're trying to say is very clear. They're marrying the two things very smartly. The message and the action that goes with it. It's not shoving it down your throat.

Q: Did the fact that the film had a message make it more interesting for you to do?

MG: Indeed it did. It means you have to work harder for the point. The other two films tended to be slightly nihilistic [*laughter*]!

Q: Now that you can pick and choose your projects more freely, does the message of a film mean more to you than it did in the past?

MG: No. I've always considered pretty carefully what I've done, except for a couple of occasions. And that was in the beginning. But that's where you learn not to. You've got to burn your fingers a couple of times.

No, I always look at it from the most basic way I can possibly think of it. Emotionally, and just how it hits me.

Q: How did you feel about the dubbing of *Mad Max I* in America?

MG: I thought it was a bit unusual since we were all speaking English. But, apparently, they couldn't understand it.

Q: Do you think that *Mad Max* has had a good effect on your career?

MG: Oh yeah! They've been well liked by a big audience.

Q: How's George Miller as an actor's director?

MG: He's very good. He doesn't think he is, but he is. He's got his own way of dealing with that, which is perfectly fine as long as you can crack his code a little bit. Because I think the dominant force in him is as an artist and a filmmaker, not as an actor's director. He achieves performances through framing. He can do that so he can alter you somehow and it works even better.

Q: And what do you think of George Ogilvie?

MG: George has a characteristic of really being able to talk to actors, and he's learning a lot of film technique off of George Miller. So that they complement each other rather well.

There's no ego involved here, you see, only healthy stuff. Which leaves a great freedom in exchange of ideas, borrowing. Two heads are better than one, if the two heads can handle it.

Q: Have you noticed changes in George Miller as a director over the three films?

MG: Sure! He's always coming out with little surprises and new things. And that's good because I know it's exciting to him that he's progressing.

Q: Is it exciting to you to work with him?

MG: Sure it is. Because he's taken me with him. I mean, he's not selfish with his knowledge at all. It rubs off on you. And really, he's just good to work with.

There's a kind of simplicity about him. But I find in most cases people who are fairly brilliant at what they do have the knack of being able to undo the complexities and just focus on the basics and build up from there. Rather than just sort of clutter a basic thing with a lot of bullshit [*laughter*]! He doesn't do that.

Q: I know that a lot of times things will change between the script and the final shot. Is that sometimes disconcerting to you?

MG: No, not at all. It's exciting. Because it's only in the practical assertion of filmmaking that you can really find out if it's working and how it works. Then you're on your mettle, right? And you can't blindly plow through it and stick to some blueprint. You've got to go with the flow of what's right, or what feels right. George is very good at doing that. He's very adaptable, very willing to sort of throw it away and start again. That's courageous, and that's a true artist. Which he is.

RETURN OF THE
JEDI (1983)

B y the time *Return of the Jedi* rolled around, there was no question that the final episode of the beloved *Star Wars* trilogy would rank as one of the highest grossing films of all time. In essence, director Richard Marquand had a hit on his hands before a single frame of film was shot.

All of the familiar characters returned for the conclusion of the saga—which also launched a new set of television movies, as well as a merchandizing line in the cuddly Ewoks.

Even though the film was a tremendous hit, however, the success belonged not to Marquand but to creator-producer George Lucas, as it had when Irvin Kershner directed *The Empire Strikes Back*. And despite helming a movie that soared to the top of all-time box-office champions, Marquand did not immediately join the ranks of superstar directors. While Kershner was able to parlay his *Star Wars* gig into such mediocre cinema sequels as *Never Say Never Again* and *Robocop 2,* Marquand disappeared into relative obscurity with the drowsy romance *Until September* and the disastrous flop *Hearts of Fire,* starring Bob Dylan, which was finally, and quietly, released on video.

Whether Marquand would ever have achieved another hit that even approached the magnitude of *Return of the Jedi* is something we will never know, for the young director died in 1988.

Interview with Richard Marquand

Richard Marquand loves the *Star Wars* saga. And it is a good thing he does. It would not look too good if the director of *Return of the Jedi* had rather be working on a movie version of "Dukes of Hazzard."

You might say that Marquand, a youngish and affable Englishman, is a movie publicist's dream. Why? Because he can say a lot of good things about a film without giving away any of the surprises or letting anything potentially embarrassing slip out.

And in the case of *Return of the Jedi*, that has been unusually important. The pre-premiere interest in such plot essentials as "Who is the other?" "Is Darth really Luke's father?" and "What happens to the Leia-Solo romance?" has been rather intense. So intense, in fact, that Lucasfilm officials have given actors phony scripts and the like to keep plot twists secret until they absolutely have to be revealed to the cast.

So it is no big surprise that Marquand is tight-lipped when it comes to *Return of the Jedi*. But when it comes to *Star Wars* in general, the man can talk forever.

"When I went to see *Star Wars* I was completely bowled over by the experience, by the mythological story line as well as the incredible creations in the story and the way it was technically made," Marquand said, relaxing in his sparsely decorated digs at Lucasfilm's San Rafael headquarters. "I had never seen anything like it as an emotional human being or as a moviemaker."

In short, he did not ask for his money back.

> I felt an enormous surge of pleasure when I discovered there was going to be another one. It was as though a group of long lost members of my family had phoned to say they were stopping by the house. I don't think it would have been possible to do what I've done on *Jedi* for

two years of my life with the intensity that I have without being a total fan.

He may be a total fan, but he does not relax around the house in *Star Wars* pajamas.

When I say total fan, I don't say I'm the type of person represented by many of your readers who are *total* fans. I don't put myself in that category. I couldn't indulge to that extent. I like the films and stories as they exist on the screen; I don't need to take it further than that.

So how did a director, whose previous credits included a handful of documentaries ("Search for the Nile," "Birth of the Beatles"), a disappointing chiller (*The Legacy*) and the film adaptation of the bestselling Ken Follett thriller *Eye of the Needle*, get the chance to planet hop with Han Solo, Luke Skywalker, Chewbacca, and the others?

"I've almost come to the conclusion that it's better to ask somebody else that question because I always end up extolling myself, which is something I don't like to do."

He was aware that producers George Lucas and Howard Kazanjian had made up a list of potential directors and were talking to various agents. Marquand's agent gave the director a call, asking him to seriously consider the idea of helming the third *Star Wars* adventure.

Marquand did not think he had a chance—not until he heard what Lucas and company were looking for. He explained:

I fit the bill in that it seemed like they were looking for a younger man who has a lot of experience and can work hard and fast and make up his mind and stick to it and run a crew very quickly. I knew then what George was looking for was not the old school movie director who would wait for the weather to get the shot he wanted. He was looking for someone who could improvise, think on his feet.

Though his name was eventually added to the coveted list, Marquand put the whole thing out of his mind until the winter of 1981, when George Lucas gave him a call. Recalled Marquand:

> George was in London doing the music for *Raiders of the Lost Ark* at the time and it was a very convenient moment for him to come see what was then a rough cut of my *Eye of the Needle*. His people called my cutting room and asked if we would screen it for him. I said by all means. At that stage, you don't particularly want to show your movie because it's still in a very embryonic stage. But, I thought, he's a moviemaker and I admire him so let's show it to him. And I was proud of it. I felt I had achieved, for the most part, what I wanted to achieve.

Lucas sat through the whole movie and asked Marquand if they could get together and chat that evening. It may have been short notice, but Marquand accepted the invitation.

> When we met, I felt extremely comfortable. It was one filmmaker talking to another filmmaker. It was very good. We talked about our films and how we dealt with certain problems. It was not in any sense an interview or the kind of thing that happens in Hollywood where you have to put on a tremendous performance to impress somebody.
>
> Then after that came a series of different meetings, during which time I supplied Howard with films of mine and I began to be aware of the names on the list. There were a lot of names. And the list was slowly whittled down until it was just me and an American director. It was at that point I realized I had to get this job and I really cared about it.

He got it. Then the question was, could he actually do it. After all, Marquand had never really been involved in a film which required the special effects knowledge or had the broad scope the movie would have.

> I said to George if I was going to direct this adequately I would need loyalty and support in the areas that were new to me. In a way, being a movie director of a film of this size is rather like being the president of the Ford Motor Company. You don't necessarily have to know how to weld a car door but you have to make damn sure the guy who is doing it for you is someone you know and [who] knows his skills and you know he will do a good job.

Because *Star Wars* is so much George Lucas's baby, so heavily identified with George Lucas by the fans, and so dependent on George Lucas's far-reaching story line, how much creative input could Marquand really have?

Was the relationship between George Lucas and Marquand like the *Poltergeist* case, where producer Steven Spielberg was said to have directed the film himself while credited director Tobe Hooper was just a figurehead?

> If you are the director you are really the man who says what goes. There are always stories in the movie industry about directors getting pushed around by producers. But all producers are people who really don't understand how movies get made. You can only really have one person doing that job. The good thing about George is he knows that.
>
> All you can do is tell the story your way, the best that you can. I must say I like the way George made *Star Wars*; the way he set it up and did it was extremely clever. He made it seem to have a very simple surface but in fact it had a very dense, complex background to it.

I preferred that surface naïveté to the much more sophisticated way Kershner told his story. His style was very much suited to this rather more dark, metallic second section of the saga. I think in this third segment they will see a different kind of glow and flavor to it. But I tried to make it simple because the textures in *Return of the Jedi* are so very, very complex. There's a world of new people and some of them are incredibly difficult to appreciate at first meeting.

Marquand said he made a "considerable" contribution to the story while it was still in the writing stages.

Once George and I selected a writer (Lawrence Kasdan), we then locked ourselves in a room for about two weeks. It was very exciting. Larry, George, Howard, and I literally just gave our ideas. Each of us had a different way of seeing how the story could be structured and slowly it was built up. There was a lot of stuff I wanted to introduce, characters I wanted to bring in, and I think in every way George was absolutely ready to listen, and Larry and I saw eye to eye about a lot of new things we wanted to do.

He contributed to the writing out of necessity. "You could not, as a director of this extremely complicated saga, go away to England and start working unless you had examined the screenplay very closely. If you work on the script, you know the script."

He may know it, but he is not telling what he knows. What Marquand withholds in the way of facts, however, he more than makes up for in unrestrained enthusiasm and in a seemingly endless stream of superlatives to describe *Return of the Jedi*.

This is an extremely unusual film. I don't think there's ever been a movie quite like this before…

It's big in scope, big in dimension, big in the extraordinary multiplicity of the characters....

It's just amazing, a huge, huge, huge movie. I can't think of anything quite like it....

It's like *Star Wars* and *The Empire Strikes Back* rolled into one....

It's not a cartoon serial, for me it's more akin to an agnostic religious experience.

No kidding. He does not seem to think there is a danger of building up the film too much, of making the fans expect a film that is just too huge, too amazing, too big, and too breathtaking an experience to be true.

But maybe he is right. Maybe that is what the fans want to hear. And in the absence of any real facts about the film, maybe they are willing to suspend their disbelief and be immersed in the pure joy of the hype and hoopla.

Has Lucasfilm gone overboard security-wise? The film was shot on location under the title *Blue Harvest* to avoid publicity, high prices, gawkers, and the like. Script pages were given to actors in sealed envelopes just before they were to play their scenes. Phony scripts were passed around.

He smiled awkwardly. He looked as though he might say "I'm sorry, you know too much," pull out a gun from his desk drawer and sigh, "I'm afraid it's time for you to die." He replied, quickly and defensively:

The actors who needed to know knew well in advance of shooting what was going to happen had their scripts. Any actors that we felt were security risks were given other (phony) scripts. There was one particular actor who gave an interview to the English press about the plot of the movie, which upset us a lot. But we knew that actor was a security risk and we had actually not given him the right lines of dialogue. He fell completely into the trap.

And there he was having lunch with the English press one day and the next morning the paper came out and printed all this totally misleading information.

Marquand said Kazanjian called the actor into his office and had a talk with him, explaining to the actor that there were certain secrets which had to be kept in order for the story to remain "fresh."

"We were very disappointed that he did it. He was very apologetic and he said he was a very weak man. When the press phoned him, he found it very hard to turn them down."

There was a silence. Was the man, er, eliminated?

No, security was not that tight. The actor finished his work on the film, unharmed.

Carrie Fisher's performance as Princess Leia in *Return of the Jedi* is something of which Marquand is particularly proud.

She gives a tremendous performance in this and I, as an actor's director, really pride myself on being able to help actors over what are problematic areas. I actually feel that she and I together brought out depths in Princess Leia's character [that] hitherto had not been seen.

She has become very well-rounded metaphorically and physically as a character in this movie. I think at last you will see what a good actress she is. In the past, by necessity, there often wasn't very much room for depth of character. She really has some emotionally deep scenes which she handles wonderfully well.

Marquand calls himself an actor's director because he says

[I am] very interested in directing actors—a lot of directors direct cameras. I think the actors felt very lost on *The Empire Strikes Back*. I think they felt they were almost neglected. The special effects sort of rode through the movie in terms of the actors being left alone.

I was lucky in this film, the major actors who were carrying the story and dialogue were by now very experienced at this nightmarish way of working and they were used to it and [knew] how to deal with it.

Unlike most directors, Marquand films his rehearsals.

The reason I do that is because it makes the crew suddenly realize we are actually shooting film. There's a different quality to the way people act when they know film is going through the gate than if it's just a rehearsal and we're moving the camera around.

He says the performances given during rehearsal are often very different from those he elicits when they get into the now-we're-filming-quiet-on-the-set mode.

Very often you find that the first take has a quality to it, it's sort of an angst, that the adrenaline is really pumping and often you get some wonderful stuff. It's money well invested to get as much on the negative as you can in one day.

With the principal photography in the can, Marquand was hard at work "every day and every night shooting more special effects. We have a colossal space battle in this movie which, for me, is a tremendously stretching experience."

Marquand does not view *Return of the Jedi* simply as a science fiction film.

> A lot of people get completely carried away by the super-
> ficial science fiction aspect of the movie. That's like being
> completely enthralled with the frame around a Picasso.
> Science fiction is not really what it's about. It happens to be
> set in that world because that's where the saga works best.
>
> I don't want to get pompous here, but it *[Jedi]* does set
> up some echoes in your mind and in your heart. It deals
> with life and death of man, which is very important stuff.

Marquand does not see *Return of the Jedi* as just a sequel,
either.

> There are sequels and there are sequels. Is this a sequel?
> What this film does is end the third chapter of a coherent
> story. *Superman III* isn't the coherent end of anything; it's
> just a remake of the same movie. *James Bond* is merely a
> remake of an old movie and you just hope that this time
> they can remanipulate your characters and come up with
> something slightly different.
>
> The actual *Star Wars* saga from chapters one through
> nine is a total symphony, if you like, though it's actually
> just a movie. You know what I mean. I'm not making a
> sequel. I'm doing the third movement of a piece of music.
> The themes are being developed and ended here. That's
> why it's satisfying. I don't know if I could do a sequel.

And what does the end of *Return of the Jedi* mean for fans?
For Marquand, it will mean the end of the hardest job of his
career:

> [It was a] profoundly rich experience that I am very grate-
> ful for. There are some deeply sad moments. Not every-
> thing ends as you necessarily expect it to. There are such
> interesting revelations about them and there are still open

endings for most of them. There are places to go for those who don't die.

Oh no! He did not slice Luke Skywalker into little Space Food Sticks, did he? Come on, he would not melt down R2-D2? Will Han Solo's next adventure be six feet under on some asteroid? Will Chewbacca be the new rug at Darth's summer place?

Marquand will not say.

But he will say filming the ending, which was the first thing they shot, was not easy.

> It was an enormous responsibility getting the ending right. Endings are always a problem. This film has such a complex ending that your problem as a director is to make it clear, make it work, and make it emotionally satisfying. Your job is to enable the audience to overcome some of the sadness of the film. And there are some deeply sad moments.

With *Return of the Jedi* behind him, Marquand will soon be off to Paris, where he will direct a low-budget romance starring Karen Allen. And then? Are there more space epics in his future?

> I would like to do one of the early ones in the *Star Wars* saga. I'm already fascinated with them; the way the society works in those early ones is something that appeals to me very much. It sounds like a very intriguing world.

ROBOCOP (1987)

H alf man, half robot, all *cop*.

 Robocop was one of those ideas that seemed so commercial, so obvious, it was hard to believe no one had bothered to do it before.

But rather than being just a derivative action movie with lots of special effects, *Robocop* managed to mix in a healthy dose of black comedy and dark social commentary. Perhaps most of the credit for that belongs to director Paul Verhoeven, known for such Dutch favorites as *The Fourth Man* and *Soldier of Orange*. Early drafts of *Robocop* were what one would expect from the concept, but under Verhoeven's care the script evolved into a far richer story than perhaps was originally intended.

For a glimpse of the lesser *Robocop* that might have been, one need only look at the sequel, *Robocop 2,* under Irvin Kershner's direction. It was every bit as flat and unimaginative as the original might have been had Verhoeven not been involved.

Audiences were not thrilled with *Robocop 2* either. Still, Orion smelled a moneymaking franchise—à la James Bond or Indiana Jones—on their hands, and ordered a third, albeit cheaper, installment with Fred Dekker *(Monster Squad)* at the helm and a different (that is, less expensive) actor than Peter Weller in the robot suit. Completed in early 1992, *Robocop 3* remained shelved for almost three years. A box-office bomb, it did not harm the sturdy high concept franchise. A *Robocop* television series premiered in 1994.

Interview with Robocop *Screenwriters Edward Neumeier and Michael Miner*

When budding filmmaker Michael Miner went into Universal executive Edward Neumeier's plush office, he hoped Neumeier would give him a job making movies.

It is a typical situation: one replayed about every five minutes in Hollywood. The meetings usually go one of two ways. The executive gives him a job, or he does not.

This time, the executive did neither.

And that is why today Orion is about $60 million richer, Michael Miner is making movies, and just about everybody in America thinks the future of law enforcement is *Robocop*.

So, about that meeting...

Edward Neumeier was a "junior exec who wanted to make vp," who sat in "this lavish office in my Italian suit" and felt constantly "hassled and harried." It was his job to slog through piles of scripts looking for blockbusters and to sit bleary-eyed through scores of student films, hoping to catch the next Spielberg. One of those movies was "a 45-minute art film with no linear structure" by Miner, a UCLA project Neumeier says "I only started to understand last week."

It did not matter whether Neumeier understood the film. He had *seen* it. Miner quickly dashed to Universal—where the Red Sea is parted every 10 minutes on the back lot for gaggles of tourists—to see if he could finagle a miracle, a deal.

"Michael came into my office and said 'Hey, man, I want to make movies,'" says Neumeier. "I liked him right away."

So they schmoozed for a while and met the next day for lunch. While power munching at some Hollywood hot spot, Miner told Neumeier about a robot-themed rock video he was doing, which prompted Neumeier to blurt out an idea he had called *Robocop*. Says Neumeier:

> I had this vision of a far-distant, Blade Runner-type world where there was an all-mechanical cop coming to a sense of real human intelligence. It had been bugging me for years, but when you're an executive, the idea of actually sitting down and focusing on one project is difficult.

It was not hard for Miner to focus. He could see the possibilities of *Robocop* very clearly.

"Michael said 'That's great! Let's do that!,'" says Neumeier. "We both saw the same movie, which is the key to a collaboration. We were of the same mind."

So a partnership between these two relative strangers was forged. "We were never friends before we did this, we just immediately started working together," says Neumeier. "We worked at my house nights and weekends for about two months while we both did other demanding jobs."

Neumeier left Universal and worked as a development executive for several independent producers, including Martin Ransohoff, for whom he found *Big Town*. Miner continued working on rock videos.

In their free time they struggled with their story and each other. "Developing our relationship really took time," says Miner. Because they didn't know each other very well, Neumeier says they were "very polite to each other," and that had to change. Says Miner:

> It took a while to cut through the bullshit. It takes time to get strength to get your ideas rejected and still throw out more ideas. It takes time to learn how to throw out somebody else's ideas in a way that's constructive.

Says Neumeier:

> When you sit down alone with somebody and try to write, the whole game boils down to not so much whether you

agree, but whether or not you are able to share the same ideas. A lot of people you work with won't understand you, they won't see the same thing immediately. Michael and I always do.

They took their first draft, gave it to some friends to read, and skipped out of town for a month. When they came back, they discovered their script had circulated—and that they had an offer from director Jonathan Kaplan and his friend, producer Jon Davison. Relates Neumeier:

> What attracted them was that it was funny. We always intended this to be funny; we were always fighting this battle with people who said "No, this is a robot movie, this can't be funny." The first draft had a certain adolescent silliness about it.

Sure, it may have been silly. But Davison liked it, and so did Orion.

So that is how Michael Miner got that job in moviemaking he was looking for when he strolled into Edward Neumeier's office. And that is how Neumeier went from wading through scripts to writing his own and gladly "fell back into my slovenly ways" of wearing t-shirts and jeans.

They sat down immediately and produced a second draft. "The option from Orion kicked us into high gear," says Miner. "It really gave us a reason to make the second draft a good read, a draft to convince them they really had something."

Kaplan left to pursue other projects, but Davison stuck with it, "encouraging the humor," Neumeier says. "He said the reason I bought this was because it was funny. He said make it funny."

Davison also entertained them. "He would take us down to the screening room," says Neumeier, "and our treat would be to watch his prints of *Road Warrior, Madigan, Dirty Harry* and *On*

Dangerous Ground, because he understood that was the genre we were dealing in."

"So we write the second draft," says Neumeier. "We are really amused with it. Davison is actually pretty happy with it. And Orion gives it a green light. We will now make this picture if you can put together the right package."

Originally, Michael Miner had harbored dreams of directing *Robocop* himself, but he says "when it became a big Orion project I stepped away from that and a little bone was thrown to me of second unit director." He ended up tossing that bone back, choosing instead to write and direct Empire's *Deadly Weapon.* Neumeier, however, succeeded in angling himself in as coproducer, as he relates here:

> When we met, we both had things we wanted to do. I wanted to get a movie and be in on it on every level. Michael wanted to direct. Originally, we tried to combine both of those interests into a single goal. But as the picture got bigger, it got more difficult. The first thing that happened was Orion said, "Why should we hire this guy who has never directed anything before to do this $7 million picture?" which eventually became $13 million. So at Empire, Michael got what he wanted to do: direct.

The chance to direct *Deadly Weapon* probably took the edge off any resentment or jealousy Miner felt toward Neumeir. Says Miner:

> Because we are human beings, there are jealousies. I was probably a little bit jealous of Ed's position as producer because I was locked out of the room sometimes, but ultimately it protected my interests as well as his. Ed may have felt a little jealous of me going off and doing a picture. But the bottom line is I see in Ed a really talented person. I

want him to do all the things that he wants to do creatively, and that cuts through all the bullshit about jealousy.

After searching for six months for the right director for *Robocop*, they finally settled on Paul Verhoeven, the acclaimed filmmaker behind *Fourth Man* and *Flesh and Blood*.

He rejected it. Says Neumeier:

> I heard he saw the title page and said "Ah, one of those," and threw it over his shoulder. So we were dead. The project couldn't find a director. Davison said, "Fuck it, I'll do another movie." In the meantime, Orion convinced Paul to read it again, and Paul reconsidered.

But Verhoeven insisted on some big changes, says Neumeier:

> Paul said, "I want to make this much more like my pictures. It has to be real." So, the humor level was threatened seriously. This became [a] story about a real cop with a real live family and this terrible thing happened to him. We wrote about ninety pages of a third draft and we showed it to Paul and we were both sick and tired and the script was not working. Paul, bless him, read this thing and said, "Well, this is a piece of shit, I was wrong, we go back."

The next hurdle was finding the right actor to play Robocop. It had to be someone accomplished enough to pull off the challenge, but not somebody who would drive the budget into the stratosphere. Says Miner:

> Peter Weller was actually the best we could get. We saw Keith Carradine, James Remar, and Peter. Buckaroo Banzai was a factor because he already had a cult following

in science fiction movies. He is also the most stylized actor
and has a personality that is uniquely suited to be *Robocop.*

They were set. The movie went before the cameras. Michael
Miner went off to direct *Deadly Weapon,* and Neumeier changed
hats from screenwriter to coproducer.

> Being coproducer of *Robocop* was the most traumatic and
> most difficult thing I have ever done. I was like a zombie
> when I came off of production and it was rather nice to see
> Michael, who was vibrantly in [the] middle of a produc-
> tion on *Deadly Weapon.* For me, it showed me there's hope,
> because I was just destroyed.

His mood quickly changed when *Robocop* premiered—and
became the surprise hit. Suddenly, Neumeier and Miner went
from being unknown to everybody's best friend.

"What seems immediate really isn't," says Miner. "But to the
movie industry, in July 1987 we were born in Hollywood."

Of course, Orion was hungry for a *Robocop* sequel. Neumeier
explains:

> We've always had another story in mind, but we were so
> sick of *Robocop.* Luckily for us, Oliver Stone went to [Orion
> president] Mike Medavoy and wanted us to do a politi-
> cal comedy for him. We were able to have a bumper put
> between Robocop movies. I don't think *Robocop II* would
> have been any good if we had [had] to go right into it.

Orion narrowly escaped an X rating from the MPAA on
Robocop by slicing some of the more violent sequences. *Robocop*
squeaked by with an R rating. For *Robocop 2,* Orion has made
no secret of its preference for a PG—a rating that lets kids come

in droves without having to bring their parents, babysitters, and older siblings in tow.

"Yeah, we'll see," says Neumeier. "Sure, that would be wonderful for the studio guys, they'd make more money, but we aren't sure if going for a PG would violate the tone."

They will not talk about the story. Although Verhoeven will not return, star Peter Weller will, with the small proviso that the robot suit be more comfortable. "The big battle for us," Neumeier says, "is not to screw it up." Because, if they do not, there could be a lot of *Robocop* movies in their future.

But for now, the two screenwriters are toiling in a Wilshire Boulevard office—"the spoils of *Robocop*"—on their Oliver Stone script. Says Miner:

> We started spending more time together in September and had forgotten what the struggle was. There's this great quote: "You struggle with your friends and you fight with your enemies." We were getting in some huge arguments at the beginning.
>
> Then I realized Ed is a great guy, Ed is my friend, and the reason why it's not a fight is literally 30 seconds later, one of us says, "OK, what does this character say next?" And you just keep going. It's part of working together. Our friendship survives because of a sense of mutual respect.

Some of their biggest blow-ups came during a trip to Central America to research the Stone script. "I'll tell you what it was," says Neumeier. "Michael had just finished directing a picture. A director, in [the] middle of a picture, has to envision that he has the largest penis around."

Despite the enormous success of *Robocop*, their lives and their partnership have not changed much. Sure, they have a few more bucks, but people think they are swimming in it.

"It hasn't really changed our lives in that way," says Neumeier. "The money isn't that great."

Miner agrees:

> It really isn't. But the workload has increased. People come [up] and say, "Gee, you've got so much more money," and I say "I got more work." The money may come in later. Money is great, I would love to have it, but ultimately I think being able to make a picture that 20 million people see is what it's about.

THE STAR TREK
MOVIES (1980-88)

Quite a bit has been written about "Star Trek," and understandably so. Beyond its artistic and cultural merits, the story behind the survival of the series has all the makings of legend—a classic David and Goliath story. How else can one describe a flop television series that miraculously rose from the dead not only once, but time and time again to conquer every dramatic medium one can imagine?

Perhaps the best way to describe "Star Trek" is *unstoppable.*

The first "Star Trek" pilot was rejected by NBC as too cerebral. That should have been the end. But creator Gene Roddenberry was able to coax NBC into a second pilot by promising a more action-oriented approach—and it sold the series. The series was canceled after its second year. That should have been the end. But fans rallied to its support and NBC relented, ordering a third season.

When the series was canceled again, the end seemed certain. But off-network reruns proved surprisingly popular, and the characters returned in an animated series.

Once a series becomes a cartoon, it is all but over. Who can take it seriously after that? No doubt, this was the end. But the success of *Star Wars* proved that science fiction could sell—so in 1979 Paramount revived "Star Trek," this time as a feature film, the first time a television series had been revived on the big screen. *Star Trek—The Motion Picture* was a lumbering whale of a film, a colossal bore that went millions over budget. Although fans flocked to see it, the film was considered a $50 million bomb.

No one makes a sequel to a big-budget bomb. Surely, *Star Trek* had finally been laid to rest. But what if the film had not cost as much? What if you were to try again, but approach the movie like a television episode instead of an epic? Paramount took the gamble and put veteran television producer Harve Bennett in charge. He went back to the original series for inspiration, and *Star Trek II: The Wrath of Khan* became another milestone—the first time a television episode spawned a theatrical sequel. More importantly, it was a hit, sparking four sequels and becoming the first television series to evolve into a *theatrical* series.

Although 1992's *Star Trek VI* supposedly put the series, in its original form, to rest, we would not bet on it.

Star Trek II: *Interview with Jack Sowards*

Jack B. Sowards killed Mr. Spock with just a few taps on the keys of his homemade computer.

"But there ain't nothin' wrong with Spock that five minutes at my typewriter can't fix," says Sowards with a vaguely devilish grin.

For a man who shuns fame ("I'm the best kept secret in Hollywood"), he should never have written *Star Trek II: The Wrath of Khan*. The hordes of loyal trekkies who have paid nearly $100 million this summer to see the further adventures of the Starship *Enterprise* will no doubt elevate him to sainthood as they have every other person, from William Shatner on down to the studio custodian, ever connected with the show.

When the trekkies got word that Sowards had doomed Mr. Spock to an astral tomb they threatened Paramount Studios with a boycott of the Nicholas Meyer-directed sequel to *Star Trek—The Motion Picture*.

"They said 'You killed Mr. Spock' and I'd say 'That's not the point of the movie. It's something that happens in the movie, and when you see it you'll understand it,'" Sowards says, pulling out a tattered copy of the *Hollywood Reporter*.

"Look at this," he says, pointing to an ad taken out by the trek-kies which reads: "Special thanks … it is a far far better thing you've done than has ever been done before. We salute you and anxiously await *Star Trek III*." He smiles and nods as if to say "case closed."

The pointy-eared Vulcan would no doubt appreciate the dollars and cents logic behind killing off the character. The entire cast was signed for the sequel except Leonard Nimoy, who finally strapped on his tricorder and beamed aboard the project when Sowards offered him the chance to play Spock's death.

Sowards says he became involved with *Star Trek II* when producer Harve "Six Million Dollar Man" Bennett, then just an acquaintance of his, called him up one day "and asked me 'What do you know about *Star Trek*?' I lied and said 'everything.'"

Before Sowards put pen to paper himself Bennett worked up three-quarters of a page worth of approach to the movie: "you know, basically he had Khan's return, the relationship between David and his mother, and a 'problem' somewhere in the universe Kirk would be involved in, that Khan would get involved with, that would eventually bring Kirk and his son together."

William Shatner as Capt. Kirk.

Leonard Nimoy as Mr. Spock.

The artistic failure of the first film weighed heavily on Sowards and Bennett in December 1980 when they began drafting the *Star Trek II* story line, a continuation of the 1967 TV episode "Space Seed." Says Sowards:

> We went and saw it [*Star Trek*] again and again and again. I think they got carried away with the special effects and I don't think they had a good people story. It was a magnificent attempt, but it was wrong, that's all. It was the most obvious story you could have for a *Star Trek* movie. It was mechanical.

The first step in avoiding the same mistakes was to stop thinking of *Star Trek* as a big-budget cinema event and remember its humble beginnings on a 12-inch television screen. "Basically, what we tried to do was a good episode—first," Sowards says, adding that he got a big kick out of critics who panned the movie for being a glorified TV episode. "What do you think the trekkies wanted? They didn't want a bunch of effects, they wanted a good episode. And once you have that, you take it and blow it up into a feature."

He openly admits they worked very hard to "duplicate the technique" of the television series, right down to the "Star Trek" theme and old-style communicators. Oddly enough, the sequel worked so well on a TV level that it may signal the start of a new "Star Trek" TV series. Recalls Sowards:

> It was my understanding that the origins of the movie being made was that one of the networks went to Paramount and said, "Make us another 'Star Trek' pilot." Paramount balked and said it was too expensive. The network said "Why don't you make another movie and we'll use that as a pilot and we'll give you a certain amount of time to distribute the movie so you can recoup your costs." So they were considering, and still are as far as I know, doing a series again with a new cast, headed by Saavik and David. Maybe Scotty and Sulu and Chekov would be in it too.

Sowards says the training mission plot line in *Star Trek II* could boost the chances of a TV or movie series evolving.

The man behind the original TV series, Gene Roddenberry, was billed as executive consultant on the movie, a title which suggests he was given a hefty check and shooed out of an airlock.

That was not the case, Sowards says.

"You can't do *Star Trek* without Gene," he says. "Most of the stuff we developed on paper we sent to Gene and he sent us his notes on it. Let's face it, Gene Roddenberry is the daddy of the whole thing."

Roddenberry turned in six to eight pages of questions and criticisms of Sowards's final script. "Apparently, we violated some law of the universe, the primary rule, or something," Sowards recalls. "I don't remember what it was, but we corrected it."

The supporting cast of *Star Trek* (seen here in *Star Trek II*) shown clockwise: Walter Koenig as Chekov (top left), Nichelle Nichols as Uhura, George Takei as Sulu, and James Doohan as Scotty.

While Sowards stresses his desire to "keep a low profile," he would like more credit for *Star Trek II* than the *New Yorker*'s film critic Pauline Kael gave him.

> She gave complete credit for the script to Nicholas Meyer. She said although Harve Bennett and Jack Sowards have their names on it, I can recognize the work of Nicholas Meyer. Yes, he did add some lines to it that were uniquely Nicholas Meyer, and I think they are marvelous. I'd love to have him hang baubles on my tree any time. A writer

erects a tree somewhere and everybody is going to hang a bauble on it of some kind. You cannot decorate a tree that doesn't exist.

Nearly two decades after his guest starring role in the TV series "Star Trek," Ricardo Montalban again portrayed Khan in the theatrical sequel, *Star Trek II: The Wrath of Khan.*

Apparently, some of Meyer's changes left plot holes and inconsistencies in the story which were not in Sowards's final draft. Many fans have left *Star Trek II* mumbling, "But Chekov wasn't in 'Space Seed.' How did Khan recognize him?" Sowards laughs, explaining "that's one of 25 holes I could give you in *Star Trek II*." His script has Chekov (Walter Koenig) screening a library tape on Khan (Ricardo Montalban) before meeting the megalomaniac space villain. That scene was cut and the dialogue sightly reworked, creating the hole.

Paul Winfield as Capt. Clark Terrell in *Star Trek II: The Wrath of Khan*.

Saavik's crying jag during Spock's funeral is another error. Why did Kirstie Alley fret for the cameras? "Because someone dumb probably told her to," Sowards says, frowning. "It was ridiculous."

However, most of Meyer's changes in script did not rub Sowards the wrong way. "Spontaneous changes on the set make the show breathe; those changes have to be done."

The changes that do bother Sowards were those made before the film began shooting.

In Sowards's final draft, turned in to Harve Bennett on April 9, 1981 (two days before the notorious writers' strike), Khan was depicted as a "mystic" rather than, as Sowards puts it, "Attila the Hun."

DeForest Kelley as Dr. McCoy.

One of the things I had with the mystic approach, which I liked better than the way they did it in the film, was that Khan met Kirk face to face in the Genesis cave. I like that better than them always off in space together making phone calls.

In Sowards's final script Kirk and his landing party beam down to Dr. Carol Marcus's (Bibi Besch) space station, where several survivors of Khan's vicious attack hold Kirk prisoner and try him for murder, blaming the slaughter of their fellow officers on the admiral. David (Michael But-trick) pronounces a death sentence for Kirk, only to be stopped from killing him when Dr. Marcus explains that Kirk is his father.

The script then progresses as it did in the movie, however. Once in the Genesis cave and after the death of Terrell (Paul Winfield), Khan accepts Kirk's challenge to beam down and meet face to face.

Khan materializes in the Genesis cave, where he is greeted by Kirk and David.

Paul Winfield (left), as Capt. Clark Terrell of the USS _Reliant,_ and Walter Koenig, as Comm. Chekov, explore the apparently lifeless surface of the hostile planet Ceti Alpha V in Paramount's _Star Trek II: The Wrath of Khan._

I invested Khan with certain powers. He could make you see things that didn't actually exist. When Khan comes into the room he gestures at David, who rolls up in a ball of pain. Kirk tells David, "It's all in your mind, David. None of this is really happening, fight it." Suddenly, Kirk and Khan appear on a beach. Both of them have these Romulan whips with scorpion things on them. They fight with those to the point where Kirk is almost beaten. Then Khan shifts them to a desert, where, with new weapons, Khan beats the shit out of Kirk again, inflicting terrible punishment.

Then, knowing Kirk's love for ancient weapons, Khan switches the scene to a cavernous stone hall. Lying on a table between them are two foils. Khan motions for Kirk to choose a weapon and the fight begins again.

"While Kirk is saying the whole time 'this isn't really happening,' Khan is cutting him up and asking, 'How are you feeling, Kirk?' Kirk just is not good enough for Khan."

The villain, with fiendish delight, disarms Kirk and runs him through; Kirk buckles up in agony and then slowly convinces himself that what has happened is not real, stands up again, and faces Khan, who returns them to the reality of the Genesis cave.

Ricardo Montalban (left), as the villainous Khan, threatens Starship USS *Reliant* officers Walter Koenig (center) and Paul Winfield in Paramount Pictures' *Star Trek II: The Wrath of Khan.*

"It's when Khan can't win through force of will that he goes back to his ship," Sowards says.

In all the 400 pages of discarded drafts and approaches (in which *Star Trek II* was titled "The Undiscovered Country," "The Next Continent," and "The Vengeance of Khan," among others) Spock's death scene was always the same, Sowards says, noting that one slight alteration was made in the adaptation of his script to screen.

> Someone jazzed it up. I sent Spock into the room, which was bathed in a deep blue, cobalt light. In the movie you see things spurting out at him and all that. The way I had it he walks into the room just as he would walk onto the bridge, knowing from the moment he steps inside that he's dying. It was just the fact that you knew he was dying while he was in there, adjusting knobs and pressing buttons like he was cooking his eggs for breakfast. I didn't have all that stuff spurting out.

(Kirk's line to Spock early in the film—"Aren't you supposed to be dead?"—Sowards says was his way of acknowledging and playing upon the fact that the ending would leak out and the audience would already know about Spock's death when they came into the theater.)

Sowards does not know who decided to cut those scenes or why, but he speculates they may have simply fallen prey to rereading:

> I gave the script to them in April, and they started shooting in September or October. In that four or five months everyone has read that script seventy-three times. On the seventy-fourth time they say "What is this boring, trite, stale piece of shit we have here? My God, I've seen this all

before." Of course they've seen it all before—seventy-three times. They forget that when you read a script you must retain the first impression. And you must say I don't care what it reads like the hundred and fourth time I read it because I read it the first time and it read good. Don't play with something that's good.

With Paramount's scanners firmly locked on the moviegoing audiences' pocketbook, it is safe to assume Sowards will not go hungry ("this could be my retirement fund if I want it to be"). So it would not surprise anyone if he drove a Mercedes, lived in a fancy Brentwood estate, wore his shirt open to his waist, and had lots of hot "projects" and "concepts" and "vehicles" in the works.

But while he may not be strapped for cash, he is hardly living like a king. And as for his next cinematic effort…

"I think Pauline Kael was upset I didn't have another feature in the works and that I was going back to TV (working on CBS's "Falcon Crest"). So, consequently, it brings me down the scale in someone's mind," he says, propping his feet up on the patio table of his small, sparsely furnished Studio City home. "You see how I live. They're coming in today to put in drapes, thank God. I don't have a Mercedes, I don't have a home in Brentwood. I put the money in the bank so I don't have to go to work if I don't want to work."

Sowards taught himself how to build computers and "could sit at my computer 18 hours a day and be just as happy as writing a script."

Now that he is finished his stint with "Falcon Crest," he busies himself by reading up on PASCAL, a computer programming language.

He began scriptwriting after playing a cop for two years on "Peyton Place," before realizing "acting is no way for a grown man to make a living."

His first script sale to "Bonanza" led to writing jobs with other western series, experience that he says helped when it came time to draft *Star Trek II* ("It's a western set in a different place").

> No one knows who I am because I don't care. I can't let it mean anything to me. If I did, I'd start writing for all the wrong reasons. If I'm gonna impress them with money, Christ they all have money. I'm a good ole boy from Texas who's still trying to find out what I'm gonna be when I grow up.

Kirk's midlife crisis in *Star Trek II,* his obsession with foiling the no-win situation, and his newfound need for bifocals are all reflections on Jack Sowards.

Sowards has to slip on bifocals now to toy with the intricacies of his computer or to read the fine print on an H. Uppmann cigar wrapper. He also feels young—young enough to still look at tomorrow with childlike wonder.

> I'm not the age I am and I'm not settled. I've still got an awful lot to do, to accomplish; I don't want to just settle in and be permanent anywhere. There's a lot of me philosophically in the script; I don't believe in the no-win situation, the Kobiashi Maru (named after the people he lived next door to in Hancock Park). Kirk's solution to the Kobiashi Maru was legitimate. Nothing limits you except yourself.
>
> What we in Hollywood try to do is talk about the business and figure out how it works so we can make it work for us; we don't want to work within the business.
>
> I feel 19, it's the work which keeps you young.

Don't expect to see Sowards at any "Star Trek" conventions or on the credits for *Star Trek III: In Search of Spock*. Sowards is turning down speaking invitations because he does not want to devote time to re-creating what is already behind him. He balks at boldly going where no man has gone before again in order to avoid becoming the Star Trek writer (as Richard Maibaum is with the James Bond series). Harve Bennett is scripting the next film, which Sowards says he knows nothing about.

Paramount, however, has disclosed that Khan may return to harass Kirk again. Is Sowards bothered by that farfetched plot machination?

"Nope, not at all. What I've done is done. And it's on film and it's shot. What they do now that it's finished, locked up, and it's in cement is part of the future. What I did is part of the past."

Interview with Star Trek II *Director Nicholas Meyer and Producers Harve Bennett and Robert Sallin*

Nicholas Meyer adapted and directed *Time After Time* (1979), in which H. G. Wells perfects a time machine and chases Jack the Ripper into twentieth-century San Francisco. He is also the author of the Sherlock Holmes novels *The Seven Percent Solution* (which was adapted in 1976 into a movie starring Robert Duvall and Nicol Williamson as Holmes and Watson) and *The West End Horror*. His other writing credits include *Judge Dee and the Monastery Murder* (1974), a mystery based on Robert Van Gulik's famous Chinese sleuth, and *The Night That Panicked America* (1975), a dramatization of the events that followed Orson Welles's famous radio broadcast of *The War of the Worlds*.

He was joined in the interview by producer Harve Bennett, whose television writing and producing credits include "Six

Million Dollar Man" and "Mod Squad," and line producer Robert Sallin.

Q: Nicholas Meyer, how and why did you decide to do *Star Trek II*?

NICHOLAS MEYER: A friend of mine, named Karen Moore, who at the time was working for Paramount, was visiting one night. I had done nothing since *Time after Time*. I had turned down a lot of stuff, trying to get my own script of a movie called *Conjuring*—with no success, I might add! So I wrote the book *Confessions of a Homing Pigeon,* which came out in October 1981. This was just before that ....

Karen said to me, "You know, if you want to learn how to direct movies, you should direct." She suggested the *Star Trek II* movie, and said that the two guys producing it were very nice.

They sent me the script, which I loved. I met Harve and Bob, and I thought they were wonderful, and I haven't changed my views since! As far as making the film was concerned, I could not have been better partnered to not look like a fool, because of the expertise and support that I was given.

ROBERT SALLIN: Nick is a very intelligent man, as you can tell *[laughter]*, and that special effects stuff is horrendous. Frankly, we've talked amongst ourselves about this, and none of us individually could have done this film. It's the kind of picture that cannot be really turned out without everybody's cooperation.

NM: The miracle of it was that we were always making the same movie! Because where everything could have really been unstuck was if we had started going off in different directions. But there was never a substantive disagreement about the tone or the action. Details, yes.

Q: Had you liked the TV series before?

NM: I never saw it before! I don't particularly like SF. I'm interested in good stories first. I loved *Star Wars* and *The Empire Strikes Back,* which, I thought, were very exciting and a lot of fun. I saw some "Star Trek" stuff after it was offered to me, and they ran the first movie for me too. I didn't like that very much. I thought that it was spectacular in some ways, but I didn't like the way the people looked, and I didn't like what I considered to be an absence of story and human interaction.

There are really two reasons to do remakes and sequels, aside from financial consideration. One is because, for some reason, it's been so long and people really didn't see the original except on late night television. The other reason is that there was something wrong with it. It didn't fulfill what it was supposed to do, or could be improved upon.

I looked at the first film, and I thought that there was no way that we were going to make a movie as filled with ennui as that one, and that we could do it for a quarter of the cost, so that we would probably look like heroes!

Q: The characters were more dimensional than in the TV series. Was that part of your intention?

NM: That was definitely the aim, yes! I have always thought, to the extent that I've had any clear thoughts *[laughter]* about "Star Trek," that it was something that for one reason or another never quite fulfilled its promise. Either because in terms of a TV show, they couldn't afford the sets or the effects, or, because in the first movie, they had dropped the ball somewhere. This was an opportunity to make something right, that had never quite been on the nose before!

The more specific you get, the better. It was not necessary for me to see Admiral Kirk go to the bathroom, but why couldn't he read a book? That's very specific, and from the book, we got the glasses, and that's specific too, and that's real! From all of that comes age....

I think it's fair to say that our movie would not have been as good as it was if it hadn't been for the first picture. We definitely learned, in the broadest sense, that they had made a picture based on a technical nature, with runaway production costs, and we said we wouldn't do that.

I had the sound guy from the first film walk down the set and show me what went wrong. Every time he pointed to a motor that made noise, we ripped it out. That saved us a lot. But it's also conceptual differences. The first movie was short on story. I couldn't have the script written while we were working. I'm too inexperienced to work that way. I don't know what to do with a page here and there. It's got to be really organized ....

So we owe the first film a debt. We tend to feel very superior to it, and I think we're right to feel superior. But, at the same time, they had their own stuff to work out, and they're lucky they got the movie on film.

Q: How did you decide what to keep, and what to change within the *Star Trek* formula?

NM: Very simple, I decided to keep what was good, and change what was bad.

I decided that I owed allegiance to what was good in either the first movie or, more importantly, the television series. And that I owed no allegiance and no respect to things that were bad. So what that really boiled down to was the characters. I had to keep characters as who they were, and I had to redesign everything I could—the uniforms, make the sets look different, etc. Again, it was in the context of what they were, the overall shapes, I couldn't do anything about. But I could add twinkling lights whenever possible. I tried to get away from that gray look.

Philosophically, I said that I was simply going to take these characters more seriously and more literally than anyone has ever taken them before.

Q: Yet there was a lot of humor in the characters, [which was] absent from the first film.

NM: The humor in *Star Trek* is the tragicomic view of life: that of people talking, real people. It seemed very difficult for me to do the movie without including a lot of that. It's a fine line to walk. I didn't want to be camp, but I wanted it to be affectionate and to be real.

By deciding to take them seriously, I didn't mean that they had no humor. I meant that I took them seriously as if they were real people. We said, at the very beginning, when we sat around talking—I said I'd do it under one condition: "Let's make it real, because anything else is either camp, or bland." I said "Let's play it up to the armpit, and if we're going to kill Spock, kill him." Because the unforgivable thing is to fake it, to rip people off that way, to manipulate them. That is tasteless.

HARVE BENNETT: You have to define reality. By traditional filmmaking terms, the "Star Trek" reality is very operatic. That's one reason why we thought Nicholas would like the film, and why he was exactly the right choice for it.

NM: Yes, when I think of opera, it's like life in stone! It's like something that's really real to me. What music does for opera is that it provides the emotional subtext and underpinning. The guy is saying something, and the music is telling you what he's thinking or what he's feeling. *Star Trek* works a bit like that.

Q: You chose to deal with the age of the characters in a different way than the first picture did. Why?

NM: The subject of the screenplay, the theme of this movie is about age and death. That may have originated out of the fact that they're all much older now, but I said "Look, instead of trying to avoid that, or throwing out a couple of lines about it, let's make that the subject." So that's what we decided to do.

It has another effect of making them seem younger, because they deal with it in a more head-on way, and we don't have to look at somebody being ludicrous, pretending to be a leading man when they're character actors.

Q: What were your first tasks when you came in?

NM: When a movie goes forward, several things happen simultaneously. One is that I had to meet with the people at Industrial Light and Magic and go over at least every shot. Robert Sallin was then in charge of making sure all of those special effects were what we thought, and kept up with whatever changes we were making.

At the same time I had to cast the movie, although that, too, was a collaborative process. At the same time I spent two hours a day with my cinematographer on the bridge of the *Enterprise,* with a book of blueprints. Since most of the action takes place on that bridge, and that was a very difficult set, we planned every camera angle.

Q: Were you frightened to do a picture with so many special effects?

NM: I'm frightened all the time! Of everything! So being frightened of this was nothing new!

Q: Was it hard to work with an ensemble of actors that had known each other for so many years?

NM: No, I didn't notice; I just loved it! I loved my actors. I thought they were wonderful. They were nice to me, they didn't pull rank, they were real professional. Everyone came on the set and did their job.

Q: Did you have a good relationship with Harve and Robert Sallin?

NM: I think we all worked very well. I was astounded, the big miracle to me was that we would argue and fight about the details of things, about the effect that would be achieved if we did "A" as opposed to "B," but in the end it was always in the creative overall context of achieving the same objective. That was remarkable!

Q: Did having to rush the film to meet the release date fixed by Paramount hurt you in any way?

NM: Sure! There are mistakes in the movie. There are things in the sound mix that aren't always perfect. There are about three effects shots that are wrong. When the *Enterprise* is leaving dry dock, for instance, there's a black stripe down on one side of the screen.

Q: Do you think all of this was attributable to the film being produced by the TV division?

HB: Well, the real reason for this originally was that, at the time of the industry's shakes over *Heaven's Gate* and of massive spending of money on giant pictures, etc .... someone conceived of giving this kind of film to the people whose background and training was essentially the more cost-conscious arena of television—which may be a first, as far as we know.

I think they chose wisely because they also chose good storytellers and not just people who make pictures for controlled budgets. It was never seriously, however, a television project! The minute the script began to shape up, it was clear to all that we had something terrific. It was designed for theatrical release, and we had an original release date of June 4, which then could not be changed.

NM: Yes, by the time I came on, it was already a feature. I never could follow that stuff about who could sign the checks! I could never understand the distinctions between the TV department and the film department .... I've learned since!

Q: Did budgetary concerns make the story more human-oriented rather than heavily into special effects, like the first movie?

NM: I don't think that was the reason. Our take on the movie was that we wanted to emphasize the people. The budgetary restrictions made us inventive within the context of what we were doing. It made us very creative, very ingenious. We came up with interesting things as a result of these constraints. But they had nothing to do with the orientation of the story.

HB: I'll give you one simple example. When we began this, we were told that we had the set, the bridge, the models, etc .... used in the first picture. It all turned out to be in total disrepair. Everything had been stolen by souvenir hunters! Two or three models of the *Enterprise* also turned out to be gone, and nobody had even reported it to the insurance company! It was like $250,000 that was supposed to be already in our cost, that was really nothing, useless.

Out of the idea that we had some models, Bob and I were already conceptualizing what some of the special effects would be like at the earliest stage of the story. At that moment we thought that if another Starfleet vessel attacks the *Enterprise,* we already had two models. That's what we started thinking. So we designed the whole first movement of the story with two *Enterprises* locked in combat, painted differently. One of them had D-Day-like stripes, I think....

Then it turned out that we didn't even have one model! So we had to start all over again. Of course, that elevated us into different concepts, and then the story changed, and so on. But that's basically how we started. We started very bare, we had to stretch every nickel!

RS: I'll give you another small example, which could be multiplied several times. Remember the sequence in the torpedo bay? The guys put those great things up, etc.... Nick had designed a great shot, but he wanted the camera down there, following the departure of the torpedo. When the torpedo tube was designed, we discovered that between overtime, construction, etc., it would have cost anywhere between $5,000 and $10,000 to structurally brace the side of the tunnel so that the camera could get into position and move. So what we did was to build a tubular dolly track inside the tunnel, and make it look like it belonged there! Then we put the camera on a dolly on wheels and that was it. It cost only $29.

HB: Incidentally, you're looking at the two great space craft designers of the future [he points to himself and Sallin]!

After we found that we had to spend money to build new models, we thought "So what's the *Reliant* going to be?" We thought about it and realized that now we could solve our problem of mistaken identity, because the ships wouldn't look alike, they would be different.

I remembered that a fan had already sent me a model of the *Enterprise,* a simple wooden model, and it was sitting up on my desk. I said "Bob, we've got it!" and I turned the model upside down, and he said he'd take it from there. Off he went to ILM and designed the *Reliant,* which is basically an upside-down *Enterprise* with a roll bar addition across the top!

Q: Was ILM your first choice for special effects?

RS: Not initially. We went through a whole process of examination and bidding. Once we had designed all of the special effects shots, we had bidding meetings, where I laid out all of the specifications of every shot. We had a number of special effects companies here in town come in, and we had three-or four-hour sessions with each of them laying out the specs that came down with budgets and schedules. ILM was one of them.

As the time dwindled and the schedule became more compressed, and we were facing the immovable June 4 release date, it became very apparent that everything had to be done at one place. That somewhat narrowed the choice down more, to these companies which had the capability of handling this volume of work in that amount of time, within reason.

After that, we talked and it became very clear to all of us, really, that the work of ILM, their reliability, their understanding about what we were trying to do, was what we needed. They were not, however, by any stretch of imagination, the lowest bidder....

Q: But they have a reputation to sticking to their bid and keeping costs down.

RS: Oh yes, they're beautifully organized. They have a great attitude.

NM: But it's expensive to do this stuff, and to do it right. Their reputation is not based on ..., well, what I mean is if you bring a movie in under budget, but it's a terrible movie, you're only a hero for 15 minutes! ILM is the Rolls Royce of special effects houses, and it doesn't mean that it gets 10 miles to the gallon! It does mean that when the stuff gets delivered, it's the best. And it is really, they care a lot. They've been doing it ever since George Lucas set them up, so there's a certain system and methodology and organization to it.

RS: Each of the individuals involved up there has this wonderful attitude. They are committed to helping you. They are sensitive, they adjust to changes and shifts....

NM: It's like a strange combination of great technical sophistication and real childlike souls. That is to say, on the one hand, they're talking some kind of technical stuff, but the enthusiasm and the idea that what they do for a living is to make dragons and Ceti eels and starbursts etc.... they get off on that as much as anybody!

Q: Nicholas Meyer, did their knowledge help you? It was, after all, your first big effects picture.

NM: I told them they had the wrong guy. The first time I met them, I told them that what I knew about special effects could be put on the head of a pin. And I'm not talking about a very large pin! I'm talking about a small pin.

If you don't believe me, look at *Time after Time*, which has about two minutes of special effects in there, and they're really very crude. That was fine for that movie, because that's not what it was all about. But really, Bob was the one who organized for me all of the special effects. I would say "This is what I need," and not only would he get it, but his mania for perfection, I think, was astounding, to both me and Harve. We'd look at the film, and think that it looked fine to us, and he'd say that he wasn't happy with the way the shadows were falling on the ship or something.

I suppose that partially comes from his background in commercials, where you really become obsessive about the effect of your stuff....

HB: His mania wasn't astonishing to me. I've known Bob for 30 years and he was there specifically to keep Nicholas from getting cuckoo.

Q: Did you use some of the special effects footage from the first picture?

NM: Just about a few shots at the beginning, the docking sequences, the attack of the Klingon warships.

HB: As you can imagine, the studio, or certain people at the studio, said "Listen, you can use a lot of the stuff from the first movie." But the fact of the matter was that, when we looked at it very carefully, we felt that we had our own movie to make, a unique movie, and that any shot from the other movie would discredit the originality of our work. We started out using the space docking sequence because it was intrinsic to the story line of the film. It was probably the best single visual from the first movie, as far as I was concerned.

NM: We also had what I thought was kind of an in-joke on my part. The docking sequence went on for 15 minutes in the first film, and everybody was oohing and aahing. I thought it would be funny to have the thing last 30 seconds, and Kirk read a book through half of it, then look up and go "oh, yes, hmm." So it was sort of a backhanded comment on that original sequence.

HB: I was forwarded a bill for two stuntmen, and I said, "What stuntmen?" These turned out to be the two stuntmen outside, hanging on the dock, waving. Residuals!

Q: What was Gene Roddenberry's role?

HB: Well, if you want a definition of his role, Gene Roddenberry is as you know credited as executive consultant. Although he has been involved in this project, he was at arm's length, which I define as not intimately involved, but certainly involved. We have exchanged memos at every step of the way. We've talked. He and I had a lot of meetings early in the game, and then memos from wherever he was. He saw the picture, read the reviews in the papers, and I was delighted to get a wonderful call from him saying, "You guys have kept the faith, I'm very proud of this movie."

I think there were some problems between his concept and ours, but nothing that didn't get worked out. A lot of his notes were very seriously incorporated at various stages. I think he's very happy with the picture.

Q: Was the "Star Trek" cult any problem?

NM: No. There was a social problem, however. We wound up saying that there was more than one ending, so that we could go about our business and make the movie without being pounced on.

There were a lot of letters. There's a fringe element to that following that is not particularly pleasant, or at least they don't behave pleasantly. But I answered all of the letters that I got, and said, "Look, I understand your concerns, but I cannot be responsive to them, I cannot promise you anything except that I'm going to try to make the best *Star Trek* movie ever, and you're going to have to trust me.

"Art does not get made by a committee, by a vote, or by a popularity contest. Also you think you know what you want and what you don't want, but I don't think you really know either."

I didn't say this in so many words, but that was my private feeling, and I think the movie has borne out my contention.

Q: I would think many fans would be surprised at Kirk having an illegitimate child. Heroes don't normally behave this way.

NM: Not true! If you're really talking about heroes, heroes are often illegitimate themselves! Hercules was an illegitimate child. Heroes with illegitimate children are also common; at least if you're talking about real, classical heroes as opposed to television.

But this movie was not being made by the networks; it was being made by me! I thought that if Kirk was real, did it mean that he never put out the wrong foot, never [did] a bad thing?

People get very worried [that] if heroes are human beings instead, then we are going to lose affection for them. I think, on the contrary, that we gain affection for them! I think finding that they did something once not to be so proud of makes them more real, and you have compassion. In some cases, when a hero has a great weakness, and functions despite that weakness, it serves to throw heroism in sharper relief.

Q: You have a tendency to refer to, and use, forms already in existence: Sherlock Holmes, "Star Trek," etc. Why?

NM: The advantages of working with forms that already exist is that you don't have to have a lot of exposition. I don't have to set these people up.

If they're already given, then I can devote myself exclusively to their internal processes, and use them to say whatever I want them to say.

There are certain things that are common preoccupations of mine, and one of them is what it means to believe and to be a human being. It's no accident that H. G. Wells and Kirk, in highlights of both stories, say the same line ....

Q: What really happened with these multiple endings rumors?

NM: Well, it started with me, Harve Bennett, and Paramount. I think Michael Eisner of Paramount originally thought of it, and it turned out to be a nifty way to keep the heat off us. Paramount actually suggested that we shoot multiple endings, but I told them we had barely the time to shoot the movie as it was! Besides, what possible other ending could there be!

Past a certain point I became irritated because it made the people who make the movie look very manipulative, as though we really didn't care, as though a story such as the one we were telling was arbitrarily susceptible to cutting and pasting!

Q: Are you going to be involved with *Star Trek III?*

NM: No. I feel that I've done my space movie, now I want to go back and do what I want to do.

Star Trek III: *Interview with Harve Bennett*

Producer Harve Bennett can be credited with expanding the appeal of "Star Trek" light years beyond that of the original TV show—without ignoring fans of the series (as exemplified by references to such Trek paraphernalia as the Tribbles in *The Search for Spock*. Bennett explains:

> *Star Trek*'s core audience is quite large. They deserve to be treated like family. So the task is to make them feel like they're once again back in their land, speaking their language. But not doing it so excessively that someone who doesn't speak French, for example, can't follow the opera. In fact, I have often used that analogy. *Star Trek* is an opera, in the very nice sense of the term. It has stylized issues and performances, and everything is on the grand stage level. And I've always thought that it's in a foreign language. Those who understand it, having seen the series and the reruns, get a maximum value from it. But those who don't speak that language can still enjoy the music and the theater.
>
> I once used a different analogy. When I first took over the job, I had a nightmare. I dreamed that I was in World War II and that I had been given an assignment by the O.S.S. to parachute behind the lines into Poland and set up a Polish underground to help win the war. And, I remember saying to the general, "But I don't speak Polish!" And he said, "That's all right. You'll learn on the way down!" That's how I felt when I came to *Star Trek*. I knew little about the series, except maybe generalities. Twenty years ago I did a television program called "Mod Squad," and in its first year we were scheduled against "Star Trek." So, understandably, on those nights, I used to watch my program instead of "Star Trek." I didn't

discover the series until reruns, some years later. So I really had to do a crash course. I saw all the episodes in one two-month period.

Now, several years and two films later, Bennett has virtually become *Star Trek*'s new guiding light. "It's been a long, slow process, and it took two movies," he comments, "but I have a feeling that we've succeeded in making people who love *Star Trek* trust this team. Certainly Gene [Roddenberry] does. It's been a very good experience."

Now Bennett is hard at work on *Star Trek IV*, to be directed by Leonard Nimoy, but this time scripted by someone else. He remarks:

> This will be my third *Star Trek* picture. I didn't want to write this one because I also wanted to save time for other projects—both feature and television. When you do write as complex a screenplay as *Star Trek*, it really puts you into a room for six months, exclusive of wife, children, and other projects. That was the primary reason I didn't want to do it again. If I have to go back to the typewriter to rewrite this work, it will be a different task, and a task I've faced countless times. It's a totally different emotional experience. In this case we've got two wonderful writers. They've had tons of input storywise, from Leonard and from me. Our hopes are very high, based on what they've done in the past, their love for *Star Trek* and all that.

The story of *Star Trek IV* remains a secret, but Bennett intends the picture to be a full continuation of the two earlier pictures. He comments:

> It's the third part of a trilogy. We're being more ambitious, and the budget feels, at this time, a little heavier. It relates

entirely to the two previous pictures, as a three-volume set. *Star Trek IV* suddenly offered an opportunity to close the ring on a trilogy, and to rebound from "life," "death," and back to "resurrection," which is what we've been dealing with for two pictures.

The tone of the film, however, may surprise the fans, for Bennett wants *Star Trek IV* to be in a lighter [vein] than its two predecessors. He explains:

> Our aim is that, in addition to the *Star Trek* corps tradition and feeling, we want to have some fun. That is, as you know, part of the tradition—and we had some fun along the way in both of the other pictures. This one will be even more lighthearted. Because I think our audience deserves it, and I think if we were still doing a TV series, every third show would tend to be: "let's lighten up, folks."

There have been many rumors that actor Eddie Murphy, a "Star Trek" fan himself, would join the cast in order to contribute his own particular brand of humor. Bennett remains vague.

> The vehicle is designed for the *Star Trek* family. It's no secret that Spock will again be central as a character. But we also have a marvelous guest star part. I know rumors abound that it will be played by Eddie Murphy. My comment on that is, actor that he is, Eddie Murphy could play it. He is hardly committed to play it, and he has plans of his own. He loves *Star Trek,* like many millions of people do, and if he is available, I know he'd love to play it. He's the biggest box-office star in America, and although he's said, "I'd love to do a *Star Trek*," who knows? Tom Selleck has also

said that to me. But every time I call him and ask, "How'd you like to play a Klingon?"—which frankly, I did—he was either doing his series or making his in-between pictures. I believe Tom was as genuine as Eddie in expressing his desire to be in a *Star Trek* movie, but it's a long way between that and the release date.

The release of the yet unsubtitled *Star Trek IV* was, in theory, due to take place in the summer of 1986; but there may be delays. Bennett comments,

> The studio would love to have it on the same schedule, that is June every two years. We lost an inordinate amount of time for two reasons. One was the Shatner hold-out; but to an even larger extent, we lost time because of the management change. The management change in turn affected the Shatner hold-out. That is to say, I believe that the old management would have resolved that problem much more swiftly. In addition to that, when everybody leaves, and the chairs are empty for four or five months, it's irretrievable time. So, right now, we are six months behind any best schedule we've ever had. It is, therefore, to me unthinkable to try to do this for June 1986. Particularly now that Shatner is going back into production on "T. J. Hooker," and is not available to us on our terms, but only when he finishes shooting, which may be December.

But then, making the *Star Trek* pictures was ever a challenge. Bennett reminisces how he felt when he took over *The Wrath of Khan:*

> The first obstacle that we had to overcome was that *Star Trek: The Motion Picture* had left *Star Trek* in a state of

disarray. It had not whetted the public's appetite for more *Star Trek* movies. So when they asked me to do another one, I figured we could probably make a more interesting movie by being faithful to what Gene had done. Of course, the other problem was like being the new kid in town, and getting comfortable and integrated not only with the cast and with Gene, but also with the fans.

The Wrath of Khan went on to make over $80 million, and Bennett was pleased, and even somewhat surprised. Then he realized almost immediately that there was to be a *Star Trek III*—which he decided to script himself.

I decided to write the third film because I had such a clear idea of where we were going. It seemed like a script that would write itself in a way. And that's what it proved to be. There was a lot of input from Leonard, as well as Gene, and it went fairly well. Once I began writing *The Search for Spock,* the one thing that was clear was that they were a two-volume set and that they would stand together as one. I'm sure they will be played together as a revival double bill. At the same time it was important to me, as a writer and producer, that you did not have to have seen *The Wrath of Khan* in order to comprehend *The Search for Spock.* To the best of my own observation, I think we succeeded in that.

At the time *The Wrath of Khan* ended, it was not absolutely clear whether Spock would be coming back—and how. Bennett explains how he had to solve that problem.

It became my task to paint myself as a writer out of the corner that I, as a producer, had painted myself into at the end of *The Wrath of Khan.* Originally, the film had ended

with Spock's funeral. But I think the studio was concerned that the film was an irrevocable downer. So we felt
we could be more hopefully ambiguous and we designed
what became the current ending, with the capsule landing on Genesis and Bill saying things like, "As Spock is
fond of saying, there are always possibilities, and I must
come back here someday." Then we did an insert, which
was an enhancement of something that was in the film—a
close-up of Spock doing a mind meld with McCoy, saying
"Remember." When I asked Leonard to do that, he said,
"Why are we doing it?" I said, "I don't know. But if there is
a *Star Trek III*, it will be something that is a breadcrumb.
Clearly it has all kinds of potential." But at the time I really
didn't know why.

Bennett felt happy to put on his writer's hat again for *The
Search for Spock.*

I feel I demonstrated what those people close to me knew,
that even though I hadn't written in a while, I was still a
highly competent screenplay writer, and had been in all of
my television career. But, frankly, I hadn't done a from-
scratch original in a couple of years. It was great to do it,
and to flex the muscles. Having written a screenplay is the
greatest satisfaction in the world. It is the hardest thing to
begin and the greatest thing to have done. It's a high that
rivals any other achievement that I've ever had.

For *The Search for Spock,* Bennett had to wear two hats, that
of writer and that of producer. But instead of seeing this as a
handicap, Bennett thought of it as an asset.

One of the virtues of having grown up in television as both
a producer and a writer is that you're forced to function at a

rapid tempo. You really don't have time to overthink. And, in my mellow, middle years, I'm finally recognizing that it's the greatest asset that I could have learned. I see people in the feature business, agonizing over treasured scenes and treasured words, and stuff that makes no sense to shoot. It is the stuff of which colossal disasters come, like *Heaven's Gate* and other famous disaster pictures. No one wants to part with a vision. Well, in television you don't have time for those extravagances and you are much more into committee thinking. Now all of these things bear negative connotations in our society, but the good side of real collaboration between trained professionals is that no one steps on anyone else, but there is a tremendous give and take of ideas in a rapidly changing situation. And when you hit the thing that's working, everyone tends to sense it and they come together. It's like selecting a candidate. If it's right, everyone puts their differences aside and go[es] on to the next problem.

Bennett the writer provides an example of one of the many changes made by Bennett the producer.

One of the most interesting changes was that I had written the script for Romulans. Then Leonard felt that the Klingons were more exciting, more theatrical. I thought about it a while, we kicked it around, I went back to some episodes, and I realized he was quite right. Also, a sampling of fan mail indicated that they wanted to see Klingons. So I rewrote my script and "Klingicized" the characters. But I didn't change their ship. Because I remembered a piece of trivia that said that there was a mutual assistance military pact between the Klingons and the Romulans for an interchange in which the Romulans supply military equipment to the Klingons, including spaceships!

The decision to kill off David, Kirk's son, was another such hard decision. Bennett explains how the production arrived at the conclusion that David had to die.

> One step followed another. With the Genesis device, we had crippled ourselves in terms of storytelling. Because, in future *Star Trek* pictures, it would be used as an all-powerful saving device, or the ultimate negative force, the H-bomb of the twenty-fourth century. Something operated in my mind, which comes directly as most of my work does, from films I've liked. This one came from *The Man in the White Suit,* which is a lovely science fantasy film on a small scale. Its theme is that for every great advance, you pay a price. Putting protomatter into the hands of David had created an impossible situation, and then suddenly we were dealing with guilt. So I found myself writing a scene in which I was playing Russian roulette with three characters. I thought, "This is a great scene." Then I walked into Leonard's office and I said, "I've just painted myself into another corner. If we don't kill someone, we've really cried wolf in a very desperate situation." So we wrestled with that for a couple of days. And, frankly, there were literally times where we were behaving like the film itself, passing the knife over Saavik. The one person we couldn't eliminate was Spock. So it went back and forth between David and Saavik, with the exigency of it having to be real. Then, finally, because we felt that was the logical choice, we committed to it.

Although the character of Saavik was not eliminated for *The Search for Spock,* actress Kirstie Alley, who had created the role in *The Wrath of Khan,* did not come back—over an alleged dispute concerning her salary. Bennett comments,

The crew of the starship *Enterprise,* with newcomer Kirstie Alley as Lt. Saavik, prepare to confront *The Wrath of Khan.*

It was all very unfortunate. I think both Leonard and I would have loved to have had Kirstie in the picture. But it wasn't just a dispute we had. It was relative to the rest of the cast and what they are paid, which is substantial enough. I can only describe the dispute by saying that she wanted an amount that would have had her outrank most of the cast members, which we felt was unfair. You've got seven people in the show, two big stars and a third costar, DeForest Kelley. Jimmy Doohan is himself a costar, not to mention George and everybody else. So it would have been very bad not only business wise, but for the cast relations. That's a very tight family, and had any one of them found out what she was making, had we chosen to give her that, or even half of that, we would have had awful resentments.

It was like having a baseball team, and having a rookie of the year come at you and say, "I'm now a free agent, and you've got to pay me $1 million a year." You say, "But you're not seasoned yet." That was the reason. And there was no give. We had three serious discussions, where we told them it was not the ballpark, and they shouldn't play games with us, by starting very high and expecting us to come halfway. We were much lower. In negotiations, somewhere you establish the parameters and it's all whittling wood in the tunnel. But when you're so far outside the tunnel, all you can do is say, "We don't have a game here." They didn't believe that, three times. Finally, we said, "If you don't come back to reality within a certain period of time, we've got to move on, because we can't play this game." And they never called us back.

Instead, actress Robin Curtis was chosen to replace Alley. Bennett explains,

A funny thing is that there is a qualitative difference between Kirstie and Robin. Essentially, Leonard cast Robin. He was very much in her corner. I think the reason was then, and is now, that she's more Vulcan. I think somewhere deep in Leonard's unconscious he preferred that, because he thought, with his own background, he could get a better performance out of her that way. Originally, she was designed as half Vulcan, half Romulan. Kirstie really helped make that background work. But Kirstie also had a contemporary quality that Robin has less of. Robin has a certain style and elegance. I would like to exploit the character a lot more.

Although *The Wrath of Khan* was directed by Nicholas Meyer, and *The Search for Spock* and *Star Trek IV* by Leonard Nimoy, it is Bennett who is very much in charge of overseeing the series. He describes how he worked with each director.

For *The Wrath of Khan,* I had Nicholas Meyer, who is a very stimulating, unconventional, irreverent iconoclast, both as a writer and as a director. Leonard is quite the opposite. He's a meticulous, contained, very thoughtful, very prepared man. He doesn't like to deviate once he's set a course for himself. He is very Spock-like in that. So I have the experience of collaborating with hot and cool. It's interesting, because the pictures are quite different, yet they are clearly of the same piece of cloth.

With *Star Trek IV* at least six months away from the theaters, Bennett once again goes back to the source, the television series, and points out how the films took the characters in areas where no television character had gone before.

When you come to a movie or read a novel, there is an element of surprise that needs to be watered or refreshed.

You've got to do the unexpected from time to time, because in a television series you know you can't. You know that Kirk will be back on the bridge of the *Enterprise* at the end of the episode, because there are reruns. For that reason, the plasticity of television is that nobody dies. Nobody dies, nobody changes. And the one thing that we were committed to in this series of films was that both death and change will be dealt with. Particularly change. These people are getting old. In *The Wrath of Khan*, with Nicholas, I attempted to deal with the fact that they were middle-aged people, instead of waxy replicas of themselves as younger.

You see, the interesting problem which you face with *Star Trek*, which Gene did not face with the series, is that, when you're doing a show a week, you can get very radical and turn Spock into the heavy, turn Kirk into a homosexual, do all those daring things and then bring them back to where you want them in the next episode. In a feature, because of the time delay—it is two years between films— it's hard to make such radical changes and leave people out or in. On the other hand, you can't, in a series, do things like we did to Spock or David.

After *Star Trek IV*, whence Bennett? If the film repeats the success of its predecessors, the producer might very well find himself hard at work on yet another sequel. But he refuses to consider it for now.

Beyond this, I'm not looking to "Star Trek V." If it presents itself as a wonderful opportunity, I may think about it. Paramount treats me like a king. They would love to have me stay here for 15 years and do seven or eight more. But, after all, *Star Trek* is Gene Roddenberry's gift to people, and that limits my own sense of commitment. I got more satisfaction from the Emmy for "Golda" because there I was making a statement deep from my own roots, from my own storytelling and from my own admiration. It was my gift to people.

Star Trek III: *Interview with William Shatner*

Q: Are you committed to another *Star Trek* film? WILLIAM SHAT-NER: No.

Q: It seems that the emphasis in the latter two films has been more on the characters than on "the planet of the week" style story. Do you see that as a continuing trend, and are you pleased to have that emphasis on humanity?

ws: It's true that the series always used to have what I called the monster of the week. And that's the nature of episodic television. We liked to think on the series that there was a level of humanity and philosophy that stood out every so often. I think it was one of those elements that made the series so popular. When I first heard the conversations about *Star Trek I,* it was directly after the success of *Star Wars,* and I think the studio had always held back from doing anything with "Star Trek" because of their reluctance to believe, very naturally so, that something like that could have a viable economic life. When *Star Wars* hit, they decided to do a "Star Trek" in the same manner. So *Star Trek I* was in my view, an attempt to catch up to *Star Wars,* which meant making it big, spending $40 million in special effects, etc. Although it made a lot of money, when that was not a good ... I mean it was not a terrific film; it was good but it was not terrific. It was not in the tradition of "Star Trek," because by that time, everybody in the management who knew what the elements were, had died off or moved away.

Those of us who did know, and said, "Come in for a close-up on this face" were told, "Close-up? This is movies! You guys don't know movies, you're used to television. We need grandiose, epic proportions." So, of course, it being their money, they won and this mold of *Star Trek* was struck.

Now they had a conflict. It made them a great deal of money, but it was not "Star Trek." And they had spent so much money on it, even though it had large box office, they didn't make much profit. So they said, "If we make a next one, let's spend less money and do what you guys want to do, a little humanity."

I think it's an interesting confluence of economics and art that became these last two shows, which is that at one point in the series when we didn't have much money for special effects, [it] almost forced us to do more human stories. Now, we have more money, but they want to save it for special effects, so they're doing more human stories.

Q: How was it to work with the three different directors on the films?

ws: Each director has their own characteristics. Robert Wise came to that film with a justifiably legendary reputation. When he said "We're going to put the camera over here and go over there," you said, "Yes, Sir," because he had won all these Oscars, and it meant a great deal. One didn't question the father figure who knew all. Not that he didn't allow us certain freedoms, but he was Robert Wise, one of the great directors in Hollywood. Nick Meyer had written the script, and we were so in love with the script and we were so impressed with his creative abilities that, although it was only the second picture, we felt that his imagination should be given full flower. So here he was, he had written the script, but he hadn't directed very much. Whatever help we could give him was proffered, and he would accept it or not accept it, depending on what he felt was right or wrong. But he had written the script, and therefore brought to it another unquestionable aspect.

Leonard and I are dearest, good old friends. We have shared a mutual struggle with the management in various things that we struggled with. Whether it was the script, or prop, or concept, or dressing rooms, we were always united. We would go into a dressing room and say, "Well, what do you think?" We'd have a plan whenever we had something to deal with with management. We were together, we were brothers in flesh and in spirit. Now, suddenly my brother was saying, "Well, I think you should do this." And I was saying, "Now, wait a minute, I think I should …," and I felt alone. So there was an awkward period of time for me, and I don't think for Leonard, or maybe so; I never really talked to him about it. But there was a period of a couple of weeks in which I felt alone in anything that I might have objected to, although I had no reason to. Both Harve Bennett and Leonard Nimoy, and in fact the whole of Paramount's management, have given nothing but love and affection in most areas. But, from my point of view, it was more awkward in the beginning than [with] either of the other two directors. But that slowly erased itself as I realized that Leonard had a point of view and knew what he was doing.

Q: Have you ever asked to direct one of the *Star Trek* films?

WS: No. I didn't say that, until recently!

Q: Is that going to be part of your deal if you make another one?

WS: That's a difficult question, because I'm so tied up with "T. J. Hooker" and I'm directing here. But the truth of the matter is that I'd like to. It's just a matter of whether I can.

Q: Was there ever any trepidation at the idea of bringing a character back to life?

WS: It was never anticipated, an accident happened. Maybe it wasn't an accident if you don't believe in accidents. It was really very strange. We were getting ready to do the death scene of Spock in *Star Trek II*—and this wasn't scripted—and Leonard pinched DeForest and DeForest fell, then he put his hand on DeForest's forehead, and he was looking for something mysterious, so he put his hand up and said, "Remember." Then he took off and Spock died. Because Leonard didn't want to play Spock anymore.

They argued and went through every possible permutation and combination to get Leonard to play Spock. Leonard said, "Look, I've spent my adult life playing Spock. I want to go on to other things. It is stifling my career, stifling my creative impulses. I need to stop." Very understandable. We were all very pained, but we understood completely. This was the death of Spock.

But, for some reason, Leonard said, "Remember." It was mysterioso, it was Vulcan. It was meaningful to somebody in *Star Trek,* but we didn't know what. And that was the end. Spock was dead, and the question was would there be a *Star Trek III* and how would we do it without Spock, and that was a whole other question. But as far as everybody connected with *Star Trek* was concerned, Spock was dead.

Then the possibility of Leonard directing the film came up. Leonard said, "If I can direct the film, I'll play Spock." Then the problem was, how do we bring him back to life? And Harve Bennett in a tremendous creative leap, used that "Remember," and brought him back in a very viable, valid, science fiction way. So it was an accident, or fortuitous circumstance, or fate.

Q: Do you feel stifled playing Kirk?

ws: No. Because the character is different, because he is in effect the hero, and heroes are universal. I never did feel stifled in the series. And I think that any actor would have paid the management money, rather than received money to tackle the roles that I've been asked to do in the last two films.

I just love being Captain Kirk in the way they've been writing him.

Q: What would you like to see happen in future films, since now it is totally open-ended?

ws: Yes, it's totally open-ended, unless Harve has got some plots in his mind that he hasn't talked about. I have two things that I'd like to see. They're contrasted, and yet they're unified. One is that I'd like to see romance, and I'd like to see gritty realism, with handheld cameras and dirt under the fingernails.

Q: Is there a particular director you would like to work with on a future film?

WS: There are a number of bright, young directors that are making their mark now. It seems to me that the best thing that we can do with *Star Trek* is to bring some brilliant, young director, where he wouldn't be afraid to try new things and not let stodgy tradition get in his way. I don't think I should mention any names. It's just that there are a group of fine directors who are doing the best work, and I'd love to see them come and do a *Star Trek* movie.

Q: Why did you do *Visiting Hours?*

WS: I shouldn't have done it. I made a mistake. I think at that time there was a lot of money involved. I regret doing it.

Star Trek IV: *Interview with Leonard Nimoy*

During its original run in the 1960s, "Star Trek" was always thought of as a series with a social conscience, exploring themes such as liberty and racial prejudices.

Now, with the fourth in its series of theatrical motion pictures, director Leonard Nimoy (who also plays the Vulcan science officer Mr. Spock) has chosen to go back to those "activist" roots by highlighting the plight of an endangered species—the humpback whale.

The story of *Star Trek IV: The Voyage Home* has the crew of the now gone Starship *Enterprise* returning to earth, where a giant space cloud is causing devastating damage. Captain Spock discovers that the cloud is sending a signal that requires a response from a humpback whale—a species extinct for several hundred years. In a last ditch effort to save the world, the crew undertakes a dangerous journey through time to bring a breeding pair of whales back to the future!

In the midst of the film's postproduction, Nimoy took time to discuss his choice of subject for the picture.

Q: When did you know that you were going to begin on *Star Trek IV*?

LEONARD NIMOY: I was asked by the administration of the studio to do another *Star Trek* about three weeks before *Star Trek III* opened.

Q: So you've had a long time to contemplate it, then?

LN: Well, it's been a long time coming. I started working on it immediately. In fact, I started working on the ideas for this film around the time that *Star Trek III* opened, which would be about two years ago.

Q: Did you have trouble coming up with a way to get the crew out of the situation in which they were left?

LN: That was the job, wasn't it? No trouble, no. It was a creative process, developing ideas. We quickly had a pretty good fix on what general direction we wanted this movie to go and what kind of tone we wanted it to have. There were certain strong feelings that I had about what this picture should be about, and what it should not be about. Most important, I felt that we had done two pictures in a row with a kind of black-hat heavy: Ricardo Montalban as Khan in *Star Trek II*, and Chris Lloyd as Kruge in *Star Trek III*, and I thought we'd had enough of that.

The series did not depend on black-hat heavies each week, and I felt strongly that the films shouldn't be a series of us—good guys—versus them—bad guys. I insisted that this picture would not have that kind of a tone, and that if there was a problem, it would not be a problem created by a bad person. It would be a problem created by misunderstandings, by ecological problems, by scientific problems, failures, breakdowns, that kind of thing, but nobody with no-good intentions. And in this film such a problem is discovered, that we have to try to deal with and try to help.

I also felt, very strongly, that the picture should be lighter in tone than the last two were. We'd had lots of life and death situations, and friends of ours dying, and I think we've had enough of that for a while.

Q: Did you ever contemplate not taking the crew of the *Enterprise* back into the fold of the Federation? Maybe letting them take that *Bird of Prey* and set out…

LN: And work as renegades? No, not really. I heard that idea bandied about, but I didn't take to it very well. I didn't want to do it.

I think it would be out of character for them not to at least come home and deal with what they had to deal with. After that, whatever happened remained to be seen. I really believe that it would have been totally out of character for them to avoid coming home for trial, if there were going to be a trial, and just say, "Well, we're not coming. We'll stay out in space." I didn't like that idea at all.

Q: Did you consider writing the script yourself?

LN: No, I didn't want to. I had very strong feelings about the kind of writing that was needed, and I had very strong feelings about the story ideas that were in the film, but I did not want to write it.

I thought it was enough that I would be directing it, and I did a lot of acting in it, a lot more than in *Star Trek III*. But I did want a certain kind of writing tone, which we finally got.

Q: Is that why you decided to have Nicholas Meyer and Harve Bennett work on the script together?

LN: Harve is a very fine constructionist, and Nick has the kind of humor and social comment, gadfly attitude, that I wanted very much in this picture.

Q: Did you feel that it was easier for you to direct and act this time than it had been last time?

LN: No, not really. In fact, it was harder in certain respects, because I am in this film much more than I was in the last. In *Star Trek III* I was on my back for two or three small moments, then on my feet playing one major scene at the end of the movie. It is quite the contrary in this picture. I'm on my feet throughout.

Q: One of the days that I was on the set, you were all stuck on the *Bird of Prey* in the tank. Did you feel frustration being over there, and not being able to look at what was going on?

LN: Oh yeah! It would be much easier if I were only doing one job or the other. It was tough. I wouldn't recommend it!

Q: Are you going to do it again?

LN: No, at least not on *Star Trek,* and certainly not on the next one. My understanding is that Bill Shatner will direct the next picture. I think he should. He's very talented and energetic, and I'd love to have him do it. I'd love to have his energy come in now and take over some of it.

Q: It will be a little vacation for you to just act …

LN: It will certainly be a lot easier than this picture!

Q: How did you focus on the whales as being the right problem to be solving?

LN: Well, back in February 1985 I was doing extensive research to determine what the motivating factor of this film was going to be about. We had agreed—the studio, myself, and Harve Bennett—that the concept of this film would be essentially a time travel story. We wanted to lighten the tone and we wanted to have a little more fun and adventure than we had in the last few pictures. Harve and I had written a concept, which the studio accepted, and that concept was that there was time travel, but we hadn't decided which period we were coming back to. We gave ourselves several different choices, but we all agreed it would be wonderful to come back right now. And to San Francisco, home base of the Federation of Planets.

Now, when you decide to do a time travel story like that, the next question that comes up is, why are we traveling through time? Is it accidental or is it intentional? Are we on our way home and something goes wrong with the *Bird of Prey,* and we find ourselves going through the time fabric? Or does somebody accidentally go through the time fabric, and we have to chase and find them, as we did in "City on the Edge of Forever," one of the better episodes. Or do we find ourselves being chased into the time fabric, and we're forced to go into time to escape? These are all the various possibilities.

So I did a lot of research which had to do with contemporary scientific concerns about the future. And, of course, one of the big, big scientific concerns is about endangered species and loss of species. I came across a book written by a biologist named Wilson who works at Harvard. I called him and had a wonderful conversation with him in February 1985.

This is the key. He says in his book, among other things, that by the 1990s we'll be losing 10,000 species per year off this planet, at the rate we're going now. That's one species per hour. Many of those species will be unrecorded scientifically. We'll never even know they existed, they'll just be gone, long before the biologists have even had the chance to research them and find out what they are. Then, of course, there are the major endangered species that we all know and talk about, like certain whale species.

There are what he refers to as certain keystone species. The keystone theory. Meaning that, if you build a house of cards, you can take this card out and the house won't fall down. You can take that card out and the house won't fall down. At a certain point you get down to the keystone cards which really hold up the ecological structure of the planet. We may not even be sure of which ones are the keystone species. But you pull one out and the whole thing starts to crumble.

Scientists have told me, during my research, that one of the things they're terrified of, really scared of, is that the attitude on this planet seems to be that if something goes wrong, the scientists will fix it. That's not necessarily true. We may reach a point where it's too far gone. We turn to the scientists and say, "Fix it," and they can't, it's too late, they don't have the time or the wherewithal or the means. They're worried about that. I would be too if I were them.

So I became intrigued with the idea that we have a problem erupting in the twenty-third century that can only be resolved by using an element—something—from a species that became extinct, that was allowed to die, was killed off. The scientists are at a loss because they cannot synthetically replace this natural thing that's gone. Without giving away any more of the story than is already given away, let's just say that the only way to solve the problem is to go back 300 years and pick up a couple of hump-back whales. We have to come back to the twentieth century, pick them up in the *Bird of Prey*, fly them into the twenty-third century, drop them in the ocean, and hope that solves the problem.

In any case, that's essentially what the idea's about, and that's how it evolved. I was sitting with a scientist friend of mine after I'd had this conversation with Wilson, and after I had meetings at Harvard, MIT, and UC-Santa Cruz with scientists, talking about all those concerns. He happens to also be a science fiction buff, and we were talking about various species being lost, and it came down to whales.

Q: Have you always had ecological concerns?

LN: Yes. I don't consider myself an activist, but I am concerned about conservation. I do belong to a number of organizations and I send them money. I've been sending money to Greenpeace for a long time.

All of that sounds pretty grim! The fun in the picture happens when we come to the twentieth century and spend time walking here on earth, San Francisco 1986, and have to make our way through this society to accomplish a task that's been set for us. It's fun; it's a fun picture.

I talked with the scientists about time travel. You know, there's this ongoing concern that you go back and inadvertently change the flow of time, or change some event. Well, there's another theory that says you can't: it's impossible. You cannot do that because it's going to happen the way it did happen. If you follow that theory, you can go back into time and buy a gun, load it, put it to somebody's head, and pull the trigger, and the gun wouldn't work if that person's not supposed to die at that moment. You couldn't do it! So it's a fun game to play, and we have a little of that in the picture. But, essentially, we're playing it pretty straightforwardly. We do what we came to do and go back.

Q: When you decided on having whales in the story, did you immediately start exploring how you were going to show them on-screen, and come up with alternative possibilities?

LN: Yes. There will be footage of whales done in a variety of different ways. We're using actual footage of humpbacks that we've had shot for us around Maui by Debby and Mark Ferrari. We had pieces of humpbacks built for us here on the lot by our special effects people. We used those in the tank in conjunction with the *Bird of Prey*. And we have four miniature, radio-control humpbacks being built for us by ILM, which will be photographed underwater by them. So we have various ways of doing it.

Q: Did you consider doing it all with models and not getting any real footage?

LN: No, I wouldn't say we did. But I would say we covered ourselves so in case we could not get the right kind of whale footage we knew that we would be able to get it down anyway. But we do have some good actual footage that will work for us.

Q: Did you consider going with the Ferraris when they were shooting?

LN: I wasn't available. The timing is bad you see. The best time to shoot underwater footage of humpbacks is when they start gathering around the islands in January. That was a bad time for me; January was when we started shooting here. So, to take time off to go shoot whales would have been impossible. Particularly since I wouldn't have really been helpful to them.

Q: Do you regret it? Just from the standpoint of it being such a rare experience?

LN: I'll go next year!

Q: Did you feel under strictures to give all of the cast members fair shares of on-screen time?

LN: I don't think I had to concern myself with that consciously. I just feel that way. I feel they all make a contribution, they're all important to us. And I certainly wanted them to know as quickly as possible that I feel that way. They're all deserving of opportunities. It is difficult to keep everybody happy all the time. They know that and I know that. We have tried from picture to picture to see that there was a balance from one picture to the next. A person who perhaps had a little bit less to do in one, would hopefully have a little bit more the next time. We try to do that. But our intentions are good, and I think they know that. I try to see that they have a good time working on the picture, and that they are well used in the picture. I do the best I can.

I think they're all happy with the experience they had making the picture. I think they're all excited about what the picture can be. We all are. I'm very pleased with what I've seen. It's very promising.

Q: Have you tried to take Spock in any new directions?

LN: This is a different Spock than you've ever seen. Quite different. We pick Spock up in the sense that when we left him in the last movie he was kind of disoriented. He was trying to figure out who's who here, and he finally manages to recognize Jim, I think! So it's quite a different Spock than we've seen before and, I feel, funny and charming.

Q: Do you think that having been able to "wipe the slate clean" last time gave you the chance to try things with the character you couldn't have done before?

LN: Yeah. We see him going through a kind of growing up process in this picture; kind of bemused and wondering what's going on, and what am I supposed to do about this? His memory is back, we find out very quickly that he's been training his memory and feeding himself on large quantities of information: facts, figures, data, history, and so on. But on the other hand, his sensitivities and sensibilities, his awareness of social attitudes and conduct, and how to function in society are still a little bit askew. So he's really looking for, "How do I do this?" I think it's a lot of fun.

Q: Did that give you a lot of enjoyment as an actor?

LN: Oh yes. It was the most fun I've had playing Spock in a long time!

Q: Do you think that being able to start out this way, that in future pictures you'll be able to develop Spock further?

LN: I hope so! You know, there's always that question about what's next. Well, we've still got a long way to go on this one. I've got five months to go yet on this picture, and I'm concentrating on that and having a great time with it.

Q: Saavik doesn't have a very big part in this picture...

LN: No. We see her, but it's not a major thing. It wasn't really the kind of story that called for a function by that character. So we have her in the film so people know we haven't just dropped her.

Q: I heard a rumor that she may be pregnant by Spock?

LN: I haven't seen a medical report....

Q: Were there any aspects of the film that were frustrating for you from a directorial standpoint?

LN: There's always the question of "Do we have enough time to do this the way we would like to do it?" I always feel a certain responsibility to the studio on the scheduling. They were extremely supportive and very happy with everything that they were seeing. But my sense of responsibility keeps driving me to get on with it. And, as I say, the acting and directing both are sometimes frustrating. Particularly when you have to be in a scene, and you know that there are things going on behind you that you cannot see, and you'd like to be able to have an eye in the back of your head, and you just can't do that. But I had very good support from a very good camera department, and Bill Shatner was helpful when he wasn't in a shot he was watching, and the other actors I trust. Everyone was helpful. They got you past the tough times.

It's been said before. You start out to make a movie with an enormous amount of energy and enthusiasm, and there comes a point about half or two-thirds of the way through, when you just want to get finished with it. You get so tired!

Maybe one of the biggest frustrations I had was that on some days I had to sit in the makeup chair for two hours, in addition to the hours that I was putting in as a director, shooting the picture all day, then looking at film at night. I found myself getting very tired, very short on sleep. But on the other hand, I was constantly aware of what an opportunity this was. It's a wonderful script. We developed it over a long period of time with a lot of love and a lot of talent. And a lot of talented people came together and had a wonderful time making it.

Q: Vis-à-vis the other films, do you feel happier with this one so far?

LN: I think this is more my personal film. The last film was kind of a film that we all got together to do. I was the director, and responsible for what got up on the screen, but there was more of a sense of people coming together, a sense of collaboration. This is much more of a personal statement. This is a Leonard Nimoy film by title, and I took that responsibility very seriously. I said, "I want to make my movie." So, in that sense, I feel a greater sense of growth here. I feel the training wheels have come off, and they said, "Go ahead and do it." In fact, those are exactly the words the studio used when I finished *Star Trek III* and they asked me to do this one. They said, "The training wheels are off, make your vision of the *Star Trek* movie."

Q: Did you feel more comfortable this time with the technical details of the special effects?

LN: Yeah. I was not uncomfortable on *Star Trek III*, but I was still in a kind of learning process. I'd been around them enough so that I knew what was going on. It wasn't like a new world to me. But this time I'm a little ahead instead of running astride of it. I'm a little ahead in anticipating the questions and problems, and maybe pushing the right buttons a little earlier than I did last time.

But there's a lot of wonderful stuff in this film that does not at all depend on effects. I'm talking about most of this film is stuff that we play on earth in 1986. This is not a special effects film. There's very little special effects in it. It's very fresh, fun, a personal kind of film.

Q: Obviously, this is a more "human" kind of movie, not a technical movie...

LN: No, this is not a technical movie at all. Strangely enough, I believe that our special effects people, who did the whales, are entitled to very serious consideration for Academy Awards for their work on this picture. But at the same time, it's not a technical picture.

Q: *Star Trek II* and *Star Trek III* were both done under the aegis of the television division, but this film is being done under the motion picture wing. Have you noticed any differences in that?

LN: I'm not sure that I could say if I did. The simple fact is, that on *Star Trek III* we agreed on a budget, and I shot the film, and brought it in on that budget, and that was that. *Star Trek IV*, we agreed on a budget and I did the same thing. That budget is much larger on *Star Trek IV*, but a lot of that has to do with inflation. On *Star Trek III* the budget was $16 million. On *Star Trek IV* the budget is over $23 million. But I think we were able to demonstrate that if we did *Star Trek III* today, it would cost $22 million to make it, because of inflation factors. So we're only adding a couple of million real dollars to the cost of making this film. One could argue that if we were doing this under the television division, they might not have let us have those $2 million. I don't know. But I must say I've been very well treated by this studio on the making of both pictures, whatever the department involved. They're all very supportive.

Q: What were some of the most interesting moments for you in doing the film?

LN: That whole storm thing that we did in the tank, I got the biggest kick out of that, because people were coming from all over to see that. It was like old-fashioned Hollywood moviemaking, creating this whole drama using all of these various kinds of wonderful talents of people who know how to do this. I loved seeing that happen. And it [works] just wonderfully.

Q: How was shooting on location in San Francisco?

LN: It was great. People like us, they know who we are, they like the *Star Trek* movies. At times we had a little problem with crowd control. But for the most part, people were very helpful. Certainly, the San Francisco Police Department saw to it that we got the job done. I loved being there. I loved the whole idea of bringing *Star Trek* home to today.

Q: How did not having the *Enterprise* affect this film?

LN: We did have the Klingon *Bird of Prey.* That becomes the vehicle, and we're going home in that. The adventure starts in the *Bird of Prey,* with us using that ship. That was a little unusual because, obviously, we were in a different ship than what we were used to, and we had to accustom ourselves to that. I had to get that ship designed in such a way that it would be different from the *Enterprise,* but still we would all be comfortable and learn how to function in it very quickly. We had to have the feeling that this is not the *Enterprise,* but that we had studied it while it was on the ground and knew how to fly it.

So, that was a major difference. The lighting of it, the construction of the consoles, the construction of the equipment on the ship, how to shoot it, what were its best angles. The *Enterprise* we knew. We built a new interior bridge for the *Bird of Prey,* by the way. Because the one we used in *Star Trek III* was okay for the short period of time we were in there for that film, but in this picture we were in it for a much longer period of time. We say, in fact, that we've revamped it on Vulcan. And we did a lot with it, a lot of terrific looking stuff. That was a major physical difference.

And that set, because it needed to be tilted at a particular moment of the show, was built on a steel frame, and the whole thing together weighed 20 tons. We brought in an enormous crane to lift it from one end, to tilt the whole bridge. So we got into some production ideas on this picture that were quite challenging.

Q: Why did you decide to do that instead of the old trick of tilting the camera and everybody throwing themselves from side to side?

LN: Well, because we did a lot of camera tilting in the series, and it's not quite the same. When the actors stand up and walk in a tilted set, you see the difference. You really see and feel the difference. When water or something drips in a tilted set, you see the angle of the tilt, because what's dropping is dropping toward the tilt. If you just tilt the camera, things drop wrong. Things falling off the consoles and so forth happen because of the tilt. It's quite different. I feel very strongly that it was the worth the energy and the money and the time to tilt the set and get that effect.

On the Set of Star Trek IV

When the moving picture business first began, the big Hollywood studios built large back lots that could be used to provide locations for anywhere and any when a director could desire. Over the years, however, these back lots have often given way to the realistic look of location filming. But for several of the sequences of *Star Trek IV: The Voyage Home,* the latest escapade in the adventures of the gallant crew of the late Starship *Enterprise*, there was a feeling of what it must have been like in the old days.

One of the most outstanding features at Paramount Pictures is a gigantic, freestanding painting of a beautiful, brilliant, blue sky. Many visitors ask themselves why, in the midst of southern California's almost endless summer, such a thing would be necessary. Considerations of smog aside, *Star Trek IV* provides one of the answers.

Last April visitors at Paramount were surprised to discover that the parking lot located in front of that painting had been emptied of cars and filled with water. For, in point of fact, the lot is really a gigantic water tank of 200 feet by 200 feet, up to five feet deep in some spots. Whenever a film needs scenes to take place in water, and there is no real need to go to the ocean, this tank is used instead. Miniature battle scenes for "The Winds of War" all took place in the tank.

Star Trek IV executive producer Ralph Winter explains that using the tank is not as easy as it looks.

> First, we had to secure permission from the studio to get people to abandon these parking spots for about a month and a half, and that's a serious problem at Paramount! Then we filled the tank with one million gallons of water, and it only gets filled on the weekend, because it lowers the water pressure in the entire studio. The water had to be filtered, and we heated it to seventy-two to seventy-five degrees for the actors, and it needs to be continually cleaned.
>
> We had to plan everything out so that, once we put the water in, we could shoot everything in sequence, because it's too expensive and time consuming to drain the tank and then fill it again. Everything had to be planned to happen in exactly the sequence in which it's shot. So there's a lot of coordination that happens there, from making a

small mock-up to choosing the color of the floor, repaint-
ing the base, washing it down, cleaning it, setting the par-
allels, etc.

For half of the scenes using the tank, the painted blue sky
background that stands next to the lot is mostly covered with a
second background to simulate a cloudy sky. Overhead are 100
feet of white silk suspended on wires, to diffuse the sunlight and
keep the tank in shadow. It is now ready to serve as a set where
the Klingon *Bird of Prey,* that serves as a replacement for the lost
Enterprise, is partially submerged in water.

The story of how this ignominious situation arose is as fol-
lows: approximately three months after the events of *Star Trek
III: The Search for Spock,* the crew of the late Starship *Enterprise*
decide that they are prepared to return to earth to face the consequences of their actions. They set out in the repaired *Bird of
Prey,* which Dr. McCoy coyly dubs the H.M.S. *Bounty.* Director
Leonard Nemoy, who also plays Mr. Spock, explains:

> I think it would have been out of character for them not to
> at least try to come home and deal with what they had to
> deal with. After that, whatever happened remained to be
> seen. I really believe that it would have been totally out of
> character for them to avoid coming home for trial, if there
> were going to be a trial, and just say, "Well, we're not com-
> ing. We'll stay out in space." I didn't like that idea at all.

So the former *Enterprise* crew do return to earth. But in the
meantime, a gigantic alien probe has approached the planet,
sending out signals that are causing catastrophic, ecological
destruction. If the signals are not stopped, earth will soon be
covered in impenetrable clouds, created by an unprecedented
evaporation of its oceans. When Spock discovers what the probe
really seeks, the crew of the *Bounty* must go back in time to 1987,

and they must attempt to save the earth once more. The rest of the plot must remain secret until the release of the film.

While shooting in the tank, it was necessary for the cast to stay in a completely soaking wet state for long stretches of time. Luckily, the weather during this part of the filming had been sunny and hot, with temperatures circling the 90 degree mark. They were probably the only ones on the film who were really comfortable.

As the cameras got ready to roll, two huge, incredibly noisy fans were started up. These blew water spray and smoke to help simulate a stormy atmosphere. At the same time, three wave-generating machines pounded the water in the tank. This had to be carefully coordinated in the proper rhythm to give waves of just the right speed and size. The tank was then filled to over-flowing, so that its edge would be covered with water, creating the illusion of an endless horizon. When everything was working together, it was very easy to believe that the heroes of *Star Trek IV* were lost in a stormy sea.

After many weeks filming in a very closed-in soundstage, where visitors could not be accommodated, the outside sets were quite popular with the cast. Among those watching on one day were the Los Angeles mayor, Tom Bradley, and "Star Trek" creator Gene Roddenberry and his family. During a break, actor Jimmy Doohan (Scotty) proudly states:

> I have much more to do in this film than in any of the others. In fact, I just got a great compliment from Leonard. He said, "I think we've got a marvelous film, and you are marvelous in it." Not only that, but he said it in front of a bunch of people, which made it even better.

The actor was delighted to have been able to get away from the usual sets at Paramount and escape on actual location shootings in the San Francisco Bay area.

There was lots to do in this film. It's a very busy, active picture, and so much of it was shot on location. Of course, we were thrilled with that because we never did any of that before. What they wanted, in the past, they built. Even in the first picture, Leonard went up to Yellowstone, but they didn't like what they shot there, so they ended up bringing Yellowstone down here and building it at the studio.

But on this day, traditions were very much alive. Another of the sequences filmed took place on Vulcan, before the departure of Admiral Kirk and crew. For this scene, the alien landscape of Planet Vulcan was once more reconstituted on the set. A large part of the bright green *Bird of Prey* rose into the sky. Visible behind it were several painted backgrounds of the reddish-brown Vulcan countryside, while underneath were several tons of reddish-brown dirt, which covered the usual tarmac surface of the back lot.

Surrounding the ship were a variety of large, futuristic crates and containers, all lettered in Vulcan and Klingon. The Vulcan workers were dressed in beige tunics and loose-fitting trousers. On their feet they wore red boots with curled up, pointy toes. Their hats were about a foot tall and ended in a point that curved toward the front. The design is said to be modeled after the headgear worn by Shinto monks.

The *Bird of Prey* was an impressive sight. It was hard to believe that it was not real, but only made of wood. It gave a strange feeling to walk behind it and see the scaffolding that securely held the facade. But from the right angle, except for the cameras and crew, it would be easy to believe that it was really a ship preparing to depart [from] a distant world.

The scene being shot had Kirk walking past his crew: McCoy, Scotty, Uhura, Chekov, and Sulu, asking them if they were prepared to return to earth to face the consequences of their actions.

Then they were all to file away and enter the ship. Missing from the lineup was Captain Spock.

Careful inspection revealed, however, that he was indeed present, only he wore a white shirt and dark pants, and his ears did not exhibit the least sign of a point. Leonard Nimoy was at his post behind the camera, directing the action. After two or three takes, all interrupted by the seemingly interminable circling of a Los Angeles Police Department helicopter, Nimoy finally pronounced the scene to his liking.

Nimoy comments on the difficulties of being both the director and one of the main stars of the picture.

> Being in this film, in fact, was harder in certain respects than being in the previous one because I am on screen much more than I was last time. In *Star Trek III* I was on my back for two or three small moments, then on my feet playing one major scene at the end of the movie. It is quite the contrary in this picture. I'm on my feet throughout. I suppose it would be much easier if I were only doing one job or the other! It was tough. I wouldn't recommend it!

During a lull in the filming, Nimoy's assistant, Kirk Thatcher, whose duties included everything from writing scientific jargon for background in the script, to coordinating events between various departments, describes some of his experiences on the picture.

> Something that I thought was really interesting is that Leonard Nimoy has an incredible sense of humor. A lot of people don't know that. When you meet him, you think he's a very serious, thoughtful guy, and he is, but there's also a very funny side to him. He does funny voices and noises! That makes it even more terrific working for him.

313

Another funny thing about Leonard came when we were writing all the scientific angles to the script. We tried to make the stuff we wrote have some sort of background in science, and be real science fiction, not fantasy. The character of Spock is so strongly identified with Leonard that you automatically assume that he knows a lot about science. And he does, but in a well read layman's version. We'd go to him with things and he'd say, "Well, I don't know." It just seemed funny.

Thatcher points out some of the differences between this film and the ones that have preceded it. "*Star Trek* has generated a universe, like *Star Wars*. Having worked on the *Star Wars* universe, too, I'd say it's very textural. Everything is dirty and grungy, and kind of off-beat. Things stick off at weird angles for no apparent reason. *Star Trek* is very ordered, and everything's very clean. This one has more of a synthesis of the two. Look at the *Bird of Prey*. It's a dirty ship. It has hoses hanging off of it and shoots smoke. That's never been in a *Star Trek* before. I think it's a good cross. Our D.P., Don Peterman [*Splash, Cocoon*] is really helping with that look." Thatcher continues:

The bridge of the *Bird of Prey* changed from *Star Trek III*, because that original set was so tiny, and not meant to be shot on for very long. So we said, "Okay. Scotty's taken this original ship and retrofitted it with Vulcan parts and Federation bits." That ship is a lot of fun, because it sort of looks like a cross between *Alien* and *Star Trek*, as if there was some order here, but it all got kind of messed around and rewired, so humans could work on it.

For the aliens we played a little bit. We stuck an Andorian in there and Tellarites, but new Tellarites. They don't look so rubber-masky, I hope. We tried to maintain the *Star Trek* look throughout, but bring it up to date. They were done by a guy named Richard Snell. Actually, we interviewed about five or six companies, and I'd met Richard when I was art directing rock videos. We'd worked together on an alien mask for a Rick Springfield video. He did incredible work. He does these amazing soft contact lenses, where you can change your eyes and make them look like cat eyes, solid blue eyes, or whatever.

While most of the other sets used in filming have already been dismantled, the *Bird of Prey's* bridge is being refitted on a nearby soundstage. The set is mounted on a platform, about eight feet off the ground. Usually, when a scene is filmed where the ship undergoes a shock of some kind, only the camera actually moves, while the actors hang on to furniture at an angle and throw themselves, appropriately, from side to side. For such shots in this film, however, the entire bridge set was lifted and shaken by a crane for a more realistic effect. According to one source, "When you see a look of terror on DeForest Kelley's face this time, it's real terror!"

An interesting footnote: at the other end of the soundstage from *Star Trek IV: The Voyage Home* is a large sewer set from *Golden Child*, Eddie Murphy's new film. Murphy's proximity is a reminder that he was once rumored to have a role in the new [Star] *Trek* film. It was, however, only meant to be a small part with Murphy unrecognizably made up as a Klingon official, a role that was instead filled by character actor John Shuck.

As the filming recommences under the competent hand of Nimoy, the assistant director is pointed out. "That's Frank Capra, III," a visitor is told. "It was great when Jane Wyatt was here filming. Everybody was hugging, because, of course, Frank Capra directed her in *Lost Horizon*."

Star Trek IV may very well be Nimoy's last directorial assignment on the *Star Trek* series. But if *Star Trek IV* does well at the box office, the show will remain in the family—of sorts. He reveals,

I won't do it again, at least not on the next one. My understanding is that Bill Shatner will direct the next picture. I
think he should. He's very talented and energetic, and I'd
love to have him do it. I'd love to have his energy come in
now and take over some of it.

Star Trek V: *Interview with William Shatner*

"I find film direction to be the culmination of any artistic activity, it is the pinnacle," says William Shatner, the Canadian-born
actor who created the part of Captain Kirk in "Star Trek."

Shatner plans to follow in the footsteps of fellow actor
Leonard Nimoy, who directed *Star Trek III: The Search for Spock*
and the recent *Star Trek IV: The Voyage Home,* to be in the directorial chair for the forthcoming *Star Trek V,* currently in preproduction at Paramount Studios in Hollywood. "I have led my
life as an actor. That seems to me to have led to this place. I am
ready for this moment, to take a large motion picture and create
something. If I fail, it won't be because I'm not ready."

But are the other members of the *Star Trek* cast ready for
Shatner? Jokes Shatner:

> I've been directing them for years, now I'll have to be paid
> for it. Human problems? I don't anticipate any. Just the
> pleasure of trying to fix some things in people's perfor-
> mances nobody has ever told them. Directors don't talk to
> us actors much. That's a shame because we need to get fresh
> ideas. Leonard felt that way too. We would talk frequently
> about "Let's try it this way." I have the same feeling. There
> are things in the playing of scenes I want to correct, ten-
> dencies people have, things they do that I would like to fix.

Shatner is, of course, not inexperienced. He has already
directed several episodes of his own television show, "T. J. Hooker."

I've done a lot of directing and I feel I know actors and how to dramatize a scene. So I'm not looking at the joy of creating and filming a scene in the manner I think it should go. The difficulties with this movie will be the special effects of which I need to be aware. There are many technical aspects to directing a science fiction film which I'm not too sure about. But I'll have plenty of technical help.

What are Shatner's plans for *Star Trek* V? The actor-director, who plans to involve himself in the story, is understandably cagey about them.

Movies that have a message are boring to me—usually, not always. It's my preference to think of entertaining. The thrust of the idea, if it has a message, communicates itself to you individually, and you just come away with what you think it is.

I have a mind to use action cameras for lack of a better term using hand-held cameras for close impact cuts in a kind of style that I've learned from the streets of Los Angeles shooting action shows. "T. J. Hooker" has a great deal of running and jumping and pounding people on the back of the head. I thought that was kind of fun and entertaining. If we could combine it with some of the other basic tenets of *Star Trek,* it could be equally entertaining.

I also like the battleship shoot-outs and stuff like that. They're good fun. I use the word a lot but what I mean is entertaining. It's what you expect in a science fiction film— at least, I do. I love those shots of the ship coming over the frame's top. So I would like to keep as much of that as possible, but I also have in mind different ideas that are universal and should add some depth.

It certainly has to look like characters will die. Lives have to be threatened to make it sing. Everything about drama is jeopardy. That's a central problem in writing *Star Trek*. How to create jeopardy when all those characters have to live.

Indeed, can the *Star Trek* movies go on forever with an increasingly older cast of heroes? Shatner confronts the issue candidly.

> As you get older, just the mere hint that you can't bend over as easily as you used to will remind you of your mortality. Even if a guy is dumb, stupid, has no sense, the age alone makes you think certain thoughts. The aging process brings about questions, no matter what level of sophistication you're at.
>
> Since this series of movies is unique in that we are writing for the aging process, we're not trying to pretend we are still as we were twenty years ago. Then the issues we deal with can be as various as what the person who is getting older thinks about.

Obviously, the Paramount executives are aware of this, since *Star Trek V* is not the only *Star Trek* saga looming over the horizon. As announced in the media, next fall Paramount will release a new syndicated television show entitled "Star Trek: The Next Generation." That show, once again produced by "Star Trek" creator Gene Roddenberry, will take place more than a century after the current "Star Trek" series and will feature an entirely new cast.

I think "Star Trek: The Next Generation" is a mistake. To call a series "Star Trek" that doesn't have the cast and the ship in it is an error. The error seems to me the overexposure of the "Star Trek" name and the possibility of not having the "Star Trek" quality we've become accustomed to. It remains to be seen.

2010 (1984)

I n *2010* the future of mankind hung in the balance. So did the future of MGM/UA. The beleaguered studio was wagering its very existence on this $30 million sequel to Stanley Kubrick's legendary *2001: A Space Odyssey.*

Insiders at MGM had doubts about the wisdom of mounting a sequel to a film of such a lofty reputation—especially one over a decade old that was very much a product of its time and that, when all the pennies were counted, only did decently at the box office. A sequel would have to be at least as good as the original, probably better, if it were to succeed.

To bring off a picture of this epic scope, and to top what Kubrick had done (since he refused to do it), they would need a director of incredible artistic vision. What they hired instead was a workhorse—Peter Hyams, a mediocre writer-director of tepid action films like *Star Chamber* and *Capricorn One.* Hardly a director of Kubrick's caliber. Nonetheless, MGM paid him $1 million not only to write and direct but also to function as producer *and* cinematographer.

According to Peter Bart's *Fade Out: The Calamitous Final Days of MGM,* when Freddie Fields, MGM/UA's head of production, argued that Hyams's work was "wooden," studio chief Frank Yablans felt that concern was outweighed by the fact Hyams could get the project out by Christmas.

The subject was closed.

So while Hyams labored in smoky soundstages (he positively *loved* smoke), MGM did its best to manufacture all the hoopla and anticipation that it could. The script was kept secret (although anyone interested could have read Arthur C. Clarke's novel *2010: Odyssey Two* on which the movie was based), ID badges were required to enter the soundstages, and *Thus Spake Zarathustra,* played against trailers of a black monolith, echoed in theaters nationwide.

But despite dazzling special effects and a strong cast, the film was as leaden and uninvolving as Hyams's other films. A black monolith turned out to be not only the perfect image for the film, but it also became a giant tombstone for MGM/UA and the Frank Yablans regime.

On the Set of 2010

> *The time has come... to talk of many things. Of shoes and spaceships and sealing wax, but mostly of mono-liths and malfunctioning computers...*

By itself, there is nothing very interesting about the two-story, yellow plywood ball that occupies a blue-draped corner of MGM's cavernous stage 30. But if you squint and use a little imagination, the sunlit soundstage suddenly becomes deep space. You are floating beside the sulphur-stained, derelict *Discovery* as the spacecraft does its carousel spin in front of an ominous black shape that is set against the stars like some kind of tombstone.

This is just a part of writer Arthur C. Clarke's captivating vision, a story that began 15 years ago with director Stanley Kubrick's *2001: A Space Odyssey* and is now being continued in *2010,* a cinematic sequel based on Clarke's best-selling follow-up. Director Peter (*Outland*) Hyams has adapted Clarke's novel, and armed with a $25 million bankroll, he has brought together an international crew of actors, artisans, and technicians to capture the long-awaited saga on film.

Hyams, in attempting to follow up *2001*, has taken on a seemingly impossible task. *2001* was a landmark film, science fiction and moviemaking as no one had ever seen it before. Clarke and Kubrick created a sweeping, philosophical movie that traced mankind from its infancy to its first contact with life from another world. Utilizing state of the art special effects and a classical music score, *2001* had a depth and intensity far beyond the cartoonish cinematic science fiction that had dominated the movie screens for decades.

But the technological wizardry that made *2001* unique is commonplace today, thanks to the continuing efforts of folks like George Lucas and Steven Spielberg. The streamlined, sterilized look of Kubrick's spacecraft [has] also been outdated by the first-hand experience we have all had watching the Apollo landings and the space shuttle flights. And the use of Richard Strauss's *Zarathustra* theme to characterize the majesty of space is now a cliché. All Hyams has left to work with from *2001* is the story and the questions it left unanswered.

2010 star Roy *(Blue Thunder)* Scheider recalls:

> I don't think it's possible to repeat *2001*. The first time is the first time. When I saw *2001* it blew my mind just like it did everyone else's. But the choice Kubrick made to make it particularly dull, deliberately dull, in that very modern situation was a wonderful conceit that can only work once when you see the film for the first time. After that, the characters must become very, very dull. I think Peter was right to avoid that. You can't pull the same stunt twice.

The real feat facing Hyams, who is also handling the duties of cinematographer and producer, is to imbue *2010* with enough original and compelling qualities so that the film can stand on its own *and* live up to the example set by its predecessor.

Hyams has, in consultation with Clarke, altered the story line of *2010*, and one of the film's production crew commented that moviegoers can expect the sequel to be "exciting and full of action, something you couldn't say about *2001*. While *2001* was more cerebral, *2010* will be more accessible."

2001 star Keir Dullea agrees. "It's a different style, and it has more plot than *2001*, but I think it dovetails very well."

"I think the plot of this film will be much clearer than in *2001*," Scheider says. "There's a story you can hook onto here and ride to the end, which you couldn't do in *2001*."

"I'm happy with the changes Peter's made with *2010*," says actor Bob *(Close Encounters of the Third Kind)* Balaban, who plays HAL's creator in the sequel. "I like to think of the book as an outline for a good movie. Based on the script and the actors in this, this could really be an exciting movie and not just, you know, 'ta-da, here's the sequel.'"

The material artifacts of Clarke's tales lay scattered about the mammoth soundstage 30. HAL, the coldly efficient computer that murdered astronaut Frank (Gary Lockwood) Poole and doomed colleague David (Keir Dullea) Bowman to an uncertain fate, is a harmless wooden box full of red plastic strips and fluorescent lights. The exterior and partial interior of the *Leonov* pod bay rises from a grimy pit that once, long ago, was filled with bright blue chlorinated water so Esther Williams and a dozen swimsuit-clad starlets could frolic for the cameras. And off to one corner is the *Discovery* pod bay set where the legacy of *2001* and the promise of *2010* will meet.

Just a few steps away, in another huge soundstage, the new environs of *2010* reside safely outside the shadow of *2001*'s memories. Here is the entire interior set of the *Leonov*, the Russian vessel that journeys to Jupiter to investigate the fate of the *Discovery* and astronaut David Bowman, whose last message—"My God, it's full of stars!"—continued to perplex scientists long after he disappeared into the monolith.

The *Leonov* is inhabited by a team of U.S. and Soviet scientists. The U.S. scientists are Heywood Floyd (Scheider), who uncovered the lunar monolith; Walter Curnow (John Lithgow), an engineer who is an expert on the *Discovery* design; and Dr. Chandra (Balaban), returning to fix HAL, his malfunctioning creation. The Russian crew is headed by Tanya Kirbuk (Helen Mirren), the *Leonov* commander (whose name is "Kubrick" spelled backward) and Max Brailovsky (Elya Baskin), an engineer.

The Soviet contingent includes several other expatriate Russian actors in addition to Baskin. Among them are Vladimir Skomarovsky, once the best Soviet actor in his home country; Savely Kramarov, the popular star of 42 Russian comedies; and Natasha Shneider, who was the lead singer of a Western style Russian rock and roll band before immigrating to New York, where she began a new group, White Russian.

Keir Dullea reappears in the *Discovery* pod bay as a disembodied David Bowman; Douglas Rains once again gives HAL his voice; and Arthur C. Clarke turns up in a cameo as a drunk on a Washington, D.C., park bench.

"I guess I have a sort of proprietary interest in the *2010*," Dullea says of [his] second turn as Bowman. "I'm very glad I was able to be a part of it." Makeup expert Michael Westmore, who transformed actor John Lone into a neanderthal for *Iceman,* will supervise Dullea's physical agings and regressions.

This is *the* big movie on the MGM lot, so despite the fact that the movie is based on a well-read book, everyone is "hush-hush" about the film. The set is closed. Guards stand watch inside and outside the soundstages. Those few, authorized visitors must wear dated, laminated identification cards that change color daily. The lone exception was Prince Andrew, who visited Los Angeles during the shooting and was led on a royal tour of the sets by Scheider. The prince's press entourage was left outside to stare at the grey soundstage and gape at the leotard-clad "Fame" dancers strolling to work.

Actor Elya Baskin, who emigrated from Russia in 1976 and recently costarred in *Moscow on the Hudson,* found the rigid security on the set, and the sense of importance implied by it, stoked his confidence and creativity.

> Everyone, starting with Peter Hyams right on down to the costume and prop people, are so confident that we are doing something meaningful and important. It's very impressive. They take this work very seriously. You can feel it, walking on the set, that this is something with extra meaning for everyone involved. This is far from routine work. It gives me great confidence, that, and working with such a cast. I feel very privileged.

Yet despite the sense of importance they have attached to their work, Balaban says the emotional temperature on the set stayed comfortably warm.

> The atmosphere around here is rather pleasant. When you walk on some movie sets you sometimes get an immediate impression that there is ice flowing in a lot of people's veins. The atmosphere here is due to Peter, mostly, and it flows down from there. Everybody's attitude is that this is going to be a long movie to shoot, a meaningful movie, so let's be smart, let's be happy, and let's be as creative as possible.

The inside of the *Leonov* soundstage is dark. A hazy cloud of gritty smoke flows thickly over the floor. When Hyams first came on the set, a crew members recalls, the director took a deep breath, exhaled slowly and grinned, "Ahhh, smells like filmmaking." The smoke is spewed out frequently between takes by a machine that lets out a hacking, mechanical cough that grates on the ears. The camera does not see the smoke, but it plays on the light, adding a depth of field.

Hyams huddles in front of a television screen several yards away from the cramped *Leonov* communications room set, where Roy Scheider and Bob Balaban prepare for a scene. The two actors are doing their part of the initial *Discovery* reconnaissance trip that Lithgow and Baskin, suspended by wires in front of a blue screen, filmed a few days earlier.

Movie directing has become something of a video game with the Louma crane Hyams is using. It is a camera, on a telescoping crane, that can snake into the narrow *Leonov* corridors and follow the cast. Hyams controls the crane from a station where he can see through the camera's eye on a video screen. The Louma crane, which was used recently on *Iceman,* allows Hyams to create a more claustrophobic feel and squeeze into areas a camera and crew cannot go. It will be extremely useful when Balaban enters HAL to bring the computer "back to life."

Wandering through the *Leonov* set is an education in set-making and detail. Stop at an airlock, a control panel, one of the space pods, any place where there is fine print to read. Look closely. It is always going to be the operating instructions for the zero gravity toilet from an early scene in *2001.* It is an in-joke moviegoers will never notice. The camera will see only indiscernible lines of type. But there are other details, which moviegoers *can* see, that are far more interesting. Production designer Albert Brenner is the man to talk to.

The *Leonov,* Brenner stresses, is a different sort of ship than the *Discovery.*

> We're machinery, floating hardware. The feel of the *Leonov* is entirely different. We had a problem with this film, we had to stay close to *2001* and also take into account the new visual sense of the audience. The *Discovery* is slick and

streamlined with nothing showing. Audiences don't see space travel as so sleek anymore. The *Leonov* is more like a flying tugboat or submarine.

"Hundreds of miles" of wiring, some serving a real function and some used only as set dressing, are strewn over the gray and white interior and plywood exterior of the set. Over 120 TV monitors dot the *Leonov*'s halls. Yet, Brenner says, that is not even enough. The monitors serve double, sometimes triple duty and are yanked out when the action changes locale to fill other portions of the *Leonov* set and parts of the *Discovery*. The abundance of monitors and other instrumentation is visual futurist Syd *(Blade Runner)* Mead's fault.

"I gave Syd the sketches and he filled in the details," Brenner says. "You know, the television sets, readouts, and stuff. It was just a bunch of garbage in my sketches. Instrumentation is Syd's specialty."

There is no room in the *Leonov* set for the traditional, bulky, movie lights, and that is intentional. Explains Brenner:

> Peter likes to work with available light. Tight, claustrophobic sets aren't amenable to lighting. So we turn on all the monitors and switches and that's it. Peter uses fast film. There's a tremendous amount of fluorescent and incandescent light. All the banks of plastic switches are lit from behind by fluorescent tubes. The intensity of the light is cut down by the colored plastic switches.

The *Leonov* is also a "wild set," meaning many sections are removable to allow the camera to poke through and film from several angles. Original plans to film "up through the floor," Brenner says, were scrapped. So the set is on the ground and the corridor floors are simply hard, plastic, industrial pallets used for shipping materials.

The *Leonov* flight deck, however, is suspended over a hole in the soundstage and built on an axle-like mount. Inside the *Leonov* flight deck, the chairs are refitted; armor-plated helicopter seats "that weigh a ton," Brenner groans. "We retrofitted things onto them to give them this look. They're wonderful." At one point in the film, we have to get away in a hurry. So there is a rapid acceleration. When that happens, everything falls backwards under the force of the thrust. So we strap the actors into those seats and take the entire set, turn it 90 degrees and let everything fall."

"But," he grins playfully, "the real secret to all of this is Joe's Plastic in Vernon, California. He gets scrap plastic from everywhere and recycles it. I found the place and acted like a kid in a candy shop. This ship is full of pieces from Joe's Plastic."

Brenner sweeps his hand expansively over the set, inviting the visitor to look around at the details of the *Leonov* interior for "anything unusual." It is not easy. And Brenner, smiling, knows it.

> Right here is a little device that is really one half of a ski tote. Those, over there, are small motor housings from lawn mowers. That brown object protruding from the wall over there is a child's carseat turned upside down and spray-painted. That, by the door, is a Sparklett's water bottle, that's a pool filter, and that is a car bumper.

Welcome to the future, folks.

Brenner laughs, strolling through the *Leonov*'s dark corridors.

> Joe never thought he'd be in the movie business. Everything that looked interesting I bought. I just pointed things out, I asked for 20 of those, a couple hundred of these. I had a huge mountain of plastic hauled down here. As the set was being built, I went through the rubble and picked out pieces, roamed around the set and put 'em on the wall.

I had a picnic in my backyard last June and had ice cream cones. Cones come in a box and [are placed] in this styrofoam packaging. The packaging is interesting, something you'd usually throw out without looking at it. I'll show it to you on the walls.

The entire *Leonov* set is littered with, well, litter, and it is liberally polished with several coats of imagination. Baskin found it a fascinating contrast to Russian filmmaking and a further incentive to give his best efforts to his role. Says Baskin:

In Russia, money is not limited. If a film requires a high budget, the government gives it. So seeing a big set or whatever isn't such a big surprise. To see such a masterfully crafted set, that was a big surprise. I was really shocked when I saw the work Albert Brenner and Sid Mead have done. During the whole filming, I was still wandering around the set touching things. I was very fascinated. And then Al took me to the special effects place. That was even more impressive. I tell you, working with such fine craftsmen and such experienced actors helps you to do your very best.

Brenner began designing the sets while Hyams was still busy hammering out the screenplay. "I began working from the book though the set is laid out for the geography of the screenplay."

Reconstructing the *Discovery* proved to be a challenge. Brenner explains.

We had to go through the film, pull out frames, and work backwards from there because the blueprints for the sets were destroyed. So we pulled out maybe 50 frames, and based on the size of the people, we plotted out how large the set actually was. We've reconstructed the airlock, flight deck, corridor interior, and pod bay. We've also done some exterior pieces of the *Discovery*'s front ball and the spine that leads back from it to the engine.

As difficult as it was, they were successful. "The sets from the *Discovery* have been reproduced exactly and I hadn't seen them in 10 years," says Keir Dullea. "To walk on the set was like going through a time machine."

"This movie is going to be something," Dullea says, a strange smile creeping across his face, "something *wonderful*."

Interview with Keir Dullea

The twisted reality of a dream, with its blurred lines between illusion and substance and its commingling of past, present and future, engulfed him as he stood in the twilight darkness of the *Discovery* pod bay. His familiar, sharp features were hidden by the scratched and withered visage of a man who has lived a millennium.

"I don't believe it," Keir Dullea whispered to himself as he stepped onto the dark *Discovery* set. "I'm back."

Dullea, aged by layers of skillfully crafted makeup, was once again portraying David Bowman, the astronaut doomed by a malfunctioning computer in Stanley Kubrick's 1968 film *2001: A Space Odyssey* to undergo an unexplained alien regeneration and suffer an eternal existence in a mystifying netherworld.

2001 was a sweeping, philosophical space saga told with state of the art special effects and embellished with a classical music score. It left an indelible mark on moviegoers and a sequel's worth of unanswered questions.

Nearly two decades later, *2001* creator Arthur C. Clarke got around to answering those questions in his bestseller *2010*, which MGM has spent $30 million to transform into what they hope will be 1985's first big box-office hit. In a Kubrickesque turn, Peter (*Outland*) Hyams produced, wrote, and directed the sequel, which stars Roy Scheider, John Lithgow, Bob Balaban, and the voice of Canadian Douglas Rains as HAL, the malevolent computer.

For Dullea, his cameo role was simultaneously a "lonely exhilaration," a "time warp to the past," and an "exciting new experience." They were three of the strangest working days of his career.

"To walk on the set was really like going into a time machine," Dullea says. "It was like 18 years had never passed."

The strangest moments of all came during his reunion with HAL, the murderous computer which sent Bowman hurling into the black monolith orbiting Jupiter and into the unknown territories charted in the sequel.

> We are, in a sense, taking this journey together. It was a remarkable and moving experience to work with HAL's voice again. It wasn't even being filmed, it was all done off camera. In this particular scene, I'm a totally disembodied entity. You just have the empty halls of the *Discovery* with these two voices bouncing off the walls.

2010 doesn't strike him as a belated attempt to cash in on the tremendous success of *2001*. He read Clarke's sequel "out of curiosity" and was delighted to find "that it wasn't a copy of the first, it really was its own entity and didn't read like an excuse."

Likewise, he says:

> [I think the film version] dovetails with *2001* very well. It has a different style and there's more plot than in *2001*. It's certainly a nice attempt at answering the questions posed by *2001*. It will also have a different visual appeal. The cinematography, which Peter is handling, has a totally different

quality. It will be more like *Alien* in terms of its look than *2001*. That film had a clean, sterile look to it. The ships in *2010* will look dirty, full of recycled air.

The passage of time between the two films did not hamper Dullea's ability to become David Bowman again. He recalls:

> In the original film, the character was fairly close to myself. It wasn't like I was doing a characterization the way you would do in the theater or in some films. It was just a matter of being truthful and honest under slightly different circumstances.

At first, Dullea was not even sure there would be a part for him in *2010*.

> I read the book and in it, my character was a disembodied entity. I figured my character would be played by a special effect. Well, I'm back. But the audience is going to see some remarkable visual effects on me because I change form constantly while I'm talking with Roy Scheider. I go through all the aging processes, shifting from fetus to old man to myself, all in one scene.
>
> The character I play has been so transformed by his experience with the aliens that what I express in the film is quite different than the concerns Bowman had in *2001*. In that film, he was basically an astronaut. Now he has been transformed and is on such a different plane that I really had something new to play.

Being the link between the two films gives him a special sense of pleasure, though he admits if the sequel had been made only a few years after *2001* he might have thought twice about coming back.

The only other film I can think of that compares is *Psycho II*. But the similarity lies only in the many years between original and follow-up. Other than Anthony Perkins and the set, there really wasn't much in common with the original. *2010* is based on another book by Clarke, I'm back and so is HAL, and I think that gives it some legitimacy. And Peter is repeating what Kubrick did. Kubrick was also cowriter, producer, and director. It's like being reunited with one's old friends in a weird way.

In a sense doing *2010* is coming full circle for me. I took HAL apart in the first film. In this film, he's been put back together and we're alone again on the ship. He says "I'm afraid." Boy, did I get a weird feeling then. He says "Where will I be?" and I say "You'll be where I'll be."

He shrugs. "I guess that will always be true."

An Interview with Roy Scheider

If you look at Roy Scheider's hard, lined face, you can understand why killer sharks, New York street gangs, devious helicopter pilots, and international assassins think twice about messing with him. This guy is tough.

Even the alien intelligence that sparked the evolution of mankind on earth and stuck an ominous black monolith next to the planet Jupiter might have second thoughts about tangling with this guy. But they are going to have to anyway, because Scheider, as intrepid scientist Heywood Floyd, is coming to get them and find out what happened to his ship, *Discovery*, and the crew that was aboard it.

This is the story of *2010*, director-writer-producer Peter Hyams's long-awaited, $30 million sequel to director Stanley Kubrick's classic *2001: A Space Odyssey*. Scheider is taking over the role originated by William Sylvester, an unfamiliar actor whose lack of popular appeal seemingly precluded his involvement in the sequel from the outset.

"I was Peter's first choice," Scheider says, taking a break between shots in his trailer beside MGM's mammoth stage 30. Clad in his crew jumpsuit, he looks out of place in the drab, familiar environs of a mobile home.

> Peter had me in mind while he was writing the screenplay from Clarke's book. I read the first 80 pages of the script, which he hadn't finished yet, and I was interested. He explained to me what he planned to do with the rest of the story and I agreed to do it.

Scheider was seduced by the dramatic conflicts [that] would be swirling around Floyd.

> That's what I look for first in a screenplay. Is whatever happened to him interesting to the audience, does anyone want to look at him, will they care? And is there enough there to interest me as an actor? When you get those two together, where the character is interesting and challenges me as an actor, that's a real plus.

Clarke's novel *2010* was not required reading for Scheider's role. "I deliberately avoided the book because I'm performing the screenplay," he says. "I don't want to confuse the two."

Nor did he rush out and see *2001* again for many of the same reasons that he avoided Clarke's book. But the memory of past viewings still lingers.

> When I saw *2001* it blew my mind just like it did to everyone else. The actors were never the stars of *2001*. The special effects were. If anything, HAL was the major actor. As I've seen it more and more times since then, I still marvel

at the technical things. But the choice Kubrick made to make it particularly and deliberately dull in a very modern situation was a wonderful conceit that can only work once when you see the film for the first time, and after that it just becomes very, very, very dull.

Which is one of the reasons [why] *2010* will be so much different [from] its predecessor.

Peter made a good point when he said to me that he didn't want the people in this film to be dull like that, because the device won't work twice. That grandiose space movie Kubrick did can't be done again. You can't pull the same stunt twice.

That is why few members of the cast or crew will refer to *2010* as a sequel. They prefer to look at it as an entirely new film.

This is a whole new deal. For instance, one reason I did not go [to] see *2001* before seeing this film [was] because they are not related at all until we get up in space and find *Discovery*, and then the two stories connect. I would say that 80 percent of this movie really hasn't got much to do with *2001* except that it has the same setting: space.

It is a setting that involves the utilization of many special effects. Scheider is no stranger when it comes to working with the technical side of movie magic. In *Jaws* and *Jaws 2* he worked with a mechanical great white shark and in *Blue Thunder* he scorched across the skies in a helicopter that resembled a flying tank.

It is a difficult relationship between the actor and the special effects, and Scheider is trying to reach an amiable accord.

My only problem with them is the amount of time that has to elapse between shots to get the special effects set up. It's debilitating. The hard thing is to keep the energy level up and maintain continuity. I would never adapt my acting style to work around special effects. I always consider special effects the enemy. I know they are necessary, but for actors they just get in the way.

Special effects, though, play a far less important role in *2010* than they did in *2001*. As the *2010* staff repeats time and time again, this film will emphasize character over hardware.

It's also a much better story. I think the audience will have a better time with this film than they had with the first one. I think the film's plot will be much clearer than in *2001*. There's a story you can hook onto here and ride to the end, which you *couldn't* do with *2001*, which was all kind of marvelous and mind-blowing, but if you ask anyone on the street how *2001* ends they can't tell you. And that includes me. The only person who knows is Kubrick, and it really doesn't matter because that movie went off on an extraterrestrial flight at the end, which is okay, because how the hell are you going to end a movie like that anyway?

That *does not* mean, Scheider stresses, that the impression audiences got from the first one will be lost or ignored. Keir Dullea's return as David Bowman packed a wallop for everyone involved in *2010*.

"It was rather eerie playing a scene with Keir Dullea," Scheider says. "We all felt strange. He felt just as eerie about being there as we felt about seeing him."

What the basic difference between the two films comes down to, Scheider believes, is that *2010* should be "more fun and more exciting to watch," while still solving many of the questions raised in the first film "and presenting a whole new set of mysteries that will be easier for the audience to hold on to. It's pretty fantastical. I think the audience will leave the film with their minds expanded."

He grins and shrugs.

> I mean, it's pretty fantastical what happens at the end. If you want to think about the possibilities of there being a new sun in the sky and the possibility of a whole new universe, that sets up a frontier that's pretty exciting and makes what's going on on earth seem pretty trivial.

What's happening on earth during Floyd's trek aboard a Russian spacecraft to Jupiter is that tensions mount between the two superpowers and pose the possibility of a world war. The animosity on earth reaches out into space and touches the international crew journeying to delve into the mysteries of the *Discovery.*

"That's the real conflict of the story," he says, "the cold war heating up between the Russian and American crew while they are out in space."

When it came to conflict on the *Blue Thunder* film, heating up between director John Badham and screenwriter Dan O'Bannon, Scheider admits there were some problems.

> *Blue Thunder* went through *a lot* of changes. The script I read was *not* the script that ended up being shot. They had two more writers come on and then a third and then they went back to the original two guys who got the screen credit (O'Bannon and Don Jakoby). I mean, what attracted everyone in the first place was what really made the story good so they went back to the drawing board.

O'Bannon was offended by the ad-libbed dialogue Badham encouraged between the actors. The screenwriter, now directing

Return of the Dead from his own script, took it as an insult to his writing.

> A lot of the stuff between Daniel *(Diner)* Stern and myself, you know that bullshit macho dialogue in the helicopter, was mostly ad-libbed stuff and John Badham encouraged us to do it. He did that because it worked for the film; it helped establish a relationship and that's hard to do on paper.

O'Bannon's displeasure baffles Scheider.

> Since the movie did about $80 million worldwide, I don't think O'Bannon should be too unhappy. I know for a fact that John never treated those guys with anything less than respect and invited them to the set and showed them dailies. As a filmmaker, I think John is a little more sophisticated about how things will affect an audience than they [O'Bannon and Jakoby] are. And I'm a guy who believes that the writers are absolutely the number one creative force in any movie.
>
> I make it my business to meet the screenwriter, oh yeah, because where are you going to find out more about your character than from him? You find out what compelled him to write the screenplay in the first place.... If I like the script, and I choose to do it, it means that I like the character to begin with and anything I bring to it is just maybe an embellishment on what the writers already have. So I don't have conflicts with writers.

Scheider can sympathize with a writer's position on a movie and her or his anger when an actor "takes over" a role.

> How would you like it if you wrote the movie, and they cast the part, and the actor signs a contract to play the character

for X amount of dollars and on the first day of shooting the actor says "I don't like the character." How would you feel? So an actor can't do that; he can't say "wait a minute, I'm not playing this guy because I have a better idea." That's why some actors get fired the first week of shooting.

Scheider is well respected by both the movie industry and the audiences. Moviegoers first got a glimpse of him as Jane Fonda's slimy pimp in the detective film *Klute,* then as a cop opposite Gene Hackman in director William Friedkin's *French Connection.* Both films were Academy Award winners. *The Seven-Ups, Jaws, Jaws 2, Marathon Man, All That Jazz, Still of the Night,* and *Blue Thunder* followed.

He was born in New Jersey and had a serious bout with rheumatic fever when he was a child, which he weathered by reading lots of books. His college career began at Rutgers and continued at Franklin and Marshall, a small school in Lancaster, Pennsylvania, where he had a serious bout with the acting bug. He never got over it. From school, however, he followed an ROTC commitment with two years in the Air Force. Flunking flight school with low math scores, he became an air traffic controller.

Once discharged, he and his new wife moved to New Jersey and he pursued an acting career. The marriage fizzled but he was making his mark in Shakespearean theater. He married actress Cynthia Bebout, who is now working as a film editor, and his critical accolades for his stage work soon led him to the screen.

A heavy percentage of his movies are action/adventure fare. So you have to wonder if those are the kind of films Scheider likes to see.

Yeah, they are. I wouldn't make them if I didn't like to see them. For instance, when I read *Blue Thunder* I found the helicopter a fascinating concept. If you've read the papers lately and you look at what's being built at Hughes and being used at the Olympics you'll see it's nearly the same machine. So I felt that it has some historical significance. And *Jaws,* of course, was just about the most exciting blast of a yarn I had read in a long time. I like to do movies I would like to go out and see.

He must be doing something right. After all, most of Scheider's films have inspired sequels of one type or another. There was *French Connection 2,* which Scheider was not in but he "liked it a lot. I loved the way they unleashed Popeye Doyle, this New York barbarian, on French society. But, I think it suffered from sequelitis." There was talk of a *Blue Thunder* sequel, and then Columbia opted for a TV series instead. Was Scheider offered the starring role? "Yep," he nods.

And what did he say to them?

"No," he shakes his head emphatically, "Absolutely no."

He wasn't able to say the same when Universal asked him to do *Jaws 2,* though he would have liked to.

I did *Jaws 2* because of a contractual obligation to Universal. It wasn't my choice. It was a plain sequel. I don't think it stood on its own as a movie. That wasn't a natural sequel at all. I don't think it was necessary to have that shark appear again. There isn't any way to top the first film.

Getting Steven Spielberg to direct again, though, would have been a good start. When the original director of the film was ousted after a few weeks of shooting (executives thought the film's look was "too gothic"), they asked Spielberg to do it.

"He agreed to do it if they would give him five months to develop what he considered a worthwhile story," Scheider says. "They wouldn't give him that time. I was all for it but they didn't want to wait the extra five months."

The final film, directed by "Night Gallery" veteran Jeannot Szwarc, was a disappointment to Scheider but it did well financially. Spielberg, according to Scheider, "didn't think very highly of the film at all." Still, it was financially rewarding enough to merit yet another sequel, the ridiculous *Jaws 3-D*. "I didn't see it," Scheider says, "I had absolutely no curiosity at all."

Although *2010* closes with some open-ended questions, and Clarke is toiling on *another* sequel, Scheider doubts there will be another cinematic follow-up. "There are certain stories that lend themselves to sequels," he says. "This isn't one of them."

WAR GAMES (1983)

A teenager inadvertently hacks into NORAD with his PC and nearly sparks nuclear Armageddon. Is that a high concept or what?

At the heart of *War Games* was a simple, extraordinarily commercial idea—one that shrewdly tapped into society's casual acceptance and emerging dependence on computers.

In the early 1980s, computers were becoming as common in the American home as a television or a transistor radio. In fact, they were everywhere and were so nonthreatening, even a child could master them.

Perhaps it was inevitable that someone would craft a story in which an ordinary PC brings the world to the brink of apocalypse. When Lawrence Lasker and Walter F. Parkes wrote the script, they had no shortage of suitors. But the journey to the screen was not a smooth one. After enduring several false starts at several studios, they finally got the go [ahead] from MGM/UA, only to have the studio fire their director, Martin Brest, two weeks into shooting.

Producer Leonard Goldberg replaced Brest with John Badham, who was at the time supervising the editing of *Blue Thunder.* It turned out to be a fortuitous change.

The film was a smash, affirming Badham as one of the top action/ adventure directors and pumping sorely needed cash (and generating positive public relations) for Kirk Kerkorian's beleaguered studio.

Interview with Director John Badham

Q: Had there been much done by Martin Brest before you got started?

JB: He had shot for about three weeks, I think. I would say that 90 percent of what he shot, I had to redo. I went back and started almost from scratch, working first of all with the kids in their room. The 10 percent that remains in the film is very nice. A lot of it is mixed up in different things, with bits and pieces here and there.

Q: Do you know what the creative differences were between Martin Brest and MGM/UA?

JB: All I can tell you is that, from their point of view, they were not getting the kind of film they expected. In order to get what they wanted, they felt they should make a change.

Q: Was your interpretation of the story different?

JB: Yes. I did a fairly extensive set of revisions on the script. I essentially returned it to what Larry Lasker and Walter Parkes had originally written. I tightened it as I went along the way, and injected a lot more humor into it than there had been when they were first shooting. Larry and Walter had a lot of humor in it originally, and that humor had been eliminated. It had a much darker view than the film presently takes.

Q: Would you say that Brest's version was more "preachy"?

JB: No, I wouldn't say it was preachy, but I would say it was darker. For example, one of the things I did for the lightening up was that I wrote in a lot of jokes in the existing structure. There is a lot of humor that has been put in there. I also recast the father. They had a very good actor in there, but he was playing it like a real tyrant. I recast the schoolteacher and reshot his scenes. He was playing it too much like a real jerk.

You see, usually you can go out and cast one of the nicest guys you meet for these characters, because the lines themselves will convey "jerk." You don't need to cast somebody who plays a jerk. So I went out and got real, nice fellows and let them play it that way. In the situation, they appear to be the kind of people that they are. That way, we are not being so heavy-handed about it. We also lightened up the kids considerably. They were kind of serious about their changing of the grades. Everything was very, very serious.

Q: Were there any other cast members that were changed, or other problems that you faced, because you were stepping into a production that was already underway?

JB: Not really. There was a terrific production crew there. They had done good work and good preparation. If they weren't so well organized, I might have thought a little longer before getting involved. But they were in good shape.

Q: Was it a difficult decision to decide to get involved with a film that was already started?

JB: Well, the script, with whatever little qualifications I mentioned, was good. It was long, it needed these other things, but you could see a terrific story there. That is a big factor right there. If you've got a good script, somehow you're going to make it work.

Q: Is there much of a difference in the version of *War Games* that is out now and Lasker and Parkes's original script?

JB: I would say it's reasonably close, although there are certain differences all over the place. I don't think that in their script Falken was so interested in dinosaurs and so on. But it's the same story, refined and tightened all the way.

Q: What was your motivation for having Falken change his field of interest to dinosaurs?

JB: Actually, that was a contribution of Wally Green, the interim writer picked by Brest. He wrote and directed a picture called *The Hellstrom Chronicles* some years ago, and he has a certain fascination with extinction and replacement of the species. Seeing a man who says to himself, "What happened to the dinosaurs? They failed to adapt, they failed to learn, and the world outgrew them. Eventually they were replaced, they became extinct. That will happen to us, too. Maybe we'll be replaced by the bees." That's pure Wally Green. It's a bit dark, yet for that character it was right.

Q: Did you have any other input in the story line?

JB: I had to create characters in some cases where there were none. The character of the general is a creation of mine. He was very flat, dull, pompous, and boring in the previous versions. I, on the other hand, knew that most of the general staff of the military comes from the South and the West. It is a little like law school and medical school to New York boys, it's their way out. That's why the military is staffed with many people who talk with funny, country-boy accents, and yet who are not to be messed with. Eventually, he is the person in authority that comes down on the side of human beings.

Q: Other than the father and the teacher, were all the other parts cast with people that you kept?

JB: No, as I said, I cast the general. He's my contribution. Most of the smaller characters in the war room were also cast by me.

Q: Didn't that cause quite a delay in the shooting?

JB: Not really. We shut down for three days. I work fast. I had a Labor Day weekend in there somewhere, while they were negotiating my deal, where I rewrote the script. Then I paid attention to the other stuff that needed to go on.

Q: Did you have storyboards or anything for this?

JB: No. There was no time for storyboards. I threw out the storyboards that were there before. They were impossible. I just did it out of my head.

Q: Were the sets already designed, or did you make changes there?

JB: They were pretty much designed. The big sets were deep into work. I had a hand in the designing of the missile capsule, Falken's house, the computer center, and a few things like that. The big NORAD set was basically the way it was.

Q: Is that the way NORAD really looks?

JB: NORAD should be so lucky! NORAD built a facility 25 years ago underneath the Cheyenne Mountains, and they could only chisel out so much granite. They put in what was state of the art then. Our set is state of the art today, and I'd bet that they would probably like to have it!

Q: Does the technology in the war room really work? Or is it merely an artist's rendition?

JB: Everything was researched as carefully as we could: the screens with constantly updated projections, video read-outs of all that stuff, etc. I suppose you could put the same logo on the front of *War Games* as we have on the front of *Blue Thunder*: "the technology here is real stuff."

Q: All of the computers used in the film were high-tech and very realistic. Why was WOPR designed to look like something out of a 1950s SF film?

JB: For one thing, the man who designed it is supposed to have died 10 years previously, so that will tell you something. He was designing something that he put a great deal of himself in, which had a more anthropomorphic bent to it than just a lot of blank boxes with disk drives and tapes running. So it does have a more human appearance to it. Also, if you're going to have it as a major character in a film, you'd better bloody well not have a blank box sitting there, unless you just enjoy boring the audience!

Q: Did you have any military cooperation on the film, in order to have the fighter planes in it?

JB: The same fellows that gave us all that help on *Blue Thunder* came right on over to *War Games*! [On *Blue Thunder* Badham had to use miniature F-16s, built by the Dreamquest special effects company because he was prohibited from filming real planes.] Actually, we did luck out on finding a couple of nice pieces of stock footage, which were good, and we could use those. We needed a lot more on *Blue Thunder*, so we just had to make our own. But on this it was sufficient to have those couple of little pieces.

Q: Have you gotten any feedback on what the people in Washington thought after seeing the film?

JB: I heard all kinds of good things. There was a lot of enthusiasm at the screening I went to in Washington. They were talking it up quite a bit, and everyone stayed around for an hour afterward. There were a lot of right-wing, left-wing, and centrists there, and they seemed quite taken with it. David Stockman [President Reagan's budget director at the time] did leave with a "No Comment," as did William Casey, the head of the CIA. But, what the hell, you can't please everybody!

Q: How long did the shoot take once you got started on it?

JB: About 10 weeks. Nothing unusual. I pulled about 10 days out of the schedule and reshot stuff that had to be reshot and just accelerated everything right along. They were really in need of a little help in the budget department. I was trying my best to accommodate them. It stayed pretty much in line once they accounted for the stoppage and the changeover in personnel, etc.

Q: Were there any humorous incidents that occurred during production?

JB: I will say that the biggest laugh in the picture was improvised on the spot by Barry Corbin, who plays the general. The famous "Piss on a sparkplug" line was done by him, when he and I were trying to find a line that would be good. We weren't having any luck and I forgot about it, and suddenly we were in the middle of a take and he lays that one on us! It was like having gold fall out of the sky, when you hear a line like that.

Q: How was working with the two kids?

JB: They are very good actors. Matthew is just a wonderful talent, and Ally is quite good too. They're able to hold their own in pretty big scenes against some very important actors. Matthew is a big star, though nobody knows it yet.

Q: Can you go through the shooting of a particular scene?

JB: The missile commander scene at the beginning was quite a detailed shoot, and one that was a real labor of love, because it was the beginning of the movie and also a very important sequence. I didn't realize until we got into it that it was the first day in the motion picture business for one of our actors.

Wally Hasida, who cast him, had found him. He walked in off the street in Chicago while she was interviewing and she liked him a lot. She had told me that he hadn't done a movie or any professional stuff before, and at the time I had said, "It's all right, we'll go ahead with him." But those words hadn't really sunk in till we got there, and I suddenly realized that the guy didn't know anything about marks or anything!

But Wally was right, he was a terrific actor. Since I've always maintained that you can learn all that technical stuff about films real easily and quickly, I had to stick by my own words and teach him. He did great. He's since gone into the pilot of "Diner" as a regular. I'm really excited for him, because I thought he was just wonderful.

While we were shooting that scene, we had a couple of real missile commanders with us, the guys who had sat down there for those 24-hour shifts for five years. They were checking us on every detail that we were doing, making sure that we didn't overstep our bounds. It was a very interesting sequence. Another interesting sequence is the end of the movie, in the war room .... All the work there was very complicated. Getting six rear projection screens and six front projection screens all working at the same time, functioning beautifully in dead sync with 75 video screens, is a huge, mind-boggling kind of task. It looks very easy, and once it's cranking along you say, "Oh, isn't that nice!" But there were a lot of Excedrin headaches on that one, I can tell you!

Q: Other than that, were there any problems with the special effects?

JB: It went so boringly well that you could go to sleep on how well it worked. It was prepared brilliantly. Most of the stories you hear about how things went wrong come from places that didn't do their homework in advance. These guys, you can't say enough good things about how carefully they had everything ready. This was a whole different set of guys from *Blue Thunder*, mostly electronics people as opposed to the mechanical effects people that we used on that. Mike Fink was the chief guy responsible for coordinating everything. Colin Cantwell designed and supervised all the computer graphics.

Q: Do you think the message is stronger than *Blue Thunder*'s?

JB: I think it's more strongly put. I think it's laid out for the audience more strongly, and that's important. It is also put there gently enough so that you can take it or leave it, whatever you please. So far, it'd seem that people get it. What you are trying to say is very clear to them, and they are happy to have it said.

Q: Were you trying not to be too "preachy"?

JB: To coin a phrase—you will lose friends by influencing people. By this I mean, nobody wants to be preached to. Also, I believe that it is wrong to ask somebody to pay $5 for a movie and then, once you've got them in the seats, start hammering them with your own beliefs. If you want more message, then you should go see a different movie. For example, you should go see Dr. Helen Caldicott's *If You Love This Planet,* which is a brilliant film on the subject of nuclear disarmament.

Q: Would you agree that *War Games* could be called a modern-day *Dr. Strangelove*?

JB: I would agree that there are similarities, and I would certainly point out that the humor in *Dr. Strangelove* is certainly more cynical and black than in this film, where there is a much more innocent humanism at work.

Q: How would you describe *War Games* in just a few words, as to what it means to you?

JB: I hope that it does something to raise the level of consciousness of the audience somewhat. Set them thinking about the potential of nuclear disaster.

www.ingramcontent.com/pod-product-compliance
Lightning Source LLC
Chambersburg PA
CBHW020419030726
47495CB00006B/1585